The
DAUGHTERS
of
IRELAND

Also by Santa Montefiore

The
DAUGHTERS
of
IRELAND

SANTA
MONTEFIORE

wm

WILLIAM MORROW
An Imprint of HarperCollinsPublishers

Originally published as *The Daughters of Castle Deverill* in Great Britain in 2016 by Simon & Schuster UK Ltd.

HarperCollins books may be purchased for educational, business, or sales promotional use. For information, please email the Special Markets Department at SPsales@harpercollins.com.

FIRST WILLIAM MORROW EDITION PUBLISHED 2017.

Designed by Diahann Sturge

Library of Congress Cataloging-in-Publication Data has been applied for.

ISBN 978-0-06-245688-5 (paperback)
ISBN 978-0-06-269868-1 (library edition)

18 19 20 21   LSC   10 9 8 7 6 5 4

To Sebag
with love and gratitude

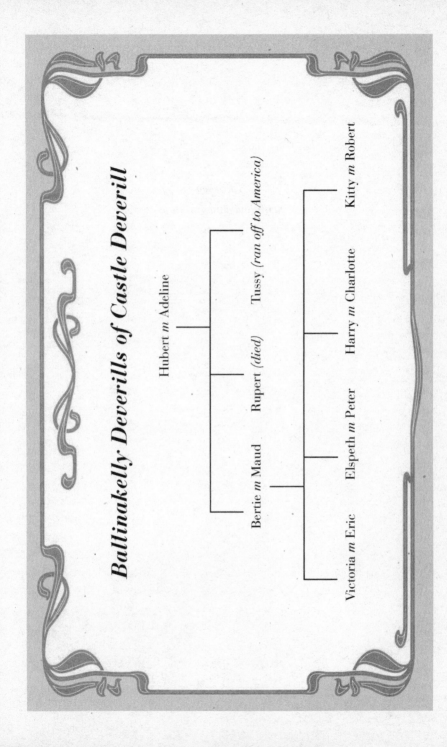

Ballinakelly Deverills of Castle Deverill

Hubert *m* Adeline

Bertie *m* Maud — Rupert *(died)* — Tussy *(ran off to America)*

Victoria *m* Eric — Elspeth *m* Peter — Harry *m* Charlotte — Kitty *m* Robert

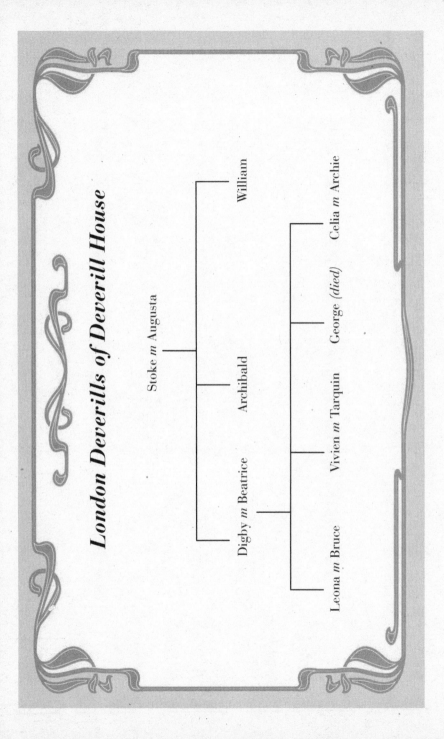

London Deverills of Deverill House

Stoke *m* Augusta

William

Archibald

Digby *m* Beatrice

Celia *m* Archie

George *(died)*

Vivien *m* Tarquin

Leona *m* Bruce

Barton Deverill

Asalty wind swept over the white beaches and rocky cliffs of Ballinakelly Bay, carrying on its breath the mournful cry of gulls and the crashing of waves. Gray clouds hung low and a gentle drizzle misted the air. Swathes of green pastures and yellow gorse rendered it hard to believe the violence of Ireland's history, for even in that dull, early spring light, hers was a flawless, innocent beauty. Indeed, in that moment when the seemingly impenetrable canopy above thinned sufficiently to allow a beam of sunlight to filter through it, Barton Deverill, the first Lord Deverill of Ballinakelly, vowed to heal the scars of Cromwell's brutality and bring comfort and prosperity to the people over whom he now presided. Wrapped in a velvet riding cape of the deepest crimson, a wide-brimmed hat with a swirling plume placed at a raffish angle on his head, high leather boots with silver spurs and a sword at his hip, he sat astride his horse and ran his eyes over the vast expanse of land bestowed on him by the recently restored King Charles II in gratitude for his loyalty. Indeed, Barton Deverill had been one of the leading commanders in the fight against Cromwell's conquest of Ireland. After the defeat at Worcester he had fled across the sea with the King and accompanied him during his long exile; a title and land were satisfactory recompense for Cromwell's confiscation of his family's lands in England and the years he had devoted to the Crown. Now he was no longer a young man, thirsty for combat and adventure, but a man in middle age eager to put away his sword and enjoy the fruits of his endeavors. Where better to lay down his roots than here in this startlingly beautiful land?

The castle was taking shape. It was going to be magnificent, overlooking the sea with towers and turrets and high walls thick enough to repel the enemy, although Lord Deverill would have rather seen an end to the violence. Protestant though he was and an Englishman to his marrow, he didn't see why he and the Irish Catholics couldn't respect and tolerate each other. After all, the past lived only in one's memory, whereas the future was forged on the attitudes of today; with understanding and acceptance in the present a peaceful land could surely be attained.

He signaled to his large retinue of attendants and the group continued slowly toward the small hamlet of Ballinakelly. It had rained heavily during the night and the road was thick with mud. The sound of squelching hooves heralded their arrival, striking fear into the hearts of the people who had witnessed too much blood to be complacent about Englishmen on horseback. Men watched them warily, having not until that moment laid eyes upon their new lord and master. Women blanched, hastily sweeping up their children and retreating into their houses and slamming the doors behind them. A few intrepid youngsters remained barefoot in the drizzle like scarecrows, wide-eyed and hungry, as the English gentlemen with fine leather boots and plumes in their hats rode into their midst.

Lord Deverill halted his steed and turned to his friend, Sir Toby Beckwyth-Stubbs, a portly man with a sweeping auburn mustache and long curly hair in the fashionable cut of the Cavaliers. "So this is the heart of my empire," he said, gesticulating with his gloved hand, then added with sarcasm, "I can see that I am well loved here."

"Years of bloodshed have made them wary, Barton," Sir Toby replied. "I'm sure with a little gentle persuasion they can be brought to heel."

"There'll be no persuasion of that nature here, my friend." Barton raised his voice. "I will be a beneficent lord if they'll swear me their allegiance."

Just then, a woman in a long black Bandon cloak stepped into the track. It seemed as if the wind dropped suddenly and a stillness came over the village. The ragged children melted away and only the woman remained, her dress trailing in the mud.

"Who is this?" Lord Deverill demanded.

The estate manager brought his horse alongside his master's. "Maggie O'Leary, milord," he informed him.

"And who is this Maggie O'Leary?"

"Her family owned the land you are building on, milord."

"Ah," said Lord Deverill, rubbing his beard with a gloved hand. "I suppose she wants it back." His joke caused his attendants much amusement and they tossed their heads and laughed. But the young woman stared at them with such boldness the laughter faded into a few nervous chuckles and no one had the courage to outstare her. "I am happy to pay her something," Lord Deverill added.

"She is clearly mad," Sir Toby hissed anxiously. "Let us be rid of her at once."

But Lord Deverill raised his hand. There was something in the confidence of her stance that aroused his curiosity. "No. Let's hear what she has to say."

Maggie O'Leary gave a quiver of her white fingers and, with a movement so light and fluid that her hands might have been a pair of snowy birds, she pulled back her hood. Lord Deverill's breath caught in his chest for he had never before seen such beauty, not even in the French court. Her hair was long and black and shone like the wings of a raven, her face was as pale as moonlight. She curled her lips which were full and red like winterberries. But it was her light green eyes that severed the laughter from their throats and moved the facto-tum to cross himself vigorously and whisper under his breath. "Keep your wits about you, sire, for surely she's a witch."

Maggie O'Leary lifted her chin and settled her gaze on Lord Deverill. Her voice was low and mellifluous, like wind. "*Is mise Peig Ni Laoghaire. A Tiarna Deverill, dhein tú éagóir orm agus ar mo shliocht trín ár dtalamh a thógáil agus ár spiorad a bhriseadh. Go dtí go gceartaíonn tú na h-éagóracha siúd, cuirim malacht ort féin agus d-oidhrí, I dtreo is go mbí sibh gan suaimhneas síoraí I ndomhan na n-anmharbh.*"

Lord Deverill turned to his estate manager. "What did she say?" The old factotum swallowed, afraid to repeat the words.

"Well?" Lord Deverill demanded. "Speak up, man, or have you lost your tongue?"

"Very well, my lord, but God protect us from this witch." He cleared his throat and when he spoke his voice was thin and trembling. "Lord Deverill, you have wronged me and my descendants by taking our land and breaking our spirits. Until you right those wrongs I curse you and your heirs to an eternity of unrest and to the world of the undead." A collective gasp went up behind him and Sir Toby reached for his sword.

Lord Deverill scoffed, turning to his men with an uneasy smile. "Are we to fear the empty words of a peasant woman?" When he looked back she was gone.

PART ONE

Chapter 1

Ballinakelly, 1925

Kitty Trench kissed the little boy's soft cheek. As the child returned her smile, her heart flooded with an aching tenderness. "Be good for Miss Elsie, Little Jack," she said softly. She patted his red hair, which was exactly the same shade as hers. "I won't be long." She turned to the nanny, the gentleness in her expression giving way to purpose. "Keep a close eye on him, Elsie. Don't let him out of your sight."

Miss Elsie frowned and wondered whether the anxiety on Mrs. Trench's face had something to do with the strange Irishwoman who had turned up at the house the day before. She had stood on the lawn staring at the child, her expression a mixture of sorrow and longing as if the sight of Little Jack had caused her great anguish. Miss Elsie had approached her and asked if she could help, but the woman had mumbled an excuse and hurriedly bolted for the gate. It was such a peculiar encounter that Miss Elsie had thought to mention it to Mrs. Trench at once. The ferocity of her mistress's reaction had unnerved the nanny. Mrs. Trench had paled and her eyes had filled with fear as if she had, for a long time, dreaded this woman's arrival. She had wrung her hands, not knowing what to do, and she had looked out of the window with her brow drawn into anxious creases. Then, with a sudden burst of resolve, she had run down the garden and disappeared through the gate at the bottom. Miss Elsie didn't know what had passed between the two women, but when Mrs. Trench had returned half an hour later her eyes were red from crying and she was trembling. She had swept the boy into her arms and held him so tightly that Miss Elsie had worried she might smother him. After that, she had taken him upstairs to her bedroom and closed the door behind her, leaving Miss Elsie more curious than ever.

Now the nanny gave her mistress a reassuring smile. "I won't let him out of my sight, Mrs. Trench. I promise," she said, taking the child's hand. "Come, Master Jack, let's go and play with your train."

Kitty went around to the stables and saddled her mare. As she brusquely pulled on the girth and buckled it tightly, she clenched her jaw, replaying the scene from the day before, which had kept her up half the night in fevered arguments and the other half in tormented dreams. The woman was Bridie Doyle, Little Jack's natural mother from a brief and scandalous affair with Kitty's father, Lord Deverill, when she had been Kitty's lady's maid, but she had chosen to abandon the baby boy in a convent in Dublin and run off to America. He had then been taken by someone from the convent and left on Kitty's doorstep with a note requesting that she look after him. What else was she to have done? she argued as she mounted the horse. As far as she could see she had done Bridie a great favor for which Bridie should be eternally grateful. Kitty's father had eventually come to recognize his son, and, together with her husband, Robert, Kitty had raised her half brother as if he were her own child—and loved him just as dearly. There was nothing on earth that could separate her from Little Jack now. Nothing. But Bridie was back and she wanted her son. *I had to leave him once, but I won't do it a second time,* she had said, and the cold hand of fear had squeezed Kitty's heart.

Kitty stifled a sob as she rode out of the stable yard. It wasn't so long ago that she and Bridie had been as close as sisters. When Kitty reflected on everything she had lost, she realized that her friendship with Bridie was one of the most precious. But with the unsolvable problem of Little Jack between them she knew that reconciliation was impossible. She had to accept that the Bridie she had loved was long gone.

Kitty galloped across the fields toward the remains of her once glorious home, now a charred and crumbling ruin inhabited only by rooks and the spirits of the dead. Before the fire four years before, Castle Deverill had stood proud and timeless with its tall windows reflecting the clouds sweeping in over the sea like bright eyes full of dreams. She recalled her grandmother Adeline's little sitting room that smelled of turf fire and lilac and her grandfather Hubert's penchant for firing his gun at Catholics from his dressing-room window. She remembered the musty smell of the library where they'd eat porter cake and play bridge and the small cupboard at the bottom of the servants' staircase where she and Bridie had met secretly as little girls. She smiled at the memory of stealing away from her home in the Hunting Lodge close by to seek entertainment in the affectionate company of her grandparents. In those days the castle had represented a refuge from her uncaring mother and spiteful governess, but now it signified only sorrow and loss and a bygone era that seemed so much more enchanting than the present.

As she galloped across the fields, memories of Castle Deverill in its glory days filled her heart with an intense longing because her father had seen fit to sell it and soon it would belong to somebody else. She thought of Barton Deverill, the first Lord Deverill of Ballinakelly, who had built the castle, and her throat constricted with emotion—nearly three hundred years of family history reduced to ash, and all the male heirs imprisoned within the castle walls for eternity as restless spirits cursed never to find peace. What would become of *them*? It would have been better for her father to have given the ruins to an O'Leary, thus setting them all free and saving himself, but Bertie Deverill didn't believe in curses. Only Kitty and Adeline had had the gift of sight and the misfortune of knowing Bertie's fate. As a child Kitty had found the ghosts amusing; now they just made her sad.

At last the castle came into view. The western tower where her grandmother had set up residence until her death was intact but the rest of it resembled the bones of a great beast gradually decaying into the forest. Ivy and bindweed pulled on the remaining walls, crept in through the empty windows and endeavored to claim every last stone. And yet, for Kitty, the castle still held a mesmeric allure.

She trotted across the ground that had once been the croquet lawn but was now covered in long grasses and weeds. She dismounted and led her horse around to the front, where her cousin was waiting for her beside a shiny black car. Celia Mayberry stood alone, dressed in an elegant cloche hat beneath which her blond hair was tied into a neat chignon, and a long black coat that almost reached the ground. When she saw Kitty her face broke into a wide, excited smile.

"Oh my darling Kitty!" she gushed, striding up and throwing her arms around her. She smelled strongly of tuberose and money and Kitty embraced her fiercely.

"This is a lovely surprise," Kitty exclaimed truthfully, for Celia loved Castle Deverill almost as much as *she* did, having spent every summer of her childhood there with the rest of the "London Deverills," as their English cousins had been known. Kitty felt the need to cling to her with the same ferocity with which she clung to her memories, for Celia was one of the few people in her life who hadn't changed, and as she grew older and further away from the past, Kitty felt ever more grateful for that. "Why didn't you tell me you were coming? You could have stayed with us."

"I wanted to surprise you," said Celia, who looked like a child about to burst with a secret.

"Well, you certainly did that." Kitty looked up at the facade. "It's like a ghost, isn't it? A ghost of our childhood."

"But it will be rebuilt," said Celia firmly.

Kitty looked anxiously at her cousin. "Do you know who bought it? I'm not sure I can bear to know."

Celia laughed. "Me!" she exclaimed. "*I* have bought it. Isn't that wonderful? I'm going to bring back the ghosts of the past and you and I can relive the glorious moments all over again through our children."

"*You*, Celia?" Kitty gasped in astonishment. "*You* bought Castle Deverill?"

"Well, technically Archie bought it. What a generous husband he is!" She beamed with happiness. "Isn't it a riot, Kitty? Well, I'm a Deverill too! I have just as much right as anyone else in the family. Say you're happy, do!"

"Of course I'm happy. I'm relieved it's you and not a stranger, but I admit I'm a little jealous too," Kitty said sheepishly.

Celia flung her arms around her cousin again. "Please don't hate me. I did it for *us*. For the family. The castle couldn't possibly go to a stranger. It would be like giving away one's own child. I couldn't bear to think of someone else building over our memories. This way we can all enjoy it. You can continue to live in the White House, Uncle Bertie in the Hunting Lodge if he so wishes and we can all be terribly happy again. After everything we've suffered we deserve to find happiness, don't you think?"

Kitty laughed affectionately at her cousin's fondness of the dramatic. "You're so right, Celia. It will be wonderful to see the castle brought back to life and by a Deverill no less. It's the way it should be. I only wish it were me."

Celia put a gloved hand on her stomach. "I'm going to have a baby, Kitty," she announced, smiling.

"Goodness, Celia, how many more surprises have you in store for me?"

"Just that and the castle. How about you? Do hurry up. I pray we are both blessed with girls so that they can grow up here at Castle Deverill just like we did." And Kitty realized then that Celia had placed herself here within these castle walls for more than merely the annual month of August. She was one of those shallow people who rewrote their own history and believed in the absolute truth of their version. "Come on," Celia continued, taking Kitty's hand and pulling her through the doorframe into the space where once the great hall had been. "Let's explore. I have grand plans, you know. I want it to be just the same as it was when we were girls, but better. Do you remember the last Summer Ball? Wasn't it marvelous?"

Kitty and Celia waded through the weeds that grew up to their knees, marveling at the small trees that had seeded themselves among the thistles and thorns and stretched their spindly branches toward the light. The ground was soft against their boots as they moved from room to room, disturbing the odd rook and magpie that flew indignantly into the air. Celia chattered on, reliving the past in colorful anecdotes and fond reminiscences, while Kitty was unable to stop the desolation of her ruined home falling upon her like a heavy black veil. With a leaden heart she remembered her grandfather Hubert, killed in the fire, and her grandmother Adeline who had died alone in the western tower only a month ago. She thought of Bridie's brother, Michael Doyle, who had set the castle ablaze, and her own foolish thirst for recrimination, which had only led to her shame in his farmhouse where no one had heard her cries. Her thoughts drifted to her lover, Jack O'Leary, and their meeting at the wall where he had held her tightly and begged her to flee with him to America, then later, on the station platform, when he had been arrested and dragged away. Her head began to spin. Her heart contracted with fear as the monsters of the past were roused from sleep. She left Celia in the remains of the dining room and fled into the library to seek refuge among the more gentle memories of bridge and whist and porter cake.

Kitty leaned back against the wall and closed her eyes with a deep sigh. She realized she was ambivalent about this canary, chattering away about a house whose past she barely understood. Celia's voice receded, overwhelmed by the autumn wind that moaned about the castle walls. But as Kitty shut off her sight, her sixth sense at once became sensitive to the ghosts now gathering around her. The air, already chilly, grew colder still. There was no surer feeling than this to drag her back to her childhood. Gingerly, she opened her eyes. There, standing before her, was her grandmother, as real as if she were made of flesh and blood, only younger than she had been when she had died and dazzlingly bright as if she were standing in a spotlight. Behind her stood Kitty's grandfather, Hubert, Barton Deverill, the first Lord Deverill of Ballinakelly, and other unfortunate Deverill heirs who were bound by Maggie O'Leary's curse to an eternity in limbo, shifting in and out of vision like faces in the prism of a precious stone.

Kitty blinked as Adeline smiled on her tenderly. "You know I'm never far away, my dear," she said and Kitty was so moved by her presence that she barely noticed the hot tears spilling down her cheeks.

"I miss you, Grandma," she whispered.

"Come now, Kitty. You know better than anyone that we are only separated by the boundaries of perception. Love binds us together for eternity. You'll understand eternity when it's your turn. Right now there are more earthly things to discuss."

Kitty wiped her cheeks with her leather glove. "What things?"

"The past," said Adeline, and Kitty knew she meant the prison of the long dead. "The curse *must* be lifted. Perhaps you have the strength to do it; perhaps *only* you."

"But Celia's bought the castle, Grandma."

"Jack O'Leary is the key that will unlock the gates and let them all fly out."

"But I can't have Jack and I don't have the castle." The words gripped her throat like barbed wire. "With all the will in the world I can't make that happen."

"Who are you talking to?" It was Celia. She swept her eyes over the empty room suspiciously and frowned. "You're not speaking to those ghosts of yours, are you? I hope they all go away before Archie and I move in." She laughed nervously. "I was just thinking, I might start a literary salon. I do find literary people so attractive, don't you? Or maybe we'll hire a fashionable spiritualist from London and hold séances. Gosh, that would be amusing. Oliver Cromwell might show up and scare the living daylights out of us all! I've got so many capital ideas. Wouldn't it be a riot to bring back the Summer Ball?" She linked her arm through Kitty's. "Come, let's leave the car here and walk with your horse to the Hunting Lodge. I left Archie to tell Uncle Bertie about us buying the castle. What do you think he'll say?"

Kitty took a deep breath to regain her composure. Those who have suffered develop patience and she had always been good at hiding her pain. "I think he'll be as happy as I am," she said, making her way back through the hall at her cousin's side. "Blood is thicker than water. That's something we Deverills all agree on."

BRIDGET LOCKWOOD SAT at the wooden table in the farmhouse where she had been raised as Bridie Doyle and felt awkwardly out of place. She was too big for the room, as if she had outgrown the furniture, low ceilings and meager windows from where she had once gazed upon the stars and dreamed of a better life. Her clothes were too elegant, her kid gloves and fine hat as incongruous in this house as a circus pony in a cowshed. As Mrs. Lockwood she had become too refined to derive any pleasure from her old simple way of life. Yet the girl in her who had suffered years of clawing homesickness in America longed to savor the familiar comfort of the home for which she had pined. How often had she dreamed of sitting in this very chair, drinking buttermilk, tasting the smoke from the turf fire and the sweet smell of cows from the barn next door? How many times had she craved her feather bed, her father's tread on the stair, her mother's good night kiss and her grandmother's quiet mumbling of the rosary? Too many to count and yet here she was in the middle of all that she had missed. So why did she feel so sad? Because she was no longer that girl. Not a trace of her remained except Little Jack.

The farmhouse had filled with locals keen to welcome Bridie back from America and everyone had commented on her pretty blue tea dress with its beads and tassels and her matching blue T-bar shoes, and the women had rubbed the fabric of her skirt between rough fingers, for only in their dreams would they ever possess such luxuries. There had been dancing, laughter and their neighbor Badger Hanratty's illegal poteen, but Bridie had felt as if she were watching it all from behind a pane of smoked glass, unable to connect with any of the people she had once known and loved so well. She had outgrown them. She had watched Rosetta, her Italian maid and companion whom she had brought back from America, and envied her. The girl had been swung about the room by Bridie's brother Sean, who had clearly lost his heart to her, and by the look on her face she had felt more at home than Bridie had. How Bridie had wished she could kick off her shoes and dance as they did, and yet she couldn't. Her heart was too heavy with grief for her son—and hatred for Kitty Deverill.

Bridie yearned to slip back into the skin she had shed when she had left as a twenty-one-year-old, pregnant and terrified, to hide her secret in Dublin. But the trauma of childbirth, and the wrench of leaving Ireland and her son, had changed Bridie Doyle forever. She had been expecting *one* baby, but was astonished when another, a little girl the nuns had later told her, had arrived, tiny and barely alive, in his wake. They had taken her away to try and revive her, but returned soon after to inform Bridie that the baby had not lived. It was better, they had said, that she nurture the living twin and leave the other to God. Bridie hadn't even been allowed to kiss her daughter's face and say good-bye. Her baby had vanished as if she had never been. Then Lady Rowan-Hampton had persuaded Bridie to leave her son in the care of the nuns and she had been sent off to start a new life in America.

No one who has given away a child can know the bitter desolation and burning guilt of that act. She had already lived more lives than most do in their entire lifetime, and yet to Sean, her mother and her grandmother, she was still their Bridie. They knew nothing of the sorrows she had suffered in America or the anguish she suffered now as she realized her son would never know his mother or the wealth she had, by accident and guile, amassed. They believed she was their Bridie still. She didn't have the heart to tell them that their Bridie was gone.

She reflected on her attempt to buy Castle Deverill, and wondered, if it had succeeded, would she have been willing to stay? Had she tried to buy it as an act of revenge for the wrongs inflicted on her by Bertie and Kitty Deverill, or because of a purer sense of nostalgia? After all, her mother had been the castle's cook and she had grown up running up and down its corridors with Kitty. How would they have reacted on discovering that poor, shoeless Bridie Doyle had become Doyenne of Castle Deverill? The smile that crept across her face confirmed that her intention had been born out of resentment and motivated by a desire to wound. If the opportunity ever arose again, she would take it.

When Sean, Rosetta, Mrs. Doyle and her grandmother Old Mrs. Nagle appeared in the parlor ready for Mass, Bridie asked them all to sit down. She took a deep breath and knitted her fingers. The faces stared anxiously at her. Bridie looked from her mother to her grandmother, then to Rosetta who sat beside Sean, her face flushed with the blossoming of love. "When I was in America I got married," she declared.

Mrs. Doyle and Old Mrs. Nagle looked at her in astonishment. "You're a married woman, Bridie?" said Mrs. Doyle quietly.

"I'm a widow, Mam," Bridie corrected her.

Her grandmother crossed herself. "Married and widowed at twenty-five, God save us! And not chick or child to comfort." Bridie winced but her grandmother did not know the hurt her words had caused.

Mrs. Doyle ran her eyes over her daughter's blue dress and crossed herself as well. "Why aren't you in mourning, Bridie? Any decent widow would wear black to honor her husband."

"I am done with black," Bridie retorted. "Believe me, I have mourned my husband enough."

"Be thankful that your brother Michael isn't here to witness your shame." Mrs. Doyle pressed a handkerchief to her mouth to stifle a sob. "I have worn black since the day your father was taken from us, God rest him, and I will wear it until I join him, God help me."

"Bridie is too young to give up on life, Mam," said Sean gently. "And Michael is in no position to stand in judgment over anybody. I'm sorry, Bridie," he said to his sister, and his voice was heavy with sympathy. "How did he die?"

"A heart attack," Bridie replied.

"Surely he was too young for a heart attack?" said Mrs. Doyle.

Bridie's eyes flicked to Rosetta. She wasn't about to reveal that Mr. Lockwood had been old enough to be her father. "Indeed, it was most unfortunate that he died in his prime. I was planning on bringing him here so that Father Quinn could give us his blessing and you could all meet him . . . but . . ."

"God's will," said Mrs. Doyle tightly, affronted that Bridie hadn't bothered to write and tell them of her marriage. "What was his name?"

"Walter Lockwood and he was a fine man."

"Mrs. Lockwood," said Old Mrs. Nagle thoughtfully. She clearly liked the sound of it.

"We met at Mass," Bridie told them with emphasis, feeling the sudden warmth of approval at the mention of the Church. "He courted me after Mass every Sunday and we grew fond of each other. We were married only seven months, but in those seven months I can honestly say that I have never been so happy. I have much to be grateful for. Although my grief is deep, I am in a position to share my good fortune with my family. He left me broken-hearted but very rich."

"Nothing is more important than your faith, Bridie Doyle," said Old Mrs. Nagle, crossing herself again. "But I'm old enough to remember the Great Famine. Money cannot buy happiness but it can surely save us from starvation and hardship and help us to be miserable in comfort, God help us." Her wrinkled old eyes, as small as raisins, shone in the gloomy light of the room. "The road to sin is paved with gold. But tell me, Bridie, how much are we talking?"

"A cross in this life, a crown in the next," said Mrs. Doyle gravely. "God has seen fit to help us in these hard times, for *that* our hearts must be full of gratitude," she added, suddenly forgetting her daughter's shameful blue dress and the fact that she never wrote to tell them about her marriage. "God bless you, Bridie. I will exchange the washboard for a mangle and thank the Lord for his goodness. Now, to Mass. Let us not forget your brother Michael at Mount Melleray Abbey, Bridie. Let us do another novena to St. Jude that he will be saved from the drink and delivered back to us sober and repentant. Sean, hurry up now, let us not be late."

Bridie sat in the cart in an elegant green coat with fur trimming, alongside her mother and grandmother, wrapped in heavy woolen shawls, and poor Rosetta who was practically falling out of the back, for it was not made for so many. Sean sat above in his Sunday best, driving the donkey who struggled with the weight, until they reached the hill at which point Bridie and Rosetta walked with Sean to lighten the animal's load. A cold wind blew in off the sea, playfully seeking to grab Bridie's hat and carry it away. She held it in place with a firm hand, dismayed to see her fine leather boots sinking into the mud. She resolved to buy her brother a car so that he could drive to Mass, but somehow she knew her grandmother would object to what she considered "*éirí in airde*"—airs and graces. There would be no ostentatious show of wealth in this family as long as she was alive.

Father Quinn had heard of Bridie's triumphant return to Ballinakelly and his greedy eyes settled on her expensive coat and hat and the soft leather gloves on her hands, and knew that she would give generously to the church; after all, there was no family in Ballinakelly more devout than the Doyles. He decided that today's sermon would be about charity and smiled warmly on Bridie Doyle.

Bridie walked down the aisle with her chin up and her shoulders back. She could feel every eye upon her and knew what they were thinking. How far she had come from the ragged and barefooted child she had once been, terrified of Father Quinn's hellfire visions, critical finger-wagging and bullying sermons. She thought of Kitty Deverill with her pretty dresses and silk ribbons in her hair and that fool Celia Deverill who had asked her, "How do you survive in winter without any shoes?" and then the girls at school who had called her a tinker for wearing the dancing shoes Lady Deverill had given her after her father's death, and the seed of resentment that had rooted itself in her heart sprouted yet another shoot to stifle the sweetness there. Her great wealth gave her a heady sense of power. *No one will dare call me a tinker again*, she told herself as she took the place beside her brother, *for I am a lady now and I command their respect.*

It wasn't until she was lighting a candle at the end of Mass that she was struck with a daring yet brilliant idea. If Kitty didn't allow her to see her child she would simply take him. It wouldn't be stealing because you couldn't steal what already belonged to you. *She* was his mother; it was right and natural that he should be with *her*. She would take him to America and start a new life. It was so obvious she couldn't imagine why she hadn't thought of it before. She smiled, blowing out the little flame at the end of the taper. Of course such inspiration had come directly from God. She had been given it at the very moment she had lit the candle for her son. *That* was no coincidence; it was divine intervention, for sure. She silently crossed herself and thanked the Lord for his compassion.

Outside, the locals gathered together on the wet grass as they always did, to greet one another and share the gossip, but today they stood in a semicircle like a herd of timid cows, curious eyes trained on the church door, eagerly awaiting the extravagantly dressed Bridie Doyle to flounce out in her newly acquired finery. In hushed tones they could talk of nothing else: "They say she married a rich old man." "But he died, God rest his soul, and left her a fortune." "He was eighty." "He was ninety, for shame." "She always had ideas above her station, did she not?" "Ah ha, she'll be after another husband now, God save us." "But none of our sons will be good enough for her now." The old people crossed themselves and saw no virtue in her prosperity, for wasn't it written in Matthew that it is easier for a camel to go through the eye of a needle than for a rich man to enter the Kingdom of God? But the young were both resentful and admiring in equal measure and longed with all their hearts to sail as Bridie had done to this land of opportunity and plenty and make fortunes for themselves.

When Bridie stepped out she was startled to find the people of Ballinakelly huddled in a jumble, waiting to see her as if she were royalty. A hush fell about them and no one made a move to meet her. They simply stared and muttered to each other under their breaths. Bridie swept her eyes over the familiar faces of those she had grown up with and found in them a surprising shyness. For a moment she was self-conscious and anxiously looked around for a friend. That was when she saw Jack O'Leary.

He was pushing through the throng, smiling at her reassuringly. His dark brown hair fell over his forehead as it always had, and his pale wintry eyes shone out blue and twinkling with their habitual humor. His lips were curled and Bridie's heart gave a little start at the intimacy in his smile. It took her back to the days when they had been friends. "Jack!" she uttered when he reached her.

He took her arm and walked her across the graveyard to a place far from the crowd where they could speak alone. "Well, would you look at you, Bridie Doyle," he said, shaking his head and rubbing the long bristles on his jaw. "Don't you look like a lady now!"

Bridie basked in his admiration. "I *am* a lady, I'll have you know," she replied and Jack noticed how her Irish vowels had been worn thin in America. "I'm a widow. My husband died," she added and crossed herself. "God rest my husband's soul."

"I'm sorry to hear that, Bridie. You're too young to mourn a husband." He ran his eyes over her coat. "I've got to say that you look grand," he added and as he grinned Bridie noticed that one of his teeth was missing. He looked older too. The lines were deeper around his eyes and mouth, his skin dark and weathered, his gaze deep and full of shadows. Even though his smile remained undimmed, Bridie sensed that he had suffered. He was no longer the insouciant young man with the arrogant gaze, a hawk on his arm, a dog at his heel. There was something touching about him now and she wanted to reach out and run her fingers across his brow.

"Are you back for good?" he asked.

"I don't know, Jack." She turned into the gale and placed her hand on top of her hat to stop it blowing away. Fighting her growing sense of alienation she added, "I don't know where I belong now. I came back expecting everything to be the same, but it is *I* who have changed and that makes everything different." Then aware of sounding vulnerable, she turned back to him and her voice hardened. "I can hardly live the way I used to. I'm accustomed to finer things, you see." Jack arched an eyebrow and Bridie wished she hadn't put on airs in front of him. If there was a man who knew her for what she really was, it was Jack. "Did you marry?" she asked.

"No," he replied. A long silence followed. A silence that resonated with the name Kitty Deverill, as if it came in a whisper on the wind and lingered there between them. "Well, I hope it all turns out well for you, Bridie. It's good to see you home again," he said at last. Bridie was unable to return his smile. Her loathing for her old friend wound around her heart in a twine of thorns. She watched him walk away with that familiar jaunty gait she knew so well and had loved so deeply. It was obvious that, after all these years, he still held out for Kitty Deverill.

Chapter 2

London

"Good God!" Sir Digby Deverill put down the receiver and shook his head. "Well, I'll be damned!" he exclaimed, staring at the telephone as if he wasn't quite able to believe the news it had just delivered to him. He pushed up from his leather chair and went to the drinks tray to pour himself a whiskey from one of the crystal decanters. Holding the glass in his manicured, bejeweled fingers, he gazed out of his study window. He could hear the rattling sound of a car motoring over the leaves on Kensington Palace Gardens, that exclusive, gated street of sumptuous Italianate and Queen Anne mansions built by millionaires, like Digby, who had made their fortunes in the gold mines of Witwatersrand, hence their nickname: Randlords. There he lived in Deverill House, in stately splendor, alongside a fellow Randlord, Sir Abe Bailey, and financier, Lionel Rothschild.

He took a swig, grimacing as the liquid burned a trail down his throat. Instantly he felt fortified. He put down his glass and pulled his gold pocket watch out of his waistcoat by the chain. Deftly, he flicked it open. The shiny face gleamed up at him, giving the time as a quarter to eleven. He strode into the hall, where he was met by a butler in crimson-and-gold livery talking quietly to a footman. When they saw him the footman made a discreet exit while the butler stood to attention awaiting Sir Digby's command. Digby hesitated at the foot of the grand staircase.

He could hear laughter coming from the drawing room upstairs. It sounded like his wife had company. That was not a surprise, she always had company. Beatrice Deverill, exuberant, big-hearted and extravagant, was the most determined socialite in London. Well, it couldn't be helped; he was unable to keep the news to himself a moment longer. He hurried up the stairs, two steps at a time, his white spats revealed beneath his immaculately pressed gray checked trousers with every leap. He hoped to snatch a minute alone with his wife.

When he reached the door he was relieved to find that her guests were only his cousin Bertie's wife, Maud, who was perched stiffly on the edge of the sofa, her severely cut blond bob accentuating the chiseled precision of her cheekbones and the ice-blue of her strikingly beautiful eyes, her eldest daughter, Victoria, who had acquired a certain poise as Countess of Elmrod; and Digby's own mother Augusta, who presided over the group like a fat queen in a Victorian-style black dress with ruffles that frothed about her chins, and a large feathered hat.

As he entered, the four faces looked up at him in surprise. It wasn't usual for Digby to put in an appearance during the day.

He was most often at his gentlemen's club, White's, or tucked away in his study on the telephone to his bankers from Barings or Rothschild, or to Mr. Newcomb, who trained his racehorses in Newmarket, or talking diamonds with his South African cronies. "What is it, Digby?" Beatrice asked, noticing at once his burning cheeks, twitching mustache and the nervous way he played with the large diamond ring that sparkled on the little finger of his right hand. Digby was still a handsome man, with shiny blond hair swept off a wide forehead and bright, intelligent eyes, which now had a look of bewilderment.

He checked himself, suddenly remembering his manners. "Good morning, my dear Maud, Victoria, Mama." He forced a tight smile and bowed, but couldn't hide his impatience to share his news.

"Well, don't stand on ceremony, Digby, what is it?" Augusta demanded stridently.

"Yes, Cousin Digby, we're all frightfully curious," said Victoria, glancing at her mother. Maud looked at Digby expectantly; she loved nothing more than other people's dramas because they gave her a satisfying sense of superiority.

"It's about Castle Deverill," he said, looking directly at Maud, who reddened. "You see, I've just had a telephone call from Bertie."

"What did he want?" Maud asked, putting down her teacup. She hadn't spoken to her husband, Bertie, since he had announced to the entire family at his mother Adeline's funeral that the supposed "foundling," whom their youngest daughter, Kitty, was raising as her own, was, in fact, his illegitimate son. Not only was the news shocking, it was downright humiliating. In fact, she wondered whether she would ever get over the trauma. She had left for London without a word, vowing that she would never speak to him again. She wouldn't set another foot in Ireland, either, and in her opinion the castle could rot into the ground for all the good it had done her. She had never liked the place to begin with.

"Bertie has sold the castle and Celia has bought it," Digby announced and the words rang as clear as shots. The four women stared at him aghast. There was a long silence. Victoria looked nervously at her mother, trying to read her thoughts.

"You mean *Archie* has bought it for her," said Augusta, smiling into the folds of chin that spilled over the ruffles of her dress. "What a devoted husband he has turned out to be."

"Is she mad?" Beatrice gasped. "What on earth is Celia going to do with a ruined castle?"

"Rebuild it?" Victoria suggested with a smirk. Beatrice glanced at her in irritation.

Maud's thin fingers flew to her throat, where they pulled at the skin there, causing it to redden in patches. It was all well and good selling the castle, there was no prestige to be enjoyed from a pile of ruins and a diminishing estate, but she hadn't anticipated a *Deverill* buying it. No, that was much too close for comfort. Better that it had gone to some arriviste American with more money than sense, she mused, than one of the family. It was most unexpected and extremely vexing that it had gone to a Deverill, and to flighty, frivolous and silly Celia of all people! Surely, if it was to remain in the family, it was only right that her son, Harry, the castle's rightful heir, should have it. And why the secrecy? Celia had crawled in like a thief and bought it on the sly. For what? To humiliate *her* and her family no less. Maud narrowed her ice-blue eyes and wondered how she, with her sharp powers of observation, had never noticed the treachery in that dim-witted girl.

"They are both unwise," said Digby. "That place will be the ruin of them. It's the sort of vanity project that will swallow money with little to show for it. I wish they had discussed it with me first." He strode into the room and positioned himself in front of the fire, hooking his thumbs into the pockets of his waistcoat and leaning back on the heels of his debonair wingtip brogues.

"At least it's going to remain in the family," said Victoria. Not that *she* cared one way or the other. She had never liked the damp and cold of Ireland and although her marriage was just as chilly, at least she was Countess of Elmrod living in Broadmere in Kent and a townhouse here in London, where the rooms were warm and the plumbing worked to her satisfaction. She wanted to whisper to her mother that at least Kitty hadn't managed to buy it—*that* would have finished their mother off for good. It would have upset Victoria too. In spite of her own wealth and position in society she was still secretly jealous of her youngest sister.

Augusta settled her imperious gaze on Maud and inhaled loudly up her nose, which signaled an imminent barrage of haughty venom. Digby's mother was not too old to read the unspoken words behind Maud's beautiful but bitter mouth. "How do *you* feel about that, my dear? I imagine it's something of a shock to learn that the estate now passes into the hands of the *London* Deverills. Personally, I congratulate Celia for rescuing the family treasure, because we must all agree that Castle Deverill *is* the jewel in the family crown."

"Oh yes, 'A Deverill's castle is his kingdom'" said Digby,

quoting the family motto that was branded deep into his heart.

"Deverill Rising," Augusta added, referring to Digby's Wiltshire estate, "is nothing compared to Castle Deverill. I don't know why you didn't buy it yourself, Digby. That sort of money is nothing to you."

Digby puffed out his chest importantly and rocked back and forth on his heels. His mother was not wrong; he could have bought it ten times over. But Digby, for all his extravagance and flamboyance, was a prudent and pragmatic man. "It is not through folly that I have built my fortune, Mother," he retorted. "Your generation remember the days when the British ruled supreme in Ireland and the Anglo-Irish lived like kings, but those days are long gone, as we're all very well aware. The castle was disintegrating long before the rebels burned it to the ground. I wouldn't be so foolish as to entertain ideas of resurrecting something which is well and truly dead. The future's here in England. Ireland is over, as Celia will learn to her cost. The family motto not only refers to bricks and mortar, but to the Deverill spirit, which I carry in my soul. That's *my* castle."

Maud sniffed through dilated nostrils and lifted her delicate chin in a display of self-pitying fortitude. She sighed. "I must admit that this is quite a shock. *Another* shock. As if I haven't had enough shocks to last me a lifetime." She smoothed her silver-blond bob with a tremulous hand. "First, my youngest daughter shames me by insisting on bringing an illegitimate child to London and then my husband announces to the world that the boy is his. And if *that* isn't enough to humiliate me he then decides to sell our son's inheritance . . ." Augusta caught Beatrice's eye. It didn't suit Maud to remember that it was at *her* insistence that her husband had finally agreed to be rid of it. "And now it will belong to Celia. I don't know what to say. I should be happy for her. But I can't be. Poor Harry will be devastated that his home has been snatched from under his nose by his cousin. As for me, it is another cross that I will have to bear."

"Mama, once Papa decided to sell it, it was never going to be Harry's," said Victoria gently. "And I really don't think Harry will mind. He and Celia are practically inseparable and he made it very clear that he didn't want to have anything to do with the place."

Maud shook her head and smiled with studied patience. "My darling, you're missing the point. Had it gone to someone else, *anyone* else, I would not have a problem with it. The problem is that it's gone to a *Deverill*."

Beatrice jumped to her daughter's defense. "Well, it's done now, isn't it? Celia will restore it to its former glory and we shall all enjoy long summers there just like we used to before the war. I'm sure Archie knows what he's doing, darling," she added to Digby. "After all, it's *his* money. Who are we to say how he spends it."

Digby raised a quizzical eyebrow, for one could argue that it wasn't Archie Mayberry's money, but Digby's. No one else in the family knew how much Digby had paid Archie to take Celia back after she had ditched him at their wedding reception and bolted up to Scotland with the best man. In so doing Digby had saved the Mayberry family from financial ruin, and salvaged his daughter's future. "No good will come of it," Digby insisted now with worldly cynicism. "Celia's flighty. She enjoys drama and adventure." He didn't have to convince the present company of *that*. "She'll tire of Ireland when it's finished. She'll crave the excitement of London. Ballinakelly will bore her. Mark my words, once everyone stops talking about her audacity she'll go off in search of something else to entertain herself with and poor Archie will be left with the castle—and most likely an empty bank account—"

"Nonsense," Augusta interrupted, her booming voice smashing through her son's homily like a cannonball. "She'll raise it from the ashes and restore the family's reputation. I just hope I live long enough to see it." She heaved a labored breath. "Although the way I'm going I don't hold out much hope."

Beatrice rolled her eyes with annoyance. Her mother-in-law enjoyed nothing more than talking about her own, always imminent, death. Sometimes she rather wished the Grim Reaper would call her bluff. "Oh, you'll outlive us all, Augusta," she said with forced patience.

Victoria glanced at the clock on the mantelpiece. "I think it's time we left," she said, standing up. "Mama and I are going to look at a house in Chester Square this afternoon," she announced happily. "That will cheer you up, Mother."

Maud pushed herself up from the sofa. "Well, I'll need somewhere to live now we've lost the castle," she replied, smiling on her eldest daughter with gratitude. "At least I have *you*, Victoria, and Harry. Everyone else in my family seems intent on wanting to wound me. I'm afraid I won't come to your Salon tonight, Beatrice. I don't think I'm strong enough." She shook her head as if the weight of the world lay between her ears. "Having the whole of London society talking about me behind my back is another cross I have to bear."

HARRY DEVERILL LAY back against the pillow and took a puff of his cigarette. The sheet was draped across his naked hips, but his stomach and chest were exposed to the breeze that swept in through the open bedroom window. Making love to his wife, Charlotte, was a loathsome duty he endured only because of the mornings he was able to spend with Boysie Bancroft in this nondescript Soho hotel where no one even bothered to question their regular visits. He made his mouth into an O shape and ejected a circle of smoke. If it wasn't for Boysie he didn't think he'd be capable of living such a despicable lie. If it wasn't for Boysie his life wouldn't be worth living because his job selling bonds in the City gave him no pleasure at all. Without Boysie life would have little point.

"My dear fellow, are you going to lie in bed all day?" asked Boysie, wandering into the room from the bathroom. He had put on his underwear and was buttoning up his shirt. His brown hair fell over his forehead in a thick, disheveled fringe, and his petulant lips curled at the corners with amusement.

Harry groaned. "I'm not going in to work today. I find the whole thing a terrific bore. I can't stand it. Besides, I don't want the morning to end."

"Oh, *I* do," said Boysie, tracing with his eyes the large pink scar on Harry's shoulder where he had been shot in the war. "I have lunch at Claridge's with Mama and Aunt Emily, then I shall mosey on down to White's and see who I bump into. Tonight I might pop into your delightful Cousin Beatrice's 'at home.' Last Tuesday her Salon was rather racy with the entire cast of *No, No, Nanette*. All those chorus girls squawking like pretty parrots. It was a 'riot,' as Celia would say. I dare say your Cousin Digby gets a leg over here and there, don't you think?"

"I don't doubt he has a mistress in every corner of London but one can't criticize his devotion as a husband." Harry sighed with frustration and sat up. "I wish I could join you and your mama, but I promised Charlotte I'd take her for lunch at the Ritz. It's her birthday."

"You could always bring her to Claridge's and we could make eyes at each other across the room, perhaps sneak a private moment in the men's room. Nothing beats the thrill of deception."

Harry grinned, his morale restored. "You're wicked, Boysie."

"But that's why you love me." He bent down and kissed him. "You're much too pretty for your own good."

"I'll see you tonight at Cousin Beatrice's then."

Boysie sighed and his heavy eyes settled on Harry's face. "Do you remember the first time I kissed you? That night at Beatrice's?"

"I'll never forget it," said Harry seriously.

"Neither will I." He bent down and kissed him again. "Until tonight, old boy."

Harry walked home through St. James's Park. The light was dull, the bright summer sun having packed up and gone to shine on a more southern shore. Clouds gathered damp and gray and the wind caught the browning leaves and sent them floating to the ground. He pulled his hat firmly onto his head and put his hands in his trouser pockets. Soon it would drizzle and he hadn't bothered to bring a coat. It hadn't looked like rain when he had set out that morning.

When he reached his house in Belgravia Charlotte was waiting for him in the hall. She looked agitated. Guiltily, he panicked that he might have been found out but when he stepped inside she looked so delighted to see him he realized to his relief that he was still above suspicion.

"Thank goodness you're home, darling! I telephoned the office but they said you weren't coming in."

Harry averted his gaze nervously, waiting for her to ask him where he had been. But as he gave his hat to the butler she grabbed his arm. "I've got some news," she blurted.

"Really? Don't keep me in suspense."

"It's about the castle. I know who's bought it."

"You do?" Harry followed her into the sitting room.

"You won't believe it."

"Well, go on!"

"Celia!"

Harry stared at her. "You're joking."

"No, I'm deadly serious. Your cousin Celia has bought it."

"Good Lord. Who told you?"

"Your father telephoned about an hour ago. I didn't know where to reach you. I've been desperate to tell you. You're not angry, are you? You know I adore you with or without a castle and anyway, I wouldn't want to live in Ireland."

"My darling Charlotte, I'm not angry. I'm just rather surprised she didn't tell me herself."

"I'm sure she meant to. Bertie said she'd gone to meet Kitty. I presume she was going to tell her first. You know how close they are."

He sank into a chair and put his elbows on his knees and knitted his fingers. "Well, who'd have thought it, eh? Archie must be mad."

"Madly in love!" Charlotte gushed.

"It'll take a fortune to rebuild it."

"Oh, but Archie's fabulously rich, isn't he?" said Charlotte, not knowing that Archie's fortune came from Digby.

"You never saw Castle Deverill. It's enormous." He felt a sudden, unexpected pain deep inside his chest, as if something were slashing open his heart and releasing memories he hadn't even realized were there.

"Are you all right, darling? You're very flushed." She crouched beside his chair. "You're upset. I can tell. It's only natural. Castle Deverill was your home and your inheritance. But isn't it better that it's gone to someone in the family? It's not lost. You'll still be able to go and visit."

"*Castellum Deverilli est suum regnum*," he said.

"What, darling? Is that Latin?"

He looked at her steadily, feeling like a little boy on the brink of tears. "The family motto. It was written above the front door, that is, before the fire. I didn't think I cared," he told her quietly. "I don't want to live in Ireland, but good Lord, I think I *do* care. I think I care very much. Generations of my family have lived there. One after the other after the other in an unbroken line." He sighed and shook his head. "Papa doesn't speak about it but I know selling it has caused him enormous pain. I can tell by the amount of alcohol he consumes. Happy people don't lose themselves in drink. This has broken the family line which has continued since Barton Deverill was given the land in 1662." He gazed down at his hands. "I'm the broken link."

"Darling, you haven't broken it, your father has," Charlotte reminded him. "And it wasn't his fault the rebels burned it down."

"I know you're right. But still, I feel guilty. Perhaps I should have done more."

"What could you have done? Even *my* money wouldn't be enough to rebuild it. You have to leave it to Celia now and be grateful that it's being kept in the family. I'm sure Barton Deverill would be pleased that his castle is still in the hands of a Deverill."

"Celia will do her best to put it back together again, but it'll never be the same." Charlotte was being so kind but her sweetness curdled. He wished he could share his pain with the man he loved.

Charlotte brushed his cheek with a tender hand. "She will do her best to make it lovely, I'm sure," she said soothingly. "And one day *you* will be Lord Deverill. Give me a son, my darling, and you won't be breaking the family line." She gazed at him with fond eyes, oblivious to the fact that the thought of fathering children turned his stomach. "After all, it's only a house."

Harry looked at her and frowned. Charlotte was his wife and yet she would never understand him. How could she? "No, my darling Charlotte," he said and smiled sadly. "It is so much more than that."

KITTY RETURNED TO the Hunting Lodge, which was a short walk from the castle, with Celia, leading her horse by the reins. She held little affection for this austere, ugly house that had once been her home. It was dark and charmless with small windows and gables that pointed aggressively toward the sky like spears. Although its situation was pretty, it having been built near the river, the water seemed to penetrate the walls and infuse the entire building with a residual damp. Unlike the castle she did not cherish her memories here. She could still feel the sour presence of her Scottish governess in the nursery wing along with the unhappy traces of longing that seemed to linger in the shadows with the damp. Happiness had come naturally for Kitty in the gardens, greenhouses, woodlands and hills, and in the castle, of course, which had always been at the heart of her contentment.

Now she walked her horse around to the stables, where the groom gave it water and hay. Celia chatted excitedly about her plans for the rebuilding. "We're going to put in proper plumbing and electricity. No expense will be spared. Above all, it's going to be much more comfortable than before," she said, taking Kitty by the arm and walking toward the house. "And more beautiful than it ever was. I will hire the finest architect London has to offer and raise this phoenix from the ashes. It's all so thrilling, I can barely breathe!"

They found Kitty's father, Bertie, and Celia's husband, Archie, drinking sherry with Bertie's friend and former lover, Lady Rowan-Hampton, in the drawing room. A turf fire burned weakly in the grate, giving out little heat, and they could barely see one another for the smoke. "Ah, Kitty, what a lovely surprise," said Archie, standing up and kissing her affectionately. "I suppose Celia has told you the good news."

"Yes, she has. I'm still trying to take it in." Kitty resented Archie's enthusiasm. It was all she could do to smile in the wake of such devastating news. "Hello, Papa, hello, Grace." She bent down to kiss her friend Grace Rowan-Hampton and reflected on the miraculous healing power of time. Once, she had despised Grace for her long-standing affair with her father, but now she was grateful to her for her constant loyalty to her former lover, who looked more bloated with booze than ever. Besides Grace, Kitty didn't think her father had many friends left. In his youth Bertie Deverill had been the most dashing man in West Cork, but now he was a wreck, destroyed by whiskey and disillusionment and a nagging sense of his own failings. Even though he had formally recognized Little Jack, the child was a persistent reminder of a shameful moment of weakness.

"My dear Kitty, will you stay for lunch?" Bertie asked. "We must celebrate Celia and Archie's jubilant purchase of the castle."

Kitty thought of Little Jack and her stomach cramped with anxiety. But she dismissed her fears and took off her hat. After all, Miss Elsie had promised not to let him out of her sight. "I'd love to," she replied, sitting down beside Grace.

Grace Rowan-Hampton looked as radiant as a ripe golden plum. Although she was almost fifty, her light brown hair showed only the slightest hint of gray and her molasses-colored eyes were alert and bright and full of her characteristic warmth. Kitty scrutinized her closely and decided that it was the plumpness of her skin and the flawlessness of her complexion that were the key to her beauty; a lifetime of soft rain and gentle sunshine had been kind to her face. "Celia and Archie have taken us all by surprise," Grace said with a smile. "We've been eaten up by curiosity over the last weeks, but now we know we must celebrate. The castle is not lost to the Deverills, after all, but regained. Really, Bertie, I couldn't bear to think of it being bought by someone with no understanding of its history."

"That's what I said to Archie," Celia replied, taking his hand. "I said that it would haunt me for the rest of my days if the place fell into the hands of strangers. I just love the history. All that stuff about Henry VIII or whoever it was. So romantic." Kitty winced. No one with any real connection to the place would get it all so wrong.

"And I decided then that my wife's happiness was more important than anything else in the whole world. We hoped it would make you happy too, Lord Deverill."

Bertie nodded pensively, although Kitty didn't think her father's thoughts contained anything much. He had a distant look in his rheumy eyes, the look of a man to whom little matters beyond the contents of a bottle. "And Celia's having a baby too," Kitty said, changing the subject.

"Yes, as if we didn't have enough to celebrate." Celia beamed, placing a hand on her stomach and sliding her bright eyes to her husband. "We're both very, very happy."

"A baby!" Grace exclaimed. "How very exciting! We must raise our glasses to that too."

"Isn't it wonderful. Everything is just wonderful," said Celia as they lifted their glasses in a toast.

It was late afternoon when Kitty rode over the hills to Jack O'Leary's house. The setting sun left a trail of molten gold on the waves as the ocean darkened beneath the pale autumn sky. She had briefly stopped off at home to check on Little Jack, whom she had found happily playing in the nursery with his nanny. Kitty had been relieved to find her husband, Robert, working in his study nearby. He didn't like to be disturbed when he was writing and she was only too happy to leave him and get away. She'd tell him about Celia and the castle later. As she left the White House she was content that Little Jack was safe with Miss Elsie and Robert.

In her haste to see her lover she had forgotten her hat, so that now her long red hair flew out behind her, curling in the gusty wind that swept in off the water. When at last she reached the whitewashed cottage, she hurriedly dismounted and threw herself against the door. "Jack!" she shouted, letting herself in. She sensed at once that he wasn't there. The place felt as quiet and empty as a shell. Then she saw his veterinary bag sitting on the kitchen table and her heart gave a little leap, for he wouldn't have gone visiting without it.

She ran out of the house and hastened down the well-trodden path to the beach, cutting through the wild grasses and heather that eventually gave way to rocks and pale yellow sand. The roar of the sea battled competitively against the bellowing of the gale and Kitty pulled her coat tightly about her and shivered with cold. A moment later she noticed a figure at the other end of the cove. She recognized him immediately, shouted and waved, but her voice was lost in the din of squawking gulls squabbling about the cliffs. She strode on, leaning into the wind, brushing the hair off her face with futile swipes. Jack's dog noticed her first and bounded over the sand to greet her. Her spirits lifted when Jack finally saw her and quickened his pace. The sight of him in his old brown coat, heavy boots and tweed cap was so reassuring that she began to cry, but the wind caught her tears before they could settle and whipped them away.

"What's the matter?" Jack asked, pulling her into his arms. His melodious Irish brogue was like balm to her soul and she rested her cheek against his coat and reminded herself that home was here, in Jack O'Leary's embrace. Their adultery had started as a lightning strike of passion but now had become a way of life—none the less joyful for that. It was the pearl in her oyster.

"Celia has bought Castle Deverill," she told him. She felt him press his bristly face against her head and squeeze her tighter. "I shouldn't mind, but I do."

"Of course you mind, Kitty," he replied with understanding.

"She's going to rebuild it and then she's going to live there and I'm going to be like the poor relation in the White House. Am I being very unworldly?"

"You've suffered worse, Kitty," he reminded her.

"I know. It's only a castle but . . ." She dropped her shoulders and Jack saw the defeat in her eyes.

"It *is* only a castle. But to you, it's always been much more than that, hasn't it?" He kissed her temple, remembering sadly the time he had tried and failed to persuade her to leave it and run off with him to America. Had it been nothing more than a castle they might have been happily married by now, on the other side of the Atlantic.

"And Bridie's back," she added darkly.

"I know. I saw her at Mass this morning, swanking about in her fine clothes and jewelry. Indeed, she found a rich husband in America—and lost him. Word has it she's made a healthy donation to the church. Father Quinn will be delighted."

"She's come back for Little Jack," said Kitty, her stomach clenching again with fear. "She says she had to leave him once and she won't do it again."

"And what did you tell her?"

"That she left him in my safekeeping. But she said it was Michael who left him on my doorstep with the note. She said she's his mother and that he belongs with her. But I've told Little Jack that his mother is in Heaven and that I'll love him and look after him in her stead. I can't now tell him that she's suddenly come back to life."

"She can't have him, Kitty. She would have signed papers in the convent, giving up her right."

Kitty remembered the old Bridie, her dear friend, and her heart buckled for her. "She probably didn't know what she was signing," she said softly.

"Don't feel sorry for her," he reproached. "She's done well for herself, has she not?" He took Kitty's hand and began to walk back up the beach toward his cottage.

"I'm terrified she's going to try and steal him," Kitty confessed with a shy smile. She knew how ridiculous that sounded.

Jack looked down at her and grinned affectionately. "You've always had a fanciful imagination, Kitty Deverill. I don't think Bridie would be foolish enough to attempt kidnap. She'd get as far as Cork and the Garda would be all over her."

"You're right, of course. I'm just being foolish."

He swung her around and kissed her. "What was that for?" she laughed.

"Because I love you." He smiled, revealing the gap where his tooth had been knocked out in prison. He curled a tendril of hair behind her ear and kissed her more ardently. "Forget about the castle and Bridie Doyle. Think about *us*. Concentrate on what's to come, not what has passed. You said this wasn't enough for you anymore. You know it's not enough for me."

"It's not enough, but I don't know how to resolve it."

"Remember I once asked you to come with me to America?"

Kitty's eyes began to sting at the memory. "But they arrested you and you never even knew I had decided to come."

He slipped his fingers around her neck beneath her hair and ran rough thumbs over her jawline. "We could try again. Take Little Jack and start afresh. Perhaps we wouldn't have to go as far as America. Perhaps we could go somewhere else. I understand that you don't want to leave Ireland, but now Celia has bought the castle it's going to be tough living next door, on the estate that once belonged to your father."

Kitty gazed into his pale blue eyes and the sorry sequence of their love story seemed to pass across them like sad clouds. "Let's go to America," she said suddenly, taking Jack by surprise.

"Really?" he gasped.

"Yes. If we go we must go far, far away. It will break Robert's heart. Not only will he lose his wife but he will lose Little Jack, who is like a son to him. He will never forgive me."

"And what about Ireland?"

She put her hands on top of his cold ones and felt the warmth of his Irish vowels wrapping around her like fox's tails. "I'll feel close to Ireland with *you*, Jack. Because every word you speak will bring me back here."

Chapter 3

Bridie heard Rosetta's laughter coming from inside the barn. It was blithe and bubbling like a merry stream. As she approached she realized that in all the months they had known each other, she had never heard Rosetta laugh with such abandon and she suffered a stab of jealousy, for that carefree sound excluded her as surely as the years in America had alienated her from her home. For it came from somewhere warm and intimate, a place Bridie couldn't reach for all her wealth and prestige. Her thoughts turned to Jack O'Leary and the girl in her longed for that innocent time in her life when she had dreamed of laughing so blithely with him, when she had yearned for his arms to hold her and his lips to kiss her; when she had craved his love with every fiber of her being. But Kitty had stolen him as she had later stolen her son. Bridie pushed aside her childhood dreams with a sniff of disdain because she wasn't Bridie Doyle any longer. With a determined hardening of her heart she smothered the tenderness in it that had only brought her unhappiness, and strode into the barn. The laughter stopped at once as the light from outside was thrown across the room. Sean's surprised face appeared from around the back of the hay rick, flushing guiltily. A moment later Rosetta stepped out, the buttons on her blouse half undone and her hair disheveled.

"I need to talk to you, Rosetta," Bridie said stiffly. Then, turning to her brother, she added, "I'm sure there's something you can find to do outside." Sean grinned at Rosetta, whose brown skin was flushed from the roughness of his bristles, and stepped out into the wind, closing the big door behind him. "I see you're already helping on the farm," Bridie said, regretting, even as she spoke, the resentful tone in her voice.

"I would like to be helpful," Rosetta replied. "The country-side here is wild and romantic."

Bridie noticed the dreamy look in her eyes and her jealousy made her mean. "Believe me, there was nothing romantic about my childhood here. Hard winters and poverty are all I remember."

Rosetta's smile faded. "I'm sorry, Bridget." The two women had shared so much, they were more like friends than servant and mistress. Rosetta began to button up her blouse with trembling fingers.

Bridie's heart softened. "Forgive me," she said. "You're right. It *is* romantic and wild here. There was a time when I felt it too. But those days are gone and I can never get them back. I'm leaving, Rosetta. I'm going back to Dublin. Then I'm taking the ship to America. This time for good. I'd like you to come with me, but it's your decision." She sighed, knowing already that their adventure together was to end here. "It's time my brother married. I think he's made his choice." Rosetta blushed, lowering her eyes. "And it's plain that you like him too."

"I do, Bridget," Rosetta replied and Bridie was surprised by the degree of her disappointment and hurt. But her affection for Rosetta overrode her bitterness and she took her friend's hands.

"Has he . . .?"

"Yes, he's asked me to marry him."

"After a fortnight?" said Bridie, astonished.

Rosetta shrugged in that carefree Italian way of hers. "When you know, you know," she said.

Bridie was moved and generosity flowed back into her. Rosetta had always been strong, now she admired her resolve and certainty. "Then you must stay." She embraced Rosetta fiercely, suddenly afraid of setting off on her journey alone. "I'll miss you," she said huskily. "We've been through so much together, you and I. In fact, I realize now that you're my only real friend. It grieves me to lose you." Her voice had suddenly gone as thin as a reed. She cleared her throat and collected herself. "But there's something important I have to do. Something that matters to me more than anything else in the world."

"What will you tell your family?"

"I will write to them from Dublin and explain that I don't belong here anymore. It's like trying to put on an old dress I've grown out of. It no longer fits." She laughed to disguise her tears. "You can tell them I have left for New York. That I couldn't bear to say good-bye. I'll make sure you are all well provided for. Mam can buy her mangle and Sean won't have to worry about the farm any longer. He can buy the land now and repair the house. I doubt he'll be able to do much more than that while Nanna is alive. Write to me, Rosetta." She squeezed her hands.

"How will I know where to find you?"

"I will send you details once I have sorted myself out. It seems that I will require Beaumont Williams's assistance after all," she said, referring to her attorney.

"Are you sure you want to go back to New York?" Rosetta asked.

"Yes, I'll go back and give all those society women something to bitch about! I can count on Mr. Williams to help me. He and his wife, Elaine, were good to me when Mrs. Grimsby died leaving me a fortune. When I knew no one in New York. I know I can rely on them now." She smiled wryly. "Money has a funny way of inspiring loyalty."

"Look after yourself, Bridget."

Bridie gazed at her sadly. "And you look after Sean. He's a good man." She didn't dare mention her other brother, Michael. Rosetta would discover soon enough how very different two brothers could be. It was only a matter of time before Father Quinn released Michael from Mount Melleray.

"Good luck, Bridget. I will pray for you."

"And *I* for *you*. My family will be lucky to have you. They could do with some good Italian cooking." Bridie fought back tears.

"I hope our paths cross again one day."

"So do I, Rosetta. But I don't think they ever will."

A LITTLE LATER Bridie sat in the hackney cab that was to take her to the station in Cork. She knew it would be too dangerous to be seen on the platform in Ballinakelly. She held in her hands the toy bear that she had bought in town and hoped that the boy would like it. She hoped too that once they settled in America he would forget about Ireland and everything he had known here. She looked forward to celebrating his fourth birthday in January and rejoicing in the beginning of a new life together. She'd buy him more presents than he'd ever had. In fact, she'd buy him anything he wanted. Anything to make up for the years they had been apart. Her heart gave a flutter of excitement. If there niggled a shadow of doubt in the bottom of her conscience, she reminded herself that God had thrown light onto the darkness of her despair and inspired her to right this wrong. Little Jack *belonged* to her. As a mother, the Virgin Mary would surely be the first to understand.

Bridie asked the driver to wait in the road a short distance from the entrance to the White House, for she would bring the child through the coppice of trees and not down the main drive for fear of being discovered. She didn't anticipate any obstacles to her plan, so great was her desire that it blinded her to the reality of what she was about to do. All she saw was her son's small hand in hers and the happy-ever-after sunset into which they would surely walk, united and at peace.

It was early afternoon, but the sky was darkened by thick folds of gray cloud so that it seemed much later. The sea was the color of slate, the little boats sailing upon it drab and joyless in the waning light. Even the orange and yellow leaves looked dull in the damp wind that sent them spinning to the earth to collect in piles along the stone wall that encircled the Deverill estate. Bridie hurried down the road, searching for a place in the wall that was low enough to scale. She remembered the times she, Celia and Kitty had met at the wall near the castle to run off and play down by the river with Jack O'Leary, handsome in his jacket and cap, and she had to fight hard to suppress the wistfulness that washed over her in a great wave of regret. The sooner she left Ballinakelly the better, she thought resolutely, for memories were beginning to grow through her carefully constructed defenses like weeds through a crumbling old wall. At last she found a place where the stones had fallen into the decaying bracken behind and she lifted her skirt and nimbly climbed over, taking care not to get the bear wet.

She picked her way through the copse. Her heart was beginning to race and sweat collected on her brow in spite of the cold that was rolling in off the water. She could see the house through the trees. The golden lights in the windows made Bridie feel even more of an outcast, and she resented Kitty for belonging here. Holding the bear tightly she made her way around the back of the house, warily looking out for anyone who might see her.

When she was sure she was quite alone, she edged along the wall, peering in through the windows, searching anxiously. She was beginning to panic that she might never find her son when she spied an open window at the back of the house. Light poured out with laughter she immediately recognized by instinct: the long-lost sound of a child, *her* child.

Her chest constricted with emotion as she crept slowly over the York stone toward the voice that now called to her. In her overanxious imagination the laughter suddenly became the pleading cries of her nightmares, begging for her to find him and bring him home.

She barely dared breathe as she sidled up to the window and peered with one eye through the glass. The cries dissolved and there he was, on the floor with a man she hadn't expected to see, laughing joyously as they played with a brightly painted wooden train set. She balked at the sight of the man, whom she at once recognized as Kitty's old tutor Mr. Trench, now her husband. He was gazing down at the boy with a face full of affection. In fact, he looked quite different from the solemn man who had spent his time teaching Kitty and reading books in the castle. He had always been handsome in a bland, inanimate way, but now his features were brought to life by the laughter in his eyes and the merriment in his wide smile. She clutched the bear to her chest as Mr. Trench pulled Little Jack into his arms and pressed his lips to his face. The child melted against him and giggled. If she hadn't known any better she would have supposed them father and son. Their fondness for each other was natural and real and caused a great swell of jealousy to rise in Bridie's heart. Her eyes filled with tears and she muffled a sob into the bear's soft head.

Just then the woman Bridie had seen on the lawn a fortnight before appeared in the doorway and said something to the man. He released the boy, pushed himself up and reluctantly followed her out of the room. Bridie saw her chance. The window was open. Jack was alone. She knew she only had a few minutes.

Without hesitation she lifted the latch and opened the window wider. Sensing someone behind him, Jack turned around and looked at her in surprise. Bridie leaned in and, smiling encouragingly, held up the bear. The child's eyes settled on the toy and widened with curiosity. To her delight, she watched him jump to his feet and come running with his arms outstretched. For a blessed moment she thought that he was running to *her* and her spirits gave an unexpected leap of joy. But he grabbed the bear and took a step back to look at it. Now she had the opportunity to seize him. She could be quick, in and out in a second. She could lift him into her arms and carry him away and she'd be off into the night before anyone knew what had happened.

"If you come with me, I'll give you another one," she said softly, leaning in through the window. At this the boy's face filled with fear and he dropped the bear as if it had scalded him. His ears flushed scarlet and he burst into tears. His rejection was horrifying and Bridie recoiled as if she had been slapped. She watched helplessly as he stood rooted to the spot, bawling loudly, staring at her as if she were a monster, and the truth finally hit her like a cold slap: Little Jack belonged here. *This* was his home. *These* were his parents. She was nothing more than a stranger, a *threatening* stranger, and her resolve was at once thwarted by compassion and remorse. She put out a hand to comfort him, but the child stared at it in terror and Bridie withdrew it and pressed it hard against her chest.

She stepped back and hid as Mr. Trench and the woman came running into the room. The crying continued but grew quieter as Jack was consoled in the arms of either Mr. Trench or his nanny, Bridie couldn't see from where she stood. She sensed someone at the window and pressed herself flat against the wall, holding her breath and silently praying to the Holy Virgin Mary to protect her. A hand reached out and closed the window, then the curtains were briskly drawn and Bridie was shut out. With her heart now anchored firmly in despair she made her way back through the trees to the waiting cab.

WHEN KITTY RETURNED home, her heart full of hope and dread as she contemplated her future, she found Little Jack in his pajamas, sitting on Robert's knee. Robert's other leg, which did not bend as a result of an illness suffered in childhood, was stretched out in front of him. The boy was listening to a story about a car. He was sucking his thumb and holding his favorite rabbit with the other hand. Engrossed in the story, he didn't lift his head from Robert's shoulder, but remained there sleepy and content. Kitty hovered by the door, forgetting her plan for a moment as she gazed upon the heartwarming scene of her husband and half brother snuggled together in the warm glow of the fire. Robert glanced up at her without interrupting the narrative, and his eyes welcomed her with a smile. Kitty's pleasure was at once marred by her guilt and she retreated from the room, trying without success to picture the same scene replacing Robert with Jack O'Leary.

She found Miss Elsie in the bathroom, tidying up the toy boats Little Jack liked to play with in the bath. "How was your day, Elsie?" she asked, determined to distract herself from the gnawing teeth at her conscience. Even thinking about her flight to America set them on edge.

"Very pleasant, thank you, Mrs. Trench. Little Jack's such a good boy."

"He's tired tonight. He can barely stay awake to listen to the story."

Miss Elsie smiled fondly. "Oh, he is. But he loves his bedtime story and it's a treat to have Mr. Trench reading to him." She turned to face her mistress. From the frown that lined her brow, Kitty could see that something worried her. "He's been very needy tonight, Mrs. Trench," she said.

"Needy?"

"Yes. Something frightened him in the nursery. I don't know what it was. A fox or a bird perhaps at the window. Poor little mite was sobbing his eyes out. Since then he's been cling-ing to me or Mr. Trench like a little limpet."

Kitty felt that dreaded cold hand squeezing her heart again. "Did you see anything at the window?"

"No." Miss Elsie hesitated. She didn't want to admit that she had broken her promise and let Little Jack out of her sight or that she had found a strange bear on the floor by the window and hidden it in the bottom of the toy chest. "Mr. Trench was with him, but had to leave the room for there was somebody to see him at the door. I turned my back for only a moment and that was when he saw it. I'm sure it's nothing but I thought I should tell you since you might wonder why he's a little unset-tled tonight."

"Thank you, Elsie." Kitty hurried back into the bedroom, where Robert was now lifting the child to his bed. She helped turn the blankets down so that Robert could slip him beneath. Then he stroked his red hair off his forehead and planted a kiss there.

"Good night, sweet boy," he said. But Little Jack was sud-denly stirred out of his stupor and grabbed Robert's hand.

"Stay," he whimpered.

Kitty looked at Robert in alarm. "What is it, Jack?" she asked, kneeling beside his bed. Little Jack sat up and threw his arms around her, clinging to her as if he was afraid the mattress might swallow him up.

"The lady might come again."

"What lady?" Kitty looked at Robert in horror because she knew.

"There *is* no lady, Little Jack. There's only us and Miss Elsie," Robert reassured him.

Kitty held him close and stroked his hair. "Where did you see this lady, Little Jack? Can you remember?"

"At the window," he whispered.

"What did she want?"

"She gave me a bear, but I don't want it."

Kitty's stomach plummeted fast and far. "She must have been a tinker, Little Jack," she soothed, struggling to keep the tremor out of her voice. "Nothing to be frightened of, I promise you. She's gone now and she won't be coming back. You're quite safe. We won't let anything bad happen to you, sweetheart. Not ever."

When at last the child had been coaxed back under the bed-clothes and stroked to sleep with a gentle hand, Kitty found Robert downstairs in the sitting room, stoking the fire. "Do you think he did see someone at the window?" he asked. Kitty was as pale as ash. "What is it, Kitty?" He put down the poker.

"You know I told you that Little Jack's mother was a maid at the castle?"

"Yes," Robert replied, narrowing his eyes. "Who was she?"

"Bridie Doyle."

Robert stared at her in astonishment. "Bridie Doyle? The plain young woman who worked as your lady's maid?"

"Yes," Kitty replied.

"Good Lord. What was your father thinking?"

"I don't imagine he was thinking at all at that point. Well, after giving birth to him, she disappeared to America and we lost touch. I never thought I'd see her again. But she's come back." Kitty put her hand to her throat. "She's come back for Little Jack."

"How do you know?"

"She turned up here a couple of weeks ago. She told me she

had to leave him once, but she wasn't going to do so a second time. I think it must have been her at the window." The full horror of what might have happened robbed the strength from Kitty's knees and she sank into a chair. "I feared this would happen."

Robert flushed with fury. "How dare she!" He made for the door.

"Where are you going?"

"To tell Miss Doyle that she can't simply march in and steal a child. He doesn't belong to her. The fact that she gave birth to him is of no consequence. She gave him up and that's the end of it. He's Lord Deverill's legitimate son and entrusted into our keeping."

"Oh Robert, you can't just storm into the Doyles' house throwing accusations about. You don't know that she came to steal him. Perhaps she came to give him a present."

He raised an eyebrow cynically. "And you believe that, do you?"

"I want to."

"Then you're a fool, Kitty."

"Robert!"

"Well, I'm not going to give her the benefit of the doubt. This is our boy we're talking about. The child we love more than anything else in the world. You think I'm going to take a risk with him?"

"What are you going to do?"

"I'm going to give her a piece of my mind. I'm going to make sure she never comes near him again."

Kitty had never seen Robert so angry. His fury frightened her. It frightened her because it was fueled by love—and if he loved Little Jack so fiercely, how could she even contemplate taking him off to America?

She thrust her plan to the back of her mind and stood up. "Then I'm coming with you," she announced. "You shouldn't drive with that leg of yours."

"Very well," he replied, walking into the hall. "You can drive, but first go and tell Miss Elsie to keep a close eye on Little Jack."

They hastened down the lanes in silence. The car sped over fallen leaves and twigs swept onto the tracks by relentless winds and autumn rain. The headlights beamed onto the stone walls and hedgerows, exposing for a passing moment a pair of fox's eyes that blazed through the darkness like golden embers. Kitty shivered and gripped the steering wheel with her gloved hands.

At last they began to bump along the stony track that meandered through the valley to the Doyle farmhouse. She slowed down for tonight was not a night to get the car stuck in a pothole or puncture a tire. Kitty's heart began to accelerate as they approached the building where Michael Doyle had violated her, and although she knew Michael wasn't there, the sweat still seeped through her skin because fear does not listen to reason.

Kitty pulled up outside the farmhouse and climbed out. She caught up with Robert and took hold of his hand. "Careful now, Robert," she hissed. "I doubt Bridie's family know about Little Jack."

"I'm not about to set the whole Doyle clan onto our boy, Kitty," he retorted and Kitty felt a surge of confidence at the commanding tone in his voice.

Robert knocked loudly on the door. There was a brief pause before it opened and Sean peered out. He looked surprised and a little apprehensive to see them. Without hesitation he pulled the door wide and invited them in. Inside, Old Mrs. Nagle sat beside the turf fire smoking a clay pipe while Mrs. Doyle rocked on the other side of the hearth, busily darning. A pretty young woman Kitty had never seen before was sitting at the table. Bridie was noticeably absent.

As Kitty and Robert entered, bringing with them a gust of cold wind, four pairs of eyes watched them warily.

"Good evening to you all," said Robert, taking off his hat. "Please forgive our intrusion. We've come to see Miss Doyle."

Mrs. Doyle pursed her lips and put down her sewing.

"She's not here," said Sean, standing in the middle of the room and folding his arms.

"Where is she?" Robert demanded. "It's important."

"She's gone—"

"Gone where?" Kitty interrupted.

"Back to America."

Robert looked at Kitty and she could see the relief sweep across his face like the passing of a storm. "Very well," he said, replacing his hat.

"Can I help you with anything?" Sean asked.

"You just have," Robert replied, making for the door.

Kitty noticed that Mrs. Doyle's cheeks were damp from tears and Old Mrs. Nagle's eyes were brimming with a world-weary blend of sorrow and acceptance. A heaviness pervaded that room which Kitty would have liked to alleviate, but she was keen to be out of there as fast as possible and home, where she felt safe. As she hurried to the car she thought of the loss that poor Mrs. Doyle had suffered and she felt sorry for her.

Kitty started the engine and they set off up the track. As the car drove slowly over the stones Robert reached across the gear stick and put his hand on her leg. He glanced at her, but her features were indiscernible in the darkness. "Are you all right?" he asked.

She took a deep breath. "I am now," she replied.

"You shouldn't have come."

"I wanted to."

He grinned. "Didn't you trust me to do it on my own?"

"I don't trust you at the wheel, no. But I trust you completely in everything else, especially *this*, Robert," she said, turning to look at him. "I felt very sure that whatever happened you'd protect Little Jack; that you'd protect the both of us."

"You know, Kitty, you and Little Jack are the two people I love most in the world. I'd do anything for you."

Kitty turned back to gaze into the road, her guilt slicing a divide through the center of her heart.

BRIDIE STOOD ON the deck of the ship and watched the Irish coastline disappear into the mist. She recalled with bittersweet nostalgia the first time she had left her homeland three years before. She had traveled in steerage then with little more than the clothes on her back and a small bag, full of hope for the future and anguish for the child she was leaving behind, and watched her past grow smaller and smaller until it was gone.

She felt that she had lost Jack not once but twice. She'd had the chance to take him. She'd reached for him but the revelation that the child loved his home had taught her that the fabric of living was as powerful as the lottery of blood, and the very fact that she'd tried to lure the child with a toy shamed her. She'd abandoned him again but this time she'd debased herself in the process.

Now she watched the swirling mist engulf the island she had loved and lost, and knew from the pain in her heart that the wrench was just as severe now as it had been the first time. For in that green land rested the body of her daughter and upon those verdant fields her son would thrive, without a thought for his mother and her longing, without realizing where he really came from. Indeed, he would grow up on the Deverill estate never knowing the simple farmhouse, barely a few miles over the hills, where his roots lay deep and silent.

Tears rolled down her cheeks and she didn't bother to wipe them away. There was a strange pleasure to be found in grief, a certain satisfaction in the aching chest and dull, throbbing head, a sense of triumph in her will to go on living despite the sea below that swelled against the barrel of the boat, inviting her to taste the deadening flavor of oblivion in its wet embrace. She stared now at the black sea and found the rhythm of the waves hypnotic. They called to her in whispers and it would have been so easy to heed their summons and allow them to take away her pain. And yet she didn't. She let grief rattle through her like an old familiar friend, searching the wreckage of her soul for the last remains of sorrow. She knew that, once it had consumed all that she was, there would be nothing left and it would move on. It had done it before and it would do so again.

She closed her eyes and inhaled the damp sea air. She might be leaving her son behind but her daughter, her sweet little girl whom she had not even blessed with a kiss, was with her, for hadn't Kitty taught her that the dead never leave us? That was the only thing of value left of their friendship and she held it close, against her heart.

Chapter 4

Hazel and Laurel, Adeline Deverill's spinster sisters, known as the Shrubs, stood by Adeline's grave and admired the crimson berries they had placed there. They might have been twins, being of the same height, with round, rosy faces, anxious, twitching mouths and graying hair pinned onto the top of their heads. But on closer inspection, Hazel, who was older than her sister by two years, had bright, sky-blue eyes whereas Laurel's were the color of the mist that gathers over the Irish Sea in winter. They had not been beauties in their day, unlike Adeline with her fiery red hair and disarming gaze, but they both possessed a sweetness of nature that showed in the soft contours of their features and in the surprising charm of their smiles. Their need for each other was particularly endearing in two elderly women who seemed to have sacrificed marriage and children to remain together.

"She always loved the color red," said Hazel with a sigh.

"She loved color," Laurel agreed. "*Any* color."

"Except black," Hazel added.

"Black isn't a color, Hazel. It's the *lack* of color."

"Adeline used to say that 'darkness is simply the absence of light.' That it doesn't exist in itself. Do you remember, Laurel?"

"Yes, I do."

"She was so wise. I do miss her." Hazel pressed a crumpled cotton handkerchief to her eye. "She was a reassuring presence during the Troubles."

"Oh, indeed she was," agreed Laurel. "We've lived through turbulent times, but I do feel that peace has descended over Ballinakelly and those beasts who wanted us English out have put away their claws. Don't you think, Hazel?"

"Oh, I do. But how I wish that things hadn't changed. I do so hate change. Nothing was—"

"The same after the fire. I know," said Laurel, finishing the sentence for her sister. "No more games of whist in the library or parties—oh, how I loved the parties."

"No one threw parties like Adeline. No one," said Hazel. "All that's left are the memories. Wonderful, wonderful memories." She sighed sadly at the thought of what had once been. "It won't be the same now Celia's bought the castle."

"No, it won't be the same. It'll be different," agreed Laurel ponderously. "She'll bring it back to life, though, which will be lovely. I do hope she remembers the way it was. Should we advise her, do you think?"

"She'll be grateful for our help, I'm sure. We knew the castle better than anyone else."

"Except possibly Bertie," said Laurel.

"Yes, except Bertie, of course."

"And Kitty, perhaps?" Laurel added.

"Yes, and Kitty," Hazel agreed, a little irritably. "But we know the way *Adeline* would want it to be," said Hazel, gazing upon the damp earth beneath which their sister's body lay buried.

Laurel inhaled deeply. "We're the last of our generation here, you know."

"I'm aware of that, Laurel. One has to look to the younger generation for comfort. I'm very grateful to Elspeth and Kitty. If it wasn't for our great-nieces and their darling children, there'd be no reason to go on. No reason at all."

"Adeline was always certain we'd meet up in the end."

"A load of old rubbish," said Hazel.

Laurel stared at her in surprise. "My dear Hazel, I think that's the first time we've ever disagreed on anything."

"Is it?"

"Yes, it is."

"Well, I hope it doesn't set a precedent," Hazel added anxiously.

"I don't know. It might. Wouldn't that be awful? Suddenly at the grand old age of—"

"Don't say it," Hazel interrupted, putting a hand on her sister's arm.

"At our grand old age then, that we began to disagree."

"We couldn't have that," said Hazel.

"No, we couldn't. It would upset everything."

"Yes, it would. *Everything.*"

"Shall we go home and have a cup of tea?"

"Yes, let's." Hazel smiled with relief. "I'm so happy we agree on that!"

ADELINE WATCHED HER sisters walk out into the street and head off toward home. From her place in Spirit she could see everything that went on in Ballinakelly. Unlike her husband, Hubert, and the other heirs of Castle Deverill who were bound by Maggie O'Leary's curse to remain in the castle until the land was returned to an O'Leary, Adeline was free to come and go as she pleased. Literally a free spirit, she thought with satisfaction. It would have been easy to have left this world altogether; after all, the allure of what human beings call "Heaven" was very strong. But Adeline was bound to Hubert by a more powerful force than curiosity. She had resolved to stay with him because she loved him. She loved Ireland too, and her family who remained here. Only when *their* time ran out would she go home to Heaven; all together, as they had always been.

Adeline was intrigued by the recent comings and goings at the castle. Celia, who was staying at the Hunting Lodge with Bertie, spent a great deal of time exploring the ruins and discussing her plans with Mr. Leclaire, the architect she had brought over from London. Portly like a little toad, with a shiny round face, bald head, fleshy lips and a speech impediment that caused him to spit on his *s*'s, Mr. Kenneth Leclaire was wildly enthusiastic about this ambitious commission. Celia Mayberry was his favorite sort of client: clueless and with a bottomless budget. He had grand ideas and hopped from charred room to charred room behind the dreamy Celia, waving his arms about and describing in lavish superlatives the splendor of those rooms once rebuilt according to his glorious vision. Celia clapped her hands with glee at his every suggestion, squealing encouragement: "Oh, Kenny darling, I just love it! Import it, build it. I want it yesterday!"

Celia wanted Kitty to enjoy the process of restoration as much as she did, and Adeline, so amused by the prancing Mr. Leclaire and Celia's blinkered passion to re-create the past through the rose-tinted hue of her memories, was saddened by the sight of her favorite grandchild, wandering the ruins with her cousin as if she too were a ghost, searching for herself among the ashes.

Kitty cut a lonely, heavyhearted figure. For Kitty, the loss of her home and her beloved grandparents had caused something to shift inside her, subtly like the small movement of a cloud that repositions itself in front of the sun, casting her in shadow. But there was something else. Adeline could intuit that from her vantage point. From where Adeline stood Kitty's soul was laid bare and all the events of her life were revealed to her grandmother like the open pages of a book. Adeline saw the brutal rape in the Doyle farmhouse and the moment on the station platform when Jack O'Leary had been taken from her by the Black and Tans, and she knew that Michael Doyle had not only violated Kitty, but destroyed too her chance of happiness with Jack. His had been the hand that had swiped away her future, and yet, with the same stroke he had brought Little Jack from the convent in Dublin and placed him in Kitty's care. Adeline saw it all with absolute clarity. She also saw the plans Kitty was making to leave for America. She had missed her opportunity once before and was determined not to do it a second time. But Adeline knew that Little Jack didn't belong on the other side of the Atlantic. He was a Deverill and Castle Deverill was where he belonged.

No one had more right to Castle Deverill than Barton Deverill himself, the man who had built it and given it the family motto. Yet he was tired of haunting this accursed place. Adeline had tried to ask him about Maggie O'Leary but, unlike Kitty's, the storybook of Barton's life was closed defiantly shut. There was something in it, she sensed, of which he was greatly ashamed. She could almost see the stain seeping through the paper. Why else would he be so unhappy? Of course it made him desperately sad to see the castle reduced to rubble—it had made them all unhappy to see it so, but the excitement of Celia's plans had cheered them up considerably. Only Barton remained in his mire of misery without any desire to pull himself out and Adeline wondered why.

The curse was constantly on her mind. If it wasn't broken she knew what Bertie and Harry's fate would be. On and on it would continue to punish the Lord Deverills for what the first had done. But what *had* Barton done, exactly? Building a castle on land given to him by Charles II wasn't a crime. Maggie O'Leary had cursed him for what she felt was robbery, but Adeline sensed there was more to it. Perhaps if she could find out what he had *done*, she could figure out a way to *un*do it. When she went to her final resting place she was going to take Hubert, Bertie and Harry with her, come what may.

KITTY RODE OVER the hills above Ballinakelly at a gallop. The wet wind made damp tendrils of her hair and brought the blood to her cheeks. The icy air burned her throat and froze the tip of her nose, and the rhythmic, thunderous sound of hooves on the hard ground took her back to a time of stolen moments with Jack at the Fairy Ring, when the only obstacle to their happiness had been her father's blessing. She laughed bitterly, wishing she could turn back the clock and appreciate how simple life had been back then, before Michael Doyle, the War of Independence and the fire had complicated it beyond anything she could ever have imagined. But now she was leaving it all behind. She would start again from scratch, and forget the past. Together with her two Jacks she would create a future in a new land so that Little Jack could grow out from under the shadow of his family's tragedy. But she couldn't do it alone.

As she had done so many times in the past, she trotted up to Grace Rowan-Hampton's manor and gave her horse to the groom. Once again, Grace was the only person to whom Kitty could turn for help.

Brennan, the supercilious butler, opened the front door and took her coat and gloves. He was not surprised to see Miss Kitty Deverill, as he would always know her even though she was now a married woman. He was used to her turning up without prior warning and striding across the hall, shouting for his mistress. He wondered what it was *this* time.

Grace was in the scullery, making a large flower arrangement for the church, although, at this time of year, there was little in the way of flowers to be found in the garden. She stood in a green dress and teal-colored cardigan with her brown hair pulled back into an untidy bun, leaving stray wisps loose about her hairline and neck. When she saw Kitty she smiled warmly, her brown eyes full of affection. "What a nice surprise," she said, putting down her secateurs. "I need a break from this tedious task. Let's go into the drawing room and have a cup of tea. Brennan has lit a fire in there. My fingers are near falling off they're so cold!"

Kitty followed her into the main part of the house, which was lavishly adorned with Persian rugs and decorated with

bright floral wallpapers, wood paneling and gilt-framed portraits of ancestors staring out of the oil with the bulging, watery Rowan-Hampton eyes that had been inherited by their
unfortunate descendant Sir Ronald. "Ronald has sent a tele-
gram announcing that he's arriving the day after tomorrow
with the boys and their families, so I'm trying to warm up the
house," said Grace, treading lightly across the hall. All three of
her sons had fought in the Great War and by some miracle survived. Since the Troubles they had preferred to remain in London, where they considered the society more exciting and the
streets safer for their children. "I persuaded them all to come
home for Christmas this year even though there are few exciting parties to go to. Without the castle the place doesn't feel
right anymore. Still, it will be nice to have everyone back in
Ballinakelly again. It's lonely here on one's own."

Kitty imagined that Sir Ronald knew all about his wife's infidelity. They clearly adhered to the Edwardian mode of marital
conduct: the wife produced an heir and a spare, after which she
could make her own arrangements, provided they were discreet.
It was a given that men of Sir Ronald's class would take lovers,
but Kitty couldn't imagine how the ruddy-faced, barrel-bellied
Sir Ronald could appeal to anybody. Truly, the idea was distasteful. Sir Ronald rarely came to Ireland and Grace seemed to have
made her own life here without him. Kitty sensed Grace was
rather irritated when he showed up. She wondered whether
Grace had had other lovers besides her father. Somehow she
doubted Grace was ever really on her own.

They sat on opposite sofas and a maid brought in a tray of tea
and cake and placed it on the table between them. "I see Celia
is plowing ahead with her plans," said Grace. "It must be hard

for you and Bertie to watch her and that ridiculous little man she's hired running riot among the ruins of your home. Still, I suppose it's better than the alternative."

"It's better than many alternatives," Kitty replied. She watched Grace pour tea into the china cups. "The Shrubs are driving her to distraction with their suggestions. They think they're being helpful but they don't realize that Celia wants to do it her own way." There was a long silence as Kitty wondered how to begin.

At length Grace smiled knowingly. "What is it, Kitty? I've seen that look in your eyes before. What are you plotting?"

Kitty took a deep breath then plunged in. "I'm leaving for America with Jack O'Leary," she declared. "This time I'm really going and Michael Doyle can't stop me."

At the mention of Michael's name Grace put down the teapot and her smiling eyes turned serious. "Michael is at Mount Melleray, Kitty," she said in a tone that implied Michael had gone to the abbey for pious reasons rather than to be cured of the drink. "I'm sure he regrets many of the things he did during the Troubles, but I've told you before and I'll tell you again, he's not guilty of half the things you accuse him of." She handed Kitty the teacup. "You have to forgive and forget if you ever hope to find happiness."

"There are one or two things I will never forgive him for, Grace," Kitty retorted, but she knew that Grace wouldn't listen to a word against Michael Doyle. She hadn't believed her when Kitty had told her that Michael had been responsible for burning the castle—and Kitty hadn't told her what else Michael had done. She didn't know why, perhaps because of the close roles they had both played during the War of Independence, but

Grace *cared* for Michael. "I'm not here to argue with you," said Kitty. "I need your help."

"I thought so," said Grace, picking up her teacup and settling back into the cushions. "You're sure you want to leave Ballinakelly? You're sure you want to leave Robert?"

Kitty didn't want to think about Robert. The guilt was unbearable. "Jack and I belong together, Grace," she said, angry that she felt she had to argue her case. "Fate has separated us at every turn, but this time nothing can prevent us being together. I need to invent a story so that I can leave with Little Jack without raising suspicion. As you know, Robert writes at home, so he's always in the house. I need you to give me an alibi."

Grace's smile hovered over her teacup. "Considering the alibi you once gave me, it will be my pleasure to repay you in kind."

"So, will you help me?"

"Kitty, my dear, you saved my life after the murder of Colonel Manley. If you hadn't claimed to have had supper with me the night I lured him to his death they would have accused me of being an accomplice in his murder and put me away."

"If they had known half of what you and I got up to during the Troubles they would have put *both* of us away," Kitty added wryly.

"Indeed they would. So helping you now is the very least I can do. But it would be wrong of me, as a friend, not to advise you honestly. Little Jack has two fathers: Bertie, his biological father, and Robert, who is everything a father should be. He has yet to know Bertie, although in time I'm sure he will, but he loves Robert, that's undeniable. Think of *him* when you plot your escape. Is your happiness more important than his? By removing him from everything he knows and loves you will be causing him unknown distress. After all you have been through, surely you can appreciate the importance of firm roots and a loving home with *both* parents." Kitty's face darkened as she was forced to confront the possible consequences of her actions and the shame in building her happiness on the unhappiness of those who loved her. "I'm sorry," Grace continued. "I don't wish to be awkward, but I'm older and wiser than you, and it will be me who is left to pick up the pieces of your desertion. You may not realize it, but your father loves you dearly. He's grown very proud of his illegitimate little son. I can see it in his eyes when he speaks of him. I'm sure that if you give their relationship a chance, Bertie and Little Jack could become great friends."

"Don't forget that my father originally disowned me for taking in Little Jack. He would have preferred that I left him to die on the doorstep."

Grace was shocked. "That's not true," she interjected quickly. "He was horrified at first, of course, but once he had had time to think about it, he changed heart. He realized that nothing in life is more important than family. Didn't he recognize him in front of the whole family? Little Jack is his *son*, Kitty. He's a Deverill."

"I won't be persuaded, Grace. I lost Jack last time because I believed I had a responsibility *here*, but this time I'll take Little Jack with me."

"I don't condone what you are doing, Kitty, but I know that I owe you my life. You can say you're bringing Little Jack to London to stay with me. We'll arrange it after Christmas. I'll help you organize your passage to America and for someone to vouch for you when you get there. God help those you leave behind."

Kitty stood up to go. "Robert will get over me and Papa will survive," she said, making for the door. "After all, he has *you*."

Grace watched her leave. Kitty suspected that Grace's affair with Bertie Deverill had ended the moment Kitty had saved Grace's life. Indeed, Grace had used that as an excuse to end a relationship of which she had grown tired. She had explained to Bertie that she owed Kitty a debt of gratitude which couldn't be paid if she was sleeping with the girl's father. But that was a lie. Only Grace knew the *real* moment it had ended. When, high on the excitement of having played her part in the War of Independence and lured Colonel Manley into the abandoned house on the Dunashee Road so that Michael Doyle and the other rebels could murder him, she and Michael had fallen on each other like wild animals. It had all started then, her affair with Michael Doyle. She went and leaned on the fireplace and gazed into the fire. The flames licked the logs of turf and the smoke was thick and earthy. She wound her hand around the back of her neck and closed her eyes. The heat made her feel drowsy and sensual.

She could see him as clearly as if he were right in front of her, his brooding face close enough to feel his breath on her skin. She could even smell him, that very manly scent which was his alone: sweat, salt, spice and something feral that made her lose control and surrender herself to his every desire. He had taken her then and many times since, and Grace had grown addicted to the pleasure he gave her, for none of her previous lovers could compare to Michael Doyle. He made a mockery of all of them, even Bertie Deverill. There was a vitality about him, an earthiness, a hunger that made her wanton. He handled her roughly, impatiently, and when he was done she pleaded for more. He had reduced her to pulp, but she had never felt more of a woman than when he was inside her.

Now that he was at Mount Melleray she longed for the moment he would return. She fantasized about their reunion. His passion would be all the greater for his having been locked up in an abbey. He would be like a stallion let out into the field at last and she would be waiting for him like an eager mare. She would wait as long as it took. In the meantime, no one else would suffice.

KITTY RETURNED HOME, weary and disgruntled. Grace had been the voice of her conscience and she didn't like it. She knew that what she was planning was selfish and yet, after all she had suffered, didn't she deserve to take something for herself?

She wanted to ride over to see Jack, but she was careful not to arouse suspicion. The many times she had used her father, her sister Elspeth, who lived close by, and Grace as excuses for her long absences only heightened her chances of getting caught. She had to be discreet. It wouldn't be long before they'd have the rest of their lives to be together. Until that time she'd have to play the good wife.

After going to see Little Jack, who was having his tea, she found Robert in his study, writing. Knowing not to disturb him at his desk she went upstairs and changed out of her riding clothes. When she came down, Robert was in the hall. "Fancy a drink?" he asked, smiling at her. "I could do with one myself. I've been deep in my novel all day. I can barely see the words for the paper." He took off his glasses and rubbed the bridge of his nose. His brown eyes were red-rimmed and bloodshot. "What have you been up to, my darling?"

"I went to see Grace," she replied, stinging with guilt.

"So you did. How is she?"

"Same as always. She's expecting her entire family to descend on her in a couple of days for Christmas." She followed Robert into the drawing room and watched him make for the drinks cabinet.

"What would you like to do for Christmas?" he asked. "I've told my parents we're staying in Ireland this year, considering we've just settled here. Elspeth and Peter have asked us to join them—"

"I know," she interrupted. "But I can't bear their cold house and the chaos. Why don't we ask them and Papa to spend it here with us? After all, Mother will be spending it with Victoria at Broadmere and I doubt Harry will come over. It'll be nice for Little Jack to have his cousins here for a change. We can put up a tree over there," she said, pointing to the far corner, "and he can help decorate it." At the thought of this being Little Jack's last Christmas at the White House her chest tightened and she put a hand against her breast and sat down. The reality of her decision made her appreciate what she had and suddenly everything seemed much dearer to her than she had previously thought. In fact, the idea of losing her home, perhaps forever, made her dizzy with despair.

"Are you all right, darling?" said Robert, handing her a glass of sherry. "You look very pale."

"I'm tired," she replied with a sigh. "I'll go to bed early. That'll put me right."

"Indeed it will. Let's not talk about Christmas."

Just then Little Jack stood in the doorway in his dressing gown with his red hair glistening wet and brushed off his forehead. He was holding a wooden clown puppet on a string. "Look what Robert gave me!"

Kitty looked at her husband. "Did you?"

"I saw it in the window of the toy shop in Ballinakelly and couldn't resist."

"Isn't it fun?" said Little Jack, making it walk across the rug toward Robert.

Kitty watched the child concentrate as he laboriously moved the wooden cross in his hand to lift the clown's big red feet. He reached Robert at last and let him draw him onto his knee, wrapping his arms around his middle and kissing his cheek. "You're so clever, Little Jack. I thought it would take you much longer to make the clown walk." Little Jack beamed a smile at Kitty.

"You *are* clever, darling," she agreed. "How nice of Robert to buy you a present." Little Jack nuzzled against Robert and tears prickled behind Kitty's eyes. Grace's words echoed in her conscience and, with all the will in the world, Kitty was unable to silence them.

Chapter 5

New York, 1925

It's a very great pleasure to see you again, Mrs. Lockwood." Beaumont L. Williams shook Bridie's hand vigorously. "You look well, considering you have just endured a long and arduous journey across the sea." He helped her out of her coat, then gestured to the leather chair in front of the fire and Bridie sat down, pulling her gloves off finger by finger. She swept her eyes around Beaumont Williams's office, taking comfort from the familiar smell of it, for during the three years she had lived in New York, she had been a regular visitor to these premises. The aroma of cigar smoke, old leather, dusty books and Mr. Williams's lime cologne gave her a much-longed-for sense of home. "I'm sorry the purchase of the castle wasn't a success," he said, his shrewd eyes twinkling behind his spectacles.

"It was an impulsive idea, Mr. Williams. I saw the article in the newspaper about Lord Deverill selling it and reacted without thinking it through. As it happens, someone else got to it first, but I'm not sorry. I have no desire to live in Ireland."

"I'm very happy to hear that. Elaine and I are the winners then." He settled into the chair opposite and crossed one leg over the other. The shiny buttons on his waistcoat strained over his round belly and he placed his pudgy hands over it, knitting his fingers.

"However," she added ponderously, "continue to keep your ear to the ground. If it ever comes up for sale again, please let me know."

"Of course I will, Mrs. Lockwood. As you are well aware, my ear is always to the ground."

She laughed. "Indeed it is, Mr. Williams. Tell me, how is Elaine? I did miss her," she said, her heart warming at the thought of her old friend.

"Longing to see *you*, Mrs. Lockwood," he replied. "We didn't think you'd be returning."

"I didn't think I would," she replied truthfully. "Those Lockwoods chased me out of Manhattan but I won't be cowed, Mr. Williams. New York is a big enough city for all of us to live together without having to see each other. I considered starting again in a new place, as you once suggested. But New York is all I know outside of Ireland, and I feel at home here. I don't doubt you will find me a nice place to live and that Elaine and I will take up from where we left off and I will soon find friends."

"And a new husband," said Mr. Williams with a smile. "You're young, and if I may say so, Mrs. Lockwood, a fine-looking woman too. You will have all the bachelors of Manhattan howling outside your door like a pack of wolves."

"You make them sound terrifying, Mr. Williams," she said, but her grin told him his flattery had pleased her.

"So, tell me, what made you change your mind and return?"

Bridie sighed, her narrow shoulders and chest rising and falling on her breath. For a moment Mr. Williams glimpsed the lost child beneath the woman's fashionable hat and expensive clothes and he felt a surprising sense of pity, for he was not a man to be easily moved by the pathos of a woman. "Life is strange," she said softly. "I came here as a penniless maid from a small town in the southwest of Ireland, worked for the formidable Mrs. Grimsby, who, by some God-given miracle, chose to leave *me* her fortune when she died, so that I became a very wealthy woman overnight. Then I married a gentleman, a *grand* old gentleman he was indeed, who gave me respectability and companionship. His children might have called me many things, but I am no gold digger, Mr. Williams, and never was. I wanted to be looked after, I wanted to feel safe and I wanted to banish the loneliness forever. Nothing more than that. I was a young girl in a foreign country with no one to look out for me. Indeed I have come a long way." She dropped her gaze into the fire and the warm glow of the flames illuminated for a second a deep regret in her eyes. "I wanted things to return to the way they were, when I was a small, barefooted scarecrow of a girl with a grumbling belly but a home full of love." She smiled wistfully, sinking into her memories while the crackling embers in the grate transported her back to a simpler time. "There was music and laughter and I was as much part of the place as Mam's rocking chair or the big black bastible that hung over the turf fire full of parsnip soup. I'm not so naïve to have forgotten the hardship. The cold, the hunger and the sorrow." She thought of her father then, murdered in broad daylight in the street by a tinker, and her heart contracted with guilt and pain, for if she hadn't been with Kitty and Jack that day and discovered the tinkers poaching on Lord Deverill's land, her father might still be alive, and who knew if she would ever have left Ireland then. "But I'd suffer all that again just for a taste of what it feels like to belong." She dragged her gaze out of the fire and settled it on Mr. Williams who was listening with a grave and compassionate expression on his face. She smiled apologetically. "So, I realized I had to come back to the city that made me."

He nodded and smiled. "This city might have turned you into the fine lady you are today, but you made yourself, Mrs. Lockwood, out of sheer strength of character and courage."

"I've certainly come a long way on my own."

"When you wired to tell me you were on your way I set about finding you somewhere to live. I have an apartment for you to look at, when you feel ready. Elaine will help you put together your household. I understand you returned without Rosetta?"

"Yes, indeed. I need a new maid as soon as possible."

"Let's dine tonight. Elaine is longing to see you. We'll go out, somewhere buzzing. I hope you haven't put away your dancing shoes?"

Bridie laughed, her anxieties about her future falling away in Beaumont Williams's confident and capable hands. "Of course I haven't, Mr. Williams. I will dust them off and take them out and see if they remember the Charleston!"

Bridie spent a fortnight at the Waldorf Astoria Hotel while Beaumont Williams arranged the rental of a spacious apartment on Park Avenue, which was a wide and elegant street a couple of blocks from Central Park, home to New York's richest and most glamorous people. It felt good to be back in Manhattan. She liked the person she was here, in this faraway, vibrant city that seemed to reject the old and embrace the new in a thrilling tide of jazz, bright lights and wild parties. It was the era of Prohibition, all alcohol was banned, and yet you wouldn't have known it. The drinking was just driven underground and it was in these murky speakeasies where bootlegged alcohol was drunk to the music of George Gershwin and Louis Armstrong, Bessie Smith and Duke Ellington that Bridie could forget her past sorrows and dance until the skyline above New York blushed with the pink light of dawn. She could start afresh in the private parties on the Upper East Side where they would consume Orange Blossoms in crystal glasses and sweet-talk in dark corners, and Bridie could reinvent herself yet again, attracting a new crowd of friends who were as full of hedonistic fun as she was. Here, she was Bridget Lockwood, and the noise of the trucks, buses and automobiles, trolley cars, whistles and sirens, hoists and shovels, the clatter of feet treading the sidewalks, the singing in the music halls and the tap dancing in the theaters was so loud as to drown out the little voice that was Bridie Doyle, deep in her soul, calling her home. In the dazzling lights of Times Square she could forge a new happiness, one that came from champagne and shopping, spending money on fashionable clothes and cosmetics, and nights out at the new movie theaters. She embraced New York with a renewed fervor, determined never again to stumble back into her past.

Her apartment was light and airy thanks to its tall ceilings and large windows, and decorated in the opulent and highly fashionable art deco style. Shiny black-and-white marble floors, bold geometric wallpapers, silver and leather furnishings and mirrored surfaces gave the place a feeling of Hollywood glamour that Bridie relished. She felt she was in another world and it suited her perfectly. She gazed out of the window where modest black Fords motored up and down the street beside luxuriously painted Rolls-Royces and Duesenbergs in bright reds and greens, and noticed that there were precious few horses and carts in the city. In Ireland the horse was still the main form of transport and in the countryside very few people had a car. Everything in Manhattan seemed to belong to the future and she was thrilled to be part of this bright new world.

Elaine had found an Ecuadorian couple to work for her. The husband, called Manolo, would be chauffeur, and Imelda, his petite and quiet wife, would be her maid and housekeeper. Mr. Williams had helped her buy a car. She had chosen a sky-blue Winton, with a soft top, which could be pulled back in the summer, and plush leather seats. She was pleased with Manolo and Imelda because neither of them knew where she came from. They took her as they saw her, a wealthy young widow, and she was grateful for that. However, it wasn't long before the infamous Mrs. Lockwood who had graced the society pages of the city's magazines and newspapers only a few months before began to appear once again. But no one wanted to dwell on her past anymore; her rags-to-riches story was old news. They were now interested in the glamour of her clothes and the identity of the lucky men accompanying her out on the town.

"Oh do look, Bridget. There's a photo of you," trilled Elaine one morning, burying her head in the newspaper. "*The delightful Mrs. Lockwood attends Noël Coward's* The Vortex *in a sumptuous mink coat . . .*"

"Don't they have anything better to write about?" Bridie interrupted, secretly thrilled with the attention, for that photograph reinforced her sense of belonging.

"You're a beautiful, rich widow, out on the tiles with a different man every night. You oughtn't to be surprised." Elaine tossed her blond curls and took a long drag on her Lucky Strike cigarette. "I'm glad you wore the dress with the fringe. You look swell, like a real flapper."

"Rather a flapper than a vamp, Elaine," she replied.

Elaine grinned at her over the top of the newspaper. "You're not a vamp, sweetie, you're just having fun. I watch you, being fawned over by the most handsome men in Manhattan, and sometimes wish I wasn't married. Not that Beaumont isn't everything a woman dreams of." She gave a throaty laugh and Bridie laughed with her.

"Mr. Williams is distinguished," Bridie told her, choosing her word carefully because Beaumont Williams was not a handsome man by anyone's standards.

"Sometimes a girl wants a little more dazzle and a little less distinguished, if you know what I mean." Elaine sighed and put down the paper. "A girl needs a bit of adventure, otherwise life can get boring and boredom is the enemy, don't you think?"

"God save us from boredom," Bridie agreed. She brushed a crumb off the lapel of her pink satin dressing gown. "Having nothing to do makes me think and thinking takes me to places I don't want to go. How will we keep ourselves entertained this weekend, Elaine?"

"Beaumont has suggested I take you to Southampton. The Reynoldses are giving a Christmas party on Saturday night that promises to be one of the most lavish of the year. They're very keen for you to come. You add a bit of mystery—"

"And scandal, most likely," Bridie interrupted. "Some people have long memories in this town."

"Not Marigold and Darcy Reynolds. They're great people collectors. Anyone who is anyone will be there, you can be sure of that. We have a modest beach house in Sag Harbor, which we close during the wintertime, but we can stay there." Elaine looked shifty. "Beaumont can't come. Business, you know." She shrugged. "Too bad. We can drive out together, just the two of us. It'll be the bee's knees. What do you say?"

Bridie had inherited Mrs. Grimsby's luxurious pink chateau-style house in the Hamptons, but on the advice of her husband, Walter Lockwood, she had sold it. She hadn't been back since. She remembered gazing out of the window onto the long white beach and the frustration she had felt at not being allowed out to enjoy it. Mrs. Grimsby had been very demanding. Then, after the old woman died, she had finally taken a long walk up the sand. It was on that stroll, with the waves softly lapping at the shore and the glittering light bouncing off the waves, that she had realized she would miss her. She still did sometimes. Mrs. Grimsby's autocracy had given Bridie the greatest sense of security she had had since leaving Ballinakelly pregnant and afraid, and the hard work—and hard it certainly was—had given her a refuge from her pain. "I should like that very much," said Bridie.

On Saturday morning Bridie set off for Southampton in her new blue motor car with Elaine, who had persuaded Bridie that it would be much more fun without Manolo and was sitting confidently behind the wheel. The roof was down and they were wrapped in furs, gloves, hats and scarves to ward off the cold and chatting merrily as they jostled for position among the traffic making its way out of the city for the weekend. It was a crisp winter morning. The sky above Manhattan was a bright cerulean blue, full of optimism and free of cares. The sun hung low over the Hudson, caressing the ripples on the water with fickle kisses, and turning the rising new skyscrapers orange. As they drove over the Brooklyn Bridge Elaine broke into the song "Tea for Two" from the musical *No, No, Nanette*, which had appeared on Broadway that year and got everyone toe-tapping to the catchy tunes. Bridie joined in, although she didn't know all the words, and smiled coyly at the admiring men who glanced at them from the passing cars while their wives weren't looking.

As they left the city giant billboards lined the route, advertising cars, cigarettes and the new Atwater Kent radio set, which Elaine had insisted Bridie buy because it was all the rage. Beautiful faces smiled out from these posters, twenty feet tall, promising pleasure, glamour and happiness, and Bridie, who had bought into that world of material immoderation, delighted at being a part of it. Hers was the pretty smile in the advertisement and hers was the glossy existence behind it. Together, she and Elaine were wild, carefree and liberated, popular, fashionable and blithe.

The highway soon left the city behind and the concrete and brick gave way to fields and woodland, farm buildings and dwellings. Winter had robbed the countryside of its summer foliage and the trees were bare and frozen, their gnarled and twisted branches naked to the winds and rain that swept in off the sea. The young women sang to keep warm, their breath forming icy clouds on the air. It was late afternoon when they reached Elaine's house, which was a white cottage made of clapboard with a weathered gray shingled roof and a veranda overlooking the water. "Beaumont bought this as a young man and even though he has the dough to upgrade, he insists on keeping it. Surprisingly sentimental, don't you think?" said Elaine, drawing up outside.

"I think it's charming," Bridie replied, keen to get inside and warm up.

"Connie should have prepared it for us. Let's go and see." But before she reached the steps up to the front door, a stout little woman no more than five feet tall opened it and the welcoming smell of burning wood greeted them with the promise of hot food and comfort.

Preparing for a party is often more thrilling than the party itself. While one can't predict whether the evening will be a success or a failure, at least one can assure that the two hours or so it takes to get ready are exciting in themselves. With this in mind Elaine and Bridie laced their orange juice with gin, listened to jazz on the gramophone and danced around Elaine's bedroom in satin slips and stockings as they curled their hair and applied their makeup. Connie, who was originally from Mexico, pressed the creases out of their dresses and brushed the scuff from their dancing shoes, muttering to herself in Spanish that no good would come of two young women going off to a party without the presence of men to escort them. But she waved them off with a smile, if not a little warning shake of her head, then retreated inside to tidy up the great mess the two of them had made of the main bedroom.

The Reynoldses' grand Italianate mansion, set in sumptuous grounds overlooking the beach in Southampton, was famous for its spectacular ballroom, baronial-style fireplaces and elaborate gardens. Darcy Reynolds had made his fortune on Wall Street. His motto seemed to be, "No point earning it if you can't show it off." So the mansion, or "summer cottage" as the family referred to it, heaved with entertainments during the summer months and usually fell silent directly after the first frost. This winter, however, was Darcy's fiftieth birthday, and he had decided to celebrate with a lavish Christmas party, the like of which had never been seen on Long Island.

Bridie and Elaine were immediately struck by the lights. It looked like the entire building had been covered in stars, which shone so brightly they almost eclipsed the full moon that glowed like a large silver dollar above the towering ornate chimneys. The central piece of the circular entrance was an impressive gilded staircase that swept up in two curving flights meeting on a landing in front of a wide arched window before parting again. A dazzling crystal chandelier hung above Bridie's head and she couldn't help but remember Castle Deverill and the preparations for the Summer Ball, when the servants would help take down the chandeliers in the ballroom and lay out every little piece of glass on a vast cloth on the floor in order to polish them until they shone like diamonds.

At the far end of the ballroom a jazz band of black musicians led by Fletcher Henderson was positioned on a stage and their energizing music echoed off the walls. The floor was already crowded with fashionable people drinking champagne from crystal flutes and cocktails from slim-stemmed glasses. There were martinis and cosmopolitans and cherries on sticks, and no one gave a thought to Prohibition; if anything, it made the party all the more exiting. Some of the revelers had already begun to dance. Women with feathers and headbands, strings of beads and pearls, fringes and tassels, short dresses, short hair and short attention spans were like exotic birds among the men in bow ties and slicked-back hair. Laughter and conversation rose above the sound of brass and drum and Bridie and Elaine threw themselves into the thick of it. It seemed to Bridie that Elaine knew everyone, but it soon transpired that most people had already heard of the infamous Mrs. Lockwood. It wasn't long before they had glasses of champagne and a crowd around them of admiring suitors all vying for a dance.

"Look, darling, there's Noël Coward talking to Gertrude Lawrence and Constance Carpenter. I wonder what they're plotting?" said Elaine, gazing at the famous English playwright and actresses with curiosity. "Wouldn't you just love to be able to eavesdrop on their conversation?"

"I only have eyes for the luscious Mrs. Lockwood," said a young man who had introduced himself as Frank Linden.

Bridie gave him a quizzical smile. "You're presumptuous," she said tartly.

"How so? Is it so wrong to tell a woman she's a doll?" he replied. He watched her blush, then added, "Dance with me?"

She let her eyes wander over the dancers. Everyone looked as if they were having the most wonderful time. "All right," she replied, handing Elaine her empty champagne flute.

Frank took her hand and threaded through the crowd into the middle of the throng just as the band started to play "Yes, Sir, That's My Baby." A roar went up and a great surge of people flooded the dance floor. Bridie was good at dancing. Ever since she had been swung around the kitchen by her father in Ballinakelly she had loved moving to music. There was nothing more exciting than jazz and she danced energetically while Frank gazed at her with admiration.

Dinner was a banquet of mouthwatering dishes, each one more beautifully presented than the last. Bridie drank more champagne—she had lost count of just how many times her glass had been refilled—and sat down to eat at a round table with Frank, Elaine and a small group of Elaine's friends. She noticed that Elaine was tipsier than usual, flirting outrageously with a young man in a white tuxedo called Donald Shaw, patting his chest with a limp hand and laughing her throaty laugh at everything he said. Her headband had slipped on one side, almost over her left eye, and her kohl had smudged a little, giving her a decadent look. Bridie was glad Mr. Williams was not present to witness it. But she was too drunk on excitement and dizzy with champagne bubbles to worry about Elaine.

It was very hot in the ballroom. The music vibrated in her ears, the alcohol made her drowsy and the sheer delight of being part of such a fashionable crowd gave her a heady sense of omnipotence. So when Frank Linden took her by the hand and led her up the stairs to find a quiet room where they would not be disturbed, she happily obliged. In the darkness of one of the guest bedrooms he pressed her against the wall and kissed her. It felt good to receive the attentions of a man again and she wound her arms around his neck and kissed him back. She closed her eyes and felt the room pleasantly spin.

When she opened them again she was lying on the bed in her underwear and Frank Linden's hand was beneath her slip and caressing her breast. She was too sleepy to do anything about it and besides, the sensual feeling it gave her made her writhe in pleasure like a cat. A low moan escaped her throat and Frank, taking that as a sign of encouragement, slid his hand onto her inner thigh where it lingered for a moment, tentatively teasing. As Bridie didn't protest, rather her staggered breath and soft sighs left him in no doubt that she was willing, he slowly and gently moved his hand north, until it glided over her skin, under her silk panties, and on up her thigh until it could go no farther. Bridie widened her legs with abandon. Her moaning grew into gasps and sighs as she allowed the delicious warmth to spread into her belly.

When she awoke, Frank was lying asleep beside her. She could hear the music coming from downstairs, but it was slow and mellow, and a woman was singing. She climbed off the bed without waking him and fumbled about for her clothes. Once she was dressed she turned the brass doorknob as quietly as she could and slipped into the corridor. As she stepped onto the landing, Elaine was sitting on the top stair, smoking a cigarette. Bridie sat down beside her. "You all right?" she asked.

"Does petting count as infidelity?" Elaine asked in a dull voice.

"I think Mr. Williams would count it."

"Then I've just broken one of the Ten Commandments." She turned to Bridie and her big blue eyes shone. "Didn't I say a girl needs a little adventure from time to time?"

"I think we should go home now," said Bridie.

"You're right. I've had enough adventure for one night." Elaine narrowed her eyes. "Where's Frank?"

"Asleep."

Elaine gasped. "You didn't!"

"I have no one to betray," Bridie retorted with a shrug. "Adventures are essential for a young widow like me, are they not?"

"Are you going to see him again?"

Bridie shrugged. "I don't think so."

"Just a bit of fun."

"Yes, tonight I discovered how a girl can have fun without . . . complications." She wished she had known *that* when she had been a maid at Castle Deverill.

Elaine smiled drunkenly. "I could have told you that, Bridget."

"Are you good to drive?" Bridie asked, knowing that she wasn't.

Elaine grabbed the banister and pulled herself onto her feet. "Never been better," she giggled.

The two women linked arms and began to slowly and unsteadily descend the grand staircase. "God bless America," said Bridie, for she truly believed that America had given her a second chance.

Elaine squeezed her friend's arm. "God bless *us*," she said.

Chapter 6

Celia and Archie spent Christmas with Sir Digby and Lady
Deverill at Deverill Rising, their sumptuous Georgian
home in Wiltshire, which Digby had bought and renovated at
vast expense with the first fortune he had made in the South
African diamond mines. Originally the house had been called
Upton Manor, but that wasn't nearly grand enough for the
brash and newly rich Digby Deverill. Memories of summers at
Castle Deverill inspired him to give his home a name that
would last through history and give a sense of dynasty and substance. Therefore he swiftly renamed it Deverill Rising, en-
dowing it with the gravitas of his new status and the weight of
his historical name. Their son, George, would have inherited it
had his life not been so cruelly cut short in the Great War. This
saddened Digby and scoured the gloss from his vision. However, ebullient and always optimistic, Digby endeavored to
look for the positive. He filled it with friends at every opportu-

nity and wondered whether a grandson might one day cherish it as he did.

Joining them for the festivities were Celia's older twin sisters, Leona and Vivien, who came with their husbands, Bruce and Tarquin, and their small children. Due to the seven-year age gap between them Celia had never been close to her siblings. The twins were both blond and pretty, with long, aristocratic noses, shallow blue eyes and bland, unremarkable characters. Little could rouse them from passivity. However, ever since Celia had bought the castle and provoked their jealousy, they had shown surprising passion. Neither could believe that flighty Celia, who had shocked London society by bolting from her wedding with the best man, could have snatched the Deverill family seat for herself. It was an outrageous thing to have done and something that infuriated both girls, who lived relatively modestly with their Army husbands. What upset them even more was that their father, in spite of everything Celia had put him through, was inordinately proud of her.

Digby had initially been horrified by Celia's news, but his daughter's excitement and Archie's pride at having made the purchase possible softened his rancor and assuaged Beatrice's reservations. Archie, intent on impressing his father-in-law, told him of the architect's adventurous plans, which, Archie emphasized, included many of his own ideas. Digby requested to meet this Mr. Leclaire at the earliest convenience, for he wanted to make sure that his erratic daughter wasn't being overambitious. It was one thing to restore a castle to its former glory, but quite another to build a palace that wasn't there to begin with. "I will come to Ireland with you in the new year," he declared, his enthusiasm growing at the thought of involving himself. "It'll be good to see Bertie. Tell me, my dear, how is my cousin?"

Celia, riding on the crest of a wonderful wave, was pink in the face with happiness. "Oh Daddy, I'd love you to meet Mr. Leclaire. He's full of ideas. Really, he understands exactly what we want. Everything he suggests I tell him I want it yesterday! It's hilarious. He thinks I'm marvelous."

"You behave as if you have a bottomless pit of money," said Leona sourly.

Celia ignored Leona. "You'll adore him, Papa. We all do. He's a great character!"

"And Cousin Bertie?" prompted her mother gently.

Celia sighed. "He's as well as can be expected, I suppose," she replied, reluctant to divert the conversation away from herself. "Maud has told him that she never wants to return to Ireland and I gather from Harry that she is in the process of buying a house in Chester Square. They will continue to lead separate lives, for I doubt Bertie will ever leave the Hunting Lodge. I told him he can stay there for as long as he wants. It's his home, after all. But he's thrilled I'm rebuilding the castle. Just thrilled. Isn't he, Archie?"

"He's very interested in our plans," Archie agreed.

"I imagine he's putting on a brave face," said Vivien. "I mean how can he possibly enjoy watching someone else rebuilding his home?"

"Celia is hardly 'someone else,'" said Archie.

"Of course he's delighted," Digby interjected.

"I'm so pleased," said Beatrice. "I was worried it would create a rift within the family."

"Oh no, far from it, Mama," Celia gushed. "Everyone is so happy. Kitty especially! Our children will grow up together playing in all the places we used to play. It'll be a riot, history repeating itself. We're going to get into the Irish way of life, aren't we, Archie? Hunting and racing. Archie's going to take the dogs out to shoot snipe just like Cousin Hubert used to do. Oh, it's going to be such fun!" She clapped her hands together without giving another thought to poor Bertie, sinking sorrowfully into his bottles of whiskey.

"I hope you install some heating. As far as I remember, Castle Deverill was uncomfortable, cold and damp," said Leona.

"Oh yes, it was terribly damp," Vivien agreed. "I wore a fur coat in bed to keep warm."

"It's going to have the very best of everything," said Celia firmly.

"Shame you can't spend all that money on improving the weather," said Leona with a chuckle.

Vivien laughed with her. "Goodness, it rains all the time in Ireland, doesn't it?"

"It rains all the time in England too," said Celia, giving her sisters a withering look. "But I always remember the summers in Ballinakelly as being sunny and warm. You know, Archie and I are going to host the Castle Deverill Summer Ball. It'll be just like it used to be. The candlelight, the music, the dancing, and everyone will say that no one throws a party quite like Mrs. Mayberry. Isn't that right, Archie darling?"

Archie Mayberry smiled indulgently at his wife. Buying the castle for Celia had made him feel like a man again and restored him in the eyes of his friends and family. After her bolt from the wedding he worried that her parents might blame him for being too dull to keep her. He feared that he might never regain their esteem and it vexed him that he had been humiliated in front of his friends, but nothing makes people forgive and forget a scandal more surely than money. Digby's bribe, for that is, in essence, what it was, had enabled him not only to pull his family back from the brink of bankruptcy, but to look his own reflection straight in the eye. It was ironic, too, that he had managed to repay his father-in-law's generosity by purchasing the Deverill family seat. Digby Deverill, genial and urbane as he was, was inscrutable in the way that powerful men often are, but from the look on his face, Archie could tell that he had earned his father-in-law's acceptance, which had been his intention all along. As for respect, he hoped he would one day earn that too.

KITTY AND ROBERT had spent Christmas at the White House. Kitty's father, Bertie, had come for Christmas lunch with Elspeth and Peter and the Shrubs. Although Elspeth was seven years older than Kitty the two sisters had grown close ever since Elspeth had married Peter MacCartain and moved into his dank castle a short walk from Castle Deverill, nearly five years before. Little Jack had played with his three cousins and opened his presents with glee. Hazel and Laurel had fussed over the children while Robert and Peter had stood by the fire watching them with amusement. Bertie had put on a good show, not wanting to dampen the festivities, but Kitty could tell that he was deeply depressed. She wondered whether it was the castle he mourned, or his mother Adeline, or perhaps even Grace. She didn't imagine it was Maud.

But Bertie *did* miss his wife. It was one of those ironies of age and marriage: the couple who have bored and betrayed each other in their early years often comfort and sustain each other in their later ones. Bertie had betrayed his wife with his long affair with Grace (and before Grace many other discreet dalliances with pretty girls) but that affair was long over and now he found himself thinking of Maud often. It seemed absurd that after the great freeze that had been their marriage there might be a thawing on his part. He didn't understand it himself. He loved Grace—he would *always* love Grace—but Grace had ended their affair and now they were just friends. The light of desire that had warmed her soft brown eyes had died away and she looked on him with pity—he hated that he had become a man to be pitied. As much as she tried to disguise it, he saw through her. Maud on the other hand didn't pity him, she despised him and there was something rather magnificent about the fury in her—wasn't the opposite of love indifference, after all? Maud was certainly not indifferent. She resented him for *his* affair, but hadn't she been the first to leave the marital bed in favor of his old school chum Eddie Rothmeade's? She thought he didn't know, but he did. She had barely been able to hide her infatuation. But that was long ago and he was ready to forget it. His wife loathed him for his indiscretion with the maid, but hated him even more for having formally recognized the child born of that union. Now she resented him for having sold the castle even though *she* was the one who had encouraged him to do so. He was buying her a house in Belgravia with most of the proceeds, but he knew she wouldn't want him there. Divorce was out of the question for a woman obsessed with society's good opinion, but he wondered whether her head might be turned by another man, one who could give her more than he had been able to. That thought saddened him greatly. When he thought of cold, beautiful Maud, he wondered whether, had he behaved differently (and with less arrogance, perhaps), he might have made her happy. He wondered why, when he tried to *lose* his thoughts in whiskey, he only found them becoming more acute. In the alcohol-induced fog in his mind he saw Maud as she had been when he married her, when her elusive smile had turned on him like the warm rays of dawn. But she'd never smile on him again, he was certain of that. Perhaps the finality of it made him nostalgic for their past. Wasn't that the way of the world? One always wants what one cannot have.

The day after Christmas Kitty heard the news that Liam O'Leary, Jack's father, had died on Christmas Eve. The maid who reported it wasn't sure how he had died, only that the funeral was to take place the following day in the Catholic church of All Saints in Ballinakelly. Kitty wanted to ride over to console Jack, but was fearful that her presence there would arouse suspicion. He was sure to be with his mother and the rest of his family, and there were a good many O'Learys in Ballinakelly, she knew. Instead, she sent the stable boy with a letter of condolence. She was sure that Jack would read between the lines and get word to her as soon as she was able to visit.

The day of the funeral Kitty stood at her bedroom window, gazing out over the sea and biting the dry skin around her thumb with anxiety. She hadn't heard anything from Jack. She wondered whether their plans to depart for America would be delayed—or even canceled. Could he leave his mother so soon after her husband's death? She knew Jack had other siblings and his mother certainly had a sister, because she had heard him speak of her, but she had no idea where they lived, or indeed how intimate they were. Mrs. O'Leary doted on Jack, of that she was sure.

How she would have loved to attend the funeral. But it was impossible. Robert would consider it very strange and the locals would find it odd too, even though, as the local vet, Jack had been coming to Castle Deverill for years to look after the animals. So she waited. What else could she do?

Grace had arranged their departure for the first weekend in February. She wasn't planning on being in London until then and she told Kitty, quite unreservedly, that she hoped the month before leaving would give Kitty time to reconsider. But Kitty was certain that this was what she wanted. Her past had been marred by self-sacrifice. Now was her time and she was determined to take it.

The week before Christmas she had suffered horribly with her menstruation. She had lain in bed with severe abdominal pain and Robert had tactfully slept in his dressing room. But now there was no reason for her to banish her husband to another room, and, surprisingly, she didn't want to. She was about to leave him for the other side of the world. She was on the point of separating him from Little Jack, possibly forever. She hated herself for allowing her passion to make her selfish; after all, Robert had only ever been kind to her. He had only ever loved the two of them. Her sense of guilt was immense and her anticipation of loss drove her deep into his arms. She was like a sea creature clinging to the rock that was her home, while the current swept by to drag her away. As she let him make love to her, she realized, in the light of her imminent departure, that it was possible to love two men at once, in entirely different ways.

At last she received a letter from Jack, asking her to come to his cottage as soon as she was able. Anxious that he was about to postpone their departure she saddled her horse and galloped as fast as the animal could carry her over the hills to his house, which was situated in lonely isolation, overlooking the ocean. She could see a ribbon of smoke floating up from the chimney long before she reached it. A golden glow twinkled in the waning light from one of the downstairs windows. Fog was creeping in off the water and the horizon, usually so clear, was a gray mist in which fishing boats could easily lose themselves. There would be no moon to illuminate the path home, but she was sure she'd find it somehow.

She slipped from her saddle and tied the horse to a fence behind the cottage. She didn't bother to knock, but went straight inside. Jack was sitting at the kitchen table, staring into a half-drunk tankard of stout. When he saw her, he stood up and gathered her into his arms, embracing her fiercely. Her heart buckled at the sight of his grief-stained face and she squeezed him as hard as her arms would allow. Jack cried then. He sobbed into her neck like a little boy and Kitty was reminded of her beloved grandparents and her heart went out to him.

When his pain had passed through him, he returned to his chair and drained his tankard. Kitty put the kettle on the stove and made a pot of tea. He told her that his father had died peacefully in his sleep, but his mother had suffered a very great shock on finding him lying cold and stiff beside her in the morning. "He was a good man," he said quietly. "If it hadn't been for the war, he would have lived a longer life, I'm sure of it. The war was never ours in the first place. He should have done as I did and kept his feet firmly on Irish soil. But we didn't share the same politics. We quarreled over our views and I know he disapproved of my decision not to fight. If he'd only known the half of what I'd got up to during those years he'd have given me more than a clip about the ear. As it was he knew nothing. When he returned from the war something had been extinguished inside him. He never spoke of what he had seen and done but I know it was terrible. It robbed him of his joy. I hope he finds it again, wherever he is."

"He will," said Kitty. "He's home now."

"I love you for your certainty, Kitty." He grinned and watched her bring the pot over to the table and pour two mugs of tea. She sat down opposite and he reached for her hands across the narrow wooden table. "You're either as mad as a March hare or privy to the greatest of all life's mysteries. Whichever it is, I love you all the same."

"And I love you, Jack, in spite of your little faith," she replied with a grin.

"We're going to build a new life in America, you and I and Little Jack. I have dreamed of walking hand in hand with you for all the world to see."

Kitty squeezed his hands hard. "So have I. Life hasn't been kind to us, has it?"

"This time we'll board that boat, whatever life throws at us."

"It'll be exciting for Little Jack. He's never been on a boat."

Jack noticed the disquiet behind her cheerfulness. "I know you worry for him, my darling. But he's a lad. It'll be an adventure." He gazed at her tenderly. "We'll give him brothers and sisters. A big family. He won't have time to remember Ballinakelly."

"I hope you're right."

"He loves you, Kitty, more than anyone in the world. And

he'll grow to love me. I promise you he will. Indeed, I'll be a good father to him."

Kitty's eyes began to sting with tears. "I know you will, Jack. But I'm afraid. I want to do what's best for him, but I have to do what's best for me too. I feel I'm being torn in two. Robert . . ."

Jack's face hardened. "Don't think of Robert, Kitty!" he snapped. "He has no claim on you. You and I are like plants whose roots run very deep and intertwine. We've got a long history together. Shared memories and adventures Robert can never hope to create. He stole you from me. If you hadn't married him you'd have been free to marry me. No, don't argue. You know it's true. If it wasn't for him we'd be together." She nodded and released his hands. Taking up her mug she sipped her tea. "I know you're torn and I appreciate what you're giving up, coming away with me. Don't think I don't understand. But we deserve this, Kitty. There's no other way for us. It's this or nothing. If you can't come with me, I'll go anyway, because a future here without you is impossible."

"I'm coming with you. I promise," she reassured him softly.

He glanced at the window. The fog had gathered around the cottage and darkness had come early. "You'd better ride home now, Kitty, or you'll get lost in the fog."

"I'd know these hills blindfolded," she said, getting up.

"I'll ride with you," he said suddenly, pushing his chair out with a loud scrape.

"You mustn't. If we're seen together we'll ruin everything. I'll be fine. I've ridden these hills all my life."

He pressed his lips to hers and kissed her ardently. "To think there'll soon be a day when I can kiss you from dawn till dusk without interruption."

"Oh Jack, I can't wait. I want you to kiss me now without interruption." She slid her hand between the buttons of his shirt, but he stopped her.

"You have to ride home now, Kitty," he insisted. "If you leave it another moment it'll be totally dark. Please, my darling, you have to go, now."

Reluctantly she slipped into her coat and gloves and pulled her hat down low over her head. She swung herself into the saddle and waved at Jack, who stood forlornly in the doorway. "I long for the day when my home is your home," he said and Kitty blew him a kiss before gently digging her heels into the horse's sides and trotting off along the path that led to the hills.

ROBERT WAS GETTING anxious. It was dark and Kitty was still out with her horse. He didn't understand her need to ride all the time. If she had wanted to go into Ballinakelly she could much more easily have taken the car. He stood at the drawing-room window and stared out into the foggy night. All he could see was his own pale face staring anxiously back at him. He rubbed his chin. No one seemed to know where she had gone. Even the groom hadn't a clue. He had simply shaken his head and told Robert that Mrs. Trench had saddled the mare herself and set off without a word. She had probably just gone for a hack over the hills. But Robert was worried. She would have seen the fog closing in when she set off. Why on earth would she choose a misty afternoon in early January to go hacking over the hills?

He considered going to look for her. What if she had fallen off her horse? What if she had hurt herself? What if she was lying injured in the mud? She'd die of cold out there in the night. His heart was seized with panic. He took a deep breath and tried to think rationally. He'd never find her for a start. Besides, she could be anywhere. He couldn't go walking across the fields on account of his stiff leg, or take the car because those tracks were slippery with mud and he was sure to get stuck, or worse, crash. He felt utterly useless. He could do nothing but wait.

Perhaps she was with her father, he conceded. She had been worrying about him a great deal lately. Bertie was taciturn and melancholy and only Little Jack and his rousing ebullience seemed able to distract him from his woes. But Kitty wouldn't have ridden over the hills if that were the case. She would have cut through the woods and fields, for the Hunting Lodge was only the other side of the estate and she'd surely be home by now. She might have gone to visit Grace. The two of them were as thick as thieves. They seemed closer than sisters even, most notably in the way they spoke to each other, sometimes with impatience, sometimes with affection, but without the reserve that prevailed in most nonfamilial relationships. Indeed, their friendship seemed embedded in depths he would never know. But Grace had a house full of family and no formal invitation had been forthcoming. No, Kitty had not gone to visit Grace, he was sure of that.

When at last the front door opened and Kitty strode in, her face red from the cold and her Titian hair wild and knotted down her back, Robert was at first overcome with relief, then furious that she had caused him such concern. "Where the devil have you been?" he demanded, meeting her in the hall.

Kitty laughed. "You weren't worrying about me in the fog, were you?"

"Of course I was, you silly girl!"

Kitty was affronted by his patronizing tone. "I know those hills better than most shepherds," she retorted crisply. "There was no need for you to worry."

"Where were you?"

She shrugged and pulled off her gloves. "Out riding."

"Where?"

"Why all these questions, Robert? Are you accusing me of having a lover tucked away up there in the hills?"

Robert was stunned. "No," he replied. "That idea hadn't occurred to me. Should it?"

She flushed beneath her weathered complexion. "You're making a mountain out of a molehill. I was simply out riding, as I always do. I wasn't alarmed by the fog."

"I forbid you to ride out like that again. It's dangerous."

Kitty sighed impatiently. "Oh really, Robert. You're sounding like my tutor again!"

"When I was your tutor you were not obliged to obey me. Now I'm your husband, you are."

"I won't be told," she snapped, making for the stairs.

"Yes, you will. You have a little boy who depends on you," he reminded her. "And you have me, for better or for worse. I will not have you rampaging around the countryside in the dark. You have the entire day at your disposal. Please do me the favor of riding during daylight hours. Surely, I'm not asking too much."

Kitty, furious that he was telling her what to do and fired up with guilt about where she had been, was all too quick to inflame the argument. If she was angry with Robert it would make it all the more easy to leave him. She marched up the stairs without looking back. Robert remained in the hall until she had disappeared, then he turned and limped into his study, slamming the door behind him.

Kitty read Little Jack a story and tucked him up in bed. She planted a kiss on his soft forehead and savored for as long as possible the feel of his small arms around her neck, holding her close. Her heart mollified at the sight of him and, when Robert came in to say good night, she found it hard to maintain her sulk. However, she managed to eat her supper in silence. He attempted conversation but she thwarted it with monosyllabic answers until he gave up and only the clinking of cutlery on their plates interrupted the heavily charged silence.

Kitty went to bed alone and turned off the light. Her thoughts shifted to leaving home again and she felt the familiar sense of despair. But just as she closed her eyes she heard the door open and the sound of her husband's shuffling walk as he limped into the bedroom. She wished he would see that she was asleep and leave, but he didn't. He climbed in beside her and wrapped his arms around her, drawing her against him. "I don't want to fight with you, darling," he whispered. "I love you."

His gentle voice lured her out of her brooding and her despair was at once laid aside. She rolled over and kissed him. She kissed him tenderly, and as she did so a tear squeezed through her lashes, for, even as she knew she was betraying Jack, she knew also that she was being guided by a deeper longing. She didn't try to understand it, nor attempt to justify it. But as she undid the buttons of his pajamas and glided her hand over his chest, she knew she was sealing her fate, whichever way it would go; it was in God's hands now.

Chapter 7

After New Year's, Digby Deverill arrived in Ballinakelly with Archie and Celia to stay with his cousin Bertie at the Hunting Lodge. He hadn't been back since Adeline's funeral, when Bertie had announced to the family that he was not only selling the castle but introducing them to his bastard son, Jack Deverill. *That* had been quite a luncheon, Digby mused with a sardonic smile. Maud had stormed out and disappeared to London in a huff, bleating humiliation and hurt. Everyone else had been left speechless, which was quite something for a noisy family such as theirs. Now, a few months later, he was able to reflect on the whole episode with wry amusement.

Digby loved County Cork. He remembered with affection his boyhood summers at Castle Deverill, when he and Bertie and Bertie's younger brother, Rupert, who was later killed in the Great War, had taken the boat out to fish with Cousin Hubert, Bertie's formidable father. Digby was not a natural fisherman, but he had loved the drama of the ocean, the mystery of what lay beneath it, the wide horizon and the sense of being alone in the immense blue. He was fascinated by the local fishermen in their thick sweaters, caps and boots, their craggy faces weathered from years of exposure to the salty winds, their dry hands callused and coarse, and loved to listen to their banter when, at the end of the day, Bertie and Rupert would take him to O'Donovan's in Ballinakelly for a pint of stout. Cousin Hubert had preferred the comfort of his own home—and the security of his own kind. They would find him in the library at the Hunting Lodge (because in those days Bertie's grandparents lived in the castle), eating porter cake in front of the fire with his wolfhounds at his feet, hoping for crumbs. "Anyone for bridge?" he'd ask, and Digby would always be the first to volunteer because there had been something about Cousin Hubert that had made him long for his good opinion.

Now Cousin Hubert was gone, killed in the fire that destroyed the castle. Adeline was gone too. It was a salutary thought and one that reconfirmed Digby's belief that life has to be grabbed by the collar and lived consciously, decisively and courageously, not the way Bertie was living his, drifting rudderless on a current of whiskey and disillusionment. Something had to be done, and soon, or Bertie would be gone too and that would truly be the end of an era.

Digby had come to County Cork to meet Mr. Leclaire, but he had also come with the secret intention of rousing his cousin out of his stupor. He knew he had to await his moment. Bertie had to be in the right frame of mind to hear his advice, for there was always the danger that his cousin would take umbrage, for Bertie was a proud and fragile man, and the consequences could be dire.

While he waited for that elusive moment, Digby threw his enthusiasm into the plans for the castle. He'd seen the ruins the year before but he'd never taken the time to walk among them. Now, with the effervescent Mr. Leclaire leading the way through the rubble (and anticipating, with relish, his enormous bill), Digby wandered slowly from room to room like a dog sniffing for the scent of his past. He found it lingering in the hall where the fireplace still stood, recalling with a wave of nostalgia the Summer Ball when he had stood there with his new wife, Beatrice, who was seeing it for the first time. He remembered her face as clearly as if it had been yesterday. The wonder in it, the joy, the sheer delight at the beauty of the castle, lit up with hundreds of candles and adorned with vast arrangements of flowers.

Mr. Leclaire dragged him out of his reverie by urging him on through the hall into the remains of the drawing room. Shiny black crows hopped about the stones and squabbled among themselves. Mr. Leclaire pointed out the parts of the surviving walls that were still intact and the parts that were simply too weak and would have to be pulled down. He gesticulated extravagantly, waving his arms in the air, while Celia chirped and chattered and thought his every suggestion "marvelous." "I want it yesterday," she said in response to his every suggestion. Archie watched closely for his father-in-law's reaction, hoping that he'd approve, *wanting* him to approve.

"We will use the original stone wherever possible, Sir Digby," said Mr. Leclaire. "But where we are compelled to use new stone we will endeavor to match it as best we can. Mrs.

Mayberry has suggested we buy old stone but I have explained, have I not, Mrs. Mayberry, that the cost will soar considerably. Old stone is very dear."

"I'm sure Mr. Mayberry would like an estimate for both, Mr. Leclaire," said Digby. He smiled at his daughter and Celia slipped her hand around his arm, for she knew from experience what that smile meant: she'd have her old stone one way or another.

As they moved through the ruins toward the surviving western tower where Adeline had set up residence after Hubert was gone, Celia noticed a pair of grubby faces watching them from behind a wall. She nudged Archie. "Look, we're being spied on," she whispered. Archie followed the line of her vision. There, partly hidden among the stones, were two little boys. As soon as they realized they had been spotted their faces disappeared.

"Who are they?" Archie asked.

"Local boys, I imagine. They must be very curious. After all, this castle has dominated Ballinakelly for centuries."

"Don't you think we should say something? They're trespassing. There's a perfectly good sign by the gate telling them this is private property and trespassers will be prosecuted."

"Darling, they don't care about a sign. They're children." She laughed, rummaging in her handbag for some chocolate. Finding a half-eaten bar, she weaved her way through the debris and ash to where the boys were hiding. "Hello, you two monkeys," she said, leaning over with a smile. Startled, they stared up at her with wide, frightened eyes, like a pair of cornered foxes. "Don't be afraid," she said. "I'm not going to be cross. Here, it's hungry work being spies." She held out the chocolate in her gloved hand. They gazed at it warily. "Go on. Aren't you hungry?" The larger of the two boys held out his dirty fingers and took it. "What are your names?" she asked.

The elder boy unwrapped the chocolate and took a bite. "Séamus O'Leary," he replied in a strong Irish brogue. "This is my little brother, Éamon Óg." He elbowed his brother, who was staring at the otherworldly glamour of this English lady with his mouth agape. The diamonds in her ears sparkled like nothing he had ever seen before. As his brother speared him in the ribs he closed his mouth and blinked, but he was unable to tear his gaze away.

"I used to play as a little girl with a boy called O'Leary. Jack O'Leary," said Celia. "He must be related to you."

"He's our cousin," said Séamus. "His da just died," he added, enjoying the taste of chocolate on his tongue.

"I'm sorry to hear that," said Celia.

At that moment, Archie called to her. "Darling, we're going back now to look at the plans."

"You'd better run home before Lord Deverill sees you," she said to the boys. They scurried off without a word, disappearing behind the western tower. Celia returned to Bertie's car, where Mr. Leclaire was standing with Digby, looking up at the front door. "*Castellum Deverilli est suum regnum,*" said Mr. Leclaire, reading the inscription still visible in the charred remains of the stone.

"Now it's Celia's kingdom," said Digby.

"I'll be a beneficent landlord," she said, striding over the grass with Archie. "Once the castle is finished I'll throw a small party for the people of Ballinakelly. It will mark a new beginning."

"The people of Ballinakelly have always been loyal to the Deverills," said Digby. "The fire wasn't their doing but the actions of Irish nationalists from other parts of the county, certainly not from here. I'm sure the people of Ballinakelly will be delighted to see it restored to its former splendor. Now, let's go and have a look at those plans, Mr. Leclaire." They climbed into the car, and, with Digby at the wheel, driving much too fast in his usual daredevil manner, they made their way back to the Hunting Lodge.

It wasn't until the last day of Digby's stay that his moment came to talk to Bertie. During the fortnight Digby had watched his cousin closely. He lacked enthusiasm for anything. His heart had been sapped of its juice, his *joie de vivre* turned sour, as if life had disappointed him to the point where he resented fun. He had only gone shooting once and that was because Digby had persuaded him to. They had tramped out with the dogs and shot some snipe, but Bertie had found little enjoyment in the sport he once loved. Pleasure was no longer part of his experience but something enjoyed by other people and he begrudged them for it. The only time he had grown animated was when Kitty had brought his son Little Jack over to see him. The child had the natural charm of the Deverills, Digby thought, and he was certain that Bertie could see himself in the boy, the carefree exuberance that he had lost. Otherwise, his cousin drank too much and oftentimes was so distracted that it was impossible even to converse with him.

As it was Digby's last day in County Cork, Bertie could not deny him an excursion on the boat. The weather was fine, warm even for January, and the sea calm. It was the perfect day to take the boat out, Digby exclaimed heartily, hoping to inject his cousin with enthusiasm. Bertie agreed, reluctantly, and the two of them set off for the harbor where Bertie's boat was moored—Digby in an eye-catching yellow-and-brown Tattersall jacket, waistcoat and breeches, thick yellow socks and matching cap, Bertie in a more discreet tweed suit. Digby waited for the jokes at his expense but Bertie wasn't forthcoming. He had lost his sense of humor too.

Once out on the sea Digby seized his moment. "Now, listen here, old chap," he began, and Bertie listened because there was nothing else to do but watch his fishing line and wait for it to tremble. "You've had a tough couple of years, there's no doubt about it," said Digby. "You've suffered terrible losses: the castle, your parents and Maud. But you cannot dwell on the negatives or you'll drown in them. You have to think positively and pull yourself back from the brink. You understand what I'm saying?" Bertie nodded without taking his eyes off the fishing line, or somewhere thereabouts. Digby realized he had made no impression but pressed on valiantly. "What's the core of the problem, Bertie, old chap? It's me, Digby, you're talking to. Eh? Your cousin and friend. I see you're in trouble and I want to help." Still no response. Digby felt his resolve deflate. Like most Englishmen he wasn't good at talking about emotions and rather dreaded having to. But he sensed his cousin's survival depended on him somehow and was determined to press on even though he had rarely felt so uncomfortable. He decided to try another tack. "You remember when we were boys? Your father used to take us out on this very boat and teach us to fish. Of course, he made no headway with me." Digby chuckled joylessly. "I've never been the sporting type."

To his surprise memories began to rouse Bertie from his

languor. The corners of his mouth twitched with the beginnings of a smile. "You were pretty useless on a horse too," he said.

Encouraged, Digby continued to delve into the adventures of their boyhood. "Hubert always claimed to give me a gentle horse, but one look at me and the bloody animal was off. I think he gave me the highly strung ones on purpose."

"If he hadn't, you'd have lagged behind with the old ladies," said Bertie.

"I hate to admit it but those aunts of yours, the Shrubs, were more accomplished in the saddle than I was."

"Do you remember when Rupert scaled down the front of the castle?"

"Adeline nearly had a seizure!"

"So did your mama. I'm sure I remember her fainting flat on her back and someone calling for her smelling salts." The two men laughed. Then Bertie turned serious. "I miss Rupert," he said wistfully.

"He was a good man," said Digby. "If he was here now, and finding solace in whiskey as you do, Bertie, what would you say to him?"

Bertie's face reddened. "I'd tell him to give it up. I'd make him see reason."

"I want *you* to give it up, Bertie," said Digby softly. "It's destroying you and I can't sit back and let you do that to yourself."

There was a long silence as Bertie digested his words. Then he stiffened. "I don't have a problem," he said crisply. "We Irish like our whiskey."

"You're not Irish," Digby retorted. "And you drink too much of it."

"With all due respect, Digby, what business is it of yours?"

"I'm family," he replied with emphasis.

Bertie heaved a sigh. He turned and stared at his cousin with rheumy, bloodshot eyes. "You don't know what it's like. I've lost everything."

"That's no excuse to drown your sorrows in drink."

"Oh, it's easy for you to say, Digby. You with all your millions, a good wife and Deverill Rising that hasn't been burned to the ground by rebels intent on pushing you out of the country your family has lived in for over two hundred and fifty years. You have your parents still. You have the golden touch, Digby. The Devil's luck and probably a blonde in every port. In fact, life is just dandy, isn't it? Well, for some of us it's a struggle. I had a mistress, you know. I loved her. But I lost her too."

Digby was losing patience. "Stop feeling sorry for yourself. The truth is, you're not very attractive when you're drunk— and you seem to be drunk most of the time. She probably got sick of the stench of alcohol on your breath." Digby saw it coming, the punch that would have hit him in the jaw had he not reacted like quicksilver and caught Bertie's arm with surprising strength and agility. Bertie stared at him in bewilderment, breathing heavily like a bull at bay.

Digby bore down on him. "You're a damned idiot, Bertie Deverill. I'm not surprised Maud left you and as for your mistress, well, you've brought it all on yourself, haven't you? Weak, that's what you are, weak. You're not even fit to carry the Deverill name. If your father could see you now he'd probably punch you one himself. As he isn't here, I'm going to do it for him." Digby drew back his fist and landed a blow beneath Bertie's ribs. Bertie bent double and gasped for breath, but managed to swipe at Digby's legs, causing him to reel off balance. The boat rocked from side to side as the two men fought like boys in a playground dispute. But Digby goaded him with every insult he could think of, hoping that Bertie would eventually collapse with exhaustion and see the error of his ways. He didn't collapse, however. He flung himself upon his cousin and they both tumbled over the edge of the boat into the cold sea. A moment later their heads bobbed up, taking in large mouthfuls of salty water and air. Shocked by the cold they were unable to speak.

Digby was the first to make it back. He heaved himself up with difficulty for his clothes were waterlogged and heavy. His boots were like rocks attached to his feet, pulling him down. He flopped onto the bottom of the boat like a fat walrus, fighting for breath. Then he remembered his cousin. He scrambled up and threw himself against the side. Bertie was struggling. His clothes and boots were making it almost impossible for him to tread water. "Do you want to die?" Digby shouted. "Is that what you want? Because if you do, I'll let you go. But if you choose to live you have to give up the drink, Bertie. Do you hear me? It's your choice." Bertie coughed and gagged, sinking suddenly only to propel himself up with a desperate kicking of his legs and flapping of his arms. "What will it be, Bertie?" Digby shouted.

Bertie did not want to die. "Life!" he managed to shout, taking a gulp of salty water and coughing madly. "Please . . . Digby . . . Help . . ."

Digby lifted one of the oars out of its oarlock and carefully held it over the water so that Bertie could grab the blade and haul himself toward the boat. He remained for a moment with his arms flung over the edge, panting. "Come on, old chap.

We've got to get you home before you die of exposure," said Digby gently. He grabbed Bertie's sodden jacket and heaved him over into the body of the boat, where he lay shivering with fear as well as cold.

"You bastard," Bertie gasped, but he was smiling.

"You chose life, Bertie, and I'm going to hold you to it." Digby held out his hand and after a moment's hesitation his cousin took it. Digby pulled him to his feet.

Bertie tottered, then found his balance. "I won't let you down, Digby."

"I know you won't."

The two men embraced, wet and frozen to their bones, but the feeling of camaraderie had never been warmer.

KITTY HADN'T BEEN able to see Jack since their hasty meeting at his cottage after his father's death. He had been staying with his mother, who was inconsolable with grief. They sent each other notes, just as they had done in the old days when they had used the loose stone in the wall in the vegetable garden, but this time Kitty sent the stable boy. They met at the Fairy Ring and snatched stolen kisses, witnessed only by the gulls that wheeled above them like kites on the wind. As the day of their departure loomed Kitty felt it more like the steady approach of an ax, poised to sever her from her home. She dreaded it and longed for it in equal measure. She grew short-tempered with Robert. She snapped at Celia and she cried at the smallest thing.

And then God intervened.

Once she knew her fate a calmness came over her. A resignation that comes from total surrender. It was as if she was letting out a long, slow breath and with it came a sense of peace. She was certain now of what she was going to do. There was no question, no doubt, no indecision, her mind was as clear as crystal. Even the pain of knowing how much hurt she was going to inflict seemed dislocated, belonging to someone else.

The morning before they were due to take the train to Queenstown, Kitty rode over the hills to Jack's cottage. She didn't allow herself to cry. She set her jaw and clenched her teeth and let the cold wind numb her emotions. When she arrived she tied her horse to the fence as usual and pushed open the door. Jack wasn't there, but his bag was packed and ready in the hall. She sat down at the table and waited as the weak winter light retreated slowly across the floorboards.

At last she heard him outside, whistling for his dog. A moment later he opened the door and said her name. "Kitty."

Then he knew. Even before he saw the expression on her face, he knew. This time he didn't sweep her into his arms, promise her he'd wait for her and kiss the pain away. He stared at her in utter disbelief and exasperation, knowing that what she was about to tell him would wound him as surely as a bullet. "Why?" he demanded.

Kitty stared at her fingers, knitted on the table before her. "I'm pregnant," she replied. Jack swayed as if struck. Then she added in a quiet, steady voice, "It's Robert's."

Jack sat down opposite her and put his face in his hands. There ensued a heavy silence. So heavy that Kitty's shoulders dropped beneath the weight and her head began to ache. "Are you sure?" he asked finally.

"I'm sure," she replied.

"How could you?" He looked at her in desperation.

"He's my husband. I couldn't deny him."

"You could have. You could have, Kitty." He raised his voice. "If you had wanted to."

She lifted her chin and dared to look at him. Every twist and turn of their ill-fated love affair seemed to have dulled the light in his eyes a little further and he looked entirely desolate. He shook his head. "So this is it?" he said. "This is what it's come to? After all we've been through. After all the years we've loved each other. This is where we are?"

"I'm sorry," she said.

He banged his fist on the table. "Sorry! You're sorry!"

Kitty's eyes stung with tears. "I *am* sorry."

"Well, sorry doesn't cut it, Kitty Deverill. You're sorry for spilling tea. Sorry for putting mud on the rug. Sorry for every little fecking thing. But sorry isn't a word that even begins to put right the wrong you're doing to me. Do you understand? I've waited for you." His face contorted with disgust. "But I'm done waiting."

A tear splashed onto the table. "There's nothing more I can say."

"Did you ever truly love me, Kitty?"

A flood of emotion filled her chest. She pressed her hand against the pain. "Oh yes, I did, Jack," she gasped. "And I *do*, with all my heart."

"No, you don't. If you loved me you'd be ready to give up everything for me." He stood up and walked to the window, turning his back to her to throw his gaze over the sea. "God knows I've loved you, Kitty Deverill," he said wearily. "God knows too that I'll probably never stop loving you. It'll be a curse I'll just have to live with, but I've survived worse, so I'll survive *this*."

Kitty got up slowly, her body aching. She walked over and slipped her hands around his waist. He said nothing as she rested her forehead between his shoulder blades. She could smell the past on him. The scent of turf fires, hot tea, porter cake and horse sweat. The aroma of damp earth and brine. She closed her eyes and saw themselves as children, balancing on the wall, pottering about the river in search of frogs, kissing at the Fairy Ring, watching the sun sinking into Smuggler's Bay. Then she heard the guns, the cries of men, the shouts of the Black and Tans dragging him off the station platform and she wanted to cling to him and never let him go. He invaded her every sense until she was too overcome to hold back her grief. She held him fiercely, but he remained with his hands on the window frame, gazing stiffly out to sea, and she knew that she had lost him.

She left the cottage. Jack didn't turn around. If he had she might have buckled. She might have run to him; she might even have changed her mind. But he didn't. She mounted her horse and slowly rode back up the path, her heart a boulder in her chest. The wind dried her tears and the sight of those velveteen fields of County Cork soothed her beleaguered spirits as they always had done. Ireland was the one love she could count on.

As she headed for the hills she knew that Jack was right. A pregnancy was the only thing that could keep her from running away with him—and she had known it and allowed it to happen. Fate had played no part nor had Destiny. Kitty had prayed for a child to save her from herself. She knew as surely as she lived and breathed that she belonged here, at Castle Deverill. Not even Jack O'Leary, with the extraordinary power he had over her heart, could tear her from her home.

KITTY'S DESPAIR WAS Adeline's frustration. If Kitty married Jack and somehow returned to claim the castle from Celia, the spirits caught in limbo might at last be released. She watched Kitty ride for home and knew, as well as she knew her own heart, that Kitty's could not be changed. She had chosen Ireland, as she always had.

Adeline stood on the hill overlooking the sea. The wind blew inland off the water in chilly gusts. The waves rose and fell in ever-changing swells and their peaks extended upward as hands reaching toward Heaven. They crashed against the rocks, their efforts reduced to white foam that bubbled and boiled as the water rolled in and out in a rhythm that only God understood. But Adeline heard the melody beneath the roaring and her soul swelled like the sea as she contemplated the land she loved so dearly.

Ireland. Wild, mysterious and deeply beautiful.

"If only Hubert could inhabit these hills as I can," she thought sadly, contemplating the red sky and fiery clouds that seemed to flee the setting sun like sheep with their wool aflame. But instead he had to remain in the castle with the other Lord Deverills and in her opinion the place really wasn't big enough for the lot of them.

Death had changed them little. They were still the people they had been in life, only unencumbered by their earthly bodies. They still grumbled and moaned, argued and complained and generally made a nuisance of themselves. Adeline wondered whether Celia would rue the day she'd decided to rebuild, for Barton's son, Egerton, could be very tiresome when taken by the desire to create mischief. He enjoyed treading heavily down the corridors, making the doors creak and rattling the furniture. It was frustrating not being either on earth or in Heaven, burdened by all the grievances one had in life, only no longer limited in perspective. They had at least gained a little understanding of what their existences had been all about. Life after death was no longer an uncertainty. Time was simply an illusion. Yet, while their souls were drawn to a higher state, they were imprisoned behind bars they could not see, cursed to glimpse the light but remain in shadow, their mortal egos balls and chains about their necks.

Adeline, on the other hand, could go where she pleased. Heaven awaited her with the gates flung wide. Only love tied her to Hubert. While she waited for the curse to be lifted she could see the whole world and as she turned her thoughts to other lands she was once again drawn to the small part of Ireland, and herself, that had strayed across the water . . .

Chapter 8

Connecticut, 1926

Martha Wallace knelt on the window seat and stared in wonder at the snow that fell like fluffy white feathers onto the garden below. Today was her fourth birthday and her English nanny, the kind and gentle Mrs. Goodwin, had told her that God's present for her was snow. The little girl spread her palms against the glass and raised her peat-brown eyes to the sky to see if she could make Him out up there in the clouds, but all she could see were millions of fat flakes, constant and thick and falling fast, and Martha lost herself in the magic of them.

"Right, time to go, dear," said Mrs. Goodwin, walking into Martha's bedroom with the child's crimson çoat slung over her arm and her matching hat in her hand. "We don't want to be late for your party. Grandma Wallace has invited all the family to celebrate your big day. It's going to be tremendous fun."

Martha wrenched her eyes away from the mesmerizing whiteness and slid off the window seat. She stood before her nanny. The lady smiled tenderly and crouched down to the child's level. "You look very pretty, my dear," she said, tweaking the blue bows in her dark brown hair and running her gentle eyes over the blue silk dress with its white sash and collar, which she had taken great trouble to press so that not even the smallest crease remained. "I remember when you were a baby. Such a pretty baby you were too. Your mama and papa were so proud they showed you off to everyone. They love you very much, you know. So *you* must be good for *them*."

Martha put her finger across her lips in a well-practiced gesture of conspiracy. "Shhhhh," she hissed through her teeth.

"That's right, my dear." Mrs. Goodwin lowered her voice. "Your secret friends must remain secret," she reminded her firmly, helping her into her coat. "It's not fun if you tell everyone. Then they're not secret any longer, are they?"

"But I can tell *you*, Nanny," Martha whispered, watching as her nanny's fingers deftly fastened the buttons.

"You can tell *me*, but no one else," Mrs. Goodwin confirmed. "You're blessed with a wonderful gift, Martha dear. But not everyone will understand it."

Martha nodded and gazed trustingly at her nanny. Something caught then in Mrs. Goodwin's chest, for when she looked deeply into the child's eyes she was sure she could see the loneliness there. It wasn't that Martha was lacking in love or company but that she seemed to carry an emptiness inside her that nothing was able to fill. She had come into the world with it, this tendency to stare out of the window as if searching for something lost or longing for something only half remem-

bered. She was a melancholy, dreamy, solitary little girl—
strange qualities in a child who had every material comfort to
please her and drawers of toys to entertain her. Pam Wallace
spoiled her only child unashamedly and anything Martha
wanted she was given. But Martha didn't want much and little
that could be bought attracted her interest. She preferred to sit
with her imagination, to watch the clouds float past, to play
with insects and flowers, to talk to people no one else could
see. In her more fanciful moments Mrs. Goodwin wondered
whether Martha could hear the echo of her homeland resonating in her soul or discern the vague memory of having come
into the world as *two*, yet set off on her journey as *one*.

Mrs. Goodwin should not have heard Martha's parents discussing the child's origins—and she hadn't intended to. Goodness, if she had known what was to be gleaned, she would
rather not have eavesdropped. But as it was, she had heard and
there was nothing she could do to *un*hear it now. It had happened when Martha was about two years old. Mr. and Mrs.
Wallace's bedroom door had been left ajar and Mrs. Goodwin
had chanced to be in the corridor outside, having left the little
girl asleep in her bedroom, at the very moment that husband
and wife were discussing Martha's obvious loneliness and wondering what to do about it.

"We should have adopted another child," Mrs. Wallace had
said to her husband and Mrs. Goodwin had stopped mid-stride
as if turned to stone. Barely daring to breathe, she had lingered
there, motionless, her curiosity overriding her sense of propriety.
"We should have adopted her brother as well," Mrs. Wallace had
continued.

"It was you who only wanted one child," Mr. Wallace had

replied. "You said you couldn't cope with more than one. And you wanted a girl."

"That's because a mother never loses a daughter."

"Sister Agatha did try to encourage us to take both babies," he had reminded her. "After all, they were twins. We could always go back to Dublin and see if there are any other babies up for adoption. I'd be very happy to give another orphan a home." An uneasiness had crept over Mrs. Goodwin then as if she had suddenly realized that she was listening to a pair of thieves reviewing a terrible crime.

"If I had known how lonely Martha would turn out to be I would most definitely have taken her brother too," Pam Wallace had conceded.

Stunned and horrified, Mrs. Goodwin had managed to lift her heavy feet off the ground and retreat back down the corridor to the little girl's bedroom. She had leaned over the bed and stared at the child with pity and compassion. Martha had a brother, a *twin* brother, Mrs. Goodwin pondered, gazing at the sleeping toddler. What had become of *him*? she wondered? Did he carry an emptiness in his soul too, as she was sure now that Martha did? Did they both know somehow, subconsciously, that they hadn't always been on their own? And what of their mother? Why had she given up her babies? Mrs. Goodwin was certain that Mr. and Mrs. Wallace would never tell Martha that she was adopted—this was the first Mrs. Goodwin had heard of it and she wondered who else knew. As far as the world outside the Wallace family was concerned, mother and child looked very much alike. Both had dark brown hair, eyes the color of peat and pale Irish skin. There was nothing in their appearance to raise a question about Martha's birth—and Mrs.

Wallace loved Martha, there was no denying that. She loved her dearly. But still, there was something deeply wrong about splitting up twins as they had done—and the thought that Martha might never know where she came from, or indeed that she had a brother, was a very uneasy one.

Mrs. Goodwin took Martha's hand and accompanied her downstairs into the hall where her mother waited, fussing with her handbag. Pam Wallace was as pampered and precious as one would expect the wife of a very rich man to be. Her dark hair was cut into a chic bob that rippled with self-conscious waves, her eyebrows plucked into thin arches that gave her a permanent look of surprise and her small mouth was painted scarlet to match her long fingernails, now hidden in a pair of long white gloves. She was tall and slender with a narrow frame so that the 1920s fashion of dropped-waist dresses and flat chests showed her to her best advantage. In Mrs. Goodwin's day, for she was young at the end of the *previous* century, a woman had to have ample embonpoint, but a voluptuous bosom was no good to anyone nowadays. However, Mrs. Goodwin was no longer interested in men or fashion. After Mr. Goodwin had left her widowed she had given her life to children and she knew from experience that small babies needed something soft to lie against.

Mrs. Wallace turned to watch her daughter walk down the stairs, holding her nanny's hand in case she stumbled, and her scarlet lips spread into a satisfied smile. Martha did her credit, she knew. Her long hair had been brushed until it shone, the ribbons neatly tied into two little bows, her crimson coat done up at the front with shiny red buttons, and her shoes, oh the dainty little blue shoes, dyed to match the dress that peeped out at the bottom of her coat, were as pretty as a doll's. Mrs. Wallace was very pleased. "Well, don't you look a picture, darling," she gushed, holding out her hand. One could only just perceive her Irish accent, concealed beneath her American twang. "You look quite the birthday girl. You will outshine all your cousins!" Martha stepped forward and took her mother's hand. Her chest swelled with pleasure for she liked nothing better than to please her mama.

Mrs. Goodwin was about to put the hat on Martha's head, when a white glove stopped her. "Let's not ruin her hair," said Mrs. Wallace. "You've tied those bows so beautifully, Goodwin. It would be a shame to squash them. We'll hurry out to the car and try not to get wet, won't we, Martha?" Martha nodded, glancing swiftly at her nanny, who smiled at her encouragingly.

Mrs. Goodwin clutched the hat and nodded. "As you wish, Mrs. Wallace."

"Come along now, let's not dawdle. There are presents awaiting you, darling, and cake. Didn't Grandma say that she was going to get Sally to make you the finest chocolate cake you've ever eaten?"

Mrs. Goodwin watched mother and child walk down the steps to the driveway where the chauffeur stood to attention beside the passenger door, his gray cap already thick with snow, his hands probably cold inside his black gloves. She watched her little charge climb onto the leather seat followed by her mother. Then the chauffeur closed the door and a moment later he was behind the wheel, motoring off toward the road, leaving fresh tracks in the snow. Mrs. Goodwin wished the child had worn a hat.

Pam Wallace's mother-in-law's house was a short drive away. Martha enjoyed rides in the car and gazed out of the window at the pretty houses and trees, all covered in white. It looked like a winter wonderland and she was enchanted by it. Pam sat stiffly beside her daughter. She was too consumed by her thoughts to notice the magic of the world outside the car, too anxious about the afternoon ahead to even talk to the child. Her sisters-in-law would be there: Joan, with her four children aged between nine and fourteen, and Dorothy, with her two boys who were ten and twelve. It made Pam bristle with competitiveness just to think of them and she hoped that Martha would impress them with politeness and good manners. If she didn't, they'd simply say that Pam had acted unwisely and bought a child with bad blood.

Ted and Diana Wallace's home was a large red-bricked house with white shutters, a gray-tiled roof and a prestigious-looking porch supported by two sturdy white columns. It was the house in which Larry had grown up and lived with his two elder brothers until he had married Pam at the age of twenty-five. Larry was everything Pam's Irish Catholic parents had wanted for her: old American money, with a fine education and a respectable job in the Foreign Service—well, *almost* everything; Larry Wallace wasn't Catholic. He was well mannered, extremely well connected, impeccably dressed, good at sports, distinguished-looking and, most important, rich, but the problem of his religion was insurmountable to Pam's father, Raymond Tobin, who did not attend the wedding. Having left their home and farm in Clonakilty after their son, Brian, had been murdered by the IRA in 1918 for having fought for the British in the war, Raymond Tobin was not prepared to compromise when it came to religion. "The Tobins have married Catholics for hundreds of years. I will not give Pamela Mary my blessing to go and marry a Protestant," he had said, and he had cut his daughter loose. Hanora, Pam's mother, put aside her reservations for the sake of her youngest daughter, and did her best to accept the man Pam had chosen for love. If losing her son had taught her anything it was that love was the only thing of real value in this world.

Pam had married Larry at the age of twenty-two after a six-month courtship. They had been blissfully happy at the beginning and Pam's efforts to win acceptance from this very East Coast American dynasty, who had also had their reservations about their son marrying a Catholic, had begun to pay off. But after two years of trying unsuccessfully to conceive, Pam's doctor had confirmed her greatest fear: that she would never bear children. The agony of childlessness had propelled her, in desperation, to look into other options.

Adopting a child was most certainly *not* common in the Wallace world. Ted Wallace said that one would never buy a dog without knowing its pedigree so why would one buy a child without knowing exactly where it came from? Diana Wallace worried that it would be hard to love a child who wasn't one's own flesh and blood. But Pam was determined and Larry supported her in the discussions that flared into heated rows around the Wallace dining-room table on Sundays. Pam's father, Raymond Tobin, agreed with Ted Wallace, although the two men had never met. "You won't know what you're getting," he told his daughter. "Buy a son, Pamela Mary, but he won't be a Tobin or a Wallace, whatever name you give him." Her mother, however, understood her daughter's craving for a child and whispered that it would be nice to give a chance to one of those poor Irish babies who were born in convents to unmarried mothers too young to look after them. With her mother's help Pam found an adoption agency in New York that had links with the Convent of Our Lady Queen of Heaven in Dublin. Larry arranged to be sent to Europe to set up and advance diplomatic links with America and they went to live in London for two years—sailing over to Ireland in search of the baby they wanted so badly. Aware that what they were doing was unconventional, they had made every effort to keep it secret. Only Larry's family and Pam's parents knew, for it would have posed too great a challenge to pull off such a deception in families as close as theirs.

Martha was everything a privileged and pampered little girl should be. She was pretty, polite and charming, her features were refined and, in Pam's opinion, aristocratic. Hadn't Sister Agatha said that the baby's mother was well bred? On top of all that, Martha was the apple of Grandma Wallace's eye. This was the first time Diana Wallace had ever thrown any of her grandchildren a birthday party. Pam should have been proud, but she was too worried to enjoy the moment. Joan and Dorothy would be there with their immaculate children, who were small clones of their parents and destined to continue the bloodline, which was so important to Pam's father-in-law, Ted Wallace. Who knew what Martha's bloodline was? Pam turned to her child and there was a warning tone beneath her question. "You're going to be a good girl today, aren't you, Martha?"

"Yes, Mother," Martha replied dutifully. Sensing her mother's nervousness, she began to fidget with her fingers.

When Pam arrived, Joan, who was married to the oldest

Wallace boy, Charles, was already there, perched on the sofa in the drawing room beside Dorothy, who was married to the middle son, Stephen. Their mother-in-law, the formidable Diana Wallace, was holding court in the armchair. Joan's slanting green eyes swiftly assessed the competition, then relaxed into a lazy gaze as she rated herself the better dressed of the three Wallace sisters-in-law. Her short auburn hair curled into her cheekbones like two fish hooks. Her pale lilac-colored dress was fashionably low-waisted and worn beneath a long cardigan in the same color as her hat and adorned with a large knitted flower just below her left shoulder. The impression was one of studied glamour, for even the black shoes, with their T-bar strap, burgundy stockings and the long string of blue beads that dripped down to her waist had been carefully selected according to the trends of the day. Dorothy, who took her lead from Joan in everything, had tried and failed to create the same effect and simply looked dowdy. Pam, whose glamour was as equally contrived as Joan's, only managed to look stiff and plain by comparison.

Grandma Wallace's face lit up when she saw Martha. She held out her arms and the child ran into them, knowing she would always be welcome in Grandma Wallace's embrace. "Well, if it isn't the birthday girl!" said Grandma Wallace. "If I'm not mistaken you've grown again, young lady."

Pam noticed Joan's lips purse at this display of affection between Grandma Wallace and her niece and she allowed herself a moment of pleasure. Joan had relished the fact that Pam was unable to bear children and had enjoyed being the first daughter-in-law to produce grandchildren. Ma and Grumps, as Diana and Ted had soon been called, had doted on those children. Grumps had taken a great interest in the boys' tennis and golf and Ma had read the girls stories and encouraged them to play the piano and paint. Soon after, Dorothy had given birth to boys but Joan hadn't felt threatened by Dorothy; her sister-in-law's admiration for Joan was both eager and blatant and Diana Wallace had always had a special affection for her first son's children. Then Pam and Larry had returned from Europe with a baby.

Pam would never forget the look on Joan's face when she had first laid eyes on Martha. She had peered into the crib and sniffed disdainfully. "The trouble with adopting a child, Pam, is that you don't know what you're getting. Genes are very strong, you know. You might bring her up to be a Wallace, but she'll always be who she really is inside. And what *is* that?" She had shaken her head and pulled a sympathetic face. "Only time will tell." Pam was determined to prove her wrong.

Pam took off Martha's red coat and the little girl stood a moment in her blue silk dress with its white Peter Pan collar and sash. Not even Joan could deny the child's charm and Pam swelled with pleasure because none of Joan or Dorothy's children had ever possessed such heartbreaking sweetness. There was something about Martha that separated her from the rest. She was a swan among geese, Pam thought happily, an orchid among daisies. A moment later the other children appeared, flushed from having been tearing around the house playing hide and seek. A pile of presents had been arranged on the top of the piano and one by one Martha was presented with the shiny packages, tied up with vibrantly colored ribbons and bows. She opened them carefully, with the help of her cousins, and gasped with pleasure when the gifts were revealed. She knew better than to grumble about the ones that didn't appeal to her, and was gracious with her thank-yous, aware all the time of her mother's sharp but satisfied gaze upon her.

Tea was in the conservatory, which had been decorated with pretty paper streamers and brightly colored balloons. The children drank orange juice and ate egg and ham sandwiches and wolfed down the birthday cake, which Mrs. Wallace's cook had made in the shape of a cat. Martha's face, upon seeing the creation ablaze with four candles, had broadened with a captivating smile.

Grandma Wallace could barely take her eyes off her youngest grandchild and seized every opportunity to comment on something amusing that she either said or did. "Why, she's adorable, Pam," Diana Wallace gushed. "She hasn't even got a crumb on that darling dress."

Joan stood in the corner of the conservatory with a cup of tea and bristled with irritation. "It's only because she's adopted," she whispered to Dorothy, knowing she'd find an ally in her. "You see, Ma's overcompensating to make Pam feel better. She's overdoing it, if you ask me, for the girl's an also-ran."

"Oh, I don't think she's an also-ran, Joan," said Dorothy. Then just as Joan was about to take offense at Dorothy's uncharacteristic disagreement, she added, "She's peculiar. My George tells me that Martha has an imaginary grandmother called Adele or Adine or something. An also-ran wouldn't have imaginary grandmothers. If you ask me, I think she's psychic."

Joan narrowed her eyes. "Psychic? Why, whatever do you mean?"

"I think she sees dead people."

"You don't think they're imagined?"

"No, I think she really sees dead people. I read an article in a magazine recently about psychic phenomena. Many small children have imaginary friends who aren't really imaginary. Apparently it's very common."

"Well, none of *my* children had imaginary friends," said Joan.

"Nor mine, thank goodness, and if they had I'd have quickly smacked it out of them! I'm not sure Stephen would approve of such a thing."

"Martha might be cute now," Joan pointed out. "But she could be trouble later. At least we know with our children where their faults come from."

"Oh, we do indeed, Joan."

"Family faults are somehow palatable, but . . ." Joan sighed with ill-concealed schadenfreude. "Martha's faults will always be mystifying."

After tea when the family settled into the drawing room again, Ted Wallace strode into the house with his second son, Stephen, having enjoyed a long lunch at the golf club. Much to Ted's disappointment golf hadn't been possible on account of the thick fleece of snow covering the course. However, both men were in good spirits after eating with friends and finishing off with a game of billiards. Ted was an enthusiast of any pastime that involved a ball and Stephen had inherited not only his father's love of sport but his aptitude for it. They walked in with their bellies full of lunch, laughing as they relived their victory at the billiard table.

The grandchildren stood politely and greeted their grandfather, who was a tall, imposing-looking man with strong shoulders, straight back, thick gray hair swept off a wide, furrowed forehead and a face that, though he was fifty-nine, was still handsome. Ted Wallace was much more interested in the boys, for like him, they were keen games players, but he had a kind word or two for the girls, a comment on their pretty dresses or a question about their pet rabbit or dog. After that, the children ran off and he stood in front of the fireplace to puff on a cigar while Stephen took the place on the sofa beside his wife, lay back against the cushions and stretched out his long legs with a contented sigh.

"It's going to snow all night by the look of things," said Ted. "I wouldn't leave your departure too late. The cars will have trouble in the road with this snow. Not that Diana and I wouldn't be delighted for you all to stay over."

"Dear God, I'm not wearing the right shoes to walk in the snow! If the car gets stuck I'm getting stuck with it," said Joan. "Are you sure it hasn't settled already?" She threw her gaze out of the window apprehensively.

"It'll be good for another hour or so," her father-in-law replied. "And you haven't got far to go." It was true, Ted and Diana Wallace's sons had all managed to find houses within a few miles of their parents, such was the enduring strength of the apron strings.

"I'll call the children," said Dorothy, standing up.

"So, how was the party?" asked Ted through a cloud of cigar smoke.

"Oh, Martha's had such a lovely time," Diana answered. "She's a little treasure."

"It's so nice to see her with her cousins," said Joan. "She's really one of us, isn't she?"

"Of course she is," said Pam, a little too quickly. "It was sweet of you, Ma, to throw her a party. She's loved every minute."

Diana gave a mellifluous laugh. "I'm her *favorite* grand-mother, Pam. I have to do everything I can to remain on top."

"It's hard competing with an imaginary one," Joan said, a devilish smile creeping across her face.

"*Does* she have an imaginary one?" Stephen asked, putting his hands behind his head and yawning.

"Ah, here she is. Why don't we ask her?" said Joan as Martha trailed into the room behind the older children.

"Really, I don't know what Joan's talking about," said Pam uneasily.

"I'm not making it up. Dorothy, what is she called, Martha's imaginary grandmother?" Dorothy blanched in the doorway and looked confused. She clearly didn't want to be seen to be making trouble.

"Help us out, dear," said Joan to the little girl. Martha glanced anxiously at her mother. Joan tapped her long talons on the arm of her chair impatiently. "Well, speak up, dear. What's the name of your imaginary, or perhaps not imaginary, grandmother? We're all longing to hear."

Pam stood up and took her daughter by the hand. "Come along now, darling, we have to get home before we get snowed in." She turned to her sister-in-law and her face hardened. "Sometimes, you can be very unkind, Joan."

Joan laughed, opened her mouth in a silent gasp and pressed her hand against her chest. "Come now, Pam. It was only a bit of fun. You're much too oversensitive. It's one thing for Diana to compete with Grandma Tobin but to compete with a ghost is even beyond the capabilities of Grandma Wallace!" she said.

Diana shook her head. "There's nothing unusual about hav-ing imaginary friends. Martha is on her own so much that it's perfectly normal to invent friends to play with. I don't mind you having another grandmother, Martha. So long as she's as nice to you as I am!" Martha smiled, although her eyes glittered with tears.

Mrs. Goodwin noticed that Martha was very subdued when she returned home. Mrs. Wallace told her that the child was simply tired, but later that evening, after Martha had been put to bed, Mrs. Goodwin eavesdropped for the second time. This time she hadn't stumbled across the open door by accident but by design. It wasn't like Martha to be so quiet and solemn, especially after a birthday party. Mr. and Mrs. Wallace were in the drawing room, enjoying a drink before dinner. Mrs. Goodwin hovered outside, ears picking up the relevant snippets of conversation.

"If she were our biological daughter I wouldn't mind her faults, or eccentricities as you call them, because they'd be family faults I'd recognize, but since she comes from we don't know where, I can't help worrying that she's different. I don't want her to be different, Larry. For her to fit into the family, she has to be the same as all the other children. Don't you see?"

"I think you worry too much. She'll grow out of it when she starts going to school and making proper friends."

"I don't want to wait that long. I want to sort it out now."

"And how do you propose to do that?" Larry asked.

"I'll take her to see a doctor."

Larry laughed. "She's not sick, Pam."

"Talking to people we can't see is a kind of sickness, Larry. It's certainly not normal." Pam's voice had now gone up a tone. Mrs. Goodwin put her hand to her throat. What would a doctor make of Martha's "gift" and how would he "cure" it? She heard Mr. Wallace sigh. He didn't have much patience for domestic matters.

"Whatever you think, Pam. If it gives you peace of mind to have some doctor say it's perfectly normal to talk to daisies, be my guest."

"Mary Abercorn has suggested a man in New York who treated her son for anxiety. Bobby is now the most carefree young man you'd ever meet, so he must be good."

"Not a doctor then?"

"No, he's a . . ." She hesitated. "You know, a man who looks after the mind as opposed to the body."

"A quack."

"Really, Larry!"

"All right, a psychiatrist." There was a long pause as Mr. Wallace pondered his wife's suggestion. At last he spoke and there was a conclusiveness in his tone. "As long as he doesn't lay a finger on her," he said firmly.

Mrs. Goodwin had heard enough. She hastened to the stairs and quickly made her way up them, her tread swift and silent on the carpet. When she reached the top, she put her hand on the banister and closed her eyes. She took a deep breath and tried to assuage her fear. Yet, in spite of her efforts it lurked like a heavy shadow in the pit of her belly. She didn't know what this psychiatrist would do, but she knew for certain that no good would come of it.

Chapter 9

Martha lay in bed listening to the familiar sounds of the night: the rustling of people moving about her bedroom, the murmuring of whispered voices, the quiet buzz of activity—although in the darkness she couldn't work out exactly *what* they were doing. She just knew that they were busy, *they* being people but not people like her parents and Mrs. Goodwin; people who she understood instinctively to be not from this world.

These nocturnal goings-on had never frightened Martha because Grandma Adeline had told her that the spirits meant her no harm. "They're just curious," she explained. "This world and the next are much closer than one might imagine." Martha liked Adeline. She had a gentle smile and kind eyes and her laugh was as soft as feathers. With her mother, Martha had to be on best behavior. She had to keep her dresses clean and her shoes shiny. She had to be polite and well mannered. She

had to be *good*. Although she was much too young to understand the complex world of adults, she knew intuitively that she
had to *win* her mother's affection. She knew that her love was
conditional. With Adeline it was different. She sensed Adeline
loved her just the way she was. It wasn't anything particular
that she said. It was in the tender way she looked at her. She
made the child feel cherished.

Mrs. Goodwin had told Martha to keep Adeline secret, but
she found it hard when she was as real to her as Grandma
Wallace—well, almost. She knew her mother didn't like her to
talk about people she referred to as Martha's "imaginary
friends." But when Martha did, quite by accident, her mother's
face would change. It would grow suddenly hard. She would
suck in her affection as if it were a tangible thing, like her grandfather's cigar smoke. One moment it would be filling the space
around her and then, with one deep inhalation, it would be
gone, pulled out of the air, leaving her cold and isolated and
ashamed. During these moments Martha would try very hard
to draw it out again. She'd be exceptionally good. By and by
this had become a cycle of behavior both mother and daughter
had grown accustomed to. Pam withheld her affection in a sub-
conscious bid to assert control while Martha tried so very hard
to earn it back. All the while Adeline was there, in the background, reassuring Martha that she was special.

Martha now lay in bed, listening to the noises in her room
and finding comfort in them. She didn't realize how tenuous
her hold on that world was. She was about to find out.

The following morning Mrs. Goodwin dressed her in a
green frock with a matching cardigan and long white socks.
She brushed her hair off her face and tied it back with green

ribbons. When she was ready she was taken downstairs to the hall where her mother was waiting for her. This time she was going to New York. Mrs. Goodwin had told her how exciting Manhattan was and Martha couldn't wait to see it. She hadn't been anywhere, only as far as Grandma Wallace's house, and the thought of the big city thrilled her.

New York was indeed exciting. Martha pressed her nose to the car window and gazed out onto the tall buildings that had grown higher than trees and onto the sidewalks that were gray with slush. She had never seen so many people and so many cars, all lined up in long rows, some tooting their horns impatiently. It was in front of an elegant brownstone building that the car came to a halt and her mother hooked her handbag over her arm and waited for the chauffeur to open the door for her. As he stood to attention Pam climbed out, then took Martha's hand and led her up the steep steps to the front door.

Martha, who had been chattering happily in the car, suddenly grew quiet. She walked close to her mother and held her hand tightly. There was something oppressive about this place that made her feel afraid. The elevator frightened her too because the door was like an animal cage. It made a rattling noise when it was opened and closed and Martha felt as if she was being imprisoned. She was mightily relieved when her mother pulled it open at the second floor and she was allowed out. A lady with bright red lips and long eyelashes like spider's legs greeted them from behind a desk. Pam said her name and the lady told them to take a seat in the waiting room.

Pam had brought a picture book for Martha to look at while they waited. It was her favorite story about a kitten that gets lost but is later found. The child gazed at the colorful pictures and forgot all about the scary lift. A short while later she was interrupted by a lofty, stiff man in a dark suit and tie towering over her. He had shiny blond hair brushed into a side parting and smooth white skin. "Hello, Martha," he said and the way he articulated her name revealed his foreign origins. He extended his hand and Martha took it and let him shake it. "My name is Mr. Edlund. I'm going to talk to your mother for a moment, then I'm going to ask you to come into my office." Mr. Edlund smiled down at her but Martha was too nervous to smile back. She stared into his big blue eyes, so far away because he really was very tall, and sensed something in his energy that she didn't like. Then he walked away with her mother and disappeared into a room, closing the door behind him. Martha's stomach churned with nerves. She rested the book on her knee but she didn't read it. She just stared at the door, dreading the moment Mr. Edlund would appear and summon her.

After what seemed like a very long time, the door did indeed open and Mr. Edlund called to her. "I'm ready for you now, Martha," he said, and the little girl slipped off the chair and walked anxiously into his room. To her relief she found her mother sitting in front of a wooden desk neatly arranged with papers, books and photographs in frames. There was a chair beside her and Mr. Edlund told Martha to sit in it. She did as she was told and clasped her hands together on her lap. She glanced around the room. There was a medical bed in the corner covered in a white sheet with a standing lamp placed beside it from which a very bright bulb shone out like a demonic eye.

When Mr. Edlund spoke to her, she jumped and wrenched her gaze away from the demonic eye. "Your mother has told me a lot about you, Martha. She says you're a very good girl."

Martha glanced at her mother and saw that she was smiling. This made Martha feel less afraid. "You're an only child and you've just turned four. Is that right?" Martha nodded. "Good. Did you have a nice birthday party?" She nodded again. "Good. I hope you didn't eat too much cake." Martha blushed because she *had* eaten too much cake and had felt a little sick afterward, but she hadn't spilled anything down her dress. She glanced again at her mother, who nodded at her encouragingly.

"Answer Mr. Edlund's questions, Martha. He's a doctor," she said with emphasis. "You can tell him anything." Mr. Edlund did not correct Mrs. Wallace, for although he possessed no qualification, he certainly believed himself to be a doctor of the mind.

"Do you have lots of friends, Martha?" Mr. Edlund asked. Martha didn't know how to reply to this. She didn't really know what friends were. She played with her cousins occasionally, but most of the time she was on her own in the house. Then she thought of Mrs. Goodwin and she nodded. "Who are your friends, Martha?" he asked.

"Mrs. Goodwin," she replied quietly.

"That's the nanny," Pam told him helpfully. She laughed lightly. "She's not a friend, Martha. She's your nanny. That's different."

"Is it true that you have friends other people can't see?" Mr. Edlund continued. Now his face was very serious. Martha squirmed on her chair. Mrs. Goodwin had told her to keep Adeline secret. She looked at her mother, waiting for her to withdraw her affection, but to her bewilderment she was still smiling.

"Darling, you can tell Mr. Edlund anything. You won't be in trouble," she said.

Martha was confused. She didn't understand why she could tell this stranger about Adeline when she wasn't allowed to speak of her at home. "Yes," she said, and her voice was a mere ribbon of sound so that Mr. Edlund had to lean across his desk to hear her.

"Do you have one friend or lots of friends?"

"Lots," she replied.

He nodded. "I see. But your mother tells me you have one special friend."

"Yes," said Martha.

"What is your special friend called?"

"Adeline," said Martha.

"When do you see her?"

"In my bedroom."

"In the night?" Martha nodded. "Is she here now?"

Martha shook her head. "No," she replied.

Mr. Edlund smiled with satisfaction. He leaned back in his chair and knitted his long fingers over his stomach. He looked at Pam, who was so eager for him to cure her daughter of her strange hallucinations that she was ready to believe anything. "This is really very simple," he said, and Pam's whole body seemed to sag with relief.

"Oh, I'm so pleased," she replied.

His eyes fell on the child. "You know that Adeline isn't real, don't you, Martha?" When Martha didn't reply, he added, "She seems real to you, but she's not real. She's like a dream, that's why you see her at night when you're going to sleep. You've made her up because you're lonely and you'd like someone to talk to. Do you understand that Adeline is simply make-believe?"

Martha knew Adeline wasn't made up and she didn't only see her at night when she was going to sleep. But she looked anxiously at her mother. Pam's face was still smiling, but Martha sensed that she was about to suck in her affection and she dreaded the cold feeling of isolation that would follow. She dreaded *that* more than being put on the bed and being stared at by the demonic "eye." So she lied. Mrs. Goodwin had taught her that lying was wrong but she didn't want her mother to withdraw her love and she didn't want Mr. Edlund to ask her any more questions. "Yes," she said and her eyes welled with tears.

Her lie had a surprising effect. Pam turned to her in astonishment. "You see, darling, Adeline is in your head and isn't real at all. I'm not sure why you had to invent a grandmother when you have two perfectly good ones who love you very much." Martha wiped away a tear. Her mother turned back to Mr. Edlund. "How is it possible to invent such a person? She's been consistent about this Adeline woman since she learned to speak."

"The mind is a very complicated thing, Mrs. Wallace. Martha created Adeline out of necessity and now she believes her to be real. Children have especially strong imaginations. It is by no means uncommon. Children generally grow out of these delusions and if they don't—"

"Yes?" Pam asked anxiously.

"There are many avenues we can take. But we don't need to discuss them unless Martha continues to believe she sees people. So, in the meantime, you must make sure she is entertained. She needs friends to play with and she needs to be busy. When she mentions Adeline, gently remind her that the woman is only in her imagination. Remind her regularly because by repeating it you will override the pattern. She is young enough for this to be both efficient and effective."

Pam was very grateful. She left Mr. Edlund's office determined to find Martha little friends to play with and to keep her busy. She would organize violin lessons so that instead of gazing out of the window dreaming the child could practice scales. It was a relief to hear that Martha's fantasies were simply symptomatic of her loneliness. Pam couldn't wait to tell Joan and Dorothy. She'd tell them what Mr. Edlund had said—or rather what *Dr.* Edlund had said; she would lie about that because it sounded better coming from a doctor.

Martha followed her mother down the steps to the car. She didn't speak all the way back, but gazed disconsolately out of the window. Her mother chattered on about how wonderful *Dr.* Edlund was and how sensible his diagnosis was. She didn't realize that he had broken something in Martha: her delight in magic.

Mrs. Goodwin was waiting uneasily in the hall for Martha to return. When the car drew up outside the house it was already getting dark. Snow had begun to fall again. She could see the flakes in the golden auras around the streetlamps. Martha climbed out and walked slowly toward the house. Mrs. Goodwin knew from the way the child carried herself that she was deeply unhappy. Mrs. Wallace held out her hand and Martha took it, allowing herself to be pulled alongside her mother, who was keen to get in out of the snow.

That night when Mrs. Goodwin tucked her into bed she asked about New York. Martha told her nanny that she didn't like Mr. Edlund. "What did he say, dear?"

"Adeline isn't real."

Mrs. Goodwin was about to disagree. She knew that Martha had been born with the gift of second sight, but she didn't want to get the child into trouble. Perhaps it was better that she believed the beings she saw were figments of her imagination. That way she'd be unlikely to slip up and talk about them again. Mrs. Goodwin didn't like to think of the consequences of *that*. What would Mr. Edlund do then? She didn't want Martha to grow up thinking there was something wrong with her. She didn't want Mrs. Wallace thinking there was something wrong with her, either. "My dear, you are a very special child," said Mrs. Goodwin gently. "Sometimes children are so special that adults are incapable of understanding them. Whether or not Adeline is real doesn't matter. She is real to *you*. If she makes you happy there's no harm in that." The child blinked up at Mrs. Goodwin with love and trust. The nanny planted a kiss on her forehead. "Good night and God bless you, dear."

Mrs. Goodwin informed Mrs. Wallace that her daughter was ready for her to say good night. Pam stroked her daughter's hair and kissed her cheek. "You were a very good girl today," she said, and the weight in Martha's heart lightened a little. After she had left the room the child was alone in the darkness. A while later Martha heard the familiar sounds of rustling and shuffling and the hiss of whispers. She pushed herself beneath her blanket and began to sing. She discovered that if she sang she couldn't hear the noises.

Adeline watched her with sadness. She pitied the child's shame and lamented the mother's ignorance. She knew what would happen now, for the same had happened to similar children all through the ages: Martha would lose her gift. She would lose the ability to see the finer vibrations around her and in the process she would lose herself and become just like everyone else. There was nothing Adeline could do about it. She would simply fade like a rainbow when the sun stops shining. "I'll still be with you," she whispered into the darkness beneath the blankets. "I'll always be with you."

The following day Pam presented Martha with a present. Mrs. Goodwin had been very useful in helping her decide what to buy. She needed something for Martha to love. The child wasn't interested in toys and dolls and teddy bears. She loved real creatures like insects, birds and animals. But Mrs. Goodwin had the perfect idea. Martha put the box on the table in front of her and carefully lifted the lid. Inside, two round eyes gazed up at her warily. The child caught her breath. Her face flowered into a wide smile. "It's a kitten!" she exclaimed excitedly. She delved into the box and gently lifted the animal out. The kitten meowed, then snuggled against Martha's warm body as she held it in her arms.

"It's a boy kitten," her mother told her. "So you have to think of a name for him."

"What are you going to call him, dear?" asked Mrs. Goodwin.

Martha thought about it a moment and then a name sprang into her mind. "Little Jack," she said.

Mrs. Wallace was taken aback. She didn't know anyone called Jack. "Whatever made you think of *that* name?" she asked.

"It's a lovely name," said Mrs. Goodwin.

"Well, I'm sure he'll grow into it," said Pam. Martha lowered her head and pressed her lips against the animal's soft head. The two women caught eyes and smiled. Both hoped that, now Martha had a little friend to play with, a *real* little friend, she would no longer be lonely.

"Thank you, Goodwin," said Pam, putting a hand on the older woman's arm.

"My pleasure," said Mrs. Goodwin. "I think Martha and Little Jack were meant for each other."

Chapter 10

Ballinakelly, 1926

Spring smiled on Ballinakelly with the innocent optimism of a child. Radiant sunshine blessed the countryside and scattered the sea with golden kisses. Birds and butterflies took to the air and crickets chirruped happily in the long grasses. Hazel and Laurel made their way to church up the main street, arm in arm. The wind playfully caught the ribbons in their hats and pulled the hems of their dresses, and they responded to its teasing with predictable merriment, trying as best they could to hold on to their hats and their frocks in order to protect their modesty, while still holding on to each other.

At last they reached the church of St. Patrick. Its walls shone orange in the bright light of the sun, and the spire, rising as it did toward Heaven, uplifted the hearts of these two sisters who had suffered terrible fears during the Troubles and were still a little nervous about leaving the safety of their house. They were greeted warmly by Reverend Maddox, whose ruddy face and round belly betrayed his love of fine wine and good food and his inability to indulge in either with any sort of moderation. "My dear Misses Swanton," he said, sandwiching in turn their small hands in his big spongy ones. "Isn't it a beautiful day?" He raised his eyes to the sky in a pious manner, as if he and God were in cahoots, even about the weather.

"Oh, it is indeed," agreed Hazel, almost feeling inclined to thank him. "It is a lovely spring and I'm sure it will be a lovely summer." She sighed heavily. "Adeline would have adored the wildflowers on the hillside."

"Lady Deverill is enjoying the flowers in God's great garden," he reassured her.

"Of course she is," said Laurel.

"Adeline believed she'd be a spirit walking among us," Hazel added. "In which case, she'll be here enjoying it all for herself."

"Oh I'm sure she is," Laurel agreed. "I'm sure she's enjoying God's great garden with poor Reverend Daunt, who was such a good vicar. We are so pleased our humble parish has been sent such a fine replacement."

Reverend Maddox smiled with gratitude and ushered them into the church. "My dear ladies, why don't you step inside and enjoy the music. Mrs. Daunt has been practicing a few new pieces and she'd love you to hear them. Music has been a consolation to her during this difficult time." He watched the two women walk into the church. Two more compatible sisters he had yet to find.

Soon the church was beginning to fill up with the Ascendancy and gentry who had not been chased out of their homes by the rebels during the Troubles, and the working-class Protestants. There was an atmosphere of unity now, a sociability that hadn't existed before. The violence had herded them together in their small minority and they found comfort in each other as if a group of sheep on a windy hillside surrounded on all sides by wolves. Shopkeepers greeted the lords and ladies with sincere smiles and the grandees returned their salutations with equal warmth.

Lord Deverill sat in his usual place in the front row. Kitty was beside him with Robert and JP, as Little Jack was now known, for Kitty had felt that, at four years old, he was too big to be called "little," and considering he was christened Jack Patrick, JP suited him just as well. In truth, the name Jack gave her pain every time she uttered it.

Kitty had noticed a change in her father, subtle like the subliminal shift of a plate beneath the earth's crust. She couldn't say exactly when it had happened, but it was as if he had made a decision to amend the way he saw himself and the world. This deep shift had sent ripples through his being that affected him in so many ways. Gone was the melancholy, the self-pity and the need to drink himself into forgetfulness. He seemed grateful for life, with its small blessings. Most of all he seemed grateful for her and Elspeth, and spent as much time as possible with his little son, JP, who called him "Papa" and enjoyed all the outdoor pursuits that *he* enjoyed. The new clarity in his eyes convinced her that his feelings were genuine, but she couldn't understand what had inspired them. He even supported Celia's renovations of the castle with enthusiasm, wandering around the building site daily, where hundreds of men toiled away like an army of ants on an anthill. She wished she could share his interest in the rebuilding of his old home, but she couldn't; it caused her great anguish.

She didn't want to think of Jack O'Leary either, for that was painful too. He had gone and life had continued. She hadn't believed it possible, but it had happened. Celia had given birth to a baby daughter at the beginning of April, named Constance after her mother-in-law. Kitty's child would arrive in the autumn. Robert was ecstatic. She took his hand now and squeezed it as the jumping chords of Mrs. Daunt's organ playing resounded off the stone walls of the church. Kitty had made her choice; she had now to learn to live with it.

"Who's that man sitting with Grace?" Hazel whispered to Laurel. Laurel leaned forward and looked across the aisle to the other side of the church. There, seated beside Grace Rowan-Hampton, was a man neither Shrub had ever seen before. They both stared, and as they took in his thick silver hair, deep-set brown eyes and tidy white mustache resting above a wide and sensual mouth, time stood still. The chatter around them faded with the organ music and only their hearts, which began to race with an unfamiliar or long-forgotten tempo, resounded in their ears. United as always, the two ladies admired and feared the silver wolf in their midst. Not in the many decades of their dedicated spinsterhood had a man had such power to unbalance them. Suddenly, to their horror, he turned and his eyes met theirs, holding them captive for an excruciating moment. As they were jolted back to their senses with a flush of embarrassment, the music and chatter returned louder than before. He smiled and nodded politely. They tore their gazes away and fanned their flushed faces with their prayer books.

"Lord preserve me," hissed Laurel.

"He must be Grace's father," said Hazel.

"Has he a wife, do you think?" Laurel asked. Then she added hastily, "God forgive me for asking such a thing in His house. Don't answer that, Hazel. I don't know what's got in to me. Must be the heat. It is terribly hot, isn't it?"

"Oh, it is, Laurel. Terribly hot. I didn't see a wife. It appears he's with Grace."

"Look, Reverend Maddox is about to start the service. We must concentrate."

Hazel's fingers fluttered over her mouth. "He smiled at us, Laurel. Did you see?"

Laurel nudged her sister. "Shhh," she hissed. But her lips twitched with excitement.

Reverend Maddox gave a stirring sermon that seemed to go on and on and on. He was well known for enjoying the sound of his own voice to the point of being deaf to anyone else's, but today he was taking more pleasure from it than usual. Perhaps it was due to the sunshine, or maybe to the presence of the distinguished gentleman who was sitting beside Lady Rowan-Hampton whom he felt compelled to impress. Whichever it was, his voice rose and fell in great waves of passion, his sentences elongated like a piece of elastic only to snap back into short, brisk phrases designed to rouse the sleepy faithful.

At last, after he said the closing prayers and the Celtic Blessing he was so fond of, the Shrubs were the first into the aisle to make their escape before this devilishly handsome gentleman was able to see what a pair of quivering fools he had reduced them to.

Grace turned to her father, for indeed it was him. "I'm sorry about the rector, Papa. He mistakes the pulpit for the stage."

Lord Hunt patted his daughter's hand. "My dear, you needn't worry about me. When I am bored, which I often am in church, my mind is inclined to wander. Today, however, it wasn't my mind but my eyes that went wandering." He grinned mischievously.

Grace shook her head. "Papa, you're incorrigible. Mama would turn in her grave to see the way you behave. If you're going to live with me in this small community, you have to conduct yourself with decorum. I warn you, a town like this loves nothing more than to gossip. If you're going to misbehave you have to be discreet."

"I don't know what you're talking about, Grace." He laughed. "I'm a paragon of virtue. Besides, I'm much too old for that sort of thing." He arched a fluffy white eyebrow and smiled a wolf's smile, which told her that he was neither too old nor disinclined to "that sort of thing." Grace smiled too because in her father's lustiness she recognized herself.

They walked out into the sunshine and Grace introduced her father to Bertie and Kitty. The old rogue took Kitty's hand and brought it to his mustache, where the short hairs tickled her skin. "I must say, the women of Ballinakelly are very easy on the eye," he said, his eyes twinkling with mischief.

Kitty laughed. "You're too kind," she said, grinning at Grace, who was shaking her head in mock embarrassment.

"Papa's been here but five minutes and he's already misbehaving," she said.

"A little flirtation is the secret to longevity," said Lord Hunt. "And I intend to live a very long time."

"You must come for dinner," said Bertie cheerfully. "We'd like to welcome you formally."

"That's very kind of you, Lord Deverill. Grace has told me a great deal about your family and I admit that I am intrigued by your history. I was sorry to hear about the fire but curious to learn that the castle is being rebuilt."

"My cousin's daughter has bought it and is in the process of renovating it. Why don't you let me show it to you? It's an ambitious and extravagant project, to say the least, but I believe it's going to be magnificent when it's finished."

"I would like that very much, thank you," said Lord Hunt.

Grace looked at her former lover with tenderness. Recently she had seen glimpses of the carefree Bertie in his smile and in the light in his eyes, which seemed to her like the clear light of a new dawn. There was a fresh look about his clothes too, or perhaps it was the way he held himself in them. His tweed suit no longer looked crumpled and shabby, his hat was restored to its habitual raffish position on his head and his skin ceased to betray an excessive love of alcohol. She had noticed he had stopped drinking whiskey and wine and wondered what had come over him. She had once given him an ultimatum, her or the drink; he had been unable to live without either. Who had succeeded where she had failed?

She climbed behind the wheel of her car and waited for her father to join her. He was enjoying meeting the locals and soaking up the attention the women gave him, for even at seventy-four he was a fine-looking man. Her gaze drifted out of the window. A skinny dog limped along the street on three legs, his sharp nose in the air for he was after a whiff of something savory. Men in caps walked in groups, hands in pockets, eyes still dark with a residual wariness left over from the Troubles. Women stood chatting beneath the clear skies while children played in the road, their laughter bouncing off the walls of the houses. Then she saw Michael Doyle.

She caught her breath. Her heart stalled. The sensation was so acute it was visceral. For a moment she couldn't move. Only her eyes followed him as he ambled nonchalantly up the street with his brother Sean. She blinked, unable to believe what she was seeing, not trusting her sight, for surely, if he was back in Ballinakelly, *she* would have been his first stop? She willed him to look at her, but he didn't even toss her a glance. He strolled on, deep in conversation with his brother. She took in the face she had so often caressed, clear-skinned and glowing now that he was cured of the drink like Bertie. But she wasn't thinking about Bertie. Cast in the shadow of Michael Doyle, Bertie was invisible, as was every other lover she had ever taken. Michael Doyle was back from Mount Melleray and nothing else mattered. He was taller, broader, more rugged and attractive than ever before. A hot, prickling sensation crept over her skin and gathered in her belly. She gripped the steering wheel. He was past her now. She watched his back. Her eyes stung from the staring. How could he not feel her gaze through his jacket? How could he not sense that she was here? Why didn't he turn around? She wanted to run to him; to throw herself at him; to press herself against him and feel his rough hands upon her skin and his hungry mouth upon her lips. But she knew she had to restrain herself. She had to wait. He was only too aware of where she lived. She was certain he would come as soon as he could. Surely, his need for her was as urgent as hers for him?

"That Lord Deverill is a charming young man," said Lord Hunt, climbing stiffly into the passenger seat. He didn't notice his daughter's pale face, or the raw craving in her eyes. "Jolly nice of him to invite me to take a look at the castle. As you know, I have an enormous interest in history."

No sooner had her father closed the door than Grace started the engine and began to drive slowly up the street, her eyes frantically searching. Her father continued to share his thoughts but she wasn't listening. She was determined to see her lover; and for *him* to see *her* and the message in her gaze that told him to come to her. At last, as the car motored toward O'Donovan's, she spotted him. Then she was right beside him. She slowed down, so slow that she was crawling at the same speed as his walking pace. Sean glanced at her, but Michael was so busy talking that he was unaware of the car trailing him and of the desperate woman inside willing him to look at her.

Unable to bear it a moment longer, she tooted the horn. Both men, and the others in the street besides, turned to her in surprise. She leaned out of the window and gave a smile that exposed nothing of the torment beneath it. Desperate she might be, but Grace Rowan-Hampton was a seasoned actress and, when it came to dissembling, no one could surpass her. "Mr. Doyle," she said, without so much as a quiver in her voice.

"Lady Rowan-Hampton." Michael looked astonished to see her there. He doffed his cap and waited to hear what she had to say.

"I'm glad to see you're back. My husband is looking for strong men to clear a copse behind the house. Several trees were brought down in the winter storms. If you and your friends would like some work, will you come up to the house and see me?"

He nodded. "I'll ask in O'Donovan's," he said.

"Thank you," she replied, hoping he was reading the message in her eyes as he always used to. "I will wait for you up at the house. Sir Ronald would like the work to be done as soon as possible. I trust you'll find a few willing volunteers."

She drove on then, for there was nothing else to be said. Her father looked on in bewilderment as she checked her rearview mirror to see if he was watching the car, but he wasn't. He had disappeared inside O'Donovan's and only a cluster of scruffy youths remained in the road, admiring her shiny motor car as it rattled off.

Once home Grace hurried upstairs to change out of her church clothes into a more comfortable dress. She spent a long time at her dressing table arranging her hair, enlivening her cheeks with rouge and applying a little tuberose perfume behind her ears and between her breasts. She was sure that Michael would come.

Ethelred Hunt had claimed for himself a big armchair on the terrace, where, sheltered from the wind and warmed by the sun, he sat with his spectacles on his nose, reading the *Irish Times*. A maid brought him a glass of sherry and he lit a cigarette. He inhaled in a long, satisfying breath before releasing the smoke into the air. He didn't question his daughter's strange behavior outside the pub or the unusually long time she was spending in her bedroom, for Ethelred Hunt was a man whose concern was primarily his own pleasure and right now his attention was focused on those two birdlike ladies who had looked so startled to see him in church. He would have a great deal of fun with those two, he mused. He wasn't known as Ethelred-the-ever-ready for nothing! When at last Grace appeared, her father failed to notice, either, that she was on edge. She waited the rest of the day, but Michael didn't come.

It wasn't until the following morning that Brennan knocked on his mistress's door and announced that there was a group of lads at the front claiming to have come to clear the copse for Sir Ronald. Grace's heart gave a little leap. "Wonderful," she said. "I have told Mr. Tanner to expect them, so would you let him know and he'll look after them." As much as she wanted to run outside she knew that such a public display would be wholly inappropriate and, besides, how long had Michael been in Ballinakelly? She rather relished the idea of making him wait, as he had made *her* wait.

Brennan disappeared to find the head gardener, leaving Grace wringing her hands and pacing the room in agitation. Ethelred had gone off with Bertie to look around the castle and was then going to luncheon at the Hunting Lodge. There was a strong chance he would be gone all afternoon, for Grace suspected that Bertie would want to show him around the whole estate. Her father was a fine horseman and a keen race-goer, and since Bertie was as good as widowed, the two men had much in common. Ronald was in London, where he spent so much of his time these days. She had the house to herself until dark and was determined to make the most of it.

When Michael didn't come to her study window, or stride into her sitting room like he used to do, she began to worry. Had he gone to the copse with the other men in order to be discreet? Surely he could have made something up? She went out onto the terrace and gazed across the lawn. A rustle in the viburnum behind her gave her a start and she spun around, fully expecting to see Michael there with a lusty grin on his face, but it was nothing more than a pair of squabbling pigeons. She heaved a sigh and frowned. Why was he taking so long?

Finally, driven to distraction, she went to find Brennan in the hall. Her butler had seen men come and go over the years and had never so much as raised an eyebrow. Indeed, he had let Michael into the house many times, not bothering to announce him but letting him wander on through the hall as if he belonged there. On one occasion he had even warned him off when Sir Ronald had made an impromptu visit home. Now she asked him if Michael had been with the group of lads. Brennan shook his head. "No, my lady. Michael Doyle was not among them," he told her. Grace's face darkened with fury. How dare he humiliate her?

"Thank you, Brennan. If he does turn up, please tell him I'm indisposed." Then she went upstairs where she fell onto her bed, hugged her pillow and wondered what to do.

That evening her father returned in high spirits, full of talk about the splendid day he had had with Bertie. "Do you know he introduced me to his bastard? A bonny boy he is and as sharp as a tack too. He told me that his wife is so furious she has refused to let him move to London where he has bought her a house in Belgravia. It looks like he's going to be stuck here. I told him he should exchange her for a new one."

"Oh really, Papa," said Grace. "She's not a horse."

"From what I hear about Maud Deverill, Bertie would have had more fun with her if she was." Grace couldn't help but laugh in spite of feeling miserable. At least Lord Hunt was having fun, because *she* wasn't. She had thought of countless reasons why Michael hadn't turned up today but none of them assuaged her disappointment or her fury. His excuse had better be good, *very* good, she told herself, or he would wish himself back at Mount Melleray.

Grace drifted through the week distracted, hiding her frustration beneath a veneer of brittle cheerfulness. It seemed everyone in the county wanted to meet her father. They dined out every night and Ethelred entertained his hosts and their guests with hilarious stories and anecdotes, all exaggerated and embellished and some even totally invented, for Lord Hunt was a man of exceptional imagination. He brought laughter with him wherever he went, but no one was more taken with this witty and charming old wolf than the Shrubs, who, on the following Saturday night, were placed on either side of him at Bertie's dining-room table. They blushed, they stammered and they giggled like schoolgirls as Ethelred ensnared them in the full glare of his attention, rendering them powerless like a pair of guinea fowl, their little hearts aflutter as they had never fluttered before. As was their habit, they were in absolute agreement over the devilishly attractive Lord Hunt, but for the first time in their lives they wished they weren't.

Grace hadn't seen Michael since the Sunday before. She went to church, trying and failing to concentrate on the service, wondering how on earth she was going to seek him out without exposing herself. Her father seemed unconcerned about *his* focus on godly matters and far more interested in finding sport in the poor Shrubs, who sat across the aisle, blushing into their prayer books. As he grinned at the two spinsters and lifted his hand in a small greeting, Grace put her fingers to her lips and scowled into the middle distance.

She knew Michael went to O'Donovan's, but women didn't go to the pub and certainly not women of her class. She knew where he lived, but she couldn't very well turn up at the Doyle farmhouse, asking for him. The old network of note-passing that had worked so efficiently during the War of Independence had long ceased to exist, and even if it had still functioned a note would not bring him to her door. He was avoiding her. For whatever reason—and she convinced herself that there was a very *good* reason—he wasn't coming to see her. So she had no option but to engineer a meeting.

It is a sad fact that, in every affair, one party is keener than the other. Grace knew that only too well. But now *she* was the less desired and she couldn't accept it. Once a lover, man or woman, has given a partner unique delight it's almost impossible to imagine they no longer want it. She would pursue him. She would force him to face her and explain himself.

Her chance came at the Ballinakelly Fair, which took place on the first Friday of May. People had come from all over the county to look at the horses, buy and sell livestock and socialize. The sea breeze swept through the square with playful curiosity, dancing with sunbeams and ladies' hemlines, snatching smoke from the farmers' pipes and the boys' cigarettes. Spirits were high as the men and women flirted and the children played among the chickens and goats, earning a few bob for looking after the cows while the farmers went to the pub. There was music from a band and fortune-telling from tinker women who weaved through the crowd with baskets of heather and holy pictures. Voices rose with the peals of laughter and the mooing of cows and the bleating of sheep. Grace usually enjoyed the fair, but today she was anxious. Nights lying awake in torment had left her nerves frayed. Her father, however, was very excited. He had already met half of Ballinakelly society and was eager to meet the other half. When he bumped into the Shrubs he bowed formally and held out both arms, inviting them to show him around. It was fortunate that he had two arms, for both Laurel and Hazel were determined to take one.

Grace accompanied her father and the Shrubs, commenting on this and that without really listening to the conversation or, indeed, to her own responses. Her eyes scanned the faces for Michael's. She knew he'd be here. As a farmer he made it his business to attend every fair. Perhaps he'd even entered one of his bulls to compete for a prize?

At last she saw him right at the other end of the square: a glimpse of his head, unmistakable with its thick black curls, towering above everyone else's. She quickly left her father and the Shrubs without a word and elbowed her way through the crowd, keeping her head down for fear of getting caught by someone she knew and being compelled to stop and talk. She pushed on, eager to get to him, but it felt like she was wading through the sea, for with every step forward a wave of people came and pushed her back.

At last she lifted her gaze and there he was, right in front of her, gazing back at her with a serious look on his face. His coal-black eyes were the same but the wildness in them had gone. "Top of the morning to you, Lady Rowan-Hampton." The man he had been talking to slipped away and Grace felt as if they were alone on an island in an ocean of people.

"I need to talk to you," she whispered, barely able to restrain herself from placing a trembling hand on his forearm, just to feel him solid beneath her touch. "Why didn't you come and see me? How long have you been back? I've been waiting . . ." She despised the pleading tone in her voice, but she no longer had the will to dissemble.

"I've changed my ways," he replied solemnly, glancing about

him to make sure they weren't being overheard. "I've repented of my sins."

"What are you talking about? You went to be cured of the drink, not to become a monk!"

He lowered his eyes to hide his shame. "I've changed," he repeated, this time with emphasis. "The Michael Doyle you knew is dead. God has cured me of the drink and opened my eyes to the wickedness of my past."

Grace shook her head, unable to comprehend what he was saying. "You're still a man, Michael," she whispered, stepping closer. "God can't change that."

"I will not break His Commandments. You are a married woman, Lady Rowan-Hampton."

"But I *need* you." Even now she wanted to offer herself to him. To taste him, to kiss the sweat off his forehead, and she could scarcely keep her hands from reaching out and stroking him.

"I'm sorry, Grace," he said, this time with more tenderness.

"I waited for you, God damn it. I've waited *months* and *months*." Her voice was pleading, bordering on hysterical. "What am I? A jezebel?"

"Yes," he said with a solemnity that shocked her. "I must never look at a jezebel again. I shall never again visit Babylon."

Michael looked down at this woman who had always been so in control, of herself as well as everybody else. She had been a deadly weapon during the War of Independence, and many a British soldier had lost his life because of her, but here she was standing before him, a woman like any other, appealing to a man. He shook his head. "I think you should go before you draw attention to yourself," he said, not unkindly. Grace stared at him in disbelief, hating her submissive aching for him, longing to be rid of her dependence. Her vision began to blur but she searched his face for signs of amusement, for surely this was a joke. Surely, this was a bloody-minded joke. But Michael's face didn't change. He looked back at her with the righteous expression of a priest. She backed away, her cheeks aflame with mortification and fury. *If Mount Melleray could cure me of you, Michael, I'd be there like a shot.*

Chapter 11

On the first Wednesday in June, Sir Digby and Lady Deverill attended the Derby, the most famous flat race in the world, at Epsom Racecourse in Surrey. Accompanied by Celia and Archie, Harry and Boysie and their insipid wives, Charlotte and Deirdre, whom the two young men would have preferred to have left at home, they were in high spirits. The women wore elegant cloche hats and coats yet Beatrice had chosen a larger, more Edwardian-style hat adorned with extravagant ostrich feathers and pearls that drew the eye as well as the comments, for many of the noble ladies considered Lady Deverill rather brassy. "Who does she think she is, the Queen?" they whispered behind their race cards. The gentlemen were dressed in the finest top hats and tails but somehow Digby's shoes and hat shone with more polish than anyone else's, the cut of his collar was slightly more flamboyant than convention dictated and his confident swagger gave the impression that he was a man of great importance. Today he felt indomitable, because, running in the race for the first time, was Digby's colt Lucky Deverill, whom he had been training up in Newmarket. "I hope he has the luck of the *London* Deverills and not the *County Cork* Deverills," Boysie whispered to Celia, who swiftly reproached him with a playful smack on the hand.

"You're wicked, Boysie!"

"One cannot be chastised for telling the truth, Celia," he replied with a sniff.

"Papa says he has a very good chance of winning."

"I think he is alone in that belief," said Boysie. "Judging by the odds."

"What do they know," Celia sniffed dismissively. "Papa says he's bred to win the Derby."

"And he came fourth in the 2000 Guineas at Newmarket, yes, I know, your father told me that too."

"You will bet on him, won't you?"

"Only for you, Celia. Though I doubt it will make me a fortune."

"If he wins, his value at stud will soar. The covering fees will be enormous. Papa will make a fortune."

"Another one," said Boysie with a smirk. "Your father's rather good at making fortunes."

Wrapped in coats and hats, sheltering beneath umbrellas, the small party who had parked their cars behind the grandstand hurried inside. It was warm and exclusive in there and they were quick to help themselves to refreshments. "Goodness, there are so many people on the hill!" Celia groaned, looking out onto the rise of common land where the fairground loomed out of the rain like a mythological sea creature. "I do so hate the great unwashed!"

"The hoi polloi," said Boysie. "I'm glad they're out *there* and we're in *here*."

"Quite," she agreed. "It's hell out there. I swear the entire East End has decamped for the day."

"Darling, the whole of London has decamped for the day," said Boysie. "You'd have thought the rain would have put people off, but no, there's nothing like a free day out for the great British public."

Due to the inclement weather the trains had been restricted and the day was soon dubbed a Petrol Derby, with makeshift parking lots being set up in the large sodden fields either side of the drive to accommodate the swollen number of vehicles. The wet and dismal conditions, however, did not deter the thousands of people who arrived in cars, double-decker buses and motor coaches. Some even arrived in stagecoaches pulled by fine horses. Piled into and *on*to the coaches, the delighted passengers waved cheerfully at the crowds as policemen in capes and helmets tried to maintain some sort of order for the arrival of the King and Queen. When they appeared at last, in the middle of a long convoy of gleaming cars, the crowd stopped what they were doing to watch. The King sat stiffly beside the Queen, who was wearing one of her typically elaborate feathered hats, raising his hand every now and again to greet his people. The girls, however, were much more interested in the dashing Prince of Wales and erupted into a clatter of applause when they saw him.

Once in the relative calm of the stands Digby and Beatrice wandered around the gallery greeting their friends and acquaintances. It was there that Digby bumped into Stanley Baldwin, the prime minister, for Parliament was always adjourned for the Derby. "Ah, Prime Minister," he exclaimed, striding up to him. The prime minister swept his eyes over Digby's flamboyant purple-and-green waistcoat and pink spotted tie and grinned. For a man of his breeding there was something rather brash about Sir Digby Deverill. Mr. Baldwin lifted his top hat in salutation. "Sir Digby, Lady Deverill, I see you have a horse racing this year," he said.

"Indeed we do," Digby replied. "He's a fine colt. Young but swift. I have high expectations of him."

"I'm sure you do, Sir Digby," said Mr. Baldwin archly. "You didn't get to where you are today without the desire to be a winner."

"Nor you, if I may be so bold."

"Indeed." Mr. Baldwin smiled, acknowledging Digby's wit with a slight nod of the head. "What are the odds?"

"Sixteen to one," Digby replied.

"A long shot." Stanley Baldwin was well known as a plain-speaking man. The prime minister chuckled. It did not seem likely that Lucky Deverill would win. "Then I wish you luck," he said. "Tell me, how is work progressing on that castle of yours?"

"My daughter is pouring money into the project. If it doesn't outshine Windsor Castle in opulence and grandeur I shall be very disappointed."

"Is she intending to live there?" Mr. Baldwin asked, incredulous, for Celia's reputation as a socialite was well documented. "I would have thought a lively girl like Mrs. Mayberry would find life in County Cork dull by comparison to London." He smiled at Beatrice, noticing the large diamonds that glittered on her ears and beneath her left shoulder in the form of an elaborately crafted flower brooch. *Those Randlords!* he thought to himself with a barely perceptible shake of the head.

"Oh, but it's beautiful in the summer," Beatrice interjected emphatically.

"But not quite so beautiful in the winter, I don't imagine," Mr. Baldwin argued.

"Then we must hope that Celia shines bright enough to bring the London glamour to Ballinakelly." Digby gave his Brigg umbrella a couple of taps on the floor and roared a belly laugh that sounded like gold in a prospector's pan. "Because, by God, no one else can."

Mr. Baldwin laughed with him. Digby's ebullience was shameless but irresistible. "Of that I have no doubt, Sir Digby. Mrs. Mayberry is the very sun itself."

Beatrice was distracted by a friend who caught her eye and Mr. Baldwin raised his hat at her departure. Digby put a hand on his shoulder and moved closer. "Do let me know if I can help the Party in any way," he said in a low voice.

"I will," said Mr. Baldwin bluffly. "Your help is much appreciated."

"I hope one day I will be rewarded," said Digby.

"You've been very well rewarded already with your baronetcy," the prime minister reminded him.

"Oh, that bauble." Digby chuckled. "A viscountcy is much more to my taste."

"Is it? Is it?" said Mr. Baldwin, embarrassed at the brashness of the Randlord. "I think you've done very well already," he added.

"Up to a point," said Digby with that golden gravel laugh. "Up to a point."

Celia threaded through the crowds with Boysie and Harry, leaving their wives discussing the weather with a tedious group of Edwardian ladies old enough to remember the Crimean War. Archie was with his mother, who had slipped her hand around his arm and thus staked her claim. There would be no getting away from her until luncheon. Celia, Boysie and Harry were only too delighted to find themselves unencumbered and wandered about in search of fun people to talk to.

As they reached the steps to the upper terrace who should be coming down, surrounded by a coterie of courtiers but the Prince of Wales himself, who had left the Royal Box to go to the paddock. He recognized Celia at once and his handsome face creased into a debonair smile. "My dear Celia," he said and Celia dropped into a deep curtsy.

"Your Royal Highness," she said. "May I present my cousin Harry Deverill and my friend Boysie Bancroft?" The Prince shook hands and the boys duly bowed.

"You know I've known Celia since she was this high," he told them, placing his hand a few feet above the step.

"And I suppose you're going to tell me that I have hardly changed." Celia laughed.

His blue eyes twinkled at her flirtatiously. "You've certainly grown taller," said the Prince. "And prettier too."

"Oh sir, you're much too kind," said Celia, blushing with pleasure. "The King looks awfully well," she added. "And the Queen . . ."

"Mama's hats are so ugly," the Prince interjected. "She looks hideous in those ridiculous toques!"

Celia giggled. "Papa has a horse running in the race."

"So I see. If he wins, he'll be insufferable."

"He's already insufferable," Celia said with a smile.

"He's a *bon viveur*," said the Prince.

Celia grinned raffishly and leaned a little closer to him. "It takes one to know one, sir."

"Celia, you're incorrigible!" He laughed. "I will go and find your papa and wish him luck."

"Oh do, sir. He's quite beside himself with nerves, though he'll never admit it." The Prince chuckled and moved on into the crowd of people who were all watching him out of the corners of their eyes and hoping he'd come their way.

"The Prince of Wales rendered me dumbstruck," said Boysie once he was gone. "He's outrageously attractive!"

"The wittiest tongue in London was silenced?" said Harry, feigning astonishment.

"I'm afraid it was, old boy," Boysie replied. "Fortunately Celia's adroit enough for the three of us."

"I've known him for years. He's a darling! Come on, let's go and find some *young* people to talk to," Celia suggested, and they headed off up the stairs.

On the common ground that was the hill, the weather had not dampened the spirits of the thousands of people who had flocked to the racecourse. The noise was overpowering: coach horns tooting, bookmakers hollering their odds, salesmen advertising their wares, car engines rattling and the general public shouting in different dialects. The refreshment tents were full to bursting, the stalls busy selling wares and the fairground full of mirth. Laughter resounded from the carousel, rose up from the game tables and was swiftly smothered in the sealed booths advertising werewolves and other monstrosities. Gypsies lured the gullible into their colorful caravans to learn their futures (and the identity of the Derby winner) in exchange for a palm crossed with silver, and artists positioned themselves beneath makeshift shelters to sketch portraits of those whose hats and hairdos had not been ruined by the rain. Double-decker buses and cars were parked as close to the running rail as possible and piled with people keen to have pole position for the races while pedlars accosted them from the ground, hawking goods. The earth grew soggy but the desire to enjoy themselves kept the spectators buoyant—as did the desire to win money, for the queues at the bookmakers' were very long indeed.

Before the Derby Celia went down to the paddock with her father to watch the horses parading. Digby's jockey was a five-foot-six Irishman of almost forty years of age called Willie Maguire, notorious for his fondness of drink. Many whispered that Willie was too unreliable and that Sir Digby had been misguided to offer him the ride, but Digby was a man wise enough to take advice from those who knew better. In this case, his trainer, Mike Newcomb, had more experience and knowledge than he did and Digby trusted him implicitly. If Newcomb had appointed a seventy-year-old jockey with arthritis he would have agreed wholeheartedly.

"Oh Papa, wouldn't it be glorious if Lucky Deverill won! Willie would most certainly win the most fetching jockey in his green and white."

Digby chuckled. "He's got more mileage under his belt than all of them put together, I suspect."

"And Lucky Deverill is a fine horse." Celia ran her eyes up and down the animal's gleaming limbs.

"He's well put together, no one can deny that. He looks like he'll get the trip as he has plenty of scope."

"Plenty," Celia agreed without understanding her father's racing jargon.

"This is *our* year," Digby said to his daughter. "If ever I am to win the Derby it will be today."

"Do you really think so?"

Digby nodded thoughtfully, remembering the day he struck lucky in the South African diamond fields. "When you're lucky, Celia, you carry that luck around with you for a while. Luck attracts more luck. That's the time to exploit it."

"Can you say the same about *bad* luck?" she asked.

"I'm afraid it works both ways. Sometimes bad luck sticks to you like mud. In that case you weather it. But we're on a lucky roll, Celia my dear, and today we're going to win." He waved at Willie as the jockey walked Lucky Deverill past.

"Oh Papa, you're wonderfully confident," she gushed, full of admiration for her daring father.

"Until my luck runs out," he added.

"But it won't, surely."

"Oh, but it will," he said with certainty. Then he grinned the grin of a gambler who is as much excited by the possibility of loss as he is of gain. What mattered to Digby was the thrill of the game. "But sometimes one can make one's own luck," he added with a wink.

The horses left the paddock and paraded in front of the grandstand where the King and Queen and the Prince of Wales observed them keenly from the Royal Box. The air grew tense as the crowd watched them canter across the downs to take their starting positions behind the rope. Celia stood beside her father at the front of the gallery at the very top of the grandstand, directly opposite the winning post. "I'm a bundle of nerves," she said, shifting her weight from one foot to the other. "But terribly excited."

Digby put his field glasses to his eyes and watched the horses arrange themselves at the start. His heart began to pound in his chest like a drum. His cheeks flushed with competitiveness and it took a great force of will to steady his hands. He could see Lucky Deverill clearly, the green-and-white silks of Willie Maguire, right in the middle of the line-up. He muttered under his breath. Then the flag fell and they were away.

Celia barely dared breathe as the horses thundered off up the long incline, contracting into a tight huddle. The crowd was pressed up against the rails either side of the track and the noise of cheering was deafening. Digby said nothing. He watched through his field glasses, perfectly still, while Celia jumped and fidgeted nervously beside him. Beatrice wrung her hands while Harry and Boysie watched Lucky Deverill fall back on the outside. "Digby might have to rename him *Un*lucky Deverill," said Boysie in a low voice and Harry chuckled. He thought of the bet he had placed in support of Celia; he might as well have just burned the money.

The horses galloped up the hill, disappearing briefly behind the copse at the top before starting their descent toward Tattenham Corner, the most famous corner in racing. The inexperienced horses, fearful of the steep slope, began to slow down while the more experienced horses advanced, creating a muddle. Lucky Deverill had not yet distinguished himself. He languished behind the first six horses. Beatrice shot a surreptitious glance at her husband, inhaling sharply through her nose at the sight of his immobile profile; there was something in the barely perceptible twitch of his lower lip that caused her heart to snag. Celia put her fingers to her mouth and began to chew her glove.

It was at that moment, when the horses slowed down just

before the home stretch, that something extraordinary began to happen. The sharp bend had flung some of the horses wide into the field and Willie Maguire, being a seasoned jockey, took advantage of this, hugging the inside. To Digby's astonishment Lucky Deverill was gaining momentum—and gaining it fast. Digby's knuckles went white. He lowered his field glasses. The horses advanced up the slope toward the winning post and all Digby could see was the bright green and white edging its way past the fourth, then the third, grabbing the rising ground. It wasn't possible! His breath stuck in his throat. The noise grew more intense but he heard nothing, just the hammering sound of blood pulsating against his temples.

Everyone was now on their feet. Celia was screaming, Beatrice gasping, Harry and Boysie mute with astonishment, mouths agape, as Lucky Deverill inched ahead of the second. With only a hundred yards to go Willie Maguire rode Sir Digby's hope as if he were riding the wind. A moment later he was parallel to the first. The two horses were now neck and neck. But Lucky Deverill was propelled by the luck of the London Deverills and with one last valiant thrust Willie Maguire rode him first past the winning post.

Digby was on his feet, punching the air. Celia was throwing her arms around him. Beatrice was dabbing her eyes with Boysie's handkerchief. Harry shook his head and wanted to throw his arms around Boysie, but he thrust his hands into his pockets and swept his eyes over the crowd now pouring onto the racecourse.

Suddenly Digby was besieged. Hands patted his back, faces smiled at him, lips congratulated him. He was swept down the grandstand like a leaf on a waterfall, carried by the hundreds of surprised spectators, both friends and strangers alike. When at last he reached the ground he hastened off to the finish to meet his horse and jockey, the victorious Willie Maguire. When he saw his triumphant horse, nostrils flaring, his coat sodden with rain and sweat, he stroked his wet nose, then took him by the reins to lead him into the winners' enclosure. He was at once surrounded by journalists asking him questions and photographers clicking their cameras, the flash bulbs momentarily blinding him. "Really, it had very little to do with me," he heard himself saying. "Willie Maguire rode with great courage and skill and Lucky Deverill proved everyone wrong. It is Newcomb, Lucky Deverill's trainer, who should be congratulated and, if you don't mind, I'd very much like to go and do that myself." And with the help of the police he extracted himself from the throng of press.

"By God, he won!" said Boysie to Celia. "He really does have the luck of the Devil!"

"Papa makes his own luck," said Celia proudly.

Beatrice had now composed herself and was graciously receiving congratulations when she was interrupted by an official-looking man with a neatly trimmed mustache and spectacles. He coughed into his hand. "Lady Deverill, may I ask you to follow me. The King would like to offer you his personal congratulations."

Beatrice beamed. "But of course. Excuse me," she said to those awaiting her attention. "I have been summoned by the King." The people stepped aside to allow her to pass and Beatrice was escorted up to the Royal Box where His Majesty was waiting in the anteroom, surrounded by courtiers. A small, bearded, gruff man in tails and top hat with a row of military medals across his chest, the King had the air of a retired military colonel.

"My dear Lady Deverill," he said when she entered. He extended his hand. Beatrice took it and allowed the King to plant a kiss on her cheek, tickling her face with his beard. She then dropped into a low curtsy. "You must be very proud," he said.

"Oh I am, sir. Very." Unlike his son, the King was a man of few words, so Beatrice found herself overcompensating to disguise any awkwardness. "I shall have a hard time keeping his feet on the ground now that he's got a Derby winner." She laughed to fill the silence that ensued.

"Oh yes, indeed," said the King finally, settling his watery blue eyes on her.

"We remember with great affection your visit to Ireland," she said, recalling his state visit to Southern Ireland fifteen years before. "Did you know that Celia is now restoring Castle Deverill?"

"Is she now?"

"Oh yes," Beatrice gushed. "It is a tragedy that some of the most beautiful houses in Ireland were razed to the ground during the Troubles. It's just wonderful to think of possibly the most beautiful of all rising once again."

"Indeed," the King muttered. "Damn good shoot at Castle Deverill." At that moment an equerry sidled over and whispered something into the King's ear. "Ah, I must go and hand Sir Digby his trophy," he said.

"Of course you must," said Beatrice, dropping once again into a low curtsy. She left his presence in high spirits in spite of the uneasiness of their conversation, because, after all, the King's the King and Beatrice was dazzled by royalty.

"ONE COULD NOT really ask for very much more," said Digby to his wife when they arrived back at Deverill House at the end of the day. He poured himself a drink while Beatrice fell into the sofa, exhausted by all the excitement.

"Where do you go from here, Digby?" she asked, sighing with the pleasure of taking the weight off her legs.

"What do you mean? I'm going to win the 2000 Guineas and the Gold Cup," he replied. Digby brought his glass to his nose and inhaled the sweet smell of whiskey. His ambition would be greatly served by entering into the public arena, but he was only too aware of the skeletons rattling about in his cupboard to risk threatening his reputation by putting his head so high above the parapet. Aware that his wife was not referring to horses he added, "I have no desire to encumber my life with politics, my dear." He sank into an armchair as a maid brought in a tray of tea.

"Rubbish," said Beatrice with a smile. "You can't resist the limelight!" The maid handed her a teacup. "Ah, thank you. Just what I need to restore my energy. What a day. What a *perfect* day. Celia is mistress of Castle Deverill and my husband has won the Derby. It's all too wonderful to be true." She watched the maid pour the tea, then dug her teeth into a short-bread biscuit. "I am aware of our blessings, Digby, and I take none of them for granted. When we lost our beloved George in the war I thought my life was over. But it's possible to rise out of the ashes and live, isn't it? One simply has to keep going in a different way. One part of me shut down, but I discovered that I am more than I believed I was. Other parts of me came to the fore. So here we are, enormously fortunate, and here am *I*, grateful and proud." She sipped her tea, dislodging the lump that had unexpectedly formed in her throat.

Digby looked steadily at his wife. "I think about George every day, Beatrice," he said quietly. "And I miss him. He would have relished today. He loved horses and he had a competitive spirit. He would have enjoyed the thrill of the race. But it was not to be. I hope he was watching from wherever he is."

They withdrew into silence as they both remembered their son, and while they both felt blessed, they knew that nothing, no accomplishment, success or triumph on any level, could make up for the devastation of so great a loss.

KITTY STRUGGLED TO live with the choice she had made. She waded through her days against an incoming tide of grief and regret, the bleeding in her heart staunched only by the burgeoning life growing inside her belly. It was as if she had prized open the very body of Ireland and ripped out its soul. Without Jack the landscape was bereft, weeping golden tears onto the damp grass as autumn stole the last vestiges of summer. She kept herself busy, looking after JP and preparing the nursery for the new baby, and she tried not to succumb to the memories of the man she loved which lingered on every hill and in every valley like mist that just won't lift. Yet, in late October, hope arrived with the first frosts as Kitty was delivered of a little girl. They called her Florence, after their honeymoon in Italy, and Kitty found, to her joy, that the overwhelming love she felt for her daughter eclipsed the longing she felt for Jack.

Robert stood at the bedside and held the tiny baby in his arms. He gazed into her face with wonder. "She is so pretty," he said to Kitty, who lay in bed propped up against the pillows.

"What do you think, JP?" she asked the little boy who was snuggled up beside her.

JP screwed up his nose. "I think she's ugly," he said. "She looks like a tomato."

Robert and Kitty laughed. "You looked like a tomato too, when you were a baby," Kitty told him. "And look what a handsome boy you are now."

"She doesn't have much hair," said JP.

"Not now, darling, but it will grow," said Kitty. "You'll have to look after her and teach her to ride."

"She'll look up to you," Robert added, handing Florence back to her mother and sitting on the edge of the bed. "You'll be her big brother."

"Although, you're really her uncle," Kitty said.

"Think of that. Uncle JP. How does that sound?" Robert asked him.

The boy grinned proudly and peered into Florence's face. The baby wriggled and began to cry. JP screwed up his nose again in distaste.

Robert put out his hand. "I think you and I should leave Kitty to feed the baby," he said.

"Is she always going to make that noise?" asked JP, jumping down from the bed.

"I hope not," said Robert.

Kitty watched them wander from the room, JP's small hand in Robert's big one, his bouncy walk full of childish vigor beside Robert, whose labored stride was slow due to his stiffened leg. Her heart buckled. As hard as it had been to make her choice, she knew she had done the right thing. She gazed into the innocent face of her child and knew that *this* was where she belonged.

Chapter 12

New York, autumn 1927

Bridie had been in New York for two years. She was now an established presence in the gossip columns, at the theater, in the elegant uptown restaurants and cafés and, of course, in the smoky underground speakeasies of Harlem. Her sorrow was a silent current beneath the hard shield that she had built around herself for protection against memory and melancholy. Like ice on a river it was beautiful to look at but cold. Her life was lived on the surface where everything was superficial and gay and without a care. Happiness was acquired in the same way that she acquired everything: with money. The moment she felt a tremor of gloom she headed out to the shops to buy more happiness in the form of expensive clothes and hats, shoes and bags, feathers and sequins, diamonds and pearls. The boutiques were full of happiness and she had the means to procure as much of it as she wanted.

There were men; plenty of men. She was never without a suitor and she took her pleasure when she wanted it. In those midnight hours when darkness wrapped its soft hands around her and lovers caressed her with tender fingers the silent current swelled and grew inside her, breaking against her heart in waves of longing. Her soul cried out to be loved and the memory she had of loving shifted into focus. For a blessed moment she could pretend that the arms holding her belonged to a man who cherished her and that the lips kissing her were devoted and true. But it was fool's gold. Reality shattered the dream every time with dawn's first light and Bridie was left fighting her desolation in the shops on Fifth Avenue.

Beaumont and Elaine Williams were her allies in her new world of fickle, fair-weather friends. Mr. Williams had known her before she had inherited her fortune, when she was a naïve and humble maid, fresh off the boat from Ireland, and she trusted him. He oversaw her investments personally and his office attended to all her bills. Bridie paid him handsomely for his cunning and wisdom. With the dreary jobs taken care of, Bridie's only responsibility was to have fun, and Elaine was her constant companion. As frivolous and acquisitive as *she* was, Bridie didn't hesitate to fund her lifestyle; after all, Elaine was as vital to her as rope to a drowning man.

Just when she believed she was forgetting her past, her past remembered *her*.

It was a hot, sticky night in Manhattan. Bridie and Elaine had been to Warners' Theater to see the movie *Don Juan*, a new "talkie" with sound effects and orchestral music starring John Barrymore as the irresistible womanizer. They were in such a high state of excitement that going home to bed was not an option. "All that kissing has got me quite shaken up," said Elaine, linking arms with Bridie as they hurried across Broadway. "What shall we do now? I'm feeling in a party kind of mood."

"Me too," Bridie agreed. "Let's go to the Cotton Club," she suggested. "There's always plenty of entertainment there." She put her hand out to hail a cab.

The Cotton Club was a fashionable nightclub in Harlem where New York's most stylish went to eat fine food, drink illegal alcohol, dance to live bands and watch shows. It was buzzing, busy and boisterous and Bridie loved it especially because in that heady, loud and crowded place she could forget who she really was.

Except on this night, sitting at a round table with a group of suited men Bridie didn't recognize and being fawned over by a couple of scantily dressed showgirls, was the only man in New York capable of making her remember: Jack O'Leary.

She stood staring at him in astonishment. He had changed. His hair was cut short, he was clean-shaven and he wore a pristine suit and tie. But he was unmistakably Jack with his deepset pale blue eyes and crooked smile. People moved and jostled around her, but she remained as still as a rock until Elaine nudged her out of her stupor. "What's up, Bridget?" Elaine followed the line of her gaze. "Do you know those guys?" she asked, then she added huskily, "They look like they're up to no good, I'm telling you."

"I know one of them," said Bridie slowly, suddenly feeling sick.

"The handsome one?" Elaine asked with a giggle.

"He's from my past."

"Oh. Listen, if you're not happy we can go someplace else."

"No, we'll stay. I'm just surprised. He's the last person I expected to see in New York." As the two women stared at him Jack lifted his eyes. At first he didn't recognize her. He stared back, his face blank. Then his features softened and his eyes narrowed as he registered who she was. They remained a moment, gazing at each other through the smoke as if caught in a spell.

At last he pushed out his chair and began to make his way across the room toward her. "I think I'll leave you to talk about old times," said Elaine and she melted into the crowd of dancing people. Bridie waited, heart pounding, suddenly feeling small and lost and very far from home.

"Bridie?" he said, incredulous. "Is it really you?"

"Don't be so shocked. I've been back here for two years now. I'm the one who should be surprised to see *you*—and indeed I am."

He chuckled. "Fair play to you, Bridie." He gazed into her face as if searching for the way back to Ballinakelly.

"When did you get here?" she asked, unsettled by the intensity in his eyes.

"February last year—but it feels like ten years ago."

The sick feeling in Bridie's stomach grew stronger. "And Kitty?" she asked, suddenly realizing that they must have run off together.

But Jack's face darkened. "Let's go and sit down somewhere. Fancy a drink?"

"I'd kill for one!" she exclaimed and they made their way to a small round table in a quieter corner of the club. Jack summoned the waiter, who appeared to know him well, and ordered champagne for Bridie and a beer for himself. "I came on my own, Bridie, to start a new life."

Bridie's relief was immense. "Then it's fair to say that both you and I have run away."

"Indeed we have," he agreed, and the twist of his lips told Bridie that he was as tormented as she was. "When the drinks arrive, we'll raise our glasses to that."

"Did you find work, Jack?"

"It's easy for a man to find work here in New York. Half the city is Irish, it seems."

"So what are you doing?"

"This and that," he replied shiftily.

"Don't get into trouble, Jack," she warned.

"Don't worry. I've had enough trouble in my life. This time I won't get caught!" He grinned and she saw the old Jack of her childhood in his smile, but there was something different in his eyes—a hard glint, like the flash of a knife, which she didn't recognize.

"But you're a vet. You love animals."

"Not much demand for that in the city, Bridie. Let's just say I'm bringing a certain product over the Great Lakes. After all, I'm handy with a rifle in case some other fellas try to steal it off us."

"I would have thought your stint in jail would have taught you a little about breaking the law, Jack," said Bridie.

"I'm ready to make it in America, Bridie, whatever it takes. There are opportunities here and I'm not going to let them pass me by." Bridie watched him closely and wondered whether he missed the excitement and drama of the War of Independence, whether he had perhaps lived that life of rebellion for so long that it was the only life he knew. One thing was certain: he was up to no good.

The waiter brought their drinks on a tray and Bridie took a long sip of champagne. Jack put his hands around his beer glass and Bridie was at once taken back to the farmhouse in Ballinakelly where she'd return from working up at the castle to find Jack and her brothers sitting at the table plotting over their pewter mugs of Beamish stout.

"We're a long way from home, you and I," said Jack.

"What made you leave?"

"Da died," he said, but Bridie knew that wasn't the reason.

"I'm sorry, may he rest in peace," she said with compassion.

He took a swig of his beer, then stared into the glass. His face hardened and his lip curled. "I left because of Kitty." Bridie nodded. That came as no revelation. "She promised me she'd come with me, but she lied. She never intended to come." He heaved a sigh. "I don't imagine she ever really meant to leave Ballinakelly, or Robert. I was a fool to think so. She said she couldn't leave because she was expecting Robert's child." He took another swig, then grimaced. "She's as cunning as a fox, that's for sure."

Bridie's heart filled with resentment. Kitty was expecting a child of her own who would grow up alongside Little Jack. It didn't seem fair that Kitty should be so blessed when *she* had been so wronged. "Do you think she got pregnant on purpose?" asked Bridie.

"I know she did and I'll never forgive her. I've wasted my life waiting for Kitty Deverill."

"She stole my son," said Bridie and the relief of being able to say so caused her eyes to sting with tears. Jack was the only person in this city who would understand.

"Jack Deverill," he said.

"Named after *you*," Bridie reminded him.

He chuckled bitterly. "She'll be after changing his name now," he said, grinning crookedly again.

"He's my son," she repeated. "I came back for him but he thinks I'm dead. She told him I'd died, Jack. The woman has no heart. I couldn't very well tell him the truth, could I? I had to leave without him, God help me."

"I'm sorry," he said. "That's a terrible pain to carry."

"I try not to think about it. I came here to start again. A new life. A new me. I left the old Bridie behind. I'm Bridget Lock-wood here, don't you know."

"Indeed and you look well on it. We both left our pasts behind in the Old Country."

She smiled and Jack thought how pretty she looked when her face was animated. Back in Ballinakelly, when he'd seen her at Mass, she had been hard and defensive, but here, even though she was smartly dressed, there was a softness and a vulnerability about her that reminded him of the grubby-faced, shoeless child who had once been frightened of hairy caterpillars and rats. He smiled too. "What a sorry pair we are," he said. "Let's drink to our good health."

She raised her glass. "And to our futures."

"Indeed. May I be touched with the hand of Midas too!"

WHEN JACK MADE love to Bridie she didn't have to pretend anymore. Here was the man she had always loved. Here was the man she had searched for in the embraces of others but never found. The hands that caressed her, the lips that kissed her and the gentle Irish vowels that took her back to a safe and familiar place belonged to the only man who really knew her. Their paths had taken years to cross but now that they had Bridie was sure that they were destined to unite forever. She believed that finally, in this faraway city, she had found home.

Jack tried to lose Kitty in Bridie's arms. He had drunk so much that every time he closed his eyes it was Kitty he was making love to and in spite of his still burning fury he couldn't bring himself to open them. His heart ached with longing and homesickness. His heart ached for Kitty. He buried his head in Bridie and willed himself home.

When they lay together, bathed in the golden glow of the city's lights, they reminisced about the old days when they had both been young and innocent and full of ambition: Bridie for a better future away from Ballinakelly, Jack for a free and independent Ireland. He lit a cigarette and lay against the pillows while Bridie propped herself up on her elbow beside him, her hair falling in dark waves over the white pillows. How Jack wished that those tresses were red.

"Tell me about Lord Deverill," he asked.

"He was *Mr.* Deverill then," she said.

"You told Michael he raped you, didn't you?"

Bridie was unrepentant. "I had to or he would have killed me."

"So he burned the castle and killed Hubert Deverill instead."

Bridie looked horrified. "Don't say that, Jack. Michael wouldn't—"

"Oh, he did much worse than that." But Jack couldn't bring himself to betray Kitty so he took a long drag of his cigarette and shook his head. "You know what he's capable of," he said instead.

"He's got a good heart, deep down," Bridie reasoned. "He

rescued my son and gave him to Kitty. He brought him home where he belongs. If he hadn't, who knows where the boy might be now? He might be lost on the other side of the world. At least this way I know where he is and I know he's safe and well cared for. Michael didn't have to do that, but he did. So you see, he's not all bad."

"No one is all bad, Bridie. But Michael is no saint either. It suited him to bring Little Jack home. Ask yourself why Michael, who is so fervently anti-British, would give his nephew to an Anglo-Irish woman for safekeeping. Why would he do that?"

"Because Little Jack is my son, that's why," Bridie repeated emphatically. "But he's not just a Doyle, he's a Deverill too. Michael couldn't very well give him to Mam, could he? She'd die of shock and Nanna too. Kitty was the only person and she's my boy's half sister."

"Indeed Little Jack is a Doyle and Michael is a family-minded man," Jack conceded ponderously. "But I figure he brought the baby to Kitty's door to allay his guilty conscience. I suppose you could say that he took the life of a Deverill with one hand, but gave another life with the other. Perhaps the baby was even a peace offering to Kitty, whom he had so wronged."

Bridie was unconvinced. "He did it for *me*, Jack. He did it for my family. Maybe he even did it to shame Mr. Deverill into facing up to his crime."

"A crime which he didn't commit," Jack reminded her.

"No, rape it wasn't," Bridie agreed, but she didn't want to accept her part in the burning of the castle and the death of Lord Deverill, so she added, "However, he shouldn't have taken advantage of me. I was the same age as his daughter and I was in no position to refuse him."

"Indeed he should not have, Bridie."

She sighed, taking her mind back to those stolen moments in the Hunting Lodge when Mr. Deverill had brought her gently to womanhood. "But I loved him, you know. He was kind to me. He made me feel special." She chuckled bitterly. "No one else did."

Jack looked at her quizzically. "How close were you?"

She smiled wistfully. "I thought we were *very* close."

"How much did you share?" he asked.

Bridie was deaf to the subtle change in his tone of voice and blind to his now steady gaze, watching her through the smoke. "I told him everything," she said carelessly. "He was my friend and confidant, or so I thought. I realized what *I* was to *him* when I told him I was carrying his child. He was brutal, Jack. He treated me like I was nothing to him. After all those intimate moments, when he had made me believe that he loved me . . ." But Jack was no longer listening. He was wondering about the brave men who had fought beside him during the War of Independence, and died. How many ambushes and raids had been scuppered due to intelligence leaked on the pillow to Mr. Deverill?

"Did you not think that Mr. Deverill might repeat your idle chat to Colonel Manley?"

"I never told him anything important."

"You didn't *think* you did."

"I didn't," she retorted.

"You were bedding the enemy, Bridie."

"When we were in bed we were simply a man and a woman who cared for each other."

"You're Michael Doyle's sister, Bridie. You were present

during many of our meetings in the farmhouse. You knew what was going on."

"But I didn't betray you."

"You were playing a dangerous game."

"I'm aware of that now," she snapped. "Would I be here, thousands of miles from home, if the game I played *hadn't* been dangerous? It cost me everything. I can never get my old life back. I tried, but the door has closed forever. Mr. Deverill might have destroyed me had it not been for my resilience and good fortune. As it is I will never get my son back and he will never know his mother. I'm aware of what I did and of what I didn't do. I slept with Mr. Deverill but I didn't betray our people. I betrayed no one."

"Every action has a consequence and yours have had more devastating consequences than most."

She stared at him with black eyes and Jack suddenly saw Michael Doyle in them. "And what consequences does *this* have, Jack?" she asked.

He stared back at her and his heart grew cold. "I hope only good ones, Bridie."

Her eyes softened and when she smiled she looked vulnerable again, like the child she'd once been with bare feet and tangled hair. "We've found each other in a city of thousands. What are the chances of that? You're the only person who really knows me in the whole of America. With you I don't have to be anyone other than myself—and you can forget about Kitty. It's not hard if you really want to. Believe me, *I know.*" She nuzzled into the crook of his arm and ran her fingers over his chest. "I've made many mistakes in my life, but this isn't one of them."

Jack stubbed out his cigarette in the ashtray on the bedside table and sighed heavily. He closed his eyes and let his hand wander over her hair that soon turned from ebony to copper in the deep longing of his imagination. Bridie slept, but Jack lay awake, for his thoughts did not allow him respite from regret. Now he was sober he realized that he wanted nothing from *this*.

When her breathing grew slow and regular and the tentative presence of the rising sun began to turn the sky from indigo to gold, he edged his way out of Bridie's limp embrace and quietly dressed. He glanced at her peacefully sleeping and felt a stab of pity. She was lost here in Manhattan, but he was not the right man to find her. They had searched for Ireland in each other and only found a false dawn.

He let himself out, closing the door gently behind him. He knew that if he was to be free of Kitty he had to be free of the past, which meant leaving Bridie too. He was sorry that he was going to cause her pain in leaving her without explanation or farewell, but she had to let go of the past too. How could they possibly find happiness otherwise?

★   ★   ★

WHEN BRIDIE AWOKE she found the bed empty. She blinked into the space where Jack had lain and smiled at the memory of their lovemaking. She felt as if she had been reborn. As if she had metamorphosed into the person she had always wanted to be. She was wealthy, independent and now she had Jack. Jack whom she had always loved. Jack whom Kitty had stolen. But now he was hers.

She rolled over and strained her ears for the sound of Jack in the bathroom next door. She heard nothing but the distant rumble of cars in the street below. She frowned. "Jack?" she called. Her voice seemed to echo through the empty room. He must be in the kitchen, she thought; men are always hungry. She slipped into her dressing gown and padded across the floor to the sitting room. The morning poured through the windows in misty shafts of light, but it only seemed to emphasize the stillness of the apartment, and the silence. Then she heard the soft scuffling of feet advancing up the corridor and her spirits gave a little leap of happiness. "Jack?" she called again.

"Good morning, madam," came the voice of Imelda, her maid. The woman walked lightly into the room, clasped her hands against her apron and smiled. Bridie put her hand on her chest and felt her head spin. She knew then that Jack had gone.

PART TWO

Barton Deverill

London, 1667

Most of the Court had arrived to attend the opening night of John Dryden's new play, *The Maiden Queen*, in the Theater Royal in Drury Lane. The richly dressed aristocrats sat in the boxes in their brightly colored silks and velvets, powdered wigs and face patches, like exotic birds of paradise, resplendent in the light of hundreds of candles. The ladies passed on the Court gossip behind their fans while the lords discussed politics, women and the King's many mistresses. Lord Deverill sat in the box beside his wife, Lady Alice, daughter of the immensely wealthy Earl of Charnwell, and his friend Sir Toby Beckwyth-Stubbs. He swept his eyes over the pit below where ladies and gentlemen sweltered in the heat and whores and orange girls squawked and flirted with the fops in the thick, heavily perfumed air, like a pen full of libidinous chickens.

The King arrived with his bastard son, the Duke of Monmouth, and his brother the Duke of York. The fops in the pit clambered onto chairs and women hung over the balconies to watch the royal party enter, and Lady Alice looked out for the King's mistress, the buxom and wanton Barbara Palmer, Countess of Castlemaine, the most fashionable lady in the country.

They muttered and chattered as the royal party settled into their seats with the rustle of taffeta and the swishing of fans. Lord Deverill found the scene distasteful. The Court of Charles II had turned out to be a sink of licentious frivolity with Catholic undercurrents and he was almost starting to miss the evil Cromwell. Deverill was only here to seek an audience with the King to procure more men and arms to keep the peace in West Cork. The construction of Castle Deverill was now completed and it stood as a formidable bastion of English supremacy, but the Irish were a riotous lot and they gnawed on their grievances like wild dogs on bitter bones. While London had staggered from the Plague to the Great Fire the year before, Lord Deverill had taken refuge at his Irish seat where the clouds that hung over him were of an entirely different kind: the haunting memory of Maggie O'Leary's curse and the threat of rebellion from the Irish over the Importation Act which prohibited them from selling their cattle to England.

As he had sworn that day on the hill above Ballinakelly he was good to his tenants. Their rent was reasonable and he was tolerant of their papist church. His wife and her ladies fed the poor and clothed their children. He was indeed a beneficent landlord. His loyalty to the Crown was unwavering, but he was furious about the act, which the King had signed. Distracted by his own domestic problems, flirting too closely with the King of France and preparing to fight the Dutch, the King hadn't wanted to upset Parliament by using his power of veto. Lord Deverill feared there would be another rebellion like the one in '41 and was determined to warn the King of danger.

Lord Deverill thought of Maggie O'Leary often. He was a religious man and he did not take curses lightly, indeed Sir Toby had insisted that her threat was an indirect threat to the King himself and was adamant that she should be burned at the stake. But Lord Deverill did not want to incite further hatred by killing a young woman—a *beautiful* young woman—be she a witch or otherwise. It was not her curse that followed him like a shadow, but her strange, unsettling beauty and her almost pungent allure.

He had only seen her twice. Once when she had publicly cursed him in the road in Ballinakelly, the second time when he had been out hunting. Accompanied by Sir Toby and a retinue of attendants, he had been galloping through the forest in pursuit of a deer. Suddenly, as the deer headed off through the thicket to his left he had spotted through the tangle of trees on his right a stag, standing on the crest of a knoll. Without time to inform his men he swerved his horse to the right and quietly trotted toward it.

Alone in the wood he pulled on the reins and drew his beast to a halt. It was quiet but for the chirruping of birds and the whispering of the wind about the branches. The stag was magnificent. It stood with the dignity of a monarch, watching him haughtily with shiny black eyes. Slowly, not to frighten the animal away, he pulled out his musket. As he loaded and aimed, the stag suddenly disappeared and in its place stood a woman.

Lord Deverill lifted his eye from the gun and stared in astonishment. She wore a cloak but beneath her hood was the unmistakable face of Maggie O'Leary. He put his gun down and
gazed upon her, not knowing what to say. Her loveliness stole
his words and yet he knew, even if he had managed to speak,
that she would not have understood him. Her green eyes were
wide and inquiring and her berry-red lips curled up at the corners in a mocking smile. At once he was overcome with lust;
quite out of his mind with desire. She lifted her delicate hands
and removed her hood. Her hair fell about her shoulders in
thick black waves and her pale face bewitched him like the face
of the full moon.

He dismounted and walked toward her. She waited until he
was almost upon her and then turned and floated down the
hill, moving deeper into the forest. He followed, encouraged
by the coy glances she tossed him over her shoulder. The trees
grew closer together. The branches were a mesh of twig and
leaf, the light reduced to thin, watery beams that sliced through
the dimness. Even the birds had ceased to sing. The sweet smell
of decaying vegetation rose up from the earth. She stopped and
turned around. Lord Deverill did not wait to be invited. He
pushed her against the trunk of an oak and pressed his lips to
hers. She responded hungrily, winding her arms around his
neck, kissing him back. A low moan escaped her throat as he
buried his face in her neck and inhaled the scent of sage that
clung to her skin. His fingers tore at the laces of her bodice
until her breasts were exposed, white against his brown hands,
and his lust was intensified by the warmth of her naked flesh
and by the intoxicating smell of her. Maddened by desire he
lifted her skirts. She raised a leg and wrapped it about him so

he could more easily enter her. She gasped with satisfaction and her eyelids fluttered like moth's wings as he slipped inside with a groan. They moved as one writhing beast, their faces clamped together, their breaths staggered, their heartbeats accelerating as they took their pleasure greedily.

They reached the pinnacle of their enjoyment simultaneously, then fell limp in a tangle of limbs, clothes and sweat onto the soft forest bed. At length Maggie rolled away from him and pulled down her skirts to cover herself, but she left her laces hanging loose at her waist and her breasts exposed. She fixed him with wide, brazen eyes, as feral as a wolf's, and held him in her thrall for a long moment. Then she spoke. Her voice was as silky as a spring breeze but Lord Deverill did not understand her native language. He frowned and she seemed to find his bewilderment amusing, for she burst into peals of mocking laughter. As Lord Deverill's frown deepened she turned onto her knees and crawled toward him on all fours with the speed of a cat. She climbed astride him, pinned his wrists to the ground and pressed her mouth once more to his. She took his bottom lip between her teeth and bit down hard upon it. Lord Deverill tasted the blood on his tongue and recoiled. "By God you've hurt me, woman!" he exclaimed but Maggie just laughed louder. Her black hair cascaded in thick tendrils over her exposed breasts and her bruised mouth twisted into a secretive smile, but it was her eyes, her wild green eyes, which looked at him with a coldness that froze the blood in his veins. Suddenly she was pressing a dagger to his throat. Lord Deverill's breath caught in his chest and he stared back at her in horror. A gush of bubbling laughter rose up from her belly as she leaped to her feet. She smiled at him again, this time with playfulness, then she was gone, as quickly as she had come, and he was left alone and bewildered in the middle of the forest.

He was jolted back to the theater by a sharp jab to the ribs. "Barton!" It was his wife, Alice. "The King is waving at you. Wake up!" Lord Deverill turned toward the Royal Box. Indeed the King had raised his white glove. Lord Deverill bowed in response and the King beckoned one of his attendants with a flick of his fingers. The attendant bent down and the King whispered something in his ear. "I believe you will get your meeting with the King," said Alice, smiling with satisfaction. "King Charles will always remember those who were loyal to his father." Lord Deverill turned back to the stage just as the performance was beginning, and passed a finger absent-mindedly across his lips.

Chapter 13

Ballinakelly, 1929

C elia and Kitty stood in their finest silk gowns at the top of the castle and gazed out of the window over the sea. The sun had already begun her slow descent. Her face, which had blazed a bright yellow at midday, had now mellowed into a deeper hue, transforming the sky around her into dusty pinks and rich oranges. Later she would set the horizon aflame and the soft shades would intensify into royal crimson and gold, but by then the two women would be entertaining the large number of guests who were soon to arrive from all over the county, for tonight was Celia's first Summer Ball as mistress of the newly restored and quite splendid Castle Deverill.

The rusted gates at the entrance had been replaced by an elaborate wrought-iron creation, painted black and decorated with the Deverill coat of arms, which had been incorporated into the design in an ostentatious display of family prestige. Flares had been lit on either side of the sweeping drive, which had been resurfaced in tar and shingle and covered in gravel— an extravagance that had aroused the curiosity of the locals because tar and shingle was very new and many of the roads in County Cork were still boreens made of earth or brick. The gardens had been resuscitated, the wild, overgrown areas tamed, the tennis court reinstated and the croquet lawn mown flat and even. A kaleidoscope of colorful flowers flourished in the borders, pink roses and purple clematis climbed the walls of the herbaceous border, and raised wooden beds in the vegetable garden were home to lettuces, potatoes, carrots, parsnips and radishes and rigorously weeded by the team of men Celia had employed from Ballinakelly to train under Mr Wilcox, one of the gardeners at Deverill Rising, on loan from her father. Adeline's greenhouses had been repainted, the broken panes of glass replaced, the blancmange-shaped roofs polished until they gleamed. Inside, Celia insisted on growing orchids, which required a complicated, not to mention costly, array of humidifiers and temperature regulation. The only plant that remained from Adeline's day was the now giant cannabis, which Celia had, for some reason unknown even to herself, decided to keep. Digby had paid for the old stone Mr. Leclaire had recommended and sourced from a ruined castle in Bandon in order for Castle Deverill to retain its antique flavor so only the western tower and the few surviving walls that remained from the original building hinted at its tragic past. It looked just like it had before the fire, only newer—like a battle-weary soldier whose face has been scrubbed and shaved and whose uniform has been replaced and sewn with bright gold buttons.

Inside, however, was an entirely different matter. Besides the grand hall, where the stone fireplace still stood as it always had, and the sweeping wooden staircase, which was identical to the old one, little of Adeline and Hubert's old home remained. Celia had redesigned and redecorated according to the grandiose nature of her ambition. Gone was the shabby elegance of a home that had been loved by generations of Deverills—worn thin by their affection like a child's toy bear whose fur has all but disappeared from hugging, whose ears are ragged from games, whose nose is frayed from kisses. Celia had re-created the interiors to impress her guests, not to welcome her family home from a hard day out hunting in the rain. The hall floor was checkerboard marble, the walls papered and painted and hanging with Old Master paintings, the surfaces cluttered with Romanov antiques and Roman antiquities and anything else she could find that was fashionable. Furniture had been acquired in chateau sales in France, much of it from the First French Empire of Napoleon I and wildly opulent in rich crimsons and gold. She had bought an entire library by the yard but the cozy atmosphere of Hubert's den, where he'd once sat smoking cigars in front of the fire, reading the *Irish Times* in a tatty leather armchair while Adeline painted at the table in the bay window, was gone. Everything gleamed but nothing attracted. The charm had been consumed by the fire and the opportunity to re-create it had been lost on a young woman whose inspiration was born of her shallow nature. The warm glow of love which cannot be bought had been replaced by things that can only be acquired with money.

"Do you remember when we stood here as little girls?" said Celia, her heart fuller than it had ever been.

"We were three of us then," Kitty reminded her.

"Whatever happened to Bridie?" Celia asked.

"I believe she returned to America."

"Isn't life strange," said Celia with uncharacteristic reflection. "Who would have thought that the three of us, all born in the same year, would have ended up where we are today? I am mistress of the castle with two little girls. You are married to your old tutor and have Florence and JP. Bridie is living on the other side of the world with Lord knows how many children by now. None of us had a clue what was in store for us when we stood here as girls the night of the last Summer Ball."

Kitty was aware that Celia knew little of what *she* and Bridie had been through but she wasn't about to enlighten her. "I often think of those days," she said with a sigh. "Before things went wrong."

"Before we lost people we loved in the war," said Celia quietly. She thought of her brother George, whom she rarely considered these days, and her mood took an unexpected dive. She shook her head to dispel the memories and smiled fiercely. "But everything is wonderful now, isn't it?" she said firmly. "In fact, life has never been better." She swung around and contemplated with satisfaction the splendor of her great vision brought to completion at last. "I have poured all my love into this place," she told Kitty. "Castle Deverill is like my third child. I will now spend the rest of my life embellishing her. More trips to Italy and France, more shopping. It's a never-ending project and so thrilling. I am following in the footsteps of our ancestors who went on their grand tours of Europe and brought back wonderful treasures." She sighed happily. "And tonight everyone will admire it. Everyone will appreciate all the work I have put into it. I do hope Adeline is watching, wherever she is. And I hope she approves."

Kitty knew her grandmother was watching, but doubted she really cared what Celia had done to her home, for Adeline was in a dimension now where the material world was no longer important. "Come, let's go downstairs. Your guests will be arriving shortly," she said, moving away from the window. The two women walked through the castle to the front stairs. They hesitated a moment at the top of the landing to check their reflections in the large gilt mirror that hung there. Celia, resplendent in ice blue, admired the daring cut of her dress, which exposed most of her back, while Kitty, elegant in forest-green silk, gazed upon the two faces smiling back at her and felt keenly the absence of the third. *Where are you now, Bridie, and do you miss us too?* she thought. *Because in spite of everything, I miss* you.

A long queue of cars was slowly drawing up in front of the castle. Celia's servants were in attendance to receive the ladies in long gowns and the men in white tie who climbed the few steps up to the front door to walk beneath the lintel where the Deverill family crest had survived the fire and still resonated with Barton's passion for his new home: *Castellum Deverilli est suum regnum.* The restoration of the castle had been the talk of the county for years, and the amount of money spent on it a matter of much conjecture, and they were all eager to see the results for themselves. Celia and Archie stood in front of the fireplace that had been filled with summer flowers from the gardens, shaking hands and receiving compliments. Celia enjoyed the gasps of wonder and astonishment as her guests laid eyes on the sumptuous hall for the first time. Most had been regular visitors before the fire and were quick to compare the dilapidated old building with the lavish new one. While some were delighted by the opulence there were others who found it in poor taste.

"It looks like a beautiful but impersonal hotel," Boysie whispered to Harry as they stood on the terrace overlooking the gardens. "But for God's sake keep that to yourself or I'll never be invited again."

"I'm relieved it's nothing like it was or I should suffer terrible homesickness," said Harry.

"No regrets then?" asked Boysie, who knew Harry well enough to know that he had plenty.

"None," Harry replied firmly, knocking back his champagne. "Celia has done a splendid job."

Boysie smoked languidly. "Your mama would seethe with jealousy if she were here."

"Isn't it lucky then that she isn't?"

"She'd hate to see Celia lording it about the home that should, by rights, be hers. Celia is insufferably happy and Maud hates happy people. She loves nothing more than misery because she hopes that if it's plaguing someone else it won't have its eye on *her*. Digby is more puffed up than ever. Don't you adore the way he wears his white tie? Somehow it looks brash on him. He has a talent for brash, you know. If he wasn't Sir Digby Deverill one would assume he was frightfully common. And as for your dear Charlotte, pregnant again, I see. How do you manage it, old chap? Perhaps after two daughters you'll be blessed with an heir."

Harry looked into Boysie's eyes and grinned. "You've had two so probably the same way you manage it, old boy."

Boysie chuckled and a knowing look passed between them. "Is your father aware of your mother's little friend, Arthur Arlington?" he asked, changing the subject.

"I haven't asked him. I'm sure he is. Half of London is. Mama hasn't asked for a divorce, but I'm sure Papa would give her one. The marriage is a farce and Arthur is a drip."

"A very rich drip," Boysie added.

Harry sighed resignedly. "But life is good for Papa these days." He watched his father in a small group of people who were standing on the croquet lawn looking back at the castle. Bertie was pointing at the roof, no doubt taking them through the building process. "Strange that he takes so much delight in Celia's success, isn't it?" he said softly. "One would expect him to be bitter about it, but he isn't. I truly believe he's genuinely pleased."

"Perhaps the responsibility of being Lord Deverill of Castle Deverill has secretly weighed heavily on his shoulders all these years. Who knows, maybe he's relieved to be shot of it. I know *you* are."

"I couldn't be myself here," said Harry, recalling the brief affair he'd enjoyed with Joseph, the first footman. "It would hardly have been appropriate to put you up in one of the estate cottages. I dare say you're used to finer things."

"I am indeed, old boy. Ireland is much too damp for my tastes." He took Harry's empty glass and placed it on the tray of a passing waiter. "Now, why don't we go and pay some attention to those wives of ours, eh? For better or for worse and all that . . ."

"Capital idea," said Harry, and the two men set off into the castle.

HAZEL AND LAUREL stood in the ballroom and gazed about them in wonder. Celia had decorated it in an opulent rococo style, with white walls and lavish gold stucco designed in flamboyant, asymmetrical patterns. The chandeliers no longer held candles but blazed with electricity, which was reflected in the large mirrors that embellished the room like golden stars. "But look at the flowers, Hazel," said Laurel. "I've never seen so many lilies." She inhaled through dilated nostrils. "The smell is wonderful. Really, Celia should be very proud of herself. Tonight is a triumph."

Just as Hazel was about to agree with her, they heard the familiar and nervously anticipated voice of Lord Hunt as he strode into the room, greeting them enthusiastically. They swung around, their delight at seeing him ill-concealed. "The dear Misses Swanton," he said, taking each Shrub in turn by her white-gloved hand and drawing it to his lips with a formal and slightly exaggerated bow. Both ladies shivered with pleasure, for Lord Hunt had the ability to make them feel young and beautiful and deliciously frivolous. In the three years that he had been living with his daughter, he had gained notoriety in Ballinakelly for his breezy charm, his jocular wit and his incorrigible flirting. "May I be permitted to say how radiant you both look tonight?" He ran his astute brown eyes up and down their almost identical dresses and Hazel and Laurel felt as if he had somehow got beneath the fabric and caressed with a tender finger the long-neglected skin there.

"Thank you, Ethelred," Laurel croaked when, after a short struggle, she managed to find her voice.

"I'm going to have a terrible decision to make later this evening," he said, pulling a mournful face.

"Oh dear," interjected Hazel. "What might that be, Ethelred?"

He looked from one to the other, then sighed melodramatically. "Whom to dance with first, when I want to dance with both of you." Laurel glanced at Hazel and they both tittered with shy delight. "Is there not a dance for three?" he asked.

"I'm afraid not," said Laurel. "Although Celia is very modern, so one never knows."

"I see neither of you has a glass of champagne. Let me escort you into the garden. It's the most splendid evening. Wouldn't it be nice to enjoy our drinks in the beauty of sunset?"

"Oh, it would," said Hazel.

"It certainly would," Laurel echoed.

Lord Hunt offered them each an arm. But as Laurel slipped her hand through his left she felt the first stirring of something deeply alarming and unpleasant: competitiveness. She glanced at Hazel and for a fleeting moment she wished her sister ill. With a shocked gasp she forced the feeling away. Hazel was smiling at the object of her most ardent desire, but as he turned to smile on Laurel, she too felt the beginnings of something of which she was too ashamed to even acknowledge. Both sisters turned their eyes sharply to the double doors that led into the wide corridor and through to the hall. They could never reveal to the other the degree of their passion for Ethelred, *never*. For the first time in their lives they harbored a secret they were unwilling to share.

DIGBY STOOD IN the garden and gazed upon the castle with a gratifying sense of achievement, as if he had reconstructed it from the rubble with his own hands. It was the jewel in his family's crown, the culmination of a lifelong desire. He looked back on the years he had struggled to make his fortune in South Africa and smiled with satisfaction at how far he had come and how high he had risen. A hearty pat on the back jolted him from his thoughts. He looked up to see Sir Ronald Rowan-Hampton's red face beaming at him happily. "My dear Digby," Sir Ronald exclaimed. "What a triumph the castle is. Celia and Archie have done you credit. It's a great success, a masterpiece, an example of courage in the face of adversity. You have raised it from the ashes and, my, what a palace it is. Fit for the King himself."

"I cannot take all the credit," he replied smoothly. "It is all Celia and her vision."

"Then she is a chip off the old block," said Sir Ronald. "She has your style and your sense of proportion. Isn't it true that everything you do is larger than life, Digby?" Sir Ronald gazed at the castle and shook his head. "It must have cost a small fortune."

"It cost a *great* fortune," said Digby, unabashed. "But it is worth every penny. This is Celia's now and will be her son's one day and *his* son's after that, and so it will go on. She has not only rebuilt a castle but she has created a legacy that will long outlive her. I'm mightily proud of her." He privately wondered whether, now the project was complete, his daughter would grow bored of life here and hotfoot it back to London. He was aware of her restless nature, because she had inherited it from *him*. He only hoped she was able to stifle it.

GRACE STOOD IN the French doors of the drawing room, watching her husband talking to Digby on the lawn. The guests were now beginning to make their way upstairs to dinner in the

long gallery where Adeline had always held her dinners—
except it wasn't the same long gallery because Celia had chosen
to design hers differently. For one the faces of Deverill ancestors did not watch them impassively from the walls, as many
of the paintings had been lost in the fire; Celia had bought
paintings of *other people's* ancestors, simply to fill the gaps. It
would take years to build a collection—it had taken the Deverills over two hundred.

Grace thought of Michael Doyle. She *always* thought of Michael Doyle. He plagued her thoughts, tormented her and
drove her to distraction. She thought she might go mad with
lust and longing. Never before had a man made such a fool of
her and yet, she couldn't help her foolish behavior. She had lost
her pride that day at the fair for she had later followed him
around the back of O'Donovan's public house and thrown herself at him like a mad and wanton woman, trying all the tricks
that would normally have ensured he lost control and became
putty in *her* hand. But he had shaken her off. "I have sinned,"
he had told her.

"You cannot blame yourself for things you did in the war.
Lord knows I've done my share," she had replied.

"No, you don't understand. The things I'm ashamed of have
nothing to do with war."

"Then with what?"

At that point he had turned away. "I'm sorry, Grace. I'll
speak no more about it." He had left her then, wondering what
he had done that was so terrible, that he couldn't ever speak of,
that he couldn't tell *her*. Now she gazed out onto the lawn at
her husband and Digby as Kitty walked over to tell them to
come in for dinner, and wondered again, what did he do and

how could she find out? Surely, if she could get to the root of his guilt, she could figure a way to dig him out of it.

AT THE END of dinner, when the coffee was being served, Bertie stood up and a hush fell over the guests. This was quite a different Bertie to the swaying drunkard who had announced to the family at his mother's funeral that he was not only selling the castle but legitimizing his bastard son Jack. Now he was sober, fresh-faced, groomed and slim—dashing even. "Never before have we Deverills been so united," he said, then raised his glass. "To Celia and Archie." Everyone jumped to their feet and toasted the audacious young couple, then Digby gave a speech, thanking Bertie for his generosity of spirit and repeating, once again, the family motto, which, he explained, referred not only to the castle but to their family spirit. "Which lives in all of us," he said. Beatrice wiped her eye with her napkin. Harry smiled at Celia. Kitty looked lovingly at her father and Elspeth thought how fortuitous it was that neither Maud nor her older sister, Victoria, were here to sour the sweet feeling that encompassed their family. Suddenly, a loud snort punctured the silence. Augusta glared at her husband from the other side of the table. "Do me a favor, dear," she said to the lady sitting on his left. "Give him a sharp prod in the ribs, will you?"

Archie led Celia onto the dance floor where a jazz band, brought in from London, was playing. The Shrubs restrained themselves from squabbling over who danced first with Ethelred by both pretending to give way to the other: "No really, Laurel, *you* must go first." "No, Hazel, I insist. *You* must." At length Ethelred had tossed a coin and Hazel had won, much to the chagrin of Laurel, who had to smile and act as if she didn't care, which she did, very much. Boysie and Harry danced with their spouses, secretly longing to be rid of them and free to enjoy each other in one of the flamboyantly decorated bedrooms upstairs. Kitty threw herself into the music as she danced with her father while Robert looked on longingly for his stiff leg made dancing impossible. She tried to shake herself out of her gloom—her father was happy for Celia so why couldn't *she* be? "Our daughters will grow up here as *we* did and enjoy all the things *we* enjoyed," Celia had said when Kitty had given birth to Florence. And she was right, history would indeed repeat itself and Florence would enjoy the castle just as *she* had done. So why did Kitty feel so bitter?

"This is all marvelous," said Beatrice to Grace as they watched the dancing in front of the glittering mirrors.

"Oh, it truly is," Grace agreed. "Celia said she would bring back the old days and so she has." Although both women knew that bringing back the past was never possible they were content to indulge in nostalgia and to secretly long for a time before the Great War when Ballinakelly summers had been so golden.

It was well after midnight when Boysie and Harry found themselves alone in the hall. The grand staircase beckoned them upstairs as if the banisters were malevolent demons whispering encouragement. Their heads were light with champagne bubbles, their hearts tender with nostalgia, their longing all the more acute on account of the impossibility of their affair and their weariness of living a life of secrecy and deceit. Without a word they stepped nimbly up the stairs. The rumbling of music, thumping feet and voices receded as they made their way down the long corridors, deeper and deeper into the depths of the castle. Celia had spent a lot of money installing electricity and Harry was quite unused to bright lights where once it had only been candlelight and oil lamps. The plumbing worked too, which was miraculous considering that once the water had to be brought up in buckets by the servants. Harry was wistful for those times and, as he passed the bedroom door where Kitty had discovered him in bed with Joseph the first footman, he had to steel himself not to lose control of his emotions.

Suddenly the castle meant more to him than his lost inheritance; it also represented his failures: what had he done with his life? He had married a woman he didn't love and loved a man he couldn't have. He drifted aimlessly in London, from his club to home and home to his club, and there was no purpose to the endless round of social obligations. His job in the City was so dull and monotonous that he sometimes found himself wishing he was back in the Army where at least he had had a purpose. It seemed that the fire had taken more than his home; it seemed to have taken his rudder too. As he walked through the castle he no longer recognized, he felt a great pain expanding in his chest. A longing for what he had lost and for the man he knew he could never be.

"Boysie," he groaned.

Boysie turned around. "What is it, old boy?"

Harry couldn't put into words the sense of desolation he felt. Instead, he took Boysie's hand and retreated back the way they had come, eventually stopping outside the bedroom Celia had allocated him. Without a word he pulled his lover into the darkness inside and closed the door behind them. "This is madness," Boysie protested, but he was too giddy with champagne to resist Harry's insistent mouth kissing his.

Suddenly the light went on. They swung around in surprise to see Charlotte sitting up in the four-poster bed, her face white against the pink of her nightdress and her mouth open in a silent gasp. They stared at each other in horror. As the bubbles evaporated and Boysie and Harry were swiftly shocked into sobriety there was a part of Harry that experienced a profound sense of relief.

HIGH UP AT the top of the western tower Adeline and Hubert looked out into the starlit sky. The moon was almost full, encircled by a halo of silver mist, its eerie light throwing sharp shadows across the lawn below. "Do you remember those Summer Balls of our youth, Hubert?" Adeline asked. "Of course people came in their fine carriages back then, with men in livery driving the horses. I remember the sound of hooves on the drive as they all drew up," she reflected. "Now the guests arrive in motorcars. How times have changed." She looked at Hubert and smiled wistfully. "We lived well, didn't we?"

Hubert turned to his wife and his face was cast in shadow like the back of the moon. "But are we destined to remain here for . . ." He hesitated because he could barely utter so terrifying a word. "For eternity, Adeline? Is that what our destiny is now? Our lives were as short as a blink on the eye of time, but the eye . . . how long is the eye, Adeline?"

She put her hand against his cheek and tried to look positive. "The curse will be broken," she said firmly. "I promise you."

A voice interrupted from the armchair. "That's as likely as

them putting men on the moon." It was Barton Deverill, grumpier than ever.

Adeline ignored him. His bitterness was infectious and bringing Hubert's spirits down. "Don't listen to him, my darling. He's a sour old man with a heavy conscience."

"You know nothing of my conscience, woman," Barton growled.

"I sense it," Adeline retorted. He was really trying her patience.

"All you sense is the near two hundred and fifty years I've been rotting in this place."

"You can't rot if you don't have a body, Barton," she told him briskly, turning back to her husband. "I promise you, my darling, I'll get you out of this place. I will stay with you for as long as you are here and then we will move on, together. All of us."

Barton laughed cynically from his armchair. "So help you God."

Chapter 14

Digby sat at the breakfast table tucking into a large plate of scrambled eggs on toast, crispy bacon and fried tomatoes garnished with chives. The ball had been a great success and even though he had had little to do with the organization of the event itself, he had had a significant amount to do with the building of the castle. Having initially shied away from a project he had believed both financially suicidal and conceptually foolhardy, he had eventually succumbed to the allure of recapturing the past and inveigled his way into the plans by way of large and frequent checks. After all, hadn't those summers at Castle Deverill been the most enchanted weeks of his life? How he had envied Bertie and Rupert for growing up in this magical place. He had felt like a poor relation. Now *his* grandchildren would grow up here and he could live vicariously through them. Deverill Rising was one thing, Castle Deverill quite another: the history, the prestige, the sheer wonder of the place. He shoveled a forkful of food into his mouth and chewed with relish. Beatrice, who could read her husband's mind, smiled at him from the other end of the table.

He was enjoying his cup of tea and reading the *Irish Times* when Celia flew into the room. "Papa, last night was a triumph! I didn't sleep a wink!"

"It was a great success, my dear. You should be very proud of yourself," he said, lifting his eyes momentarily off the page to savor his daughter's beaming face. "You were the most gracious hostess."

"Everyone admired the castle!" she gushed. "Everyone complimented the decoration."

"And everyone admired *you*," her mother added with a smile.

"Oh, Mama, if I was any happier I would burst," she said. "Truly, I have never been so full of joy."

"I think you're still full of champagne," said Digby dryly, turning the page.

"In which case, you must put something else into your stomach," said Beatrice.

Celia went to the antique walnut sideboard, bought at auction at Christie's with the help of Boysie, who worked there, and helped herself to scrambled eggs and tomatoes.

A moment later Harry wandered in, ashen-faced with bloodshot eyes beneath which purple shadows shone like bruises. "Somebody had a wild night," said Celia with a chuckle, but Harry barely managed a smile.

"Good morning," he said, trying hard to be jovial. "I'm afraid I am a little worse for wear."

"Darling, come and sit down and have a cup of tea and some toast. You'll feel much better with something in your stomach," said Beatrice. "You do look pale," she added as he pulled out the chair beside her. She patted his hand with her podgy, bejeweled one and smiled sympathetically. "I suppose one must deduce that a hangover is the result of a highly successful party," she said softly.

"Quite," Harry agreed, reflecting quietly on the *un*successful way it had ended.

It wasn't long before Boysie appeared with Deirdre. The two of them looked as bright and fresh as if they had enjoyed an early night and a brisk morning walk. "What a delightful party, Celia," said Boysie, sitting beside her. "Only two bores on the guest list and I managed to avoid both!"

"Oh, do tell me who they are and I'll make sure I sit you between them next year," said Celia.

"I couldn't possibly be so indiscreet," Boysie replied with a smile. He caught Harry's eye, but swiftly turned away. "Can I help you to some breakfast, darling?" he asked Deirdre. As Boysie went to the sideboard, Charlotte wandered into the room, her face as white as a duck's egg. Beatrice looked from Charlotte to Harry and realized that their pallor had nothing to do with a hangover.

After breakfast Harry managed to talk to Boysie alone. They stood on the terrace in the warm summer sunshine while a small army of servants cleared away the debris from the night before. Boysie lit a cigarette. Harry stood with his shoulders hunched and his hands buried in his trouser pockets. "Did you want to get caught, Harry?" Boysie asked, and Harry recoiled from the hard tone of his voice.

"No . . . I mean, of course not." But he wasn't so sure.

"Damned foolish to stumble in on your wife like that. She looks none too pleased about it this morning."

"She won't say anything," he said quickly.

"She'd better not."

"She's not speaking to me, though."

"That's no surprise. It's one thing betraying your wife with another woman but quite another with a man. Poor girl. She looked as if she'd been shot in the heart."

"She had been, I suppose," said Harry. He sighed and rubbed his chin. "What a God-awful mess."

Boysie looked at him and his expression softened. "What are you going to do, old boy?"

"Nothing," said Harry.

"Nothing?"

"There's nothing I *can* do. I'll wait to see what *she* wants to do."

"See you kicked from here to eternity, I should imagine." Boysie chuckled and flicked ash onto the York stone at his feet.

"I hope not," said Harry. He swallowed nervously. "I'm hoping she'll understand."

"Celia would understand but Charlotte is not Celia. She's a sheep, Harry. Sheep follow the crowd and I'm afraid the crowd don't think very highly of homosexuality. You had better hope, no, you had better *pray* that she doesn't tell her family." He dragged on his cigarette. "Come on, let's go and find Celia." But Harry knew that Celia would be no help at all. Suddenly, he felt an overwhelming desire to talk to Kitty.

"I'm going to take a walk, old boy. I think some exercise will do me good." And he set off across the gardens in the direction of the White House.

KITTY WAS SITTING on the lawn with two-year-old Florence making daisy chains when Harry appeared at the foot of the

drive, red-faced from his brisk walk. He strode through the
gate and walked up the hill to meet her. "Harry!" she shouted
and waved. "What a lovely surprise." Harry took off his straw
hat and sat down in the shade of the apple tree that sheltered
the little girl from the sun. "Splendid party last night, wasn't
it," she said, but her eyes betrayed her struggle to find anything
positive about the newly completed castle.

"You're finding it hard too?" he asked.

"Very," she conceded. "I feel terrible admitting that, but I
know I can speak plainly to you."

"You can," he said. "My, how Florence has grown." He ran
his hand down the child's flaxen hair. "She's the image of her
father, isn't she?" he observed.

"Yes, she is," Kitty agreed, suffering a stab of pain as Jack
O'Leary fought his way to the surface of her mind, only to be
plunged back to the bottom by the superior force of her will.
"She's like Robert in every way and he dotes on her."

"Where's JP?"

"Riding. He's as obsessed as I was. There's no separating him
from his pony!" She laughed. "And he's a daredevil too. He's
afraid of nothing. He's already riding out with the hounds. Papa
is very proud. JP's a natural horseman. As for Florence . . ." She
sighed and looked tenderly on her daughter. "We shall see."

"Will you walk with me, Kitty?" Harry asked suddenly.

Kitty detected the tension in her brother's voice and sat up
keenly. "Of course." She called for Elsie and when the nanny
appeared to look after Florence, Kitty and Harry set off down
the hill toward the coastline.

"What is it, Harry?" she asked.

He replaced his hat and put his hands in his pockets. "Do

you remember that time when you found me . . ." He hesitated, unable to articulate the words.

"And Joseph," she said helpfully.

"Yes." He looked down at his feet as they paced over the grass. "I *loved* Joseph."

"I know you did," said Kitty. She glanced at him and frowned. "You don't love Charlotte, do you?"

"I'm fond of her," he conceded and Kitty sensed what he was trying so hard to say. Her heart filled with tenderness and she slipped her hand around his arm and moved closer.

"I know that Joseph loved you back. I remember the look of utter hopelessness on his face when you left to return to the Front. I saw him up at the window. He was like a ghost. I then realized that he hadn't been simply comforting you that night. At the end of the war, when you came home and you made him your valet, I knew why. I've never judged you, Harry. It's not conventional to love another man, but I love you just the way you are." Harry's throat constricted and he blinked to relieve the stinging in his eyes.

They reached the end of the path where the grass gave way to white sand and headed off up the beach. Seabirds glided on the wind and dropped out of the sky to peck at small creatures left behind by the tide. The ocean was benign beneath the clear skies, the waves breaking gently and rhythmically onto the sand. Harry placed his hand on top of Kitty's and squeezed it. "Thank you, dearest Kitty. You and I have shared many secrets over the years. I'm now going to ask you to keep another and to advise me how to proceed, because I've done a terrible thing." Kitty nodded. She dreaded what he was about to tell her. "I have been having an affair with a man for years. Ever since I came to London." He glanced anxiously at her for her reaction.

"Go on," she said encouragingly.

"I knew I had to do my duty and marry. I've given Charlotte two children and if the shock of discovering me and this man last night doesn't bring on a miscarriage, I'll have given her three."

Kitty stopped walking. "Oh Harry." She let her hands fall at her sides. "How did it happen?"

"I didn't realize she had retired early. The bedroom was dark. I pulled Boysie inside . . ."

Kitty gasped. "Boysie Bancroft?"

"Yes, didn't I say?"

Kitty shook her head. "I should have guessed. The two of you are inseparable."

"Charlotte turned on the light and saw us."

"What did she say?"

"She didn't say anything. Boysie left as fast as he could. I tried to comfort her but she just put her head under the pillow and sobbed. She sobbed all night. She still hasn't spoken to me." He raised his palms to the sky. "For the love of God tell me what I should do."

Kitty began to walk again. This time her pace quickened and her eyes focused on the ground in front of her. Harry strode beside her without speaking, hoping that she'd find the answer there in the sand. At length she stopped and turned to face him again. "Charlotte loves you, Harry, so this betrayal will have cut her very deeply. Firstly, you have to give her time to absorb it. She's made two terrible discoveries: one, that you've been having an affair, and two, that it's with a man, which as you well know is against the law and punishable by imprisonment. She will be wondering whether you ever loved her, whether you only married her to do your duty. She'll be wondering whether you hated every minute of making love to her. She'll be feeling bruised, humiliated, hurt and worried. When she comes to terms with those two discoveries, she will talk to you."

"What will she say?"

"She'll either ask for a divorce or go public and you'll have to endure a scandal that will put Bertie's scandal with JP into the shade. Mama will probably have a seizure, of course, but that'll be the least of your worries."

"God help me," he groaned.

"Or—"

"Or?" he asked eagerly. "What's the or?"

"Or she'll forgive you."

"Why on earth would she do that?"

"Because she loves you, Harry. But you must persuade her that you will give up Boysie. You'll have to convince her that it was a moment of madness. Blame it on the champagne. Tell her you love her. You love the children. You're a family man and you'll do nothing to jeopardize your family. You can do that, can't you?"

"I can't give up Boysie," he gasped, horrified.

"You'll have to. It's either Charlotte or Boysie. You can't have both, Harry."

"But I love him."

She put her hand on his arm. "I know you do. But sometimes you have to give up the person you love for the greater good." Kitty's eyes brimmed with tears. "It's hard, it's almost impossible, but it can be done."

Harry stared at her, unaware that she was speaking about herself. He hadn't anticipated having to give up Boysie when he had dragged him into his bedroom. He had willed himself to get caught only to release him from the burden of lying, not to force him to sacrifice the one person he loved above all others. What a fool he had been. He grabbed his sister by the arms and thrust his head onto her shoulder. As he wept he didn't notice that she wept also, for Jack O'Leary and her own desolate heart.

When Harry returned to the castle he found Charlotte and Deirdre playing croquet with Boysie and Celia. The Shrubs were strolling around the gardens in floral dresses and sunhats with Lord Hunt, who held his hands behind his back and was listening attentively to both. Laurel and Hazel had made a great effort with their hair and makeup and the results were surprising—they each looked far younger than their years. Digby, Archie, Bertie and Ronald were playing a men's four in long white tennis trousers and V-neck sweaters while Beatrice and Grace watched them from the bench, or at least, *pretended* to watch, sipping from tall glasses of mint and lemonade.

"Papa is leading the Shrubs a merry dance," confided Grace, watching the unlikely trio. "He's a terrible old rogue and I fear Hazel and Laurel have been totally taken in. I feel very bad about it."

"Oh, don't feel bad," Beatrice replied. "He's giving them such a lot of pleasure. I don't think they've ever had such attention from a handsome man like your father."

"He's enjoying himself immensely, but it'll be disastrous when he bores of the game, which he will. The minute it's no longer fun he'll move on to someone else. I *know* him. My mother was an exceptionally tolerant woman."

"I'm sure they take him with a pinch of salt," said Beatrice, watching Digby prepare to serve.

"They absolutely don't, Beatrice. They're smitten. They're like a pair of debutantes. I hope they don't fight over him. That would be dreadful."

"Good shot, darling!" Beatrice clapped as Digby aced his cousin. "They're grown-ups, Grace. I'm sure they're perfectly capable of looking after themselves, and each other."

"I hope you're right, but I fear the worst."

As Harry approached, Charlotte glared at him from her position beside the third hoop. Boysie watched them both warily while Celia, in a long diaphanous ivory skirt and blouse, cloche hat and pearls, lined up her ball and swung her mallet. Deirdre, who had tried and failed to find out what their fight had been about, stood beside her husband, pleased that her own marriage was free of that sort of drama. "Harry, I'm playing so badly, why don't you come and give me a hand," said Celia. "That's all right, isn't it?" she asked the others.

Charlotte dropped her mallet. "No, he can take *my* place. I've had enough." She began to stride off toward the castle, taking her sulk with her.

"Oh dear," said Celia, watching her go. "I was never that bad-tempered when I was pregnant."

"Shall I run after her?" Harry asked uncertainly, but he was afraid to hear what she might say. He glanced at Boysie and for a moment their eyes locked. How could he give him up? he thought desperately. He would rather be dead than live without Boysie.

"No, don't break up the game," said Celia, whose self-obsession had ensured that she missed the subtle tensions that coursed between certain members of the group. "Your turn, Deirdre. Leave Charlotte, Harry darling, she'll feel better after a little nap. She's probably just tired after last night, I know *I* am and I'm not carrying a child."

Harry glanced at the French doors that led from the terrace into the drawing room but his wife had disappeared. Later, when he at last plucked up the courage to talk to her, he found her lying on her bed, staring into space with a miserable, defeated look on her face. He closed the door behind him and approached her. He saw her body stiffen like a cat's, but he sat on the edge of the mattress regardless. "Darling, we have to talk about this," he began, feeling sick to the stomach with nerves. He knitted his fingers and stared into them as if working out how to *un*knit them. "I'm sorry," he said. When she didn't reply he cleared his throat and tried to remember what Kitty had told him. "I love you, Charlotte. I know that you won't believe me, after . . . after what you saw last night. I promise you, it was a moment of madness. The champagne, the excitement, the nostalgia, I wasn't in my right mind. I wasn't myself and I'm ashamed. *Deeply* ashamed and I beg for your forgiveness."

Now she turned her head and looked at him. Her face was impassive. He longed to know what she was thinking. "Do you love me, Harry?" she asked in a small voice.

"Yes, my darling, I do. I love you, I love our children, I love our family life. I'll do anything not to put in jeopardy all those things that I love so dearly."

She stared at him for a long moment. Her lips were thin and

tight, her eyes large and round and very shiny. "I cannot forgive you or Boysie. I'm ashamed on your behalf. What I saw you doing was unnatural." She turned her face the other way as her eyes filled with tears. "But I won't tell anyone. I'd rather die than tell anyone. But you won't see Boysie again, will you? You can't . . . after . . . after . . ." She began to cry hysterically.

Harry slipped off his shoes and lay on the bed beside her, putting his arm around her and drawing her close. How could he exist if Boysie was no longer part of his life? "I want you to take me back to London," she said. "I don't want to be here another minute. Say what you will, but you have to take me back to London. We'll spend the rest of the summer in Norfolk with Mama and Papa and you'll put Boysie and this shaming episode behind you." She lifted his hand off her pregnant belly. "And I don't want you to touch me."

"Charlotte," he gasped.

"I mean it, Harry. I need time. I can't easily forget what I saw. I can't pretend it didn't happen."

"It was a moment of madness."

She turned her head and her expression was hard and sharp. "And what if I hadn't been here? What then? What would you have done?" Her body shook as she began to sob again. "What would you have done, Harry?"

"Nothing. I would have done nothing. It was a kiss. That's all. A kiss." She turned away brusquely, making it clear that she didn't believe him.

Harry explained to Celia that Charlotte was suffering so much with this pregnancy that she wanted to spend the rest of the summer with her parents. "Jolly bad sport," said Celia sulkily. "She's ruined our summer. The first summer we've all been together here at Castle Deverill in nearly ten years. This was meant to be special and she's gone and ruined it." She folded her arms crossly. "Boysie won't be happy you're going. He'll be furious too. You're breaking up the party."

Harry shrugged. "I'm sorry. There's nothing I can do."

Then Celia's face brightened. "I know, she can take the children to Norfolk and you can stay here. Oh, do stay, Harry darling, it'll be just like the old days. If we could get Deirdre to go with her it really would be marvelous!"

"No," said Harry firmly. "I can't do that to her."

"Well, you're a spoilsport too and I'll find it very hard to forgive you."

"But you will, of course."

"Of course. Next time leave her at home. I don't think she likes Ireland anyway."

The car was packed and waiting on the gravel with Celia's chauffeur. Harry and Charlotte said their good-byes, managing to put on a convincing show of unity. Everyone was sorry to see them go, but none was sorrier to be going than Harry. Outside at last he helped his wife into the back seat, tucking her skirt in carefully before closing the door. Then something made him look up to the window above the front door. Boysie was standing on the landing, gazing down on him with a forlorn expression on his face. Harry's stomach gave a little flip as he remembered what Kitty had told him about Joseph. Boysie looked like a ghost too. His face was white behind the glass, his eyes like two black holes, resonating with sorrow. A lump lodged itself in Harry's throat and he remained a moment, gazing up, wanting to wave but knowing he couldn't, knowing that if he did he'd break down and cry like a boy. He wrenched his eyes away and walked slowly around to the other side of the car. As he opened the door he glanced up again. Boysie was still there. His hand was now spread on the small rectangular pane and he had dropped his forehead onto it so that his breath misted the glass in a cloudy stain. Harry inhaled deeply and forced himself onto the back seat. He slammed the door, then he put his finger in his mouth and bit down hard. If he gave in to tears Charlotte would know the truth: that he loved Boysie most of all and always would.

Chapter 15

New York

After Jack O'Leary had slipped into the dawn Bridie had plunged into a deep hole of despair out of which she had no desire, or will, to climb. She had believed that their wandering souls had at last reached the end of their searching and come to rest in each other, like a pair of blind creatures who have suddenly found the light. Yet he had gone, leaving her heart in shattered pieces about the space where he had lain, and her longing for home more acute than ever. It was as if he had taken Ireland with him and now she was completely lost, cut adrift and afraid.

She had sought solace in alcohol. Bridie discovered that a different sort of happiness could be bought in a gin bottle. She drank it on waking, when the pain of loss was at its most severe, and continued to drink it throughout the day to prevent that pain from returning. But the effects of intoxication only gave her a shallow, bitter kind of pleasure. It was like putting a ragged plaster over a seeping wound; the poison still bled through.

Elaine did everything to entice her out of her pit. She flushed the gin down the lavatory, she tempted her with shopping, new clothes and parties, but Bridie refused to be tempted and stayed at home, finding new bottles she had hidden in places that even Elaine, with her thorough searching of Bridie's apartment, had failed to find. "You're young and beautiful, Bridget," Elaine had shouted at her one afternoon, when she had found her friend still in bed with her hair matted and greasy and her eyes bloodshot and distant. "You can have any man you want."

"But I only want Jack," Bridie had replied, sobbing into her silk pillow. "I've loved him all my life, Elaine. I'll never love another. Not for as long as I live." And in her inebriated state her Irish accent was more pronounced than ever.

"You have to pull yourself together."

But Bridie had shouted back, "I'll do as I please. If you don't like it, don't come here!"

After months of steady decline Elaine was so worried about Bridie that she discussed it with her husband. "There's only one solution. You have to get rid of the bottle, Elaine," Beaumont told her firmly.

"She won't listen to me."

"She will listen to *me*," he said confidently. "*I* will talk to her."

And so it was that on a particularly windy spring morning, Elaine and Beaumont Williams rang the bell to Bridie's apartment on Park Avenue and made their way up to the top floor via the elevator. Bridie's maid opened the door and the two stepped into the immaculate hall where a large mirror seemed to open on the facing wall like a shiny silver fan. Elaine caught her anxious reflection, splintered in the various sections of the glass, but Beaumont didn't hesitate and, after giving Imelda his coat, strode straight into the airy sitting room, for he was a man who, having made a decision to get something done, was inclined not to waste time dithering. He walked over to the windows to look down onto the street below. It was a mighty fine view and he was satisfied that he had made a good decision in advising Mrs. Lockwood to rent the apartment.

At length Bridie appeared in a turquoise Japanese dressing gown, embellished with pictures of large colorful orchids, and a pair of crimson velvet slippers. For a moment Elaine thought she had been deceived, for Bridie's hair was clean and shiny and combed into a fashionable bob and her carefully applied makeup gave her face a fresh and wholesome gleam. But as she approached, Elaine noticed the unsteadiness of her step and the glassy look in her eyes that betrayed her drunkenness and her desolation, and she knew then that Bridie was simply making a great effort to disguise the truth.

"Well, this is a surprise," said Bridie, sinking into an armchair. "To what do I owe the pleasure?" But the wariness in her gaze told Elaine that she already knew.

Beaumont remained standing by the window. He turned and smiled and one could have been forgiven for thinking that this visit was simply a social one. "It's been a while since I've been here, Mrs. Lockwood. I must say, you have a very elegant home."

"Indeed I do, Mr. Williams," she replied. "Can I offer you a cup of coffee or tea? Imelda will bring it."

"No, I'm fine, thank you. Perhaps Elaine would like something."

Elaine was perching nervously on the sofa, playing with her fingers. "Coffee would be swell." She didn't dare catch eyes with her friend, in case she saw the betrayal in them.

"And I'll have a cup of tea," said Bridie.

While Imelda made the tea and coffee Beaumont chatted easily with Bridie, and Bridie, hoping that she could fool him into believing her in the very best of health, was hopeful of delaying, or even perhaps avoiding, the inevitable questions, for she knew why they had both come. After a while, which seemed interminable to Elaine, Imelda brought her a cup of coffee and her mistress a pot of tea. At that point Beaumont pulled up a chair and sat close to Bridie. As she poured from the pot her hand shook so that the top rattled noisily on the porcelain. With that simple action her poise fell apart and exposed her as surely as a mask swiped off the face of a thief. Her bottom lip trembled as she fought hard to steady her grip. Without a word Beaumont slowly and deliberately placed his hand on hers and they locked eyes. Bridie's were wild, like a cornered rabbit's, but Beaumont's were calm and full of compassion. "Allow me, Mrs. Lockwood," he said gently, and Bridie blinked at him, a child again suddenly, staring wide-eyed at a father who loved and understood her. It was that small but significant gesture that caused the tears to well. Beaumont took the pot and poured the tea and Bridie was afraid to lift the cup in case she spilled it.

"Mrs. Lockwood," he began. "Do you remember our very first meeting?" Bridie nodded. "It was in Mrs. Grimsby's parlor, was it not? You were a frightened girl, fresh off the boat from Ireland, without anyone in New York to look out for you." Two tears trickled down her cheeks, leaving wet trails in her makeup. "You've come so far from that moment and been so full of courage that if I were your father, I would burst at the seams with pride." Bridie swallowed at the mention of her dear, dead father Tomas, killed by a tinker's knife. "You have come too far to throw it all away now." Bridie dropped her gaze into her teacup. She felt uncomfortably sober. With shaking hands she lifted the cup and saucer and took a large swig of tea. "The remedy for your heartbreak is not to be found in the bottom of a gin bottle, Mrs. Lockwood, or in any other bottle, I might add. The remedy for your loss is within *you*. It is your choice to let this young man destroy you or make you stronger. You can drown your sorrow and yourself in the process or take life by the collar again, as you have done before. You are wealthy, young and beautiful. Any man would give his right arm to marry you."

"But I don't want anyone—"

Beaumont stopped her mid-sentence. "Do you remember that you once said to me that a woman without a husband has no standing in society and no protection?" Bridie nodded slowly. "You were right, but you forgot one important thing. A woman without a husband is obliged to walk life's long and often difficult road alone, and that can be a very lonely experience. We humans are not solitary creatures. We require the company of others for comfort. What you need is a husband." Bridie thought of Mr. Lockwood and for a fleeting moment she recalled the sense of security he had given her. "You have to put this Irishman out of your mind as you have so successfully done with Ireland. Heed not the voice that calls you home, but the voice that calls you forward. He's out there somewhere and we're going to find him." He gave her a reassuring smile and she put down her teacup. Elaine was so tense her shoulders ached. She sat sipping her coffee, deeply proud of her wise and articulate husband—and deeply ashamed of her *un*wise and foolish infidelity.

"Now, we're going to do this in simple steps. The first step being your commitment to giving up the booze." A shadow of anxiety passed across Bridie's face. She had been prepared to deny it, but there was no point now. Mr. Williams knew the truth. She couldn't conceal who she really was from him. "I want you to take me around your apartment and show me where it's all hidden," he said kindly. "Then we will dispose of it, bottle by bottle. It will signify the beginning of a new chapter."

With reluctance at first, then with growing enthusiasm, Bridie showed Mr. Williams the places where she had secreted her gin. Both Elaine and Beaumont were surprised by Bridie's ingenuity but neither let that show. The gin was disposed of with solemn ritual, as if they were performing an exorcism. Once again Bridie felt a sense of renewal and embraced it with both arms. Mr. Williams had thrown her a rope and she told herself that she would be foolish, suicidal even, not to take it.

Slowly and with immense effort Bridie pulled herself out of her pit. She forced herself to forget about Jack, to swallow her disappointment and regret and to focus her eyes on the future. There was a certain familiarity in her determination to leave the past behind and move forward. She had done it countless times, but it didn't get any easier; she just recognized the path for it was so well trodden. Elaine was a constant support and companion and on the various occasions that Bridie fell back, Elaine was there to encourage her without judgment.

Eventually Bridie began to take pride in herself again. She derived enjoyment from shopping and dancing, going to movie theaters and parties as she had done before, although now she was a little more subdued and a lot more cautious. She allowed a few men to court her. Her heart was still fragmented, the tears still tender, the memory of Jack still vivid. But as the months passed and the summer of 1929 blossomed into bright flowers and warm breezes, that memory dimmed and the edges of her pain were blunted. Count Cesare di Marcantonio saw her, ripe for love as a golden peach on a tree, from across the crowded garden at the Reynoldses' annual summer party in Southampton and decided to pluck.

"Who is that beautiful woman?" he asked his friend, Max Arkwright, who had brought him to the party.

"Why, that's the infamous Mrs. Lockwood," Max replied, sweeping a hand through his thick flaxen hair. "Everyone knows about *her*."

"She is married?" The Count's disappointment was palpable.

"No, widowed." This pleased the Count and Max proceeded to tell him the story, as he had read it in the newspapers and heard it in the grand dining rooms on Fifth Avenue. The Count listened intently, an eyebrow arched, his interest fanned with every enthralling detail.

Aware that she was being watched by the mysterious stranger at the other side of the garden, Bridie asked Elaine who he was. Elaine squinted in the evening sunshine and frowned. "I don't know," she confessed; she knew who most people were. "But I know the man he is with. That's Max Arkwright, a notorious womanizer. He's from a wealthy Boston family, spends most of his time in Argentina and Europe playing polo and seducing women. Unmarried scoundrel and charmer too. Birds of a feather flock together. You have been warned."

"Oh, I'm not interested in either," said Bridie dismissively, concealing her interest in *one*. "Only curious. His friend is staring at me. I can almost feel his eyes beneath my dress."

"Then you'd better move away, Bridget, before you get burned." And the two women escaped through the crowd to the wide steps that swept up to the terrace and the magnificent Italianate mansion behind. When Bridie chanced to look back over her shoulder she saw that the man was still watching her and she felt the long-forgotten frisson of excitement ripple across her skin.

Once on the terrace Bridie wandered among the vast pots of blue and white hydrangeas and mingled with friends and new acquaintances. She smiled and chatted with grace acquired over years through practice and persistence, while her dark eyes darted here and there in search of the handsome man who had caught her eye across the garden. The sun sank slowly in the western sky, bathing the lawn in a warm amber light, and the loud twittering of roosting birds died down as they settled on their positions in the branches and watched the activity below with a passive interest.

Just when she was beginning to suspect that the man had gone, she felt a light touch on her bare shoulder and turned around to see him standing before her, with an apologetic, almost sheepish look on his irresistibly attractive face. "I am sorry to interrupt," he said and his accent was so foreign that Bridie had to take a moment to understand what he was saying. "Count Cesare di Marcantonio," he said and he pronounced Cesare as "Chesaray" and the rest so smoothly that she failed to catch a single syllable. His name ran over her like warm honey and her spirits soared on the sweetness of it. "I saw you in the garden and had to come and introduce myself. It is probably not what a man should do in polite American society, but in Argentina, where I was raised, or in Italy, where I spent the first ten years of my life, it is rude not to pay homage to a beautiful woman."

Bridie blushed the color of fuchsia as his gaze swept across her face, caressing her skin. "Bridget Lockwood," she replied. "It doesn't sound as exotic as your name."

"But I'm not as beautiful as you, so there, you see, we are equal." He smiled and the lines around his mouth creased like a lion's, his big white teeth shining brightly against his brown and weathered skin. The crow's-feet were long and deep at his temples, his eyes the color of green agate, shining with mischief that at once appealed to Bridie's own sense of fun. His hair was seal-black and shone with a gloss that looked almost waxy, but the sun had caught the top of his head and bleached the hair there to a light sugar-brown and Bridie would have liked to run her fingers through it. Instead she held on to her glass of lemonade and tried not to let her nervousness show.

"So, what are you doing in Southampton?" she asked, aware that it was an inane question and wishing she could think of something better to say.

"Playing polo," he replied. "I confess, Mrs. Lockwood, I am a man of leisure." Bridie smiled, noticing how he had called her "Mrs." Lockwood when she hadn't volunteered that information. She was thrilled that he had been asking about her. "My family owns a large and highly profitable farm in Argentina so I take my pleasure where I find it. I have decided to spend the summer here, playing polo and seeing friends—one day I will take over from my father so, why not have fun before I have to take on responsibility, no?"

"Do you live in Argentina?"

He shrugged noncommittally. "I am a man of the world. I live a little in Argentina, a little in Rome, sometimes in Monte Carlo, sometimes in Paris . . . now here, in New York. Perhaps I will buy a house in Southampton; the people are certainly very charming, no?" With that he gave her a long and lingering look that made her stomach flip over like a pancake.

Impressed by his obviously moneyed and carefree existence, which was also apparent in his expensive clothes, the gleaming gold bee cuff links and matching tie pin, and in the general air of luxury and privilege that surrounded him, Bridie felt her excitement grow. She had never before met a man who exuded such mystery or had such a delightfully exotic flavor. As the conversation rattled on with ease she found herself liking him more and more. Since she had lost Jack she hadn't even tried to put back together the broken pieces of her heart, but now, suddenly, she wanted to. She wanted this stranger to have it, to hold it in his large hands and to keep it for always. Bridie allowed his gaze to consume her, and for once she didn't even think about the road home.

Curious to see that her friend had been talking to Max Arkwright's mysterious friend for longer than was decent Elaine decided to interrupt. Bridie smiled when she approached and quickly introduced her, admitting with a flirtatious smile, which Elaine hadn't seen in months, that she couldn't pronounce his name. "Cesare di Marcantonio," he repeated with a grin. "Now you say it."

"Cesare di Marc . . ." Bridie began slowly.

"Marcantonio," he repeated.

"Marcantonio," she said, then smiled triumphantly. Elaine watched with mounting unease. She might very well not have been there for these two people had eyes only for each other.

"This is my dear friend, Elaine Williams," Bridie said, putting her arm around her. "When I was new in Manhattan and had not a single friend, Elaine came to my rescue and has been by my side ever since. I don't know what I would have done without her."

Elaine looked him over coolly. "Yes, and I'm by your side right now," she said firmly. "Let's go get something to eat, Bridget. The buffet looks delicious."

"I will accompany you both," volunteered the Count to Elaine's dismay. "It will be my greatest pleasure to dine with two such charming ladies."

They made their way across the terrace and down the steps to where the tables of food were lined up on the grass. "He's certainly dishy, Bridget, but I wouldn't trust him as far as I could throw him," Elaine hissed, as they descended the steps together.

"God save me, I think I'm in love," Bridie hissed back, ignoring her friend's warning.

"Just be careful," Elaine said. "We know nothing about him."

"I know everything I want to know," said Bridie haughtily. "He's good enough for *me*."

At the bottom of the steps Beaumont appeared with two plates of dinner. "There you are, Elaine," he said. "Will you join me?"

Elaine was surprised to see her husband but she took the

plate and gave Bridie a disappointed look. "You'll be okay?" she asked.

"I'm just grand," Bridie replied and set off across the lawn with the Count.

"What's up?" Elaine asked her husband as they sat down at one of the small round tables positioned in clusters beneath lines of twinkling lights that encircled the garden.

"Bridget has found a man at last," he said with a grin.

"But is he suitable? We know nothing about him."

"Highly *un*suitable, I suspect," said Beaumont. "I doubt it will amount to much, but I think a romance is just what she needs to raise her morale."

"Is he really a count?"

"Counts are a dime a dozen in Italy," he added dismissively. "Still, he's lit her fire so we must be grateful for that. I doubt we're looking at the future Countess Cesare di Marcantonio!"

But Beaumont Williams, who was usually right about everything, was not right about *this*. The kiss that the Count stole beneath the cherry tree in the Reynoldses' garden was one of many that she would treasure. "May I see you again?" Cesare asked Bridie, taking her hand and looking into her chocolate-brown eyes as if he had discovered something precious there.

"I would like that," she replied, barely daring to believe that this beautiful man found her to his liking. "I would like that very much."

IN THE WEEKS that followed, Cesare took Bridie to watch the polo at the Meadowbrook polo club in Long Island and then to a match of his own where she sat in the stands in her summer dress and watched with her heart in her mouth as he thundered up and down the field, mallet raised. He was strong and athletic, fearless and bold, and her attraction to him intensified. She saw him as a foreign prince and her respect and admiration for him was beyond question. He told her tales of growing up in Italian palaces and then moving with his family to Argentina, where his family owned grand houses in the most elegant parts of Buenos Aires. His farm on the pampa was so large that he could travel by pony from sunrise to sunset without leaving his own land. "One day I'll take you there and show you how beautiful it is at sunset, when the plains turn red and the sky is indigo blue. You will fall in love with it."

Count Cesare seemed to relish having the infamous Mrs. Lockwood on his arm. He showed her off at fundraisers, private parties, in the dance halls of Manhattan and in the jazz clubs and speakeasies of Harlem. Wherever the fashionable people were the Count was sure to be, dressed in the most dapper suits and silk scarves with elaborate gold bees adorning the buttonholes of his shirts and jackets, stamped into the leather of his wallet and molded into the silver of his money clip. The bee emblem was everywhere. Count Cesare looked glossy and shiny with his jet-black hair as highly polished as his two-tone brogues and his dazzling white teeth matching the bright whites of his eyes. Rumor simmered and then rose in great bubbles of excitement as everyone began to predict another wedding. Flashbulbs welcomed their arrivals and journalists clamored to comment on their every move: *The ubiquitous Count Cesare di Marcantonio was once again escorting his new lady friend the socialite Mrs. Lockwood to a fundraising dinner at the Metropolitan Museum . . . She wore a gown by Jean Patou . . . Those* who despised her as an insatiable social-climber sniffed their disapproval and dismissed the Count as a "common adventurer," but those who enjoyed the colorful maid who had fulfilled the American dream and risen to be one of the richest women in the city celebrated this new chapter of her story.

Bridie let him kiss her again. And *again*. His kisses were sensual and teasing, ardent and long-lasting. He brushed his lips against hers, murmured to her in Spanish, traced his fingers beneath her blouse and dipped his tongue into the little well at her throat. He drove her to the point of madness and it was all she could do to restrain herself. And then, only a month after they'd met, he asked her to marry him.

"I love you with all my heart," he told her, bending onto one knee on the grass in Central Park where he had taken her for a picnic. "Will you do me the honor of agreeing to be my wife?"

Bridie's eyes filled with tears. She knelt in front of him and threw her arms around his neck. "I will," she replied and as he placed his lips upon hers she realized that happiness was perhaps *not* something that could be bought but something that grew out of love.

Chapter 16

London, autumn 1929

Beatrice had noticed that Digby had been somewhat subdued since the Castle Deverill Summer Ball. The event itself had been a triumph and Celia had been a radiant and gracious hostess, charming everyone with her ready smile and obvious enthusiasm for her new position as Doyenne of Ballinakelly. No one could talk of anything else for weeks afterward. The castle was awe-inspiring, the gardens the very manifestation of beauty and the guests, including the Shrubs, Bertie, Kitty and Harry, had nothing but praise for Celia and Archie's efforts. But Digby had grown morose and taciturn, which was very disconcerting for his family who knew him as flamboyant, spirited and indomitable. Beatrice wondered whether he was sinking into a mild depression on account of the castle having reached completion and his role in the project drawn to a close. A natural gambler and risk-taker, Digby had relished the undertaking, but now it was over he was back at his desk in his office speculating on the markets, plotting schemes with his solicitor and his broker and taking a keen interest as usual in his horses, but he was uncharacteristically wary and ill at ease. Beatrice noticed that he spent a lot of time standing by the window, smoking his cigars and gazing out into the road as if expecting someone or something undesirable to turn into his driveway.

Beatrice tried to distract him by filling the house with people. Her Tuesday evening Salons continued to deliver politicians, actresses, writers and socialites to her door, and she made sure that Deverill Rising was busy with Digby's racing friends at weekends. But nothing seemed to relieve him of his anxiety and restore his *joie de vivre*. When she asked him about it he simply patted her hand and smiled reassuringly. "Nothing to worry about, my dear. I've just got a lot on my mind, that's all."

Whether he had anticipated the Wall Street Crash on October 24 or his gambler's instinct sensed impending doom in the markets, she couldn't say, but the terrible fall on the London Stock Exchange a few days after Black Thursday in New York more than fulfilled his gloomy premonition. Digby locked himself in his study and remained for most of the day on the telephone, shouting. He did not emerge until very late that evening with his face red and sweating, and for the first time in their marriage Beatrice saw real fear in his eyes.

Celia had returned to London to shop for more extravagances with which to adorn her beloved castle. She had read the newspapers and listened to her mother worrying about her father but she didn't imagine that the Wall Street Crash had anything to do with *her*. When she asked Archie about the state of their finances he reassured her that they were fine, they had pots of money and no fall on the Stock Exchange could induce him to tell her to curb her expenditure. So she continued to shop in the usual way, flouncing up and down Knightsbridge and Bond Street without a care in the world, while the rest of London society trembled in their finely polished shoes and the city smog lingered in a portentous gray mist.

"It's really such a drag," she told Harry over lunch at Claridge's. "Papa's in a foul mood, which is so unlike him, and Mama is fussing around him, which makes him all the more bad-tempered. Leona and Vivien came round for tea yesterday and only made Mama worry all the more, repeating what their silly husbands have obviously told them, that we're all going to be poor and penniless and miserable. Goodness, I do dislike my sisters." She took a swig of champagne and grinned mischievously. "So, to lift my spirits, I've just bought the most gorgeous painting for the hall, to replace the one of that crusty old general with his dog that hangs at the bottom of the stairs . . ." As she rattled on Harry tried to concentrate on her words, but all he could see was her pretty red mouth moving against the roar of his thoughts, which carried in their tumultuous barrage the name Boysie Bancroft.

Celia hadn't a clue of the havoc her Summer Ball had caused, although Harry readily admitted that it was all his fault. If he hadn't taken Boysie to the room he shared with his wife . . . if he hadn't been so reckless . . . if he hadn't, in some deep and unconscious way, *wanted* to get caught. Since he had left Ballinakelly with Charlotte, he had been in a state of utter despair. Life was not worth living without Boysie. Now that he had promised his wife he wouldn't see him again the sun no longer shone, the nights were as thick as tar and his limbs were as heavy as lead. He felt as if he were walking in water and that the current was always against him. His unhappiness had engulfed him and it seemed that, while Celia was bathed in light, he dwelled in permanent shadow—and that shadow penetrated to the marrow of his bones. His misery was total and complete and yet he couldn't even begin to explain it to Celia. He had to be a master of theater, smiling in the right places, quipping as he always had, laughing in his old carefree way, while inside his heart was shriveling like a plum left on the grass at the mercy of the winter frosts.

So focused on her castle, Celia didn't even ask him about Boysie. If she had taken more notice she might have wondered why Boysie hadn't joined them for lunch. She would have questioned why he wasn't at her mother's Tuesday Salons and why, when he was such a regular visitor to Deverill House, he hadn't crossed the threshold since the summer. If she hadn't been so staunchly single-minded about herself and embellishing her new home, she might have been concerned by her cousin's pallor, by the raw pain in his eyes that no amount of dissembling could hide and by the downward twist to one corner of his mouth when his sorrow caught him off guard; but she wasn't. Celia was only too happy to tell Harry about her purchases and the fabulous plans she had for Christmas. The crowds of children they were going to have because "in a castle of that size it's only proper to fill it with family." Christmas was going to be "a riot" because they were all going to be there together instead of spending their usual fortnight at Deverill Rising.

At last she stopped motoring on about herself and put down

her empty wineglass. "Darling, I meant to ask, how is Charlotte? She was a miserable old thing at my ball. Has she cheered up?"

Harry wiped his mouth with his napkin even though it was clean. "She has," he lied. "She's had a difficult pregnancy. Spending the rest of the summer in Norfolk really cheered her up. I think she just needed to be with her family. Ours can be a little overpowering."

The truth was that Charlotte had *not* forgiven him. She had not invited him into her bedroom since they had returned from Norfolk and she had most definitely not forgotten what she had seen, nor did she intend to. She was just as unhappy as he was. Combined with the natural fatigue of pregnancy, her wretchedness was even more desperate. They existed as if in different dimensions, only coming together for the sake of the children and at social functions where their efforts went undetected and any irritability was put down to anxiety about the imminent birth on her part and the dire state of the markets on his. Most of London society felt the same about the declining economy and everyone, except Celia, was worrying about their future.

The only other person who was even more careless with money than Celia was Maud, Harry's mother. Having found a house to buy in Chester Square she had promptly set about furnishing it with the help of Mr. Kenneth Leclaire, the famous designer who had worked such magic on Castle Deverill, without a thought for her husband who had bought it for her with the proceeds of the sale of his ancestral home. Maud didn't want Bertie anywhere near her so he remained in the Hunting Lodge, courtesy of Archie and Celia, who charged him a peppercorn rent. Harry had met Maud's lover, Arthur Arlington, who was the younger brother of the Earl of Pendrith and a well-known scoundrel, twice divorced and with a notorious gambling habit. They had met at the ballet and Harry had been appalled. For a woman so desperate to be seen to be doing the right thing, Maud was very careless with Arthur, whom everyone knew was escorting her to bed as well as to the Royal Opera House. Perhaps it was because he was of aristocratic lineage, Harry mused. Nothing excited his mother more than a title.

"Perhaps you can leave Charlotte in Norfolk for Christmas," Celia continued. "She will have just had the baby. The last thing she'll want is to travel the choppy Irish Sea to Ballinakelly. Much better that she rest at home with her mama to look after her. Do you think we can persuade Boysie to leave Dreary Deirdre behind too? Perhaps he can come for New Year's. Really, why did you two have to marry? You were much more fun on your own."

"*You* married, old girl," said Harry flatly.

"That's different. Archie's such fun. Your wives are very tiresome." Her face lit up as she expressed her admiration for her husband in glowing terms: "He's denied me nothing for the castle. You should have seen the wonderful things I bought in France. We had to have it all shipped over and it took weeks—you would have thought they were sailing the Atlantic, not the English Channel! There's a sale coming up at Christie's. They're auctioning the most stunning things from Russia. After the Revolution those beastly Bolsheviks sold all the treasures. You wouldn't believe the opulence of those Russian princes. I've got my eye on a few things. I'm so excited. Would you like to come with me? I shall be bidding like crazy, waving my little hand at every opportunity. It's all so much fun. I get an enormous buzz out of it."

"I'm surprised Archie isn't reining you in, considering the present climate," said Harry, calling the waiter for the bill.

"Darling, he says there's nothing to worry about. You have to remember that I married a very clever man."

Harry wasn't convinced. "He'll have been affected by the Crash like everyone else."

"Then he must have secret reserves," she giggled. "Because I'm spending them!"

But Celia's confidence was shaken a few weeks later when her favorite couturier in Maddox Street failed to give her credit. Pale with concern she waited for Archie to return home, having enjoyed a long lunch at his club, and then she asked him.

"My darling Celia, it's simply a reflection of the times," he explained coolly. "Everyone is being extra cautious."

"So there's nothing to worry about?"

"Nothing."

Her shoulders sagged with relief. "I'm so pleased. I'd be utterly devastated if I couldn't go to the Russian sale at Christie's. I asked Harry to come with me, but he's cried off so Mama is coming instead. Really, everyone is making a fuss about nothing!" She put her arms around her husband and kissed him. "You're a wonderful man, Archie. Just wonderful. I don't know what I'd do without you."

He frowned and in her happiness she missed a certain shiftiness that made him avert his eyes. "Do you know what gives me the *most* pleasure, darling?"

"You tell me," he replied.

"Watching Papa enjoying Castle Deverill. He grew up in

the shadow of that place and he loved it and yearned to belong there as his cousins Bertie and Rupert did. All those summers in Ballinakelly made such a deep impression on him, Mama told me, that his pleasure at my ownership of it is all the more satisfying. It's as good as owning it himself, I think. You have done a wonderful thing, not only restoring the family seat, but giving it to the London Deverills. You can't imagine what that means. The prestige is enormous. I love Cousin Bertie and cherish the memories of having enjoyed the place when Hubert and Adeline were alive, but I'm happy it's fallen into *my* hands. I love it dearly and Papa does too. Thank you, my darling, for making it possible. You've made us incredibly happy."

Archie pulled her into his arms and held her close. "That's all I've ever wanted to do," he said and she felt him nuzzling his face against her hair.

At the end of November Charlotte Deverill was delivered of a boy who was immediately named Rupert after Harry's uncle who was killed at Gallipoli. The birth of their son mollified a little Charlotte's hostility toward her husband. After two daughters the arrival of a boy gave both parents something about which they could be truly happy. For a brief moment they could forget their resentment and celebrate the arrival of the heir to the centuries-old title and the future hope that Little Rupert would one day father a son who would secure the title for another generation. Harry loved his daughters but the arrival of his son affected him in a very different way. The child distracted him from his constant pining for Boysie and revived his withered heart. Little Rupert's innocence touched him profoundly and every wriggle he made induced smiles that came from deep inside him. But then as December brought windy nights and cold, dark mornings, the black dog of despair began to hound him once again.

Celia's busy little white hand impressed everyone at the Christie's Russian sale. With the encouragement of her mother she bid for almost everything and won all the pieces she had so desired. To celebrate, mother and daughter lunched in Mayfair and discussed Celia's plans for her grand New Year Ball. "It's going to be even more wonderful than the summer one," she told Beatrice. "I'm going to ask Maud and Victoria, even though I can't bear either. I think it's time to hold out the olive branch, don't you? I'd love Maud to see what I've done and to like it."

"Darling, I doubt very much she'll ever set foot in Ballinakelly again. I think it would be too much for her to see her husband's inheritance in your hands. But I'm sure she'll appreciate the gesture. I think your sisters might come this time. They spent Christmas with their husbands' families last year so it's our turn this year. I've told them you intend to host Christmas and they're rather curious to see what you and Archie have done to the place. I think they're the only members of the family who are yet to see it, having not been able to come in the summer." Beatrice smiled contentedly. "To think of all those children running around the castle gardens. They're going to have a wonderful time." Then her smile faded and concern furrowed her brow. She toyed with the stem of her wineglass. "I think it will be good for your father to get away from London. He's been very distracted lately. He's even told me to cut back where I can . . ."

"You mean to stop spending?" Celia asked, aghast.

"I'm afraid so. I'm doing my best. I'm sure the trouble will blow over, but until it does I'm being careful." She chuckled wistfully. "I haven't been careful since before I married. You know your father was a very wealthy man when I met him. He'd struck lucky in the diamond mines and then in the gold rush. He was such a dashing adventurer. But he's a risk-taker. I'm not sure what's going on, but I fear some of his gambles haven't paid off and that the Crash has robbed him of some of his wealth. I'm sure it's not too serious. I *hope* it's not too serious. But we'll weather it, won't we?"

"Papa will be fine," said Celia emphatically. The idea of her father being anything less than solid, rich and unshakable was an abhorrence. "He's much too clever to let something like this pull him down. But you're right, Christmas at Castle Deverill will make him feel much better. It makes us all feel better. It's that sort of place."

IN THE GRAND tradition of the Deverills who had occupied Castle Deverill before her, Celia invited the entire family to stay for two weeks over Christmas and New Year's, ending the festive period with a sumptuous ball that promised to eclipse all the previous parties ever held there.

Maud declined, as was expected. However, Victoria wrote to say that she would come, because, having done her duty by her husband's side entertaining the tenants and estate workers, followed by his mother, the dowager Countess, at Broadmere, their stately home in Kent, for the last fifteen years, she deserved to spend Christmas wheresoever she desired. Celia's grandparents, Stoke and Augusta, accepted too, which was a great surprise because Augusta had given every indication that she would be dead by Christmas. Celia's sisters agreed to come as did Harry and Charlotte, which dismayed Celia for she had hoped Harry might manage to leave his grumpy wife in England. Her biggest disappointment, however, was Boysie. He had written back in his beautiful brown calligraphy on luxuriously thick ivory paper from Mount Street that it was with great regret that he was unable to accept, for Celia Mayberry was undoubtedly unsurpassed not only in Ballinakelly but in London too as the greatest hostess of their age. Flattered though she was it saddened her that one of her dearest friends would not be present for her first Christmas at Castle Deverill and her first New Year Ball.

Kitty and Robert would come for Christmas Day with the Shrubs and Bertie, and Elspeth with her ruddy-faced, Master of the Foxhounds husband Peter, who now insisted on introducing Archie to the joys of Irish country living, thinking nothing of lending him a horse and sending him off with the hunt. The castle promised to be full of children—Deverill cousins all doing what Deverill cousins had always done: run around the grounds like wild dogs. Celia was as excited as a thoroughbred at the Derby and couldn't wait for everyone to arrive.

At last the cars swept up the drive and halted in front of the impressive entrance, which Celia had decorated with a wreath made of fir and red-berried holly. The butler was by the door to greet them and three footmen ready to carry the luggage to the bedrooms. The wet wind blew in off the sea and gray clouds gathered in heavy folds above the towers of the castle, but nothing could dampen Celia's joy at welcoming everyone into her expensively heated home.

The first to arrive were Augusta and Stoke. Augusta waited for the chauffeur to help her out of the car and then she stood a moment, gazing up at the walls, her face full of wistfulness as she remembered the days when she had come to stay with Adeline and Hubert, before the fire had done unspeakable things to the family. For a moment she thought she saw a face in the window of the western tower and she blinked to clear her vision. Perhaps it was a child playing up there, or a trick of light. Distracted by her husband, who walked around to offer her his arm, she turned her eyes to the entrance, where the open door gave a glimpse of the lavish hall and roaring fire beyond.

"SHE'S STILL ALIVE," Adeline commented to Hubert as their spirits gazed down from the tower window. "I suspect she'll outlive all of them."

"I hope not," said Hubert.

"She'll certainly outlive her husband. Stoke is more rickety in the legs than ever. Ah, there's another car. Let's see. Who's that?" She waited beside Hubert, who was getting increasingly difficult to entertain in the monotonous limbo that had been his for too many years now to count. Adeline smiled. "It's Harry and Charlotte." She sighed and dropped her head to one side. "Poor Harry, he's desperately miserable. Life is difficult."

"Life after life is worse," grumbled Hubert.

"Well, you had better get used to it," came Barton's voice from the armchair. "You have nothing to complain about."

"Don't bicker," said Adeline patiently. "You might as well get along because by the looks of things you're all here to stay for the foreseeable future. Ah, there's Digby and Beatrice. Do you remember, darling, how Digby used to bring you the finest

Cuban cigars?" Hubert grunted. "And Beatrice brought all of us the most exquisite silks. They were always so generous. Poor Digby's finding life difficult too. But these things are sent to test us, are they not? We were tested, weren't we, Hubert?"

"Wish I'd listened to you, Adeline," he said suddenly. "I just thought you were . . ." He hesitated then chuckled at the irony. "I thought you were a bit mad, but it was I who was mad. I thought your ghosts were in your imagination but now I'm one of them. How blind we human beings are and how misled. Look at them all." He stared down as another car slowly made its way over the gravel. "They're blind too. All of them. Only death can open their eyes."

There came a loud tut from behind them. "Be of good heart, Hubert. At least you're not in Hell."

Hubert turned to Barton. "I don't believe in the Hell that I was taught. Hell is on earth. That's very clear now."

"And that is Hell right now," said Adeline mischievously. Hubert smiled, for there, stepping out of the car, was Victoria, Countess of Elmrod, with her desperately dull and humorless husband, Eric. "Now that's going to set the cat among the pigeons," she said. "We're all in for a fortnight of entertainment. Isn't that fun!"

Chapter 17

Victoria had been in the castle for no more than an hour and already the servants were exasperated by her incessant demands. She wanted all her dresses ironed and her husband's shirts pressed. She insisted that her eight-year-old daughter, Lady Alexandra, have a lady's maid of her own, which meant that Bessie, one of the younger housemaids, had to be removed from her usual duties to look after her.

Victoria had arrived ready to criticize her cousin's audacious rebuilding of her father's former home, but to her surprise she found it very much to her liking. "It has proper plumbing and electricity!" she exclaimed in delight, flouncing into the bathroom. "Goodness, Celia's dragged it out of the Dark Ages and what a difference it makes. I think I'm going to be very happy here. I rather wish Mama had swallowed her pride and come because even *she* would be impressed with the comfort and luxury of the new castle."

"My dear, she'd find something to criticize, I assure you," said her husband, looking out of the window onto the manicured box garden below. "And her jealousy would make her stay intolerable."

"But she's spending Christmas alone in London."

"That's *her* choice, Victoria. She was asked and she declined."

"Well, I'm *not* going to let her make *me* feel guilty."

Eric laughed. "She'll make a fine job of trying."

HARRY AND CHARLOTTE were given the same room as they had had in the summer, which put an added strain on their already overwrought marriage. Harry hadn't laid eyes on Boysie in all those months, and now, finding himself back at the castle, he discovered that memories of his friend shone out from every corner, which only served to make him feel even more sick with misery and longing. He too looked down onto the gardens but his mother's jealousy was not the focus of *his* thoughts. No, Harry stared onto the box hedges below and contemplated the idea of hurling himself out the window. The thought of it came slowly yet steadily, creeping across his mind like an evening shadow. Death would be a release, he figured. He'd feel no more the pain of separation and the agony of guilt; he'd be free.

Charlotte left the room to go and check on the nursemaid and Little Rupert, who had been put at the other end of the house with the rest of the children. Harry lit a cigarette and allowed his memories to float before his eyes like ships on the sea. He remembered his first love, Joseph the first footman; the time Kitty had discovered them in bed together; the moment he had had to say good-bye and return to the Front. He remembered the war, the cracking sound of gunfire, the skull-shattering explosion of bombs and the yearning, the terrible *yearning*, when at night he had sat huddled in the trenches gazing up at the stars that twinkled like the distant lights of home. He felt that yearning now, for Boysie, and it was just as terrible.

That evening the Shrubs arrived with Kitty and Robert, Elspeth and Peter and all their children, and Bertie, who wandered up from the Hunting Lodge with a torch. Everyone embraced excitedly, for it had been so long since they had all been together, the London Deverills and the Ballinakelly Deverills, and they fell on each other with exclamations of joy. "I'm just grateful that I have been spared to see once again the magnificence of the castle restored to its former splendor," said Augusta in her stentorian voice, sinking into an armchair like a fat bantam. Her black dress ruffled up at her neck like feathers and the diamonds on her ears weighed so heavily that her lobes hung loose and floppy. She knitted her swollen, arthritic fingers so that the large gems she had managed to force onto them clustered together in a glittering display of bright colors. "I am ready to go, now that I have seen it one last time."

The men stood in the hall discussing the dire state of the economy while Celia showed her sisters, Vivien and Leona, around the drawing room and Kitty and Elspeth endured Augusta's self-indulgent soliloquy about death. Beatrice chatted to the Shrubs and noticed that there was something different about them. It wasn't the way they looked, although she had to admit that they were taking more trouble with their appearance. It was something intangible but distinctly noticeable. Something in the air between them that wasn't pleasant.

"I gather Archie is going to host the Boxing Day Meet," said Hazel.

"Indeed he is," Beatrice confirmed. "I dare say he'll be dragged off with the hunt. I don't think he's a very keen horseman."

"Ethelred is a mighty fine horseman." Laurel inhaled through her nostrils and pulled a face that could only be described as deeply admiring and reverential. "Have you met him?"

"Of course I have," said Beatrice, noticing the air had grown suddenly chilly between the two sisters.

"He will be at the Meet, certainly," Hazel interjected. "He's a *very* fine horseman."

Laurel smiled tensely. "He tried to persuade *me* to take it up again."

"And me," added Hazel, not to be outdone. "He tried to persuade me too. But I believe I'm too old."

"Well, *I'm not*," snapped Laurel. "I am considering it."

"You're not!" said Hazel.

"Why, do you think me incapable? I was a very competent horsewoman in my day, don't forget. Lord Hunt even told me that I would cut a dash in a riding habit." Laurel blushed and smiled smugly. "He does take liberties."

Hazel pursed her lips. "Ah, there's Charlotte," she said. "I'm longing to see Little Rupert. Do excuse me." And she stalked over to Charlotte, who was standing pale and shy in the doorway. Beatrice watched her go with a sense of helplessness. She turned back to Laurel and asked for news of Reverend Maddox— anything to draw the conversation away from Lord Hunt, who seemed to her like a fox in a henhouse.

Digby patted Archie hard on the back. "You're a good man, Archie, to host Christmas for my family. I do believe it'll be the best Christmas any of us have ever had." Archie basked in his father-in-law's admiration. "I must say," Digby continued, "I couldn't have asked for a better man for my daughter. You've made her very happy, which is no easy feat. She's flighty and easily distracted, but she's kept her eye on the castle all these years without deviation, which surprises no one more than me. You're the wind in her sails, Archie. You've got the measure of her, I daresay."

"Thank you, Digby," said Archie.

"Tell me, man to man. How are your affairs?"

"Very good," Archie replied.

Digby nodded thoughtfully, letting his eyes lose their focus in the middle distance. "Nothing I should worry about?"

"Nothing," Archie reassured him.

"These are trying times. I'm a gambling man, Archie. A speculator. I enjoy taking risks, but even I've had my fingers burned."

"I won't say we've come out of this unscathed," Archie conceded. "But I've been shrewd in my dealings."

"Good." Digby patted him on the back again, then he added, "If you were ever in financial difficulty, you wouldn't be too proud to come to me, I hope."

"Of course not," said Archie. Digby went to refill his glass and hoped he'd never be called upon; he was in no position to help anyone at the moment.

ON CHRISTMAS DAY the family attended church, then returned for lunch and the opening of gifts. The children, dressed in their very best velvet and silk, tore open the wrapping paper and ribbon with squeals of delight before being taken away by their nannies to play with their new toys in the children's wing of the castle. The grown-ups drank sherry, played charades and card games and watched the afternoon darken outside the drawing-room windows.

"Christmas should be a happy time," said Kitty to Harry as they stood together, looking out. "But it makes me feel nostalgic and a little sad for all that we have lost." She glanced at her brother, who was struggling to find the words to express his own sense of desolation. "You have done the right thing," she told him quietly. "Hard though it is. You have saved your family." He nodded, straining to hold back his emotion. His face flushed pink and his eyes sparkled but they remained locked, gazing out onto the slate-gray skies and inky gardens. "It will get better, you know," she continued. "The hurt never goes away, but the sharp pain you feel now will turn into a dull ache. Most of the time you'll be able to ignore it. Life has its many distractions, thankfully. Then, suddenly, when you least expect it, something will trigger it again and you'll be cut to the quick. But you push through those moments and they eventually pass. I think of Adeline and what she would say. These things are sent to test us, Harry. Life isn't meant to be easy." She looked at him again and his profile was so grave she wanted to take his hand and squeeze it, but she knew that, for his sake, she couldn't; her touch would only make him lose control.

The day after Christmas the Ballinakelly Foxhounds gathered on the lawn outside the castle for the Boxing Day Meet. It was a damp day, warm for December. Soft rain floated on the breeze that carried with it the scent of pine, wet soil and sea. Crows hopped on the grass, pecking the ground for grubs as the horses snorted smoke into the moist air. Women in their navy riding habits and hats sat sidesaddle, except for Kitty who had made a resolution the morning of the fire never to ride like that again. She sat astride her mare in a pair of breeches and navy jacket, a starched white stock about her neck, her fire-red hair falling in a thick plait down her back, almost reaching her waist. Beside her JP sat confidently on his pony. Almost eight years old he had the bold gray gaze of his half sister, Kitty, and the same red hair, but his face was broad and handsome like his father's, and, to Bertie's pride, he had already been blooded with his first kill. Eager to get going, JP fidgeted excitedly in the saddle while Robert looked on with their daughter, Florence, who was afraid of the horses. Peter had persuaded Archie to join the hunt and he sat awkwardly on his horse, trying not to show his fear. He pulled his silver flask out of his pocket and took a large swig of sloe gin, which didn't make him feel any better.

Lord Hunt, dashing in his black jacket and tan-topped boots, raised his hat to the Shrubs, who buzzed about his horse's head like a pair of flies. "It's a fine day for the chase," Ethelred told them jovially. "The air is mild. Those hounds will pick up a good scent. I really must find a way to persuade you both to take to the saddle again, if only to see you in your riding habits and veils." He grinned down at them as they elbowed each other to get closer.

Grace looked elegant in her black habit, her pale face half-hidden behind a diaphanous black veil. Her waist was, however, thinner than normal and her mouth, usually so full of sensuality, was drawn into a hard line. Ever since Michael Doyle had rebuffed her she had felt more keenly than ever the passing of her youth. She lamented that she was no longer the beauty she had once been, for surely, if she was, Michael would not have been able to resist her. Try as she might, Michael was rarely out of her thoughts and her body still ached for him with every memory of his touch. Dare she admit, even to herself, that Michael had stolen her heart as well as her desire? She hadn't taken a lover since and had to endure her husband strutting about with the smugness of a man who has a pretty woman in every city. She glanced at Sir Ronald, talking to Bertie, astride a horse that looked as if it was buckling beneath his great weight, and felt her irritation rise as he tossed back his head and laughed heartily.

Celia, who had thrown herself with zeal into the role of Doyenne of Ballinakelly, sat sidesaddle in her riding habit, her shiny blond hair tied into a neat chignon at the back of her neck and contained within a hairnet, a black hat set at a raffish angle on the side of her head. She walked her horse among the riders, greeting everyone with the graciousness of a queen. Bertie, distinguished in a pink hunting jacket, asked one of the servants passing around glasses of port to give one to Digby, who, he had noticed, was a little off-color. Leona and Vivien's husbands, Bruce and Tarquin, sat solidly in their saddles, for they were both accomplished riders in the Army, while their wives, who did not like horses, looked on.

Peter, as the Master of Foxhounds, blew his horn and the hunt was off. The hounds ran ahead, their noses to the ground, eager for the scent of fox. The lawn was suddenly empty but for the crows. Hazel and Laurel stood forlornly on the terrace. "Well, that's it then," said Hazel.

"Until tea," said Laurel.

"I'm going to go and sit by the fire in the drawing room."

"And suffer Augusta? Not for me."

"Then what are you going to do, Laurel?" Hazel asked, put out.

"I shall find three friends to play a rubber of bridge. I know Robert will join me at the table and I'm sure, with a little coaxing, Leona and Vivien will be game."

Hazel looked wounded. They had always played bridge together when Adeline and Hubert were alive. "Very well," she said, lifting her chin bravely. "As you wish. And, by the way, I *like* Augusta." The two women walked into the castle together, stinging from their unusual discord.

HARRY ENJOYED HUNTING because it forced him into the moment, just as it had done after the war when he had wanted to flee from the aftereffects of the brutality he had witnessed. Now he wanted to lose himself again. He had never liked hunting as a boy for he had been a coward then, but now he relished the speed and rode without a care for his safety, jumping hedges and fences and streams. The hounds picked up the scent and followed the trail excitedly. Harry galloped at the front, his veins pumping with adrenaline and his heart pounding against his chest, drowning out his longing for Boysie. In a moment he was beside Kitty, who rode with the fearlessness of a man, and she smiled at him as they took a hawthorn hedge and cleared it with a thundering of hooves. Brother and sister rode together relishing the danger that put them firmly in the moment, obliterating for a blessed day their impossible loves.

At length Grace, her face splattered with mud and her hair breaking out of the pins, came across a group of local men and boys in fancy dress, wandering slowly along the track that led from Ballinakelly to other small towns up the coast. With them was a small band and they were singing. She slowed down to a trot until she saw Michael Doyle among the faces and drew her horse to a halt. A young boy was holding a long stick covered in ribbons with a small bundle hanging off the end of it. She looked at Michael through her veil and he looked right back at her with his black and steady gaze. "Good morning, Mr. Doyle," she said. Then, dropping her eyes to the child, she asked him what it was that swung from the end of his stick.

"It's St. Stephen's Day, milady," said the boy, surprised that she didn't know. "This here's a wren."

Grace recoiled. "A wren? A *dead* wren?"

"Yes, indeed," volunteered one of the men.

"Why did you kill it?" she asked, directing her question at Michael, whose head and shoulders rose above the group with an air of authority and importance.

"There are three stories about the celebration to bury the wren," he said. "The first is that the wren drew attention to Jesus in the Garden of Gethsemane, which betrayed him to the Romans. The second is that a wren betrayed the Fenians when it landed on a drum and alerted Cromwell's army." Then the corners of his lips curled into a smile and he looked at her with more intensity. "But there is another story, a legend that tells of Cliona, a temptress, who lured men to their deaths in the sea with her wiles. A charm was discovered that protected them from her. Her only escape was to turn herself into a wren, to be hunted forever more for her skulduggery." He was staring at Grace with a knowing look on his face.

She lifted her chin. "Then you'd better be on your way," she said, giving her horse a gentle squeeze. The group wandered on down the track, but she called out to Michael.

He hung back until the other wrenboys were out of earshot. "Lady Rowan-Hampton?"

"I am that wren hanging from the stick," she said and bit her lip. "Your faith is your charm and I am that poor wren."

"Grace . . ."

She strained the muscles in her neck to hold back her emotions. "You know it is possible to be so heavenly as to be no earthly good, have you thought of that?"

"Then let it be thus," he said.

"You will come to your senses. I know you will."

He shook his head. "When one has experienced the light, Grace, there's no going back to the darkness."

She gave a furious groan, turned her horse roughly and galloped off to catch up with the hunt.

At dusk, when the weak winter sun smoldered through the latticework of trees like a blacksmith's furnace, the hunt made its way home. They had caught their fox and everyone was high on the thrill of the chase and the drama of the kill. Archie walked his horse down the hill toward the castle whose windows glowed with the welcoming lights that promised tea and cake and turf fires. As he approached, the towers and turrets of his home were silhouetted against a clear indigo sky, for the wind had blown the clouds inland and sent the drizzle with it. The sight was arresting. He wanted to stop awhile to savor it before the sun dipped below the horizon and the outline was lost to the dark, but the others were keen to get home to their baths and their tea so he continued, his shoulders suddenly heavy with the weight of responsibility. Castle Deverill was more than a castle and he knew it. It was at the heart of the Deverill spirit and it was now up to him to keep that spirit alive. Celia loved the castle but she didn't understand *why* she loved it. Archie did. He was well aware that it was more than the memory of good times; it was the Deverills' very soul.

When they reached the stables they handed their horses to the grooms and hurried into the castle to change for tea. Their breeches were splattered with mud, their faces stained with sweat and earth kicked up by the hooves. As Harry made his way across the hall toward the stairs, Celia hurried out of the sitting room, her face red and shining. "You'll never believe who's just turned up!" she hissed, grabbing his arm. For a moment Harry's heart gave a little leap. Could Boysie have changed his mind and come after all? "Maud!" Celia declared, trembling with excitement. "She says she's bored in London on her own and that Christmas is about family. Truly, I feel as if the wicked fairy has turned up to ruin the party!" But she didn't look at all unhappy about it. "What's your father going to say—and Kitty?"

Harry concealed his disappointment. "She hasn't brought Arthur Arlington with her, I trust?" he asked, trying to inject some humor into his voice.

"God no! Now *that* would be scandalous. She came on her own. She said she wanted to surprise us."

"She'll do that all right," said Harry, setting off up the stairs.

"Aren't you going to say hello?"

"And cover her immaculate dress in mud? I think not. I'll come down after my bath and relieve you."

"Ah, there's Papa!" She rushed over to Digby. "You're never going to guess who's shown up . . ."

MAUD SAT PRIMLY on the club fender in her pale tweed dress over which she wore a luxurious fur stole. Her blond hair was cut off sharply at her jawline, which accentuated the severe angles of her face. She passed her icy eyes around the room, missing nothing. Beatrice could almost hear the clicking of her mind as she calculated the cost of everything. Augusta watched her warily from the armchair while Charlotte, who had always been a little scared of her mother-in-law, remained on the sofa with Leona and Vivien hoping that she wouldn't direct any conversation her way. The Shrubs, who could think of nothing but Lord Hunt, sat on the other sofa, momentarily stunned like a pair of mice in the presence of a snake. Victoria sat beside her mother on the fender, a cigarette smoking in the holder that balanced between her fingers, enjoying the warmth of the fire on her back and the varying expressions on the faces of the ladies, which ranged from surprise to ill-concealed horror.

At last Maud spoke. "It's nice," she said tightly. Beatrice's mouth twitched.

Augusta gave a snort. "*We* were always taught that 'nice' is a most unimaginative word, Maud," she said imperiously.

"It's lovely then," Maud added. "It's certainly warm, which is a welcome change. Fortunately Adeline isn't alive to see how much it's changed."

"It *had* to change, Mama. One couldn't very well have made a replica of everything that was lost in the fire," said Victoria.

"But it's so different. The soul is missing."

"It's modern," Victoria told her. "I like it very much. In fact, it's just the way I would have done it, had *I* had the opportunity."

Beatrice smiled at Victoria. "You have always had such beautiful taste, my dear," she said, trying not to allow Maud to irritate her.

"I can see that no expense has been spared. Really, I had no idea that Archie was such a tycoon," Maud added.

Augusta snorted again. "It's very vulgar to talk about money."

"But hard to ignore in such lavish surroundings," Maud replied swiftly. "I do believe it's even more sumptuous than the days when Hubert's father lived here. It was extremely luxurious then."

Before Augusta could object the men appeared washed and dressed for tea. When Harry greeted his mother, Maud's resentment at Celia's inappropriate rebuilding of her son's inheritance evaporated like mist in sunlight. She embraced him fiercely and smiled with a rare display of warmth. "You will bring Rupert down, won't you, darling? I'm just dying to give that little baby a squeeze." Charlotte winced; Maud barely knew how to hold a baby. Digby hid his surprise and asked after her crossing. He wondered how Bertie was going to react to his wife setting foot in Ireland again, having sworn she never would.

Celia sat on the floor beside her grandmother for safety. She knew that Augusta would defend her from Maud's barbed comments. Part of her wished Maud hadn't come, but the other part found the drama of her surprise appearance thrilling.

When at last Bertie arrived for tea with Kitty and Robert a hush fell over the room. Maud had not spoken directly to her husband since Adeline's funeral over four years before, and everyone was curious to see what she would say, as well as a little anxious for Bertie, of whom they were all very fond.

Bertie saw Maud at once and his face flushed. Maud, who had prepared herself for this very moment, and loved nothing more than to draw the attention of the entire room, smiled sweetly. "Bertie," she said evenly. "How very good to see you." She believed her delivery to be gracious yet cool—the sort of delivery one might use when greeting the vicar or an old family friend of whom one is not particularly fond.

Bertie stalled in the doorway. He stared at her in amazement. Digby wanted to give him a nudge. Instead, he decided to break the awkward silence himself. "Isn't this a nice surprise," he said, hoping Bertie would agree. But Bertie cleared his throat and seemed to be searching for something to say— and failing miserably.

"Hello, Mama," said Kitty. But Maud's youngest daughter did not even pretend that she was pleased to see her.

"Hello, Kitty," said Maud. "How was the hunt?"

"Frightfully good. Fast and dangerous. Just the way I like it." She turned to her father. "Let me get you a cup of tea, Papa. After the day we've had, we both need to warm up." She laughed and Maud flinched; the affection between father and daughter was very apparent. She watched Bertie as the conversations in the room started up again and the awkwardness was lost in the murmur of voices. The last time she had seen him he had been fat and bloated and swollen with alcohol. Now he was slim, fit and clear-skinned. His hands didn't shake and his pale eyes were focused with the old intensity that had at first attracted her to him. He had been living well—and obviously very contentedly—without her.

A little while later Grace arrived with Sir Ronald and her father and the Shrubs were rescued from the snake by their gallant, who drew them away from the sofa to the window, where he was keen to show them the stars, which, he explained, were shining unusually bright this evening. "The temperature has dropped considerably," Ethelred said. "I believe it will snow."

"Oh, we love snow," said Hazel, thinking how romantic it would be to take a moonlit stroll around the gardens with Lord Hunt.

"We do indeed," Laurel agreed, wishing Hazel would entertain herself elsewhere so she and the silver wolf could gaze at the moon together. Lord Hunt sipped his tea and, in spite of their hopes, neither Shrub moved an inch.

Maud noticed how thin Grace was. She noticed too, much to her pleasure, that her old friend and rival was beginning to lose her beauty. She stood up and advanced. "My dear Grace," she said. "It's been much too long."

"Why, Maud. What a lovely surprise," said Grace with a faultless smile.

"I couldn't very well sit in London while my entire family is over here, celebrating without me."

"Of course not. You look well. London must suit you."

Maud smiled smugly. "Oh it does. But you, my dear, look a little thin. Being so terribly thin is very aging. Are you not eating?"

"I'm in fine health, thank you," Grace replied smoothly. "But this is the first time you have seen the castle since Celia bought it. Isn't it marvelous? I don't think there's a house in the whole of Ireland that can equal it. Everyone thinks so."

Maud stiffened. "I hope it doesn't all go horribly wrong," she said with an insincere frown. "Many a fortune has been wiped out due to the Crash. I hope theirs is secure. After all they've put into this place, it would be a great shame to lose it."

"You always were a positive person, Maud," said Grace.

"And you were always a dear friend, Grace," said Maud.

IT SNOWED THAT night. Thick white feathery flakes were released onto the frozen countryside by an army of cloud that advanced silently over the ocean under the cover of dark. The Deverills and their families slept undisturbed in their beds, oblivious of the flurry occurring right outside their windows. The castle was quiet, the winds had abated, the stars withdrawn; the snow fell softly and without a sound and yet, in the peaceful stillness, the spirits of Castle Deverill were restless; they sensed something terrible in the calm. And then, just as the first light of dawn glowed pink in the eastern sky, one of the men got up.

He dressed, taking care not to wake his sleeping wife. He buttoned his shirt and arranged his tie. He slipped into his jacket and shoes, making sure that his socks were pulled up beneath his trousers. His breathing was calm, his hand steady as he reached beneath the bed for the rope he had put there earlier. Without hesitation he crept to the door. He turned the knob without a squeak and stepped into the corridor. With the stealth of a cat he crept through the castle and out into the cold.

It was a beautiful dawn. The pink glow was turning golden right before his eyes as the sun heralded another day, cracking like a duck's egg onto the sky. He walked deliberately across the lawn, leaving a trail of indigo-colored footprints in the snow. The skies were clear now, the last of the stars peeping out from where the clouds had drifted away. Yet he was unmoved by it. He had a purpose and nothing would distract him from it. Neither the loveliness of the dawn nor the people he was going to leave behind. He was calm, resolute and relieved.

When he reached the tree, which was marked with a plaque that said *Planted by Barton Deverill 1662,* he climbed it with ease. He sat astride the branch that extended parallel to the ground and set about tying the rope around its girth. Making a noose was easy, he had enjoyed making knots as a boy. He pulled a flask out of his pocket and took a swig. The alcohol burned his throat and warmed his belly, giving him the last sense of pleasure he would experience on this earth. He didn't allow himself to feel sad or regretful: *that* might have prevented him from carrying out his plan. He thought of what he would have to face were he to continue living and knew, without any doubt, that death was preferable. Death was the only way out.

He put the noose around his neck and carefully rose to his feet with the slow agility of a tightrope walker. Pressing his hand against the trunk he held his balance. He lifted his eyes and gazed upon the castle one last time. The rising sun threw her rays upon the stone walls and like flames they slowly moved upward, consuming the purple shadows as they went. Soon it would be morning and the place would come to life. But now it was still and silent and ghostly somehow in the snow. He closed his eyes, lifted his hand off the tree and let himself fall. The rope gave a soft squeak as it jarred, then a rhythmic creaking as the body swayed a few feet off the ground.

A spray of crows took to the skies, their loud caws echoing through the woods with the eerie cry of the Banshee.

Chapter 18

Charlotte awoke to find Harry's side of the bed empty. She put her hand on his pillow. It was cold. He must have been up for a while. She clenched her fist. He was so distant these days, so aloof. She wondered whether their marriage would ever heal. Sometimes she thought that, after what she had witnessed, it simply couldn't. She dressed and went downstairs to the dining room where Digby, Celia, Beatrice and Maud were already having breakfast. The room smelled of fried bacon and her stomach gave a gentle rumble, although she didn't have much of an appetite nowadays.

"Ah, Charlotte," said Digby, smiling at her warmly. "I trust you slept well."

"Papa, the beds are the best money can buy. Of course she slept well," said Celia.

Charlotte glanced around the room for Harry. She had been so consumed by her own unhappiness that she hadn't given any thought to *his*. She wondered whether he'd gone out for an early walk in the snow and her heart lurched with remorse. He'd been spending a lot of time on his own lately.

"Isn't the snow marvelous!" said Beatrice.

"It's a sign of luck," said Celia with a contented sigh. "I'm feeling very lucky at the moment. This has been the best Christmas ever and the party we're going to enjoy on New Year's Eve will signal a prosperous year for all of us."

Digby raised an eyebrow. He didn't think 1930 was going to be a prosperous year for anyone, least of all himself. He shoveled a forkful of egg and toast into his mouth and chewed ponderously. Maud, who could always be relied on to be the voice of doom, added, "The country has just suffered the worst financial crisis in history. I can't imagine anyone is feeling particularly lucky right now, except you, Celia."

Celia rolled her eyes and was about to say something she'd regret when her mother thankfully came to her defense. "I think we are jolly lucky to be here, in this beautiful place, on such a lovely snowy morning. I don't know about you, but I'm going to go for a walk after breakfast to enjoy it."

There was a brief lull in the conversation as Victoria and Eric wandered in for breakfast, followed by Stoke, who looked as if he had given his sweeping white mustache a good brush. Amid the "Good mornings" and the courteous inquiries after the quality of their sleep, the butler appeared with a note on a tray. He hesitated a moment, unsure of whom to give it to. "What is it, O'Sullivan?" Celia asked.

"A letter, madam. It was on the table in the hall. But it isn't addressed to anybody."

"Well, bring it here," she instructed, waving her white fingers. She opened the envelope and pulled out a little typed card. As she read it her forehead creased in bafflement and her pretty lips pouted. "*I'm sorry.*"

"Darling?" said Beatrice.

"No, that's all it says: *I'm sorry,*" said Celia.

"Well, who's it from?" Digby demanded.

Celia turned over the note and then did the same with the envelope. "There's no name anywhere. Is this some kind of joke?" she looked from face to face crossly. "Because it isn't at all funny."

Charlotte burst into tears. "It's Harry," she choked. She pushed out her chair and stood with her hands at her throat, gasping for air. "It's Harry. I know it is. He's . . . he's . . ." She began to sob uncontrollably. Beatrice glanced uneasily at her daughter, who was staring at Charlotte in horror. Digby coughed into his napkin while Victoria looked appalled; this sort of emotional outburst simply wasn't done.

Maud blanched. "What's going on? What's happened to Harry? Charlotte, for goodness' sake, make some sense!"

Charlotte tried to pull herself together. "He . . . he wasn't in bed this morning. I don't know where he is."

"Let's not panic," said Eric, putting his plate of eggs, tomatoes and toast on the table and sitting down. "He's probably gone for a walk. It's a lovely morning."

"He's done something stupid. I can feel it," said Charlotte. "He's written the note and wandered off. I know he has."

"Then we must find him," said Digby, throwing his napkin on the table. "We must all search the grounds for Harry and no one is to resume breakfast until we find him."

Eric and Victoria sighed impatiently. "If ever there was a

storm in a teacup," said Victoria, but Maud was already making for the door. Stoke remained in his chair, watching in bewilderment as everyone left the room. In his late eighties he was hard of hearing and had consequently missed the entire conversation.

There was a terrible sense of urgency as news of Harry's disappearance and the cryptic note he'd typed spread swiftly around the castle. Digby put on his boots and coat and strode into the snow. He saw the footprints at once and set off in pursuit, a feeling of foreboding suddenly making him go quite weak in the knees. Beatrice, Maud, Celia and Charlotte ran after him, shouting for Harry at the top of their voices. The crows watched from the treetops, their black eyes shining with knowing.

"What on earth is he sorry about?" Maud asked Charlotte as they hurried after Digby. "I wish Digby wouldn't walk so fast. I'm sure this is nothing more than a false alarm. Harry's going to feel very silly when he comes back to find the entire castle looking for him."

Charlotte couldn't begin to tell Harry's mother about the night of Celia's Summer Ball. What if Harry felt his life wasn't worth living without Boysie? *Oh, God, what have I done?* She began to cry again. What if she had driven him to his death? Silently she prayed to any God who would listen to return her beloved Harry to her in one piece: *If he comes back I shall forgive him*, she promised, trudging through the snow. *He can see Boysie as much as he likes, as long as he's alive.*

Suddenly Digby spun around and began marching back toward them. His face was as red as a berry, his arms outstretched as if he was hoping to shield them from something he didn't want them to see. "Ladies, please go back to the castle," he said and his voice was fiercely commanding. Celia was suddenly assaulted by a wave of nausea. Behind her father, swinging from a tree, she could see the body of a man. She put a hand to her mouth and gasped. "Please. Beatrice, take the girls back to the castle," he repeated, more forcefully. In any other circumstance they would have done his bidding. But Celia, propelled by a sense of terror and dread, stubbornly strode past him, thrusting him out of the way with such vigor that he nearly fell over. Digby regained his balance and reached out a desperate hand to restrain her, but she was already running through the snow, her vision blinded by tears, her breathing labored and rasping. There, hanging pale and still like a sack of flour, was Archie.

Celia threw her arms around his legs in a vain attempt to lift him. A low moan escaped her throat as she struggled beneath the dead weight of her husband. At once her father was pulling at her, trying to unpeel her hands. His voice was soothing, encouraging, but all Celia could hear was the blood throbbing in her temples and the groans that rose up from her chest and were expelled in wild, unnatural sounds that were alien to her.

Beatrice was sobbing, Maud staring in shock at the dreadful scene unfolding before her, while Charlotte collapsed onto her knees in the snow and wept with relief. And then, amid the turmoil, Harry strode into view. They all turned to him in astonishment and Harry's eyes shifted to the limp body hanging from the noose and to Celia who was still clinging on to his legs, unaware that no amount of lifting could save him. He was long dead. Charlotte scrambled to her feet and fell against his chest. "Oh, Harry! I thought it was you!" she howled.

Harry wrapped his arms around his wife, but he couldn't take his eyes off Archie's blue face and broken neck. Slowly the full horror sank in.

At last Digby, with the help of Harry and Eric, who had been drawn to the scene by the commotion, managed to prize Celia off the body and take her back to the castle. Digby telephoned the Garda and the doctor, then he called the Hunting Lodge to inform Bertie of the dreadful news. "Good God!" Bertie swore. "What on earth made him do it?"

Digby sighed. "There's only one reason why a man in Archie's position would take his own life and that's money," he said. "I've got a horrible feeling that Celia is in for a rough ride."

"I'm coming right over," said Bertie, putting down the receiver.

It wasn't long before the entire family had assembled once again in the drawing room, muttering in low voices: "He had everything, why would he throw it all away?" "Did anyone notice he was unhappy?" "I don't think I'd ever seen Archie so content." "Appearances can be deceptive." "He must have been hiding something terrible." "Poor Celia, what's she going to do without him?"

Celia sat by the fire, wrapped in a blanket, drinking a glass of sherry. The glass trembled in her hand and her lips were quivering in spite of the warmth of the room. She was a pitiful sight, sobbing quietly. The woman who only moments before had been commenting on her good fortune was now grieving the loss of it. "He's ruined Christmas," she sniveled. "He's ruined my New Year's Eve party. How *could* he, Mama?"

Beatrice, who had drawn her daughter against her bosom and was stroking her hair as if she were a little girl again, turned to her older daughters and said, "She's in shock. Poor child." Leona and Vivien nodded, feeling guilty now for the animosity they had felt toward their younger sister who had appeared to have it all.

Kitty arrived with Robert. She flew to her cousin where she knelt at her feet and took her hands, squeezing them gently. "My darling Celia, I'm so sorry," she said.

Celia lifted her swollen eyes and smiled through a blur of tears. "We were so happy," she said numbly. "Archie was so happy. Castle Deverill and his family were his greatest achievements. He was so proud of it all. Why, when he was celebrating his success, did he feel the desire to run away? I don't understand. How could he do it to *me*?"

"He typed a note that said simply *I'm sorry*," Beatrice informed her. "It wasn't addressed to anybody. Isn't that an odd thing to do? Why didn't he write it in his hand and why didn't he explain himself?"

"He won't have been in his right mind," said Kitty wisely. "He won't have been thinking about you or his children. When people are that unhappy they think only of themselves."

"He didn't seem unhappy," said Leona.

"He seemed very happy," added Vivien.

"But he's left me a widow!" Celia stated sadly. She stopped crying as if the thought had only just then occurred to her. "I'm a widow. My children are fatherless. I am alone." And she was overcome by another wave of sobbing.

"You're not alone, darling," said Beatrice, pulling her deeper into her bosom. "You have all of us and we'll never leave you."

Kitty pulled a bag of green leaves out of her pocket and

thrust them in Beatrice's hand. "This is Adeline's cannabis," she told her. "Infuse it in tea. It will calm her down."

Augusta filled the doorway in her Victorian black dress and black shawl and stood for a long moment leaning on her stick and gazing around the room imperiously, searching for her granddaughter. When at last her eyes found her in her mother's arms by the fire, she waded through the throng that parted for her deferentially and ordered her husband, as she passed him, to bring her a very large glass of brandy "at once." She approached the sofa where Leona and Vivien were sitting and flicked her bejeweled fingers so that the two women vacated it at her command. Their grandmother dropped into the cushions and seemed to spread like a chocolate pudding until there was no space for anyone else on either side of her. Kitty, who was still at Celia's feet, moved herself to the club fender, where she duly sat alongside Leona and Vivien like one of a trio of birds on a perch.

"Well, my dear, this is a tragedy none of us could have foreseen," Augusta began gravely. "He was much too young to die. One never knows when the Grim Reaper is going to gather one, but to gather *oneself* is surely an act of the most selfish kind."

"Augusta," said Beatrice in a warning tone.

"I cannot hide my feelings, Beatrice. This young man has done a wicked, wicked thing. Celia does not deserve this. She has only ever been a good wife. Believe me, I have had moments in my life when I would rather not have woken up—but I would never have burdened my family with the shame or the misery. What on earth was he thinking?"

"We just don't know," said Beatrice, trying to be patient. She wished everyone would leave so that she and Celia could be alone together.

"Money," said Augusta with a snort. "A man only goes to such extremes over a woman or money. We can safely assume that it was not on account of a woman."

Celia sniffed. "He had pots of money, Grandma," she said.

"Well, we shall see," Augusta sniffed. She ran her eyes over all the expensive things in the room. "*This* just might have been his undoing," she said tactlessly, as her granddaughter dissolved once again into sobs.

The doctor arrived and Celia was taken upstairs by Kitty and her mother, where she was given valerian drops to calm her and put to bed, as Adeline had been the night Hubert was killed in the fire. "We're cursed," said Celia drowsily.

"We're not cursed," Kitty reassured her, sitting on the side of her bed and taking her hand. "Adeline used to say that I was a child of Mars and that my life would be full of conflict."

"Then I must be a child of Mars too," said Celia.

"You sleep now. Archie is all right where he is. You have to trust me on that. You are the one we need to look after now."

"Is he really all right? He's not still hanging from that tree?" Celia's eyes shone with fresh tears.

"He escaped that body before he even knew what was happening."

"But he's not going to rot in Hell . . . ?"

"God is love, Celia." She stroked the hair off her forehead. "And souls can't rot." She smiled tenderly at her cousin and remembered the long talks about life after death that she used to have with Adeline in her little sitting room that smelled of turf fire and lilac. "Archie was not a bad man. I suspect he took his life because he couldn't face the future. It is not a sin to lack courage. He'll be embraced by loving souls and shown the way home, I promise you." Celia's eyes grew heavy. She tried to speak but the words were lost on her tongue as she retreated into slumber.

Kitty returned to the drawing room. Everyone was talking in normal tones now that Celia was no longer in the room. "We will have to inform Archie's family," Bertie was saying, standing in a huddle with the other men.

"That's a responsibility I would not wish on my worst enemy," said Victoria from the sofa, where she was sitting beside her mother. She had lit a cigarette, which was placed in its elegant Bakelite holder, and was looking at Augusta, who had subsided on the sofa opposite and fallen asleep, her chins sinking into her bosom like a collapsing soufflé.

"I don't think I'll ever recover from the sight," said Maud weakly, sipping her second glass of sherry. "To think that might have been Harry."

"It wasn't Harry," said Victoria reasonably.

"But Charlotte put the fear of God into me," Maud continued. "What on earth was that all about, do you think?"

Victoria drew on her cigarette holder. "I haven't a clue. Perhaps they'd had a fight."

"Men don't write suicide notes because of a petty quarrel," said Maud. "I hope they're not in trouble. Our family can't cope with any more scandal." She looked up as Bertie took the place on the sofa beside her.

"I'm sorry you were frightened," he said softly. "Charlotte feels very bad for having scared you."

"Good," said Maud crisply. "Because she did. Silly girl, making a fuss about nothing."

"I suppose Harry's been suffering in silence," he said.

"Suffering? About what?" Maud asked.

"Losing his home. We've all had to put on a good show, but I dare say it hasn't been easy for any of us."

Maud dropped her gaze into her sherry. The sharp edges of her face softened a little as she let down her guard. Leona and Vivien had moved to the other end of the room and Augusta was still asleep, so they were alone, just the three of them. "No, I'm sure you're right," she said. "It hasn't been easy for anyone. Not even for me, who never really loved this place like you all do."

"That's what I thought." The tenderness in Bertie's voice took her by surprise.

"For all my stubbornness I mind dreadfully that Harry won't ever really be Lord Deverill of Ballinakelly as he ought to be, by right. The title's meaningless without the castle."

"I mind too, Mama," Victoria agreed. She grinned raffishly through the smoke. "We've all been very brave." She didn't feel it polite to add that, if the castle had been as comfortable before the fire as it was now, she would never have been so keen to leave it.

"I'm happy that you decided to come back," said Bertie, gazing at his wife with appreciation. "I'm only sorry that your stay has been marred by tragedy."

"We've endured a great deal of tragedy," said Maud, lifting her chin to show that she wasn't going to allow another to devastate her. "But we've survived. We'll continue as we always have. You Deverills are made of stronger stuff. I'm not, but you drag me along in your slipstream and that helps." She gave him a small smile. "Thank you, Bertie. Your concern is touching."

Bertie smiled back and Victoria wondered whether the embers of their marriage hadn't entirely been extinguished as she had thought.

Kitty's eyes strayed to one of the windows, where she could see a group of Gardai in their navy uniforms and peak caps carrying Archie's body across the lawn wrapped in a sheet. "Where's Digby?" Kitty asked as Robert joined her.

"In the library talking to the inspector. I dare say we'll find out shortly why he killed himself," said Robert. "He might have left a kinder note," he added. "Celia has no explanation, nothing."

"That's because he was too ashamed to articulate it."

"About what? Do you know something, Kitty?"

"I suspect he's lost all his money, like so many have. He couldn't bring himself to tell Celia that they have nothing left. I can't imagine why else he'd want to end his life. I'd put my money—the little I have of it—on shame."

"Good Lord. I hope she won't have to sell Castle Deverill."

"I hope not. If she does, then we're all in trouble."

Robert took her hand and smiled affectionately. "Whatever happens, Kitty, we'll be all right. We'll weather anything that's thrown at us because we're united and strong."

HARRY LATER FOUND Charlotte in their bedroom. She was sitting at the dressing table, brushing her long strawberry blond hair with a silver brush. "I was wondering where you had got to. I'm sorry. I should have been more attentive."

"Come and sit down," she said, replacing the brush on the dressing table and turning around on her stool. "I have something important I want to say."

Harry pulled up a chair and sat facing her. He dreaded that she was going to request a divorce. He didn't think his mother would survive divorce, especially after the horrors of today.

Charlotte gazed at him and he noticed that her blue eyes had softened like water in springtime. They were no longer frozen with resentment but glowing with warmth. "I thought it was *you* who had hanged yourself today," she said quietly.

"Oh my darling. Do I look so miserable?"

She smiled sadly. "Yes, you do. When I saw the empty bed and then heard what was in the note, I assumed that you had gone and done something stupid. So I made a bargain with God."

"What sort of bargain?"

"I told him that if you were alive I would forgive you and let you see Boysie again."

"Charlotte—" he began.

"Don't interrupt. I've thought about this a great deal. I love you, Harry. I wouldn't have been so hurt if I didn't love you. I'm sure that you love me too, in your own way."

"I do," he replied.

"But I know you don't love me in the way that you love Boysie. It's not conventional, but it's not for me to judge you. Love is a wonderful thing, wherever it flows." She looked down at her hands, which were folded neatly in her lap. "I don't know whether Deirdre is aware of how Boysie feels about *you*. Perhaps she knows and it is *I* who have been naïve. But I'm not going to be naïve any longer. I love Boysie too. I'm unhappy that he is not in our life anymore. I miss him."

"Oh Charlotte . . ." Harry unfolded her hands and took

them in his. "I do love you. Do you think there's room in our marriage for the three of us?"

She laughed and blinked away the tears, all except for one, which glistened in her long eyelashes. "I think there is," she said.

The irony was, that in that moment of magnanimity, Harry realized that he loved his wife more than he had known.

Chapter 19

New York, 1929

Bridie's happiness was complete. She was engaged to the dashing Count Cesare di Marcantonio and living in a city drunk on optimism, opportunity and rising wealth. America shared her confidence. President Hoover foresaw a day when poverty would be wiped out; economists defined a "new plateau" of prosperity and predicted that the country's affluence was here to stay; ordinary people believed they couldn't go wrong buying stocks and everyone, from the shoeshine boy to the wealthiest men in the city, played the Stock Market. Bridie sang along to Irving Berlin's "Blue Skies" with the other New Yorkers who believed they had at last reached the pot of gold at the end of the rainbow, and she spent with the extravagance of someone who believes that pot to be bottomless. She ignored Beaumont Williams's warnings of an imminent crash, but Beaumont, so right about most things, was right about this.

The Crash, when it happened, was devastating, falling as it did from such a great height. Bridie listened to the wireless and read the newspapers and her first thoughts were for herself. She never wanted to return to the poverty of her youth. "How does this affect me?" she asked Mr. Williams as she settled into the familiar leather chair in his office in front of the fire, which had not been lit on account of the warm autumn weather.

"It doesn't," he replied, crossing his legs to reveal a slim ankle and a crimson sock. "I took the liberty of instructing your broker to buy you out before the panic-selling," he explained casually, as if his ingenuity were but a trifle. "You might recall that I have been expecting this for months. Stocks have been grossly overvalued for years and I decided you should take your profits. Rothschild wisely said, 'Leave the last ten percent to someone else.' You're richer than ever, Mrs. Lockwood." Indeed with unemployment rising, farms failing and automobile sales falling he wasn't the only person to sense the oncoming of disaster, but he was certainly one of the few to act in time to avoid it.

Bridie flushed with gratitude. "Why, Mr. Williams, I don't know what to say . . ."

"Your husband, Mr. Lockwood, was a shrewd man. He invested much of your fortune in gold. I predict that the gold market will recover." He opened a leather book and rested it on his knee. Then he pulled his spectacles out of his breast pocket and settled them on the bridge of his nose. "I suggest we arrange a meeting with your broker, but in the meantime I requested that he send round your portfolio to put your mind at rest. As you will see, Mrs. Lockwood, your money has been wisely invested in short-term bonds to the U.S. government, in prime property and land. I am not one to heap praise upon myself, but in this instance, I might concede that I have, indeed, been canny."

Bridie listened as Mr. Williams ran through figures and funds she barely understood. The only words that mattered to her were "gains," "interest" and "the bottom line." She watched this self-contained man, with his round belly fastened behind a pristine gray waistcoat, his clean, tidy hands and manicured nails, closely shaven face and shiny black hair and felt a flood of gratitude that she was in the care of such a sensible man. If it hadn't been for Mr. Williams, where would she be now, she wondered. What she didn't ask herself was where Mr. Williams would be without *her*—his prosperity, and he was most certainly prosperous, was more closely linked to hers than she had ever imagined.

"As you can see, Mrs. Lockwood, you have nothing to worry about. New York can crash about your ears, but you will still be one of the few people left standing."

"I am very much in your debt," she said, watching him close the book and place it on the table in front of him. She lifted her left hand and admired the diamond ring that glittered there.

"That's a very fine ring," said Mr. Williams. "May I?" He reached for her hand, drew it toward him and held it in the light. He knew a thing or two about diamonds and he could see, even without a loupe, that this one was of poor quality. "When are you going to tie the knot?"

"We haven't set a date," Bridie told him, her face glowing with happiness. "It's all happened so fast. I need to catch my breath. Cesare wants to marry as soon as possible."

"Does he indeed," said Mr. Williams, rubbing his chin thoughtfully. But Bridie was too excited to hear the concern in his voice. "Might I give you a word of advice?" he asked. Considering the amount of money he had saved her she didn't feel she was in any position to refuse.

"Of course," she replied.

"Take your time. There's no rush to marry again. Get to know the man. Meet his friends and family. After all, getting *into* marriage is much easier than getting *out* of it."

Bridie smiled and shook her head vigorously. "Oh, I know what it looks like, Mr. Williams. Of course I do. I don't know anything about him, do I? But I followed my head with Walter and look where it got me. This time I will follow my heart. Life is not worth living without love. I know that now. I can be as rich as a Rockefeller, but if I don't have love I have nothing. I do believe I have found my soulmate."

Beaumont observed her keenly. She was quite a different woman to the one she had been two years ago when she was pining for her Irishman and searching for solace in gin. Her cheeks were now flushed with the blush of a first love, her eyes shone with good health and optimism, her demeanor was both confident and satisfied, and Beaumont realized that it didn't matter whether this count was genuine or not, because Bridie loved him. After all she had been through: a life of drudgery in the service of Mrs. Grimsby, marriage to the aged Walter Lockwood, widowed at twenty-five, deserted by the Irishman she believed she loved—and those were only the facts he knew, what shadows lurked in her deeper past could only be guessed at—he realized that she deserved a taste of happiness.

"I wish you luck, Mrs. Lockwood," he said, settling back into his chair.

"Thank you, Mr. Williams," she replied and because she

was so intoxicated with infatuation, she was oblivious to Mr. Williams's reservations. However, Beaumont Williams was not a passive man. When there was something that troubled him he wasted no time in getting to the bottom of it.

Count Cesare di Marcantonio was an enigma. If Bridie knew little about him, his friends and acquaintances in New York knew even less. But Beaumont Williams had contacts in both Italy and Argentina and after a gentle digging in the right places, he was able to throw some light into the Count's murky corners. "He was born in Abruzzo, somewhere in Italy," Elaine told Bridie over lunch in Lucio's, a small restaurant on Fifth Avenue where the owner, a bearded Italian with a gift for making women feel special, always gave them the best table by the window. "But his family is really very aristocratic. His mother is a princess whose family is descended from the family of one of the popes, Barberini I think they're called, but I can't for the life of me remember which pope he was. Their names all sound the same, don't you think?"

"Go on," said Bridie, elegant in a fashionable cloche hat, olive-green dress and a string of shiny pearls that hung down to her waist.

"No one knows exactly why, but the family moved to Argentina when your count was a child. It sounds a little dubious if you ask me. They simply vanished into the night. I suspect it had something to do with owing money. Anyhow, his father is one of those men who makes a fortune, then loses it just as quickly, only to make it again. He made his first fortune in beef, then in industry, investing in railways. He bought estates and cattle, exporting the beef around the world. That's what Beaumont found out."

"And now?" Bridie asked.

Elaine shrugged. "His father, Count Benvenuto, is a notorious character in Buenos Aires. He lives the high life, takes risks investing in pipe dreams and squanders his money on his mistresses and gambling. His reputation is not entirely snow-white. Who's to say whether he's managed to hold on to his fortune or whether he's never really had one. Beaumont suspects the latter and wishes to warn you that not everything about your count is, as we say in New York, kosher." Bridie put down her knife and fork and looked thoughtful for a moment. Elaine felt bad and rushed in to soothe her doubts. "I'm not saying your Cesare is after your money, Bridget," which was exactly what she *was* saying. "But he surrounds himself with rich people who are happy to absorb him into their world. He's undoubtedly charming, entertaining and no one loves a foreign title more than the Americans." She sniffed apologetically and glanced at her friend a little fearfully. "We thought it better that you know *before* you tie the knot."

But Bridie smiled with indulgence, as if she were a parent who had just been told of her child's latest antics by a worried teacher. "I don't care about his family history, Elaine. I don't care where he comes from. God knows that *I* come from nothing. What have I got to be proud of: a farmhouse that was sinking into the mud, a few cows and barely enough food to sustain us? I didn't own a pair of shoes until I went to work at the castle. Cesare can be penniless and destitute and descended from peasants for all I care. It makes no difference to the way I feel about him. If his father's gambled all his money away, I have enough for the two of us. If he's a womanizer, I'll make him faithful. If he's an adventurer I'll give him the adventure of a lifetime. Love will carry us like the wind and our feet will never touch the ground." And there was nothing Elaine could say after that.

Bridie closed her ears and her eyes to Count Cesare's obvious faults. To her there had never lived a man more handsome and romantic and kind. Love blinded her to his arrogance and to his shameless pursuit of the rich and powerful, to his vanity and his unwavering belief in his own success. She gazed into his sea-green eyes and felt the light of his adoration reach the darkest parts of her being, reviving them like neglected gardens that are suddenly bathed in sunshine, bringing them into blossom and flower. She didn't need gifts; she needed love. And Cesare had enough of that to quench her most voracious thirst.

Cesare's charisma was so bright that it reduced to ashes any residual feelings of affection that she had for Jack O'Leary. It consumed her longing for Ireland and even quelled her yearning for her son. It raised her out of her past and carried her into a present moment where she believed that nothing and no one could ever hurt her again. Cesare would look after her now and she gladly gave him her heart. *Take it,* she told him silently as he sank his face into her neck, *and do with it what you will because I am yours and always will be.*

The wedding date was set for May, but as it was Bridie's second wedding, Marigold Reynolds had offered to host the ceremony and subsequent party in the lavish gardens of her house in Southampton. As the undisputed society queen, Marigold was only too happy to arrange another sumptuous event to which she could invite the newest stars of film, theater, media, society and sport. The Wall Street Crash might have curtailed many people's spending, but it had done little to curtail hers.

The invitations were engraved on the finest card, written in the most beautiful calligraphy and hand-delivered to the three hundred guests by one of the Reynoldses' chauffeurs.

As America descended into the most shocking economic decline in its history Bridie and Count Cesare enjoyed the happiest of engagements. They were the toast of New York and most of society welcomed a respite from the depressing news that filled the newspapers and radio waves. They began to look for a new house, which wasn't difficult as prices plummeted and those who had suddenly, from one day to the next, lost their fortunes found themselves having to sell their homes. Bridie found herself spoiled for choice.

"My darling, I need to speak with you," said Cesare, taking her hand across the dinner table in Jack and Charlie's 21 restaurant on West 52nd Street, a famous speakeasy with a secret system of levers which, in the event of a raid, tipped the shelves of the bar, sending the bottles of liquor crashing into the city's sewers.

Bridie looked concerned. "What about?"

"Money," he replied, bathing her in Latin love and shameless affection. His eyes were moist and tender, and Bridie squeezed his hand encouragingly. "My father is being difficult," he explained. "I have asked him for money but—"

In that accent, with those eyes, from those lips, money didn't sound vulgar or suspicious. It was just a gorgeous request from a gorgeous man and she wished to satisfy him immediately.

"My darling, dearest Cesare," Bridie interrupted. "I have money enough for the two of us. We don't need your father's money. I will talk to Mr. Williams, my attorney, and arrange for an account to be set up in your name and for money to be put directly into it the moment we are married. We will share everything."

Cesare tried to disguise his relief with a look of horror. "But Count Cesare di Marcantonio, descendant of the family of Pope Urban VIII, cannot accept money from a woman. It is a husband's duty to look after his wife."

Bridie held his hand tighter. "I came from nothing, Cesare. I began in Ireland as Bridie Doyle, a maid to a grand lady who lived in a castle. I came here to make a new start and worked for a wealthy old woman who died and left me a great fortune. I have been lucky. Please let me share my luck with you. I love you, Cesare. You've made me happier than I could ever have believed possible."

"It is against my nature. I cannot accept."

"Well, it is not against mine. I have suffered, God knows I have suffered, but you have restored my belief in love."

"I will write to my father again . . ."

"If you wish. But let's eat and enjoy our evening and talk no more about money."

He threaded his fingers through hers and his eyes fell heavily upon her. "I cannot wait to make love to you," he said with a smile that snatched her breath. "You are a beautiful woman and you are soon to be mine. I will take my time and explore every inch of you." He lowered his voice and leaned closer. "And when I am finished, I will do it all over again." And Bridie fell dreamily into his gaze and thought that she would buy him the world, he only had to ask.

In May the spring sunshine brought the fruit trees into blossom and warm breezes carried their pink and white petals through the streets like confetti. Yet, in spite of the change of season, the mood in the city was desperate. With growing unemployment and poverty, the atmosphere was somber, anxious and simmering with anger. However, the Great Depression hadn't reached the Reynoldses' house in Southampton. On the first Saturday of the month the road to their house was congested with chauffeur-driven Cadillacs, Chryslers and Bugattis bringing the grand and celebrated guests to the wedding. Among them were Beaumont and Elaine Williams, the only true friends Bridie had in New York. Everyone else was glitter and sparkle—people she knew would melt away at the first sign of her decline. But she didn't care, for today she was marrying the man she loved.

She wrote a brief letter to tell her family that she was marrying again but omitted to mention his aristocratic title. She didn't want them assuming that she had married him just for that. She posted the letter, then forgot all about them. She was so detached from her old life that she barely gave them a thought. Distance didn't dim her memory, infatuation did. While she was in Count Cesare's brilliance the shadows of her past could not reach her. Dressed in an ivory Chanel dress, covered in pearls and beads and sparkling in the sunlight, she walked down the aisle of white roses to where the manifestation of all her dreams stood waiting to take possession of her. Mr. Williams stood in for her father and handed her to the Count, while Elaine walked ahead as her maid of honor. Marigold sat at the front, satisfied that all the most prominent writers, actors and socialites from New York were there. But Bridie saw only Cesare. She took his outstretched hand and stepped in beside him. The priest read the vows, which they both repeated, and then it was over and the party began. Everyone drank champagne and ate from the bountiful feast and danced beneath the flower moon that rose over Long Island, pink in the light of the setting sun.

Cesare held his bride and bent his head to kiss her. The celebrations continued around them but they were a small island, rising out of the revelers who seemed to have forgotten that the party had anything to do with them. "My darling wife," he said softly. "You are now Contessa di Marcantonio, wife of Conte Cesare di Marcantonio who is descended from the family of Pope Urban VIII, Maffeo Barberini. The Barberini family coat of arms is three bees. I would like you to wear *this,* because now *you* are a Barberini too and I want the world to know it." He opened his hand to reveal a small gold bee brooch. Bridie gazed at it in awe. The magnitude of this man's ancestry made her light-headed and she swayed. Cesare slipped his fingers beneath the fabric of her dress, just beneath her collarbone, and attached the bee. "Beautiful," he said, leaving his fingers resting against her skin. Bridie saw from the way he was looking at her that he cherished her. She understood from the sleepy look in his eyes that he wanted her.

They crept away as soon as they could and closed the bedroom door behind them. The room was semi-dark, the sound of music muted by the closed windows and curtains, the air thick with the sweet smell of narcissi that Marigold had put in their room for their wedding night. Gently Cesare unhooked the back of her dress until it floated down her body, landing in a silky puddle at her feet. Bridie stood in her slip and panties, the sheen of her bare skin standing out against the silk of her lingerie. He caressed her shoulders with a light touch, then her neck, then her face, reaching behind her head to unpin her hair, scrunching it in his hands as it was released in glossy waves to fall about her body. She trembled as he lifted her slip and pulled down her panties. She stood naked before him and he admired her with lustful eyes.

Bridie had enjoyed many men, some of whom had given her satisfaction while others had been a disappointment, but Cesare took the time to pleasure her in a way that none of her lovers ever had—and he knew things that made even Bridie, with her unabashed approach to sexual gratification, blush. True to his word he explored every inch of her body, and when he was finished, he went over it once more. He brought Bridie to great heights of exultation. She moaned and murmured, sighed and finally wept as she discovered a carnal heaven made possible by her skillful and masterful lover.

If Cesare felt emasculated by Bridie's money he didn't show it. On the contrary, he lived up to his name conquering her like a sexual Julius Caesar. He was as adept in the bedroom as any man could be. The new Countess di Marcantonio relinquished control and let him take her by the hand, and *that* gave her the most exquisite pleasure of all.

Chapter 20

Connecticut

When Pam Wallace discovered that she was pregnant in the summer of 1927 she went straight to church, threw herself on her knees and thanked God for his divine intervention, for surely such a miracle, longed for and yet so elusive, had come directly from Him. She wept with joy, vowed to show her thanks with acts of charity and kindness (and never say a mean thing about anyone ever again), then hurried home to tell her husband the wonderful news.

Martha didn't know what all the fuss was about. It was as if something extraordinary had happened. Something *other-worldly*. Suddenly her mother was treated as if she was so fragile that any sudden movement might break her. She glided about the house slowly, like an invalid, but one enormously satisfied with her sickness. She moved from table to chair, chair to stair,

stair to door, making sure that her hand always had somewhere to settle in order to steady herself, just in case she tripped, and everyone did everything for her, telling her over and over again to rest "for the baby." Larry bought her flowers and jewelry in pretty red boxes, and even her father, Raymond Tobin, visited, armed with gifts, offering reconciliation. The whole house smelled like a florist's, which excited Martha far more than the thought of a baby because she adored flowers. She hovered over the petals like a bee drunk on nectar, marveling at the vibrant colors and inhaling the sweet perfume. Everyone patted her on the head and told her how lucky she was to be getting a little brother or sister and Martha secretly hoped that the baby would stay inside her mama's tummy forever, because she was very happy on her own.

The only member of the family who took the news badly, as if it were a personal affront, was Joan, who had relished the fact that Pam's child was adopted and by consequence "strange." Now that her sister-in-law was going to give birth to a genuine Wallace, Joan's competitiveness made her irritable. "I wonder if Martha will be Ma's favorite grandchild after Pam's baby is born," she said to Dorothy as they wandered around a fashionable boutique, browsing the summer dresses.

"I'm afraid I think Martha will be all but ignored once the baby arrives, poor darling," Dorothy replied. "Ted is a tribal man, for him blood is thicker than *everything*, and Diana will dote on the new arrival, because to have her own child is what Pam has wanted from the very beginning."

She has always had everything she wants, Joan thought sourly. *How galling that she's now going to get* this. Joan pulled a crimson dress off the rail and stood in front of the long mirror, holding it against her. "I have nothing against Martha. She's a child and she's very . . . sweet." It took some effort to utter the word "sweet." "I hope it's a boy. All men want sons and Larry's no different from anyone else. He'll be terribly disappointed if it's a girl." She cocked her head. "What do you think?"

"That color looks stunning," Dorothy gushed. "Why don't you try it on?"

"You don't think it clashes with my hair? I don't usually wear red."

"Oh Joan, you can get away with anything."

"That *is* true, of course. You don't think Pam will see me in it and want one too. Crimson is a better color for her and I don't want her showing me up."

"Really, Joan, you are infinitely more stylish than Pam. You know what they say about copying?"

"That it's the greatest form of flattery." She sighed. "Well, I'm not flattered, just bored. I've endured years of having her echoing my every fashion choice." She smiled with satisfaction. "At least she'll be in maternity dresses for the foreseeable future!"

Martha did not feel ignored during her mother's pregnancy because Pam was careful to include her daughter in every stage of the baby's growth. She encouraged Martha to put her hand on her belly to feel the baby moving inside. She reassured her that when babies come into the world they bring their own love with them so that there is always plenty to go around. "I won't love you less because I love this child," she told her. "I'll just have double the amount of love." Although Martha was too young to be conscious of her emotions, she began to feel secure in her mother's liking. For the first time in her life her mother's eye was not full of scrutiny and apprehension and the sucking in of her affection faded into an unpleasant memory so that, over the months before the baby was born, Martha ceased to look out for it.

Mrs. Goodwin noticed Martha's growing confidence. She was like a spring bud that had just begun to open, revealing the delicate pink and white petals inside. The atmosphere in the house became light and soft, like early evening sunshine. Pam was happy all the time. She lay on a daybed in the conservatory reading books and magazines and talking on the telephone to her friends. Ladies came to visit and drank iced tea. They shared the gossip and listened to Pam's plans for the decoration of the new baby's nursery. Martha was brought in like a little show pony and the women admired her floral frocks and commented on how much she had grown. Mrs. Goodwin was relieved that the business of Martha's imaginary friends was forgotten. It seemed that Martha had forgotten them too. She had not mentioned them since seeing the doctor and when she played in the garden on her own she no longer talked to herself or tried to catch invisible things that apparently flew about the flower beds. Fortunately, she didn't appear to suffer from their absence.

When at last the baby girl arrived in the spring of the following year the house was once again filled with flowers and gifts. Grandma Wallace, aware that Martha might be put out by all the attention her new sister was getting, brought Martha an exquisite doll's house that was the finest thing she had ever been given. It had a sweeping staircase, a grand entrance hall and nine rooms, all decorated with pretty floral wallpapers. Her mother gave her the miniature pieces of furniture, cutlery and crockery and she told Martha that the family of dolls that were to live there was a gift from the baby, who was keen to be a good friend to her sister. Martha believed her and was sure that when she was older she would make a very good friend indeed.

The baby was christened Edith and no expense was spared for this child who was so very precious to her mother. Only Pam's parents and Larry's family knew why Pam put the crib by her bed and lay on her side for hours, staring into her daughter's face. She could see Larry in Edith's features, her father about the eyes and something of her mother in the feminine pout of her lips. When Larry's family came to visit she relished pointing out the similarities to them. Especially to Joan, who bristled like a threatened cat and grudgingly handed over the gift she had bought. "She looks just like Larry," she said, peering into the crib. "I don't see you in there at all."

"Neither do I," said Pam, who didn't need to see herself in her child for she knew very well who had birthed her.

"The irony is that Martha looks more like *you*. This child is going to be fair-haired like Larry."

"She's a Tobin, Joan, as much as she's a Wallace."

Joan sniffed and sat down. "Does it feel different?"

"Does *what* feel different?"

"Having a child who is biologically yours. Do you love her more?"

Pam was affronted. "That's a horrible thing to say, Joan."

"Don't be oversensitive. It's natural to love your own child more than an adopted one, don't you think?"

"No, I *don't* think. I love Martha as much as I love Edith. It makes no difference." Joan pulled a face that suggested she didn't believe her. "You may think what you like, Joan. Perhaps *you* would love your biological child more than your adopted one were you in my position, but I'm not you. Edith has been given to me; I searched the world for Martha."

"That's a little exaggerated, even for you, Pam."

"I longed for Martha and God led me to Ireland. She was meant to belong to me from the moment she came into the world. I could not love her more."

Joan put up her hands. "All right, don't get so upset. I was only asking. Really, Pam, you're so sensitive."

"I'm not sensitive. Anyone would be offended by what you're implying."

"Trust me, it's what everyone will be thinking. Only I have the courage to say it."

"Or the lack of tact," Pam snapped. She watched Joan light a cigarette and lean back in her chair, crossing her legs. She was wearing a stunning crimson dress that clashed with her hair. Pam wondered how she could find out where she had bought it and whether they'd have another one for *her*.

MRS. GOODWIN DID not doubt that Mrs. Wallace loved her two daughters equally, but right from the very beginning Edith was indulged in a way that Martha had never been. It wasn't that Edith was more spoiled—both girls had never been denied anything on a material level—it was the way her parents responded to her behavior that was different. While Martha had always had to be mindful of her manners, aware that her every move was scrutinized by a mother so desperate for her daughter to impress and fit in, Edith could behave as she wanted and only Mrs. Goodwin ever pulled her up when she misbehaved. Things for which Martha would have been severely chastised

Edith could do with impunity. Nothing she did was ever "wrong" in her parents' eyes. She could holler and stamp her little foot, sulk, suck her thumb, spill her food, interrupt and make demands and her parents would laugh, wink at each other and make comments that they had never made about Martha: *She's so like Ma*, they would say. Or, *She's inherited her stubbornness from Grumps*. Mrs. Goodwin noticed, for the difference was stark and it saddened her, for while Martha might be too young to *see* it, she was certainly not too young to *feel* it; small children are quick to sense injustice and know things without ever being told. As little Edith grew from a toddler to a child, she was fast becoming insufferable, but her parents seemed not to notice, or chose not to care. She was their flesh and blood and their wonder at the miracle of her conception blinded them to the fact that she was growing up to be a very unpleasant child indeed.

Mrs. Goodwin tried hard to redress the balance when Mrs. Wallace was not at home. Every time Edith, now nearly three years old, took something of Martha's, she made her give it back. She was told to sit up straight, to eat with her mouth closed, not to answer back, interrupt or be rude. When she refused to share she was told she would be punished if she didn't. But Mrs. Goodwin's punishments were never severe. She'd make Edith sit on a chair in the corner or send her to her room. However, nothing seemed to correct the child's behavior because she believed herself above the laws that governed her nanny's domain. She knew she could get away with anything when her mother was around—and she was right. Mrs. Goodwin tried to keep the girls in the nursery, but Edith would escape and run through the house in search of her mama, howling her eyes out and screaming at the top of her lungs. Pam would blanch, gather her daughter into her arms and soothe her with promises and bribes and, every time she did so, Edith's belief in her preeminence grew a little stronger. Mrs. Goodwin felt a sense of helplessness. There was no doubt in the nanny's mind whom *she* loved the most.

If Martha noticed that her sister was treated differently, she made no comment. Now that she was no longer on her own she wanted very badly to find a friend in her sibling. She relished having the company of another child. Since she was six years older, she took pleasure in teaching Edith how to draw and paint and play the piano and violin. She taught her about flowers, butterflies and birds and never tired of playing games. As Edith grew she became more difficult but Martha was patient and always let her choose which character she wanted to enact and which game she wanted to play. Mrs. Goodwin tried to encourage Martha to be firm with her, not to allow her to always take the lead, but Martha was too gentle and kind and Edith's forceful character triumphed every time.

Then one afternoon at their grandmother's house, Diana Wallace took Pam aside. "My darling, don't you think Edith is becoming a little out of control?"

Pam was immediately affronted. Criticizing Edith was akin to criticizing *her*. "I don't know what you're talking about," she replied.

"Martha is so beautifully mannered and well behaved, but Edith is . . ." She hesitated. "Well, to be quite frank, she's wild." Pam didn't know what to say. In her eyes Edith was perfect. "Darling, I'm not blaming you. I'm simply suggesting that perhaps Mrs. Goodwin is not doing her job properly. If you don't enforce discipline when she's young, you'll create a monstrous adult. I fear Edith is growing up without boundaries. Bad manners are very unattractive."

Pam was hurt. "She's got character, that's all," she protested.

"Too much character, Pam," Diana replied sternly. "If she can't learn to behave you will have to leave her at home. Children who don't mind their manners should not be exposed to polite society."

Now she had Pam's attention. Having been so proud of her angelic-looking child, who was a true Tobin-Wallace, Pam worried that she wasn't fit to be seen. She was pretty, of that there was no dispute. Her heart-shaped face and cornflower-blue eyes were certainly engaging and her fair hair was long and silky like the mane of a unicorn. Her skin was as white as milk and as smooth as satin and her smile, on the rare occasions that she gave one, was enchanting. But Pam was astute enough to know that if her manners were distasteful she might as well be ugly on the outside as well.

"I will discipline her," she told her mother-in-law resolutely. "She's young and she's smart. She'll learn quickly."

"Perhaps you need a tougher nanny," Diana Wallace suggested. "Mrs. Goodwin is getting on, after all." But Pam had no intention of putting her precious child in the hands of someone she didn't know—and Mrs. Goodwin, who had come to America with them from London, was quite strict enough.

But in spite of Pam's intentions Edith still managed to have her way in everything. Having told Mrs. Goodwin to be firm, Pam then berated her for being *too* firm. Edith, although small, was an arch manipulator. She knew how to win over her mother. She was well aware of the effect her tears had and if she pushed out her bottom lip at the same time it was even more dramatic. Her mother couldn't bear her sorrow, not for a minute. As for her father, he came home late, sometimes too late to put her to bed. But on weekends she would curl up on his lap and there she was safe from Mrs. Goodwin's discipline and her grandmother's disapproving stare, because he loved her just the way she was.

Edith grew jealous of her sister's place in Grandma's heart. Diana Wallace made no secret of the fact that Martha was special to her. Joan and Dorothy could push their children forward as much as they liked, but when Diana settled her gaze on Martha it was apparent for all to see that she reserved her most tender looks for *her*. Edith was not used to being marginalized—she very much felt at the center of her parents' affection—and, as a consequence, her behavior around her grandmother only deteriorated further. Martha had every reason to be jealous of Edith but envy was not in her nature, and, in spite of their differences, Martha made every concession to be her friend.

Instead of admiring her older sister as younger siblings do, Edith was jealous of Martha. Her mother had conditioned her to believe that she was special and this only served to encourage her to resent any attention that Martha was given, from their grandmother or otherwise. Edith was only a child and her small acts of sabotage and rebellion were as ripples on the water by the feet of a gnat, but as she grew older her feet would grow bigger and the ripples would turn to great splashes of destruction.

ADELINE WAS NO longer in Martha's awareness. The child had shut her out and by the force of her will Adeline's image had receded and her voice grown distant until she was only a sensation, like a gust of wind or a ray of sunshine, which Martha chose not to feel. Yet Adeline did not desert her; Martha was a Deverill. The blood of her kin and the waters of Ireland ran in her veins. Deep in the heart of her heart Martha knew who she was. She knew where she came from. Only she had forgotten. One day, Adeline was certain, the mists of oblivion would lift and she would reconcile the longings in her soul with the land she had lost. Ireland would call to her and she would return home.

In the meantime her grandmother watched her with a keen and concerned eye. Martha loved nature, just as Adeline did, and as much as she attempted to interest her sister in the flora and fauna in the garden Edith had no sensibility for beauty. Her father bought his daughters ponies but Edith was frightened to mount. She screamed and she wriggled and she refused to be put in the saddle. But Martha found a part of herself she had left behind on the hills of Ballinakelly and felt at home with her feet in the stirrups and her hands on the reins and the feeling of the wind raking its fingers through her hair. She had no idea that her biological father had been one of the finest huntsmen in County Cork but Adeline did, and she smiled with pride as this child exhibited the Deverill spirit that was hidden in her core. Pam feared she would fall off, but Martha had never felt as safe as she did in the saddle and everyone marveled at her courage and her daring and at the speed with which she learned to master her pony.

On the outside Martha was a product of her adoptive mother. Like Pam she was dressed with polish and like Pam her movements were self-conscious and deliberate. Too much grooming had robbed her of any spontaneity and vivaciousness. She was studied, polite, gracious and always a little apprehensive. Caution was not a Deverill trait—perhaps it was a Doyle characteristic, but Adeline did not remember Bridie Doyle. However, when Martha was among nature, the magic in the trees and flowers, the twittering of birds and the buzzing of bees released something within her. She felt joy, unrestrained and profound, and Adeline knew that where Edith would only ever be aware of the superficial veneer of things, Martha was aware of the deeper mysteries inherent in the natural wonders of the world. That she had inherited from her.

"MARTHA, COME INSIDE," Mrs. Goodwin shouted from the window. "It's time for your bath." Martha, who was lying on the lawn, reading a book of poetry, sighed regretfully.

"Can't I stay out for a little longer?" she asked. "Please."

Mrs. Goodwin smiled indulgently. She looked at her watch. "Very well then," she replied. "But you must come in fifteen minutes."

"I promise." Martha rolled onto her back and gazed up at the sky. The sun was setting behind the trees and she could see it blazing like a golden ball melting into the earth. Above, the clouds were pink feathers drifting slowly on a sea of blue. She crossed her feet and put her hands behind her head and watched the pink turn to a dusty shade of indigo. The air was warm, midges hovered in clouds of gray, roosting birds sung noisily from the branches and the breeze brought with it the faint but distinct smell of the ocean. She frowned at the image that passed fleetingly through her mind, so quickly she almost missed it. She saw a coastline with high cliffs and rocks and great waves crashing against the shore. She didn't know where it had come from but it was as if a memory had been unleashed within her. Before she could dwell on it a moment longer it had dissolved, like foam, and above her the twinkling of the first star shone brightly. Reluctantly she pushed herself up and wandered inside.

Adeline watched her go. "Ireland is calling you home, my child," she said, but her voice was a whisper that was lost on the wind. "Ireland is where you belong and where you shall one day be. Love binds you to it and will eventually carry you there. I have all the time in the world to see that it is done."

Chapter 21

Ballinakelly, 1930

Mrs. Doyle sat in her usual rocking chair beside the hearth while the hunched and wizened figure of her mother, Old Mrs. Nagle, was barely noticeable in the chair opposite. Now in her late seventies and almost blind, the elderly lady toyed with her rosary beads and mumbled prayers through toothless gums while she shrank a little farther into the black dress that almost swamped her. Michael stood in the middle of the room, filling it with his physical bulk. In his hands he held a letter. He glanced at Sean and his pregnant wife, Rosetta, who sat at the table, waiting to hear Bridie's news from America, then returned his black eyes to the letter and began to read.

Dearest Mam, Nanna, Michael, Sean and Rosetta

> *I hope this finds you all in good health. I write with
> my heart full of happiness to share with you the
> wonderful news that I am marrying again. Soon I will
> no longer be a sorry widow but the wife of a gentleman
> with a new future to look forward to. I can't wait to
> bring him home so that you can all meet him and love
> him as I do. I hope you can share in my joy and forgive
> me for not informing you sooner. It has all happened so
> fast my feet have barely touched the ground. You are all
> in my thoughts and prayers.*
>
> *Your loving daughter and sister, Bridie*

Michael lifted his gaze from the page and swept it over the astonished faces of his family. Mrs. Doyle was dabbing her eye with a handkerchief, Old Mrs. Nagle had ceased to pray and suspended her thumb above the beads while Sean glanced at his wife and there passed between them a silent communication that is the fancy of young married couples. "Marrying for the second time. She's done well for herself," said Michael. He folded the letter and slipped it back into the envelope. "Indeed God has been gracious. We have much to be thankful for."

Mrs. Doyle pushed the handkerchief up her sleeve and smiled. "God has indeed been gracious, Michael. I never did think Bridie would amount to much, but as God is my witness, I admit I was wrong. We have much to thank her for," she said, thinking of her mangle and the other small improvements that had eased the burden of her work and worry.

To be sure Bridie had improved their lives immeasurably. In

spite of Old Mrs. Nagle's protestations, when Michael had returned from Mount Melleray he had set about using his sister's money as she had intended. He bought the land he rented from the Deverills, purchased more cows, repaired and extended the farmhouse and farm buildings and acquired a car—he even employed a few young lads to help with the business. Having repented of his sins and vowed to lead a pious life he was careful not to descend into extravagance and imprudence. He donated money to the church, which pleased Father Quinn and earned him the chairmanship of the Society of St. Vincent de Paul, which was a large Catholic charity set up to help the poor. He was careful not to flaunt his new prosperity but the townspeople mocked him behind his back for his sanctimonious vanity and nicknamed him "the Pope." The Doyles never wanted for anything, although their requirements were modest. There was always food on the table, there were always clothes on their backs and the house was sealed against the cold winter winds.

"She says she's coming home," said Rosetta quietly, edging closer to her husband. It had been five years since she had married Sean, and almost as many years since Michael had returned from Mount Melleray, but Rosetta still found her brother-in-law intimidating. His presence was enormous and, even though he had become a man of God, bent on doing good, Ballinakelly's own pope emanated a dark and powerful energy.

"And what is an American to find in Ballinakelly?" Mrs. Doyle asked, rocking gently on her chair, content now that Michael, whom she admired as much as she had admired his father, had given Bridie his blessing.

"I should like to meet him," said Sean.

"I long to see her again," agreed Rosetta. She remembered her friend "Bridget" whom she had met in New York when they were both lowly maids sharing their days off on the benches in Central Park. How far she had traveled, she mused with admiration. Rosetta looked at Bridie's grandmother and wondered whether she'd live to see her granddaughter again. She didn't think of her own family in America nor dare to speculate on the chances of ever seeing *them* again, nor did she think of her two small children who might never know their Italian grandparents. "She is the wife of a gentleman now," she added quietly. "A grand lady."

"A grand lady!" repeated Mrs. Doyle disapprovingly. "God save us."

"I should like to meet her gentleman," said Old Mrs. Nagle and they all stared at her in surprise for she didn't say much these days. The elderly lady's lips curled around her gums as she smiled. "My granddaughter married for the second time! Sacred heart of Jesus. What would Tomas have said, Mariah, about her wealth and her second marriage?" she asked her daughter. "God rest his soul."

"He'd have thought she'd got above herself, that's what," Mrs. Doyle replied, lifting her chin, but she couldn't disguise the pride that smoldered in her eyes. "The Lord looks on us all with one loving gaze, kings and peasants alike. Indeed Bridie is no better for being wealthy or for being the wife of a gentleman. In truth she would have led a more godly life if she had remained here with us. Who knows what kind of life she is living over the water." She began to snivel again and pulled the handkerchief out of her sleeve with a trembling hand.

"But she writes that she is going to come back," said Rosetta hopefully.

Michael settled his imposing gaze on his sister-in-law and watched her wince. "She will never come back," he said firmly. "There is nothing for her here."

Michael put on his cap and ducked beneath the doorframe, stepping into the sunshine. Summer had turned the grass a rich green and his cows grazed contentedly, growing fat on the wildflowers that flourished on the hillside. He put his hands in his pockets and thought of Bridie. He remembered her in Dublin, her belly swollen and her mouth full of lies about being raped by Mr. Deverill. He remembered bringing her child home from the convent, not before he had corrupted one of the nuns who aided him with his plan. He had placed the boy on Kitty's doorstep with a note and she had done what he was confident she would do: remain in Ireland. The baby had tied her to her home because he was a Deverill and he belonged in Ballinakelly, as *she* did. Michael had ensured that Jack was arrested by making a deal with the Auxiliaries—his freedom for Jack's capture—and Kitty had fled to London but she had come back as he knew she would. Now his rival had settled in America, for good. Jack had gone forever and Michael would never again have to endure the sight of the man Kitty had loved so fiercely. Kitty and JP were in Ballinakelly just as he had planned. He had counted on her indissoluble bond with Ireland and her strong maternal instinct and been proved right; Kitty was exactly where he wanted her.

His mind turned sharply to the time he had taken her in the farmhouse and the remorse came in such a powerful swell that he had to sit down. She had tempted him, *that* much was clear, and he had sinned. He had duly confessed to the rape to Father Quinn and been forgiven, and devoted himself to God's work. He had tried to keep his eye on the Lord so his thoughts didn't stray to Kitty Deverill, but despite all his efforts, that girl still had the power to touch him.

He plucked a head of purple heather and twirled it between his fingers. *Kitty Deverill.* The name was like a thorny rose: beautiful but capable of causing terrible pain. How he loved Kitty Deverill. He did his best to avoid her these days because the look on her face when she saw him was a stab to the heart. He had burned the castle because of the lie Bridie had told him and his anger and jealousy had driven him to do something unspeakable. But he had faced up to his sins at Mount Melleray and God had forgiven him. He was a different man now; a man of the Church. He wanted Kitty to know that. He wanted her forgiveness too.

GRACE, DRESSED IN a hat pulled low over her face, hurried up the path that led to the Catholic church of All Saints. The sunshine warmed the gray stone walls of the ancient building that had been at the very center of the Irish struggle for independence. She remembered the meetings held in the sacristy and the plans she had concocted with Michael Doyle and Father Quinn. She had thrived on the thrill of danger that had ultimately led to the killing of Colonel Manley on the Dunashee Road. That danger had thrown her into Michael's arms. She would never forget the violent excitement of that night, as Michael and she had torn at each other's clothes like wild animals. Now she was advancing up that familiar path but the danger she was about to face was of a very different kind.

She found Father Quinn at the back of the church, talking to a young altar boy. When he saw her he dismissed the child with a wave of his hand. "Lady Rowan-Hampton, please, come with me," he said, his feet stepping noiselessly across the flagstones. They walked through a low door and into the sacristy, which contained a wooden armoire for the priest's vestments, a small ceramic piscina, a large wooden table upon which stood elaborate silver candlesticks, fine candles, books and other sacred vessels. On the walls were religious paintings and a marble sculpture of Christ on the cross which hadn't been there the last time Grace had visited. She could see that Bridie's money had been well spent in embellishing God's house.

She sat down and folded her hands in her lap. "This is quite a different church to the one in which we used to meet during the war," she said.

"It has been furnished by the devout," Father Quinn replied. "Indeed it is their moral duty to dig deep into their pockets when the Lord has been generous enough to fill them."

"You are so right," Grace replied. She wasn't here to receive a homily about morality.

"Those days are over, thank the Lord," said Father Quinn. "Your help during those years was invaluable. In fact, without you and Miss Deverill, we would not have been as effective. The Irish people will never know how much they owe their freedom to you."

"Life is quiet and peaceful now," said Grace with a smile that hid her regret. She had never felt more alive than during the War of Independence. "It has given me time to look into my soul, Father Quinn."

He raised his badger eyebrows in surprise. "Indeed?"

"I feel a great longing . . ." She hesitated and lowered her eyelashes. "I'm ashamed to say it. My husband would divorce me. My children would be appalled. In fact, everyone I know would gasp in horror, but . . ."

"But?" Father Quinn, who had taken the chair opposite, leaned forward.

"I wish to convert to Catholicism."

His face flushed with pleasure. There was nothing more thrilling for the priest than a possible convert. "I cannot pretend that I am not astonished by your revelation, Lady Rowan-Hampton."

"I know. But I have felt this longing for many years now. Do you remember the days when I taught English to the children and plotted with their fathers?"

"I do indeed," said the priest.

"And the many times I met with Fenians in Dublin?"

"Of course."

"I became one of them, Father Quinn." Her eyes took on a feverish shimmer as she held his attention and the apples of her cheeks glowed pink. "I helped feed the poor with Lady Deverill and collected second-hand clothes and shoes for the children. I wanted to alleviate the poverty. I wanted to educate them, to give them the opportunity of a better life. I wanted to change things. But I also felt that I was one of them, Father Quinn. I can't find the words to describe what I felt in my heart. It was some sort of connection, I suppose. A deep and powerful connection. And then I knew it was more than a sense of patriotism. It was a religious conviction. I wanted to be Catholic." Father Quinn was listening with fascination, his head nodding and shaking with encouragement, not wanting her to stop. "It was like a thorn in my heart, Father. It niggled and hurt and every time I sat in church I felt out of place, as if I was an outsider. But I couldn't tell anyone. I had to keep my feelings hidden. Then the war was over and peace restored and I had time to think, to search my soul. I knew that if I didn't express my desire I would go mad."

"So you have made a decision?"

"Yes, Father Quinn. I want full Catholic communion and I want you to officiate, because I can trust you to be discreet. No one must ever find out about this."

"As you wish." He sat back in his chair. "As you are already Christian it need not take long."

There Grace interrupted him. "Father Quinn, I do not want to rush this. It is not a decision I have made lightly. I want to take my time and I want to enjoy the process. I have waited years for this moment."

"As you wish."

"And because of the delicate nature of my situation, I am unable to mix with the Catholic community here in Ballina-kelly. I am, however, in need of support and guidance within the community, am I not?"

"Is there anyone you trust, Lady Rowan-Hampton?"

She hesitated and narrowed her eyes, as if searching through names of people she knew. "Mrs. Doyle," she said at last. "Lady Deverill used to speak very highly of her when she worked at the castle. I know she is a pious woman and a discreet one too. When I think of what must have gone on in her farmhouse during those tumultuous years and she never breathed a word."

Father Quinn raised his eyebrows again. "That is a fine

choice. Mrs. Doyle is the most devout of my congregation and, as you know, Michael is a reformed man. They are an exemplary family."

"I know, which is why I thought of her. Would you ask her for me? Perhaps I can pay her a visit and we can talk."

"I'm sure she will be flattered."

She engaged him once again with her warm brown eyes, which were now filled with gratitude. "I would like to donate to the church," she said. "Perhaps we can discuss how I may help *you*, Father Quinn."

When Grace returned home she found her father sitting around the card table in the drawing room with Hazel, Laurel and Bertie, playing bridge. She unpinned her hat and put it on one of the chairs before it was quietly taken away by a maid. "Where have you been?" asked Ethelred, puffing on his cigar.

"Into town," Grace replied casually. She wandered over to the table and put her hand on her father's shoulder. She felt light of spirit and happier than she had in a very long time. "So, it's you and Hazel against Bertie and Laurel?" she said.

"They're quite serious competition, but we're doing all right, aren't we, Hazel?" he said, winking at his partner, who blushed with pleasure.

"Oh, we certainly are," she gushed, glancing at her sister, whose lips were pursed with jealousy. "We're a very good team," she added, dropping her gaze into her hand of cards.

"How is Celia?" she asked Bertie. It had been six months since Archie had killed himself. At first no one could talk of anything else but the horror of his suicide. Then the talk turned to speculation as to why he would take his own life, until finally the horrible truth emerged. He had lost all his money,

and that of his family, during the financial crisis but couldn't
bring himself to tell his wife, who was notoriously extravagant.
Digby had spoken of his sadness that his son-in-law had been
too proud to ask for help, but Grace wondered whether Digby
had been in a position to help him. From what she had heard,
through her husband, Sir Ronald, Digby wasn't doing very
well himself.

"She's bearing up," Bertie replied.

"And the castle, dare I ask?"

Bertie sighed heavily and dropped his shoulders. They all
looked up from their cards. "I'm afraid it's not looking good.
But I imagine I shall be the last to know."

"You don't think she'll sell it, do you?"

"She might have to. Digby has been advising her and as far
as I understand they have liquidated all of Archie's assets. But
she is heavily in debt and the money must come from somewhere. She's clinging on to the castle with her fingernails, but
I don't hold out much hope. It looks like I shall be at the mercy
of strangers, after all."

Grace felt deeply sorry for her old friend. "I wish there was
something I could do," she said.

"Besides buying the castle, I don't think there is," said Bertie.

"We'd all chip in and save it if we could," said Laurel.

"Thank you, my dear Laurel, that's very sweet of you."

The maid appeared with a tray of tea and placed it on the
low table in the middle of the square of sofas and armchairs that
was positioned in front of the empty fireplace. "Shall we have
a break?" Ethelred asked, puffing out a cloud of sweet-smelling
smoke.

"Good idea," said Hazel. "I could do with a cup of tea. How

lovely!" She got up and went to sit beside Grace, who had begun to pour from the pretty china teapot.

"Poor Celia," sighed Laurel, watching Ethelred settling into the armchair, then taking the place at the edge of the other sofa that was nearest to him.

"The whole business is simply ghastly," said Grace. "Two children without a father, Archie's parents and siblings bereft—"

"And *poor*," added Hazel bleakly.

"Oh, it's just dreadful. I can't stop thinking about it. Such a waste for a young person to throw his life away over money. Poor Archie, a long-term solution to a short-term problem."

"Folly to sink one's fortune into such an ambitious project," said Ethelred.

"Folly," repeated Laurel emphatically.

"Digby should have taken his daughter in hand," said Grace. "After all, he's a man of experience. He should have known what they were taking on."

"When I told him that Celia had bought the castle, or rather, that Archie had, he groaned and said—I remember his very words—'It'll be the ruin of them both.'" Bertie looked from face to startled face and shook his head. "Those were his very words. I don't think one can blame Digby. Celia is a very determined young lady. What she wants she usually gets."

"Goodness!" Hazel gasped.

"Indeed," Laurel agreed by default.

"I dare say Digby rather enjoyed the fact that his daughter had saved the family seat," said Grace. "He's a flamboyant, showy man. Do you remember when he won the Derby? We heard nothing else for months!"

"I'm sure he will do everything in his power to save the castle," said Bertie.

"Though I'm not sure he has the means to do it," Grace added grimly.

Ethelred puffed on his cigar and chortled. "Let's talk about something happy. Did I ever tell you of the time I bet on a winner at the Derby? It was a rather extraordinary affair . . ." He held the attention of everyone in the room except for Grace, who had heard the story a dozen times before. But no one was more enthralled by Lord Hunt's tale of adventure, deception and triumph than Laurel and Hazel, who gazed at him with doe eyes, their lips slightly parted and their breaths bated.

CELIA AND KITTY sat on the terrace as the sun set and the shadows grew longer, eating into the light on the lawn and climbing up the castle walls like demons. Wrapped in shawls they cradled mugs of Adeline's cannabis tea, which Celia had found very effective in dulling her pain. They listened to the clamor of roosting birds and the desolate cry of a lone sea gull wheeling on the wind above them.

"I thought I had had my fair share of sorrow after George was killed," said Celia quietly. "But it can come at any moment, can't it, and take everything away."

"Oh Celia, I can't stop asking myself, 'Why?'"

"Believe me, I have chewed on that word so much I'm surprised it still exists. I know *why* he did it, I just don't understand it. At no point did he tell me to stop spending. Never once did he deny me anything. I'd give it all back, all of it, if we could rewind the clock and start again. I love this place, but I could have curbed my ambition. I know that now."

"You couldn't have foreseen this," said Kitty kindly.

"That's what makes me angry. Why didn't he warn me? He didn't even try." Celia's voice cracked. She paused, giving herself time to overcome her emotions. Kitty sipped her tea and waited. The sea gull flew away, taking his sad call with him. The shadows began to blend into dusk. Soon the night would creep in, bringing Celia face-to-face with her fears, which was why Kitty now stayed with her so often; she was frightened to sleep on her own. "He didn't give me warning. We could have resolved it together, but he bailed out, leaving me alone. Leaving his children fatherless. How could he be such a coward?" Kitty didn't know what to say. Celia had never called Archie "a coward" before. "I mean, a real man would never do that to his wife and children. A real man would have sat me down and told me the situation. But Archie wasn't a real man. All the while I was blithely spending, splashing out on the castle and paintings from Italy, he was facing financial ruin. God, Kitty, it makes me so angry." She knocked back her tea and gulped. "When I think of him now I don't feel bereaved, I feel betrayed." She laughed manically. "If you see him, you can tell him how cross I am."

"You can tell him yourself, Celia. I'm sure he's watching you and wishing he hadn't caused you such pain."

"Is he in Hell?" Celia asked softly. "Reverend Maddox would tell me it's a terrible sin to take one's own life. He'd say Archie is in Hell."

"But God is forgiving, Celia."

"Well I'm not. Not yet." She sighed loudly and drained her

mug. "So I'm selling the contents of the castle. Boysie has put me in touch with a Mr. Brickworth who is coming over from London to value everything and then he's going to put it all into a big, glossy catalogue that everyone in London will see. It's embarrassing, but what can I do?"

"I'm so sorry," said Kitty. "But perhaps this way you won't have to sell the castle itself."

"I'll have to sleep on a mattress on the floor. It's ridiculous. Is it worth it?"

"No, it's not. Life is too short. Sell up and move on." Kitty smiled sorrowfully. "I could say 'it's only a castle,' but you know as well as I do that it's so much more than that."

"It's everything to me," said Celia, her eyes wide and shiny. "Everything."

"It's everything to me too," Kitty rejoined. She watched Celia pick up the teapot and refill her mug.

"Shall we just get intoxicated tonight and forget our woes?"

Kitty held out her mug. "Why not?" she said.

Chapter 22

Digby stood by the window of his study and looked furtively out onto the driveway, and beyond, to the wide avenue of leafy plane trees that ran for almost half a mile from Kensington to Notting Hill. It was, without doubt, one of the most exclusive streets in London and he was proud to live on it. He reflected on his rather less ostentatious beginnings. The youngest son of an old landed family fallen on hard times, he was always aware that his parents were more interested in climbing the social ladder than in him. Desperate to escape his mother's stifling world, he had set out to South Africa to make his own fortune in the diamond mines. There he had lived in tents, suffered the dust and heat of summer and the crippling cold of winter and yet, somehow, found in himself a strength he hadn't known he had. As he slid his eyes up and down the road, his mind wandered back to the South African diamond mines. He had been lucky, but to a certain extent he had made his own luck—after all, God only helps those who help themselves. Then a movement in the street caught his attention.

It was *him* again, standing on the opposite side of the street wearing a hat pulled low over his face, a long shabby coat and tie, a newspaper folded under his arm. He was smoking languidly, as if he had all the time in the world. Digby chuckled without mirth; if it wasn't so dire it would be funny. He looked like a comedy crook, standing there in the shadows. *Well, Digby thought resolutely, he's not going to intimidate me. Let him do his worst and see where it gets him.* But, underneath his bravado, he didn't feel quite as strong or confident as he appeared. There had been a time when he had felt indomitable, but as the years went by his confidence was gradually being eroded by loss: loss of the people he loved, loss of his youth, loss of his sense of invulnerability, and of immortality. In the old days a man like Aurelius Dupree would barely have rattled his cage. Now, however . . .

Digby had not only built a business, he had built a reputation. He was a pillar of the community, a contributor to the Conservative Party. He counted royalty, politicians and aristocrats among his friends. Not only did he give generously to charity but he supported the arts too. He was one of the main benefactors of the Royal Opera House, for Beatrice loved opera and ballet and attended often, frequently invited to watch from the Royal Box. He was on various committees and a member of elite clubs like White's. Of course he also had his racing commitments and since winning the Derby he was a man to be reckoned with—Lucky Deverill now commanded serious covering fees. Digby took pride in his seemingly unfaltering talent for making money. He was a gambler, a speculator, a risk-taker and most often his schemes paid off. But a man could only make so much luck. He was considering trying his hand at politics. Randlords weren't quite respectable but he was overcoming that with his charm and money. Perhaps he would buy a newspaper like his friend Lord Beaverbrook and get into politics that way. *If it wasn't for Aurelius Dupree*, he thought irritably, *nothing would hold me back*.

Digby watched him in the road. He looked like he had no intention of going anywhere—and he was watching Digby right back. Indeed, the two men were staring at each other like a pair of bulls, neither wanting to show weakness by being the first to look away. However, Digby had better things to do than compete in a stand-off, so he withdrew and called for his driver to take him to his club. It was a beautiful summer's day, but Digby didn't want to risk walking through the park to St. James's on account of Aurelius Dupree. The man could write letters to his heart's content, but Digby would never permit him an audience. Standing outside his house was the nearest he was going to get and with any luck, he'd see the futility of it and crawl back under the rock from where he'd come.

HARRY AND BOYSIE met for lunch at White's. It had been six months since Charlotte had permitted her husband to see his old friend again and the two of them met frequently, careful not to slip back into their morning trysts in Soho. Charlotte had given their friendship her blessing, but she hadn't said they could sleep together, even though she hadn't specifically prohibited it. Harry felt he owed her a deep debt of gratitude for her tolerance, a debt that would be quite wrong to repay by jumping into Boysie's bed. If this was all that was permitted, they were both accepting of it. Harry was just happy to breathe the same air as Boysie. He told himself that he didn't need to make love to him. But as the months passed the challenge to keep their distance grew ever greater.

They sat in the dining room, surrounded by familiar faces, for all the most distinguished men in London were members of White's. But Boysie and Harry only had eyes for each other. "It is better to be ignorant like Deirdre," said Boysie. "It's perfectly feasible to be happy that way."

"Charlotte is happy that we are friends again," said Harry firmly.

"But she's watching you, make no mistake. She's watching your every move. One slip and you're in serious trouble, old boy." Boysie chuckled but his eyes betrayed his sadness. "Is this all it's ever going to be?"

Harry looked into his wineglass. "I don't know."

Boysie sighed in that nonchalant way of his and pouted petulantly. "I'm not sure I can stand it."

"You *have* to stand it," Harry said in alarm. "It's all we're allowed. It's better than nothing. I couldn't live with nothing."

"After Archie did himself in I'm sure Charlotte has come to realize that." He grinned mischievously. "Would you really kill yourself for me?" he asked, leaning across the table, his pretty green eyes melting into Harry's.

"I thought about it," Harry replied quietly.

"Don't ever do it," said Boysie. "Because *I* don't have the courage and I certainly couldn't live without *you*. You won't go and leave me on my own, will you?"

Harry smiled. "No, of course not."

"Well, that's settled then. A weight off my shoulders. You

know that hotel in Soho is still there. No one would ever know. Not even Charlotte with her spying would know to look there."

"We can't," Harry hissed, glancing anxiously to his left and right for fear of being overheard.

"You know, Celia has told me that someone has made her an offer to buy the castle, lock, stock and barrel," said Boysie, changing the subject because Harry's reaction to *that* suggestion remained always the same. "News travels fast."

Harry's eyes widened. "When did she tell you?"

"This morning. She telephoned."

"Well? What did she say? Is she going to sell it?" Harry looked horrified.

"Of course she's not going to sell it. She adores it. She's just going to sell the contents. *Most* of them. I'm sure she'll keep a bed or two."

Harry shook his head. "It's desperate. I can't bear it for her. She's terribly lonely without Archie."

"Darling, she's lost more than Archie. She's lost her *joie de vivre*. Her *esprit*. I think we should persuade her to come to London for a while. She needs to get out, to see people, to re-member who she really is."

"She shouldn't be a widow," Harry agreed.

"Unless she's a *merry* widow. We'll remind her of her merry side, won't we, old boy."

"God, they were good old times," Harry sighed. They be-gan to reminisce wistfully about their lives before Deirdre and Charlotte had stepped in to complicate them.

Presently, Digby walked into the dining room with a great kerfuffle. With his flashing white teeth, his slicked-back blond hair and his diamond shirt studs, he greeted his friends loudly as he moved through the tables, finding something witty or charming to say to everyone. Harry and Boysie suspended their conversation to watch as he made his way toward them, his flamboyant attire and vibrant personality creating amusement and comment among the members of this most conventional of clubs.

"Ah, boys," Digby said when he reached their table. "At least there is one place in London where we are sure to be free of our wives." He laughed without realizing how true his words were to Boysie and Harry and moved on to where his guests awaited him.

GRACE KNOCKED ON the door of the Doyle farmhouse. It was the first time she had ever visited, for during the War of Independence she and Michael had met either at her house or Badger Hanratty's barn in the hills. As she pushed it open her heart accelerated at the thought of seeing Michael, "the Pope," whose piety repulsed her but whose physicality still thrilled her. She could feel his presence, for his energy vibrated strongly, like a strain of music permeating every inch of the farm, and her excitement mounted. She heard a voice and when her eyes adjusted to the darkness, she saw an elderly woman sitting on a chair by the hearth.

"Good day," said Grace and the elderly woman raised her hooded eyes and her cadaverous face registered surprise. Old Mrs. Nagle had not been expecting a lady to step into their humble dwelling. "My name is Lady Rowan-Hampton. I've come to see Mrs. Doyle."

A moment later Mrs. Doyle appeared at the bottom of the staircase. She stepped into the room, wringing her hands nervously. She was smaller than Grace remembered, her skin as lined as a map, her round black eyes the same color as Michael's. She nodded curtly. "Good morning, milady," she said.

"Father Quinn . . ." Grace began a little anxiously. She didn't want anyone to know that she was here, besides Michael, of course. *That* was the reason she had come, after all.

"Oh, Father Quinn, yes, he did emphasize discretion. You can be sure that Mam and I won't breathe a word, so help me God." She looked unsure of what to do next, then remembering her manners, she offered Grace a seat at the table. "Would you like tea, milady? The kettle is hot."

"Thank you. That would be lovely," said Grace, sitting down. She could smell Michael, as if he had only a moment ago stood before her, dwarfing the room with his wide shoulders and powerful authority. She wondered where he had gone and whether he'd be coming back soon. She didn't know how long she could sustain talking to his mother about God.

Mrs. Doyle placed a basin of tea and a plate of currant soda bread on the table in front of her and sat down, folding her hands in her lap. She waited for Grace to begin. Grace wrenched her thoughts away from Michael and tried to concentrate on the charade. She had no wish to convert to Catholicism, but if that's what it took to win Michael's heart she'd go the whole way and beyond.

"As Father Quinn will have told you, I would like to become a Catholic," she said. "This will be against the wishes of my family, but I feel I am being called, Mrs. Doyle, and I want to answer that call."

"So how can I help you?" Mrs. Doyle asked with a frown.

"I want to know what it means to live a Catholic life. Father

Quinn suggested *you* as a role model. You are a good Catholic, Mrs. Doyle. I would like you to set me an example."

Mrs. Doyle's face relaxed when she realized *that* was all that was expected of her. She certainly believed herself to be a good Catholic and was happy to tell Lady Rowan-Hampton how she lived a pious life. "Shall I—" Mrs. Doyle began but Grace interrupted.

"Tell me about your life from the beginning, yes, that would be most interesting. What was it like growing up a Catholic?" Mrs. Doyle began to reminisce and Grace's mind wandered through the house in search of Michael. Old Mrs. Nagle had fallen asleep in her chair and her head had slumped forward like a rag doll's. A dribble escaped one corner of her mouth and ran down the gray hairs of her chin, dropping onto the loose fabric about her scrawny chest. Mrs. Doyle warmed to her subject. She spoke of the angelus, her daily prayers, the rosary, Mass and the little things she did every day that were all part of her devotion. Grace listened with half an ear, nodding when appropriate. With one eye on the door she let Mrs. Doyle talk on, silently willing that door to open and Michael to stride in.

When Mrs. Doyle finally drew breath Grace had finished her tea. The room had grown a little darker and Old Mrs. Nagle had woken herself up with a snort. Grace realized that she couldn't stay any longer. She didn't think she could endure a minute more of Mrs. Doyle's flat voice and her piety. Then the door was flung open and she knew it was Michael even before she saw him. She pushed out her chair and jumped to her feet, forgetting for a moment that Old Mrs. Nagle and Mrs. Doyle were watching her with fascination, as if she were a rare bird that had chosen to mingle with geese.

Michael stared at her in surprise. He had seen her car parked outside and wondered what the devil she was doing in his house. Had she gone mad? "Lady Rowan-Hampton," he said and his tone demanded an explanation.

Grace smiled sweetly. "Hello, Mr. Doyle." She relished holding him in suspense for a moment.

He looked at his mother, who had now pushed herself to her feet. "Lady Rowan-Hampton and I have much to talk about," she said and, true to her word, she was careful to be discreet.

"About what?" he asked.

"Would you like tea?" she said, making for the fireplace. "I will boil the kettle."

"I must be going," said Grace. Her mood had lifted considerably. "Thank you so much, Mrs. Doyle. I really appreciate your time. Might we perhaps be able to meet again?"

"As you wish," said Mrs. Doyle, flattered. She had enjoyed talking about herself to someone who listened with such concentration.

Michael was perplexed. "I will escort you to your car, Lady Rowan-Hampton," he said, opening the door. Grace walked past him with her chin up, a gratified smile curling the corners of her lips.

Outside, the sun was on the wane. The tweeting of birds filled the air with the sound of summer. A light breeze drifted in over the cliffs. Michael turned to her, his face cast in shadow. "What's going on, Grace?"

"I'm converting to Catholicism," she stated simply.

Michael scowled. "The devil you are," he replied.

"Oh, I am," she insisted with a smile. "Your mother is helping me along my spiritual path. Father Quinn suggested I come and talk to her. She's an inspiring woman."

"You're not going to convert to Catholicism. Sir Ronald would divorce you."

"Ronald won't know," she said breezily. "As you're well aware we lead very separate lives. That suited you once."

He pulled a sympathetic face. "What's this all about, Grace?" he asked gently.

"It has nothing to do with you, Michael. I have moved on. You can rest assured that I will not be the temptress who diverts you from your path. I respect your devoutness. In fact, I admire it." She lowered her eyes demurely and hesitated, as if struggling to find the words. "I have done things in my life of which I am deeply ashamed," she said, lowering her voice. "I want to make peace with God. I want to ask forgiveness and I want to lead a better life. What we had was intense and I wouldn't go back and change it for all the world. But I've started another chapter. The old one is closed, forever." She walked to her car. "It's been nice seeing you. *Really* nice. I hope we can be friends, Michael."

He nodded, but his knitted eyebrows exposed his bewilderment. He watched her open the door and climb inside. Then she lifted her hand and gave a small wave as she set off up the track.

She looked in the rearview mirror and saw him watching her, the frown still etched on his forehead, and she smiled, satisfied with her plan and excited by the thrill of a new plot.

IT WAS HARD persuading Celia to return to London for a break, but Boysie and Harry were adamant that she should not be alone at the time she needed her friends the most. She protested that she had Kitty and Bertie on her doorstep and the Shrubs made it their business to visit her every day with cake soaked in whiskey. "That should be reason enough to bolt for the mainland," Boysie had said, and Celia had laughed and finally relented.

She arrived in London at the beginning of July and Beatrice made a great fuss of her. She put fresh flowers in her bedroom and arranged lunches with her dearest friends. She knew that her daughter would not feel up to going out into society, but the company of those she loved the most would be balm to her ailing spirit. Even Leona and Vivien were kind and no one mentioned Archie's suicide or asked whether she would have to sell Castle Deverill. Celia knew they were all burning with questions but was grateful for their tact and restraint. That is, until Augusta invited herself for tea.

Celia's grandmother arrived in a shiny black Bentley with a long thin nose and big round headlights that flared like nostrils. It drew up outside the house on Kensington Palace Gardens and came to a halt at the foot of the steps leading up to the grand entrance. Augusta waited for the chauffeur to open her door and offer her his hand, then she descended slowly, ducking her head sufficiently so as not to squash the feathers in her hat. The chauffeur gave her her walking stick, but knew that his mistress would not take kindly to being helped up the steps. "I'm not decrepit yet," she would say dismissively, shrugging him off.

Looking like a Victorian lady in a long black dress with a high collar buttoned tightly about her neck and her silver hair swept loosely up and fastened beneath her hat she walked past the butler without a word and found Celia waiting dutifully for her in the hall at the foot of the staircase. Augusta, who had not seen her granddaughter since Archie's death, pulled her against her vast bosom and held her in an emotional embrace. "My dear child, no one should have to suffer what you have suffered. No one. The indignity of suicide is more than I can bear." Celia was relieved when her mother appeared and the three of them went upstairs to the drawing room.

Augusta settled into the sofa and pulled off her gloves, placing them on her disappearing lap. "The whole business has been most vexing," she said, shaking her head so that the feathers quivered like a startled moorhen. "I mean, what was I to tell my friends? If it hadn't been all over the newspapers I could have made something up, but as it was, I found myself having to admit that the poor man had hanged himself. Surely, there's a way to do oneself in without drenching one's family in shame?"

Beatrice was quick to move the conversation on. They had spent enough time debating the whys and wherefores. "It is as it is," she said. "We have to look forward now and think of the future."

"The silly boy should have swallowed his pride and asked Digby for help. Digby is as rich as Croesus," Augusta said, her lips pursing into a smug smile at the thought of her son's success. "Why, out of all my chicks, Digby is the one who has flown the highest and the furthest. But pride is a terrible thing."

Beatrice handed her a teacup. "I think it was more complicated than that, Augusta," she said. Celia caught her mother's eye and pulled a face while her grandmother was dropping two sugar lumps into her tea. "How is Stoke?"

"Frail," said Augusta. "He won't last long, I'm afraid. I'm surprised when I see he's still there in the mornings. I'm as frail myself but of course I hide it."

"I thought he looked incredibly well when I saw him last," said Celia.

"That might well be. But he has his ups and downs. He must have been on an up. Sadly, the last few months have not been good. When one is as old as he is the decline is a sharp one. Still, he has had a good life." Before Beatrice could object Augusta continued stridently. "As for me, I didn't think I'd survive Archie's suicide but I'm still here. One more tragedy and I think my heart will simply pack it in. There is only so much a person can take. I've cried so much, there isn't a tear left inside me." She then proceeded to give them both a lengthy account of all her friends who were ill, dying or dead. The most gruesome tales gave her the most pleasure. "So you see, I must consider myself fortunate. When I compare myself to them I realize that shame is a small thing really. After all, no one ever died of shame."

"None of us feel at all ashamed," said Beatrice. "We just feel desperately sad for Archie and sorry for Celia. But we're not dwelling on sorrow."

"I hear from my man at Christie's that you are selling the contents of the castle." Celia flushed. "Now why would you do that? Surely Digby won't allow it."

"Digby is not in a position to help," said Beatrice, enjoying the look of surprise that took hold of Augusta's face.

"Whatever do you mean, not in a position to help? Of course he is."

"I'm afraid he is not. Most of the country has been affected by the Stock Exchange crash and Digby is no different."

"Good Lord, I don't believe it."

"I'm afraid it is true."

"I shall speak to him at once—"

"Please don't," said Beatrice swiftly. "He won't want to discuss it. You know what he's like. Like you, Augusta, he keeps everything bottled up inside. As far as anyone is concerned he is absolutely fine. But you are his mother, so you should know. Celia has to sell the contents of the castle in order to pay off Archie's debts, of which there are many." She wanted to add "and his family's debts' but she didn't want to embarrass her daughter. Celia winced at the thought of the money she had to find but hastily pushed her anxieties aside. While she sat in her mother's sumptuous drawing room she could pretend that everything was as it should be.

"And the castle?" Augusta asked in a tight voice.

Celia shrugged. "I might have to sell that too," she replied.

Augusta inhaled a gulp of air. "Then that will surely be the death of me," she said. "Shame might do me in, after all."

CELIA ESCAPED HER grandmother and the stifling heat of London and fled to Deverill Rising in Wiltshire to spend the weekend with her family. She invited Boysie and Harry, who turned up with their wives, but at least on the golf course she could be rid of them, for neither Charlotte nor Deirdre played golf. Harry and Boysie seemed just as happy to be free of them as she was.

Digby, dressed in a flamboyant pair of green checked breeches, long green socks and a bright red sleeveless sweater over a yellow shirt, was an erratic golfer. He roared with laughter when he hit his ball into the rough and punched the air when, by some miracle, he got a hole in one. His two black

Labradors headed straight into the copse like a pair of seals in search of fish, appearing a few minutes later with their mouths full of golf balls—mostly Digby's, from previous games.

Celia was a steady player while Boysie and Harry, fashionably dressed in pale, coordinating colors, were less interested in the actual sport. For them it was a way of spending a whole morning together in the company of people who didn't judge them.

"Grandma gave me a grilling," Celia told her father as they walked to the next hole. "She's incredibly tactless."

"I'm sorry to hear that, but she does like to have her say."

"She says she'll die of shame if I sell the castle."

"She'll outlive us all, mark my words," said Digby.

"She thinks Grandpa is going to pop off at any minute."

"Grandpa is not going anywhere," Digby replied firmly. "If he's survived sixty-odd years being married to her, he'll survive a few more." He chuckled. "I'm sure he's built up a strong immunity to her over the years."

Celia put her hands in her cardigan pockets. "Someone has made me an offer for the castle," she said. "A big offer. Much more than it's worth."

Digby stopped walking. "Do you know who?"

"Oh I don't know. A rich man. American."

"Are you asking my advice?"

"Yes. You know my financial situation better than I do. Really, it's such a muddle and so many noughts. I do hate all those beastly noughts."

"You don't have to sell." A shadow darkened her father's face. "At least, not yet."

"He wants to buy the castle with everything in it."

"You don't have to sell the castle," Digby said decisively, striding on. "We saved it once and we'll save it again. Now, where are those bloody dogs?"

Her father placed the ball on the tee and shuffled his feet into position. Celia noticed that his face had gone red, but she thought it was due to the exertion of walking the course. It had been a long way and the summer sun was blazing. She wondered whether he should take off his sweater. He lined up his club, patting it a few times on the green. Little beads of perspiration had started to form on his brow and his breathing had grown suddenly tight, as if he was struggling to inhale. Celia looked anxiously at the boys who had also noticed and were watching him with concern.

"Papa," said Celia. "I think perhaps we should take a break. It's very hot and even *I'm* feeling faint." But Digby was determined to take the shot. He swung his club. Just as he twisted his body, his arm went weak and he fell to his knees. Celia rushed to his side. "Papa!" she cried, not knowing where to put her hands or what to do. She felt a sickness invade her stomach. Digby was now puce. His eyes bulged and his mouth opened in a silent gasp. He pressed a hand against his chest.

Harry and Boysie helped lie him down on the grass. Harry loosened his tie and unbuttoned his shirt. His breathing was labored. He stared but seemed to see nothing. Then with a great force of will he grabbed Celia by her collar and pulled her down so that her face was an inch from his. She let out a terrified squeal. "Burn . . . my . . . letters," he wheezed. Then his hand lost its strength and fell to the ground.

PART THREE

Barton Deverill

Ballinakelly, County Cork, 1667

Charles II, six feet tall, black-eyed, black-haired, swarthy and as handsome as the Devil, was in his apartments in the rambling, ramshackle rabbit warren that was Whitehall Palace. Attended by his mistress, Countess of Castlemaine, his friend the Duke of Buckingham, and his pack of spaniels, which he referred to as his "children," he was sitting at the card table when Lord Deverill strode into the room and bowed low. "Your Majesty," he said.

"Oh join us, Deverill," said the King without looking up. "Take a hand. What's y' stake?"

The King liked winning money off his friends and Deverill tossed his into the middle of the table and sat down. "How are the girls out there in godforsaken Ireland, Deverill?"

"Bonny," Lord Deverill replied. "But my mind isn't on the girls, Your Majesty, but on the rebels . . ."

The King waved his hands and the large jewels on his fingers glittered in the candlelight and the intricate lace ruffles of his sleeves fluttered about his wrists. "We'll send you some men, of course, speak to Clarendon," he said, and that was as much business as the King wanted to discuss. Lord Deverill knew there was a strong chance that reinforcements would come too late, if at all, because the King was more concerned about the threat of invasion from the Dutch. "How considerate of you, Deverill, to marry a beautiful woman," the King continued, his lips curling into a languid smile as the Countess stuck out her bottom lip and gave a loud and irritated sigh. "We're all terribly tired of looking at the same faces and gossiping about the same people. You really must bring her to Court more often."

"She would like that very much," Lord Deverill replied. The King was unable to resist the allure of a beautiful woman and had been given the nickname "Old Rowley" after a lecherous old goat that used to roam the privy garden. Lord Deverill did not believe he would wear a pair of horns well and decided that the sooner he took his wife to Ireland the better.

However, this was not the occasion to take her to Castle Deverill. Barton left his wife in the safety of their house in London and headed for home. It was a long and arduous journey across the Irish Sea, but the weather was favorable and he reached the mainland without a hitch. With a small escort of the King's men who had met him at the port he galloped over the hills toward Ballinakelly.

The wind blew in strong gusts, propelling him on, and oppressive gray clouds gathered damp and heavy above him. Spring was but a few weeks away and yet the landscape looked wintry and cold and the buds already forming on the trees remained firmly shut. Still, in spite of the bleak light and dreary skies, Ireland's soft beauty was arresting. Her green and gently undulating fields appealed directly to his heart and Lord Deverill feared the scene of devastation that would welcome him home.

With trepidation he cantered to the crest of the hill and looked down into the valley where his castle stood, overlooking the ocean. His heart plummeted to his feet as he gazed upon the manifestation of all his ambitions, now a grisly wreck, still leaking a ribbon of smoke into the wind. Fury rose in him then like a latent beast suddenly awoken by the sharp prod of a sword. He dug his spurs into his horse's flanks and galloped down the track. His gut twisted with anguish as he approached the scene of battle. Although the castle was still standing, it had taken a terrible battering and the eastern tower had been completely lost to fire.

He recognized his friend, the Duke of Ormonde's colors at once and when the soldiers saw him they were quick to take him to their captain. "Lord Deverill," the captain said as Barton strode into the hall.

"What the devil has happened?" he asked, his feverish eyes scanning the room for damage and finding none. At least they hadn't fought their way *into* the building, he reflected.

"His Grace rushed to your aid as soon as he heard the news. We arrived just in time to secure the castle. Your men were on the back foot. Had it not been for His Grace's quick response you wouldn't have had a home to come back to."

"I cannot express my gratitude. I am forever indebted to the Duke," said Lord Deverill quietly. As loyal supporters of King Charles II during his exile in France, the Duke and

Lord Deverill had become firm friends. At the restoration Ormonde had recovered his vast estates in Ireland confiscated by Cromwell and been reinstated Lieutenant of Ireland, a position he had held under King Charles I. He was consequently the most powerful man in the country. An important ally most certainly but he was also a trusted friend; when Lord Deverill had needed him most Ormonde had not let him down.

"Who's behind this?" Lord Deverill growled. "By God I shall have their heads."

"Those who survived are imprisoned in the stables. You can be sure that the Duke will see that they are severely castigated. This is not simply a rebellion against Your Lordship, but a revolt against the King, and they shall be duly punished."

"We must make an example of them," said Lord Deverill fiercely. "Let the people of County Cork see what happens when they rise up against their English lords."

The captain rubbed his chin and frowned. "There is a woman at the heart of the plot, Lord Deverill, and she will be tried as a witch."

Lord Deverill's face drained of color. "A woman?" he said slowly, but he knew very well who she was.

"Indeed. A pagan woman called O'Leary, my lord. It is she who started the rebellion. The men are quick to accuse her of bewitching them. After all, this was her land, was it not, Lord Deverill, and it has been reported that she cursed you and your descendants. There are many who witnessed it."

Lord Deverill didn't know what to say. He could not deny the curse and any word in her favor could be counterproductive, considering what he had done to her in the woods. He pictured her face, as it appeared to him in daydreams and night terrors, and nodded sharply. "She did," he replied. His mind searched wildly for a way to help her, scurrying about his head like a rabbit in a pen, but found nothing. His jaw tensed at the thought of her inciting rebellion, at the horror of his ruined home and at her betrayal. He had no business in helping her, no business in loving her. Yet she had crawled beneath his skin and insinuated herself into his heart like an exquisite caterpillar, exploding upon his consciousness like a beautiful butterfly. Perhaps that was witchcraft too?

"What will become of her?" Lord Deverill asked.

The captain pulled a face and shrugged. "She'll most likely burn," he replied and his words made Lord Deverill wince.

"Most likely?"

"Aye, it's the decision of His Grace, His Majesty's representative, and yourself."

"Very well," he replied with a shudder, knowing there was no decision to be made; no reason to save her that would not expose *him*. "I will leave it to His Grace. I have no wish to see her." He didn't want her throwing accusations at him, although he doubted anyone would believe them; he was ashamed of having taken her in the wood.

"She was pregnant, Milord, almost to term."

"Pregnant?" Lord Deverill repeated, making a great effort to keep his voice steady. But the panic that suddenly gripped his stomach was as potent as a physical blow.

"Aye, but she lost it," the captain added. "She'll be tried now and God save her soul."

Lord Deverill took his bottom lip between his teeth and ran his tongue along the soft inside part where she had bitten him.

He could still almost taste the blood. The thought of laying eyes on her, bound like a captured animal, made him recoil. He was afraid, not just because she was a witch, but because he was frightened of his own heart and what it might rouse him to do. "Then let it be done," he said and left the room.

Chapter 23

When Beatrice was told the news of Digby's death she was overcome with grief. Once before she had clawed herself back from the brink of hopelessness, but she knew she didn't have the inner reserves to do that again. Digby had been her sails and her rudder and the captain at the helm; now that he was gone, life was a wild and lonely ocean that threatened to consume her. She withdrew to her bedroom and took to her bed, where she remained in semi-darkness, afraid of facing the world without him. Death would be preferable to living, she thought bleakly as she lay curled up beneath the quilt, and the velvet-black allure of oblivion called to her in whispers promising sanctuary in silence.

Celia was devastated and bewildered by such a great loss, coming as it did so soon after Archie's suicide. Her father had been as solid as the ground beneath her feet; dependable, unshakable, immortal. It was impossible to imagine her world without him in it. How would she get by? She had never had to think for herself. Her husband and her father had taken care of everything. She had never looked at a bill or even spoken to her bank manager—and if she had ever had a problem one of those two capable men had sorted it out for her. To whom could she turn now? Celia had no one. She dug deep to find her inner strength and found nothing but weakness.

Boysie and Harry took their wives back to London, aware that the two women would only irritate Celia and conscious of the fact that the family needed to be together. Celia enveloped them with needy arms and copious tears, promising to let them know when the funeral would be. She waved forlornly on the steps as the taxi motored down the drive.

"Death stalks the Deverills like a relentless predator," said Boysie grimly as Celia's small figure receded and finally disappeared as they turned out into the lane.

"It certainly seems so," Harry replied.

"Do your best to elude him, old boy," Boysie added under his breath.

"If a man as indomitable as Cousin Digby yields so readily what hope is there for the rest of us?"

Celia grieved with her sisters, Leona and Vivien. Tragedy brought them closer as only tragedy can. They moved into Deverill Rising to help Celia look after their mother and Celia was grateful; her mother's collapse had been almost as shocking as her father's death and she was relieved that she didn't have to cope with it on her own. During the week that followed the sisters reminisced about the old days when they had been children, shedding tears of both joy and sorrow as they remembered their father, his ostentatious and oftentimes gaudy attire and his irrepressible spirit. Digby had been a man whose glass was always overflowing. They remembered too their brother, George, when he had been a little boy following Harry around Castle Deverill like a loyal dog, and they all longed to be transported back to those summers in Ballinakelly before the Great War and the War of Independence had swept them away. They took long walks over the Wiltshire hills, finding solace in the peaceful serenity of nature, comfort in their memories and strength in each other.

Augusta did not die then as everyone, particularly she herself, was sure she would. In the great British tradition she stiffened her jaw, lifted her chin and refused to let her son's death get the better of her. She accepted condolences with fortitude— she knew that if she gave in to sorrow she might never again recover her composure—and she clung to her religion, putting her faith in God and giving up any resistance to the way things were. "Acceptance is the only way," she told Maud, who paid her a visit as soon as she heard the terrible news. "Stoke will go now, I'm sure of it. He cannot accept that Digby is gone and therein lies the folly. It is through acceptance that one finds peace. Digby's time was up and God has gathered him into His keeping. There's no point fighting it; God won't send him back. One has to accept, *that's* the key." Maud had always found Augusta trying, but she had to admire her philosophy. She wondered, though, whether the old lady let go of her control in private. The red rims around her eyes, which one might have assumed were simply the signs of her great age, told Maud that she did.

THE FUNERAL TOOK place in the village church a few miles from Deverill Rising. It was a small, family affair. Bertie, Kitty and Robert, Elspeth and Peter and the Shrubs came from Ireland, while Augusta and Stoke, Maud and Victoria traveled down from London with Boysie and Harry and their wives. Digby's two brothers came with their spouses and some of their children, but the jealousy that had seeped poison into their hearts when Digby had made his fortune in South Africa still prevented reconciliation, even in the event of their brother's death, and they left as soon as the service was over.

Beatrice, helped by her strong sons-in-law who took an arm each, was escorted to the church, then straight back home again, where she retreated once more to her bed. She didn't feel up to speaking to anyone. One more word of condolence and she would break like a flimsy raft on a wave. Sobbing quietly into her pillow, she allowed the effects of the cannabis tea Kitty had brought from Ireland to pull her under where it was still, cool and quiet.

"Hello, Maud," said Bertie, approaching his estranged wife with caution as they gathered outside the church.

But she smiled sympathetically and he saw that her icy eyes had thawed a little more since they had met at Christmas. "Why is it that we are always brought together by tragedy?" she asked.

"I don't know," Bertie replied. "We've had rather a lot of it lately, haven't we?"

"Poor Beatrice, how she must be suffering." Bertie was astonished. For once Maud was not thinking of herself. "I remember when she lost George. I didn't think she'd ever recover, but somehow she pulled herself back from the edge. Now I fear she has toppled over it."

"It was so sudden and unexpected. He was only sixty-five."

Maud's eyes shone suddenly and a shadow of fear passed across them, or perhaps it was just the reflection of the clouds. "Death could come to us at any moment. Never before have I felt so keenly a sense of my own mortality. If Digby . . ." She caught her breath. "If Digby, so strong and powerful . . . If *he* . . ." Her voice thinned. Bertie put a hand on her arm. She didn't shrug it off, but gazed at him with a benign expression softening the chiseled contours of her face.

"One has to seize the day, Maud," he said, suddenly remembering with a jolt the time Digby had shouted to him as he was on the point of perishing in the sea, demanding that he choose between life and death. "Digby saved my life," he said quietly.

"He did?" said Maud.

"Yes. If it wasn't for Digby I would have drowned myself in a bottle of whiskey."

"Oh Bertie," she gasped.

"I chose life. I pulled myself together. I vowed never to waste my God-given existence again."

Maud wiped away a tear with her glove. "I did wonder."

"Did you?" he asked, feeling his spirits soar with something close to happiness.

She nodded. "I did, Bertie, and I was pleased to see the man I married again."

"Had he really gone so very far away?" She nodded again. "Perhaps we can reach a time in our lives when we can let bygones be bygones," he ventured.

"I don't know," she said, afraid to step back into a place that had been so dark. "Perhaps."

Kitty watched her parents talking in the sunshine and wondered what they had to say to each other. As far as she knew,

Maud was still being escorted round the London party circuit by Arthur Arlington. "We're going back to the house for a cup of tea," said Hazel, tapping Kitty on the shoulder. "Are you going to come with us?"

"I could do with something stronger than tea," said Kitty, searching the faces for Robert's. She saw him talking to Bruce and Tarquin and presumed that he would hitch a lift with them. "I'll wait for Harry and Boysie," she said. "I'll walk you to your taxi."

"Do you remember Adeline's cannabis tea?" Laurel asked as they walked down the path.

"Do I ever!" said Hazel.

"If we *all* drank it *all* of the time wouldn't we be the happier for it?" Laurel said.

"Life would pass us by," said Kitty. "As pleasant as that would sometimes be, I think we are all the better for our suffering. It drives us deeper, makes us more compassionate toward others. What selfish beings we would be if we were untouched by sorrow."

Hazel frowned. "You sound just like Adeline," she said.

Kitty smiled. "Do I?" She watched the Shrubs climb into the back of the cab. "She's here, you know," she said with certainty. "I'm sure she's seen to it that Digby has found his way home."

Celia watched the cab motor off and then swept her eyes over the somber faces of the locals who had come out to pay their respects. The men stood with their hats in their hands while the women, some with small children, looked on with sympathetic faces. Among them was an old man who caught her attention on account of the fact that he hadn't removed his hat. His cadaverous face had none of the compassion or sorrow of the others; rather it had a cold, defiant expression that offended her. The man noticed that she was watching him and narrowed his eyes with contempt. He looked right at her as if his intention was to intimidate, and Celia, shocked by his visible wrath, and bewildered by it, turned away sharply and went to find Boysie and Harry. When she found them the unpleasant man swiftly slipped from her mind.

Having made sure, even in her grief, that Charlotte and Deirdre had gone with Maud and Augusta, Celia returned to the house with Harry and Boysie. "Do you know what Papa's last words to me were?" she said, staring down at her black gloves as the car rattled up the road. The boys shook their heads. "'Burn my letters,'" she told them solemnly. "That's the last thing he said. It's been bothering me, but do you think he had a mistress? I mean, I'd be naïve to believe he didn't entertain himself here and there, but do you think he loved somebody else?"

Harry caught Boysie's eye but Boysie knew better than to add to Celia's unhappiness by speaking his mind. "No, I don't imagine he did," said Boysie. "He loved your mama. That was very clear."

"I hope you're right."

"So are you going to burn them?" Harry asked.

"I don't know where they are." She laughed helplessly.

"You could start by looking in his study."

"If he has a safe I wouldn't have a clue of the code. I'm not about to break in, you know." She sighed. "If *you* were to keep love letters, where would *you* hide them?" She looked at Boysie and then at Harry and the world seemed to still for a long-drawn-out moment. She saw the two young men as if from a distance and from that fresh perspective she suddenly experienced a moment of clarity. Why had she never thought of it before, she wondered. It seemed so obvious now. Harry loved Boysie and, judging by the way they were always inseparable— and by the way Boysie's face lit up when he was with Harry— Boysie loved Harry back. They probably always had. Everything now made sense. Charlotte's grumpiness, the months Harry and Boysie didn't see each other, the fact that Boysie declined her invitation to Castle Deverill and stopped attending her mother's Salons. The two of them looked more of a couple than they did with their wives. She dropped her gaze, afraid that they might see the realization in it and be ashamed. But they had nothing to fear. When it came to love, she believed *she* loved *them* more than anyone else in the whole world. "Don't answer that," she said quickly, vigorously shaking her head. "It's a silly question. Where does anyone hide anything? In a bottom drawer? Behind a book in the bookcase? Really, they could be anywhere. I'll start in the obvious places and work my way through his study, inch by inch." She pressed a glove to her mouth and shut her eyes. "Oh, I do miss him." Both Harry and Boysie put an arm around her and squeezed her tightly.

"Of course you do, darling," said Harry. "But you're not alone."

"Lord no," Boysie rejoined. "You're never alone. You'll always have us."

AFTER THE FUNERAL Celia left her mother in the care of her sisters and returned to London with Boysie and Harry. Her father's last words had been delivered with urgency—it was her responsibility to see that his final wish was granted.

It felt strange to be in the house on her own. She could hear the reassuring rumble of motorcars down on Kensington High Street and the scuffling sound of the servants who inhabited the top floor of the building and the hidden recesses behind the green baize door. The streetlights bathed the road outside her father's study window in an amber glow that somehow made her feel less lonely. She closed the curtains. She could detect the sweetness of her father's cigars, the rich scent of whiskey and the musty smell of papers, ink and books. Or was she imagining it because she wanted to feel his presence so badly?

She slumped into his leather chair and ran her eyes over his desk. Digby was not a tidy man. There were books, documents, newspapers and notes strewn across it. He seemed to scrawl comments and observations on everything. She picked up a letter he had been writing and ran her fingers over the ink. He had flamboyant handwriting, like an artist's calligraphy. Dreading that it might be a love letter she held her breath, but it was only a thank-you letter to Lady Fitzherbert for a dinner party he had been to. She sighed helplessly. There were drawers, cupboards and bookcases, full of her father's life. Where was she to start looking for these incriminating letters?

Slowly and meticulously she began to rifle through his drawers. No one had tidied them, ever. She smiled as she remembered his continuous battle with her mother. He hadn't wanted the servants to invade his private room but she had been adamant that it had needed dusting at the very least. "It'll end up smelling like a hamster cage," she had said, to which he had replied, "Hamsters don't smoke cigars and drink whiskey, my

dear, and I'm not opposed to a thin layer of dust." At first Celia
was careful to lift everything out, piece by piece, and study it.
Attached to each item must be an anecdote she'd never hear,
she thought, rubbing her thumb over the surfaces, wondering
how her father had come by these things and what they had
meant to him. Old coins, pens, business cards, travel documents, racing cards, menus and other mementoes, all thrown
in together. Eventually she lost patience and poured the contents of the drawers onto the rug.

There were no letters, or he had hidden them in a very clever
place. If she couldn't find them, her mother certainly wouldn't.
She was relieved; she didn't want to read love letters from a
mistress. Of course she suspected that he had had mistresses, or
certainly taken lovers. After all, he had been a very wealthy,
attractive man who had mixed with socialites and actresses—
and women of ill repute no doubt; it would have been odd if he
hadn't cast his eye about. But that was a man's business. She
didn't want to know anything about it. She wanted to remember him as a good husband to her mother. She didn't want
anything to change the way she thought about him.

Celia went through the cupboards beneath the bookcases.
She felt his presence strongly as she looked through old sepia
photographs stuck into thickly bound albums. There were
photographs of him in his youth: sitting on top of a camel in a
panama hat, on safari in Africa, at Ascot Races in top hat and
tails, standing in front of the Taj Mahal and the Pyramids of
Giza. He had been dashing even then, always with a raffish
smile on his face and a mischievous twinkle in his eye. There
were a few photographs of his brothers, but they were strangers
to Celia. Her grandmother Augusta, on the other hand, had

been surprisingly beautiful then, but her grandfather hadn't changed at all. Even his sweeping mustache was the same. She dwelled on the pictures of her father. He had always been jovial, as if he had found everything in the world amusing.

With the rug almost entirely covered in her father's clutter she didn't know where to look next. She glanced at the clock on the mantelpiece. It was nearly midnight, and she was beginning to feel tired. But she was frightened to go to bed in the mansion with only the servants upstairs, sleeping like mice beneath the floorboards. The place felt uneasy, as if it understood that the master had gone and didn't know quite what to do with itself. She wished she had asked Boysie or Harry to stay with her.

Wearily she stood in the middle of the study, casting her eye about the room in search of a secret place where her father might have hidden letters he didn't want anyone to find. She hadn't even come across a safe and she had opened every drawer. Then her eyes rested on the library of books her father had never read, because it was well known in the family that her father had never read a book in his life. Why so many? For a man who never read it suddenly seemed odd. Then an idea struck her. She hurried to the shelves and began pulling out all the books and tossing them onto the floor. They clattered about her feet, releasing clouds of dust into the air. And then she found it, the safe hidden in the wall behind the row of innocent-looking books. Her excitement injected her with energy and she no longer felt tired. She didn't take long to find the key. It was sitting in an ashtray on the desk among various coins, golf tees and paperclips. Behind the door were three letters, sitting loosely on top of other documents.

With her heart thumping in her chest she took the letters to the armchair where her father used to sit and read the papers beside the fire, inhaled deeply and pulled the first out of the envelope. Just as she began to read, her father's voice came back to her on a wave of guilt. He had told her to *burn* them; he hadn't told her to *read* them. But, she reasoned, he hadn't told her *not* to read them. After a moment's hesitation her curiosity overcame any reservations and she continued to run her eyes down the page.

Her greatest fear had been love letters from a mistress but now, reading the terrible words written on the page, love letters would have been preferable to *this*. Her heart plummeted into her stomach and the blood drained from her face. The floor seemed to spin away from her as she drew the other two letters from their envelopes and hurried to read them. How she wished she had just done what her father had asked and burned them. Hadn't she been taught that curiosity killed the cat? Now she knew what these letters contained she could never *un*know it. She felt tainted by the poison contained within the words. Cursed. There was only one thing to do.

Hastily, as if the letters had a life of their own and might suddenly make off out of the house and into the public gaze, she screwed them into tight balls and threw them into the grate. She found matches on the mantelpiece and struck one. Bending down she put the flame to the paper and watched it grow into a small fire. The blaze consumed the letters until all that was left was ash, sinking into the pile of cinders left over from her father's many fires.

Aurelius Dupree. She never wanted to see or hear that name again.

Chapter 24

*L*ondon has lost its brightest—and richest—light, wrote Viscount Castlerosse in his *Express* column.

Sir Digby Deverill was one of my dearest friends and his sudden death from a heart attack has sent waves of shock through the drawing rooms of London's elite, for we all believed him immortal. It was no surprise to see his memorial service attended by the crème de la crème of British society and queens of film and theater. Earl Baldwin of Bewdley, who, it is whispered, was trying to entice the flamboyant and popular Sir Digby into politics, rubbed shoulders with Mr. Winston Churchill, the Earl of Birkenhead and Lord Beaverbrook, founder of this newspaper, and the delightful Betty Balfour and Madeleine Carroll brought the glamour of the silver screen to the somber event in Mayfair and reminded us

that Sir Digby's net was flung far and wide. The King
sent a representative, for Sir Digby was a popular
character in the racing world and I once heard that he
bought a horse from the royal stud at an inflated price, a
favor the King remembered. I was not surprised to see a
few of his fellow Randlords, among them his friend and
neighbor, Sir Abe Bailey, whom I saw chatting to the
aesthete Mr. Boysie Bancroft, one of the leading lights
at Christie's, about art no doubt; Sir Abe's collection is
said to be second to none. The black attire of mourning
did not diminish the radiant beauty of the Marchioness
of Londonderry who attended with her son, Lord
Castlereagh. But none outshone the tragic beauty of
Deverill's youngest daughter, the recently widowed
Mrs. Celia Mayberry, and the question unspoken
on everyone's lips was: Will she or won't she sell
her castle?

"Ridiculous!" Maud sniffed, closing the paper. "Nothing will induce her to sell the castle."

"She's planning on selling the contents," Harry informed her, stirring milk into his coffee.

"That's not the same as selling the castle. Viscount Castlerosse should write fiction, not fact, he'd be much better at it. Honestly, the last thing on anyone's mind yesterday was the castle."

"I'm sure Digby has left Celia enough in his will to cover any of Archie's losses," he said optimistically.

"Archie left Celia in a terrible position. Imagine doing that to one's wife. Shameful." She smiled at her son. Harry's visits did much to raise her spirits. Autumn always made her feel melancholy, with the strong winds, falling leaves and thick smog. "So what's Celia going to do now?"

"She'll sit it out here in London for a while, I think. At least until the will is read and she knows where she stands. The nanny is coming over with the children. Beatrice—"

"Beatrice," Maud interrupted, pursing her scarlet lips. "Beatrice isn't good for anything. She should remember that she has a family who needs her. I imagine Celia needs her mother very badly right now because those sisters of hers are useless, but they've never been close. You're good to her, though, aren't you, Harry? I'm sure she's taking comfort from you."

"Beatrice has returned to Deverill Rising already," Harry continued. "She doesn't want to see anyone or talk to anyone."

"She needs to eat. She's half the size she was in the summer."

"She's unhappy, Mama. I'm sure it'll pass."

"Of course it will. She'll bounce back. We Deverills are a resilient lot."

"We have to be."

"No one more than *me*, Harry. What I have been put through would have felled most normal women. But I am made of tougher stuff." Harry wondered what exactly she had been put through, besides the odd scandal and losing a castle that she never liked in the first place. He did not disagree with her, however. He knew better than to argue with his mother. "What keeps me going is my faith, my children and the certainty that I have always only ever done my best."

Harry looked around her sumptuous sitting room, which she had spared no expense in furnishing, and decided to change the subject. "You've made a fine home, Mama."

"I have, but I cannot deny that I am lonely. You are my consolation, Harry. You, Charlotte and those adorable children. I have no regrets. None." She smiled at him again and the satisfaction in it made Harry feel uncomfortable. "You have done me proud, my darling. I could not have wished for a better son."

CELIA CLOSED THE newspaper with a disdainful sniff. Her father had told her not to sell the castle. That place meant more to him than anyone could know. There was no way that she was going to give it up without a fight.

She reflected on the memorial service. What Castlerosse hadn't noticed was the strange man in the felt hat who had attended without invitation and had lurked at the back of the church, watching them all keenly—the same man as the one who had been outside the church at the funeral, staring at her with such vitriol. Celia had noticed him. She was terrible at remembering names but she never forgot a face, and his, gaunt, mottled and gray, had stuck in her memory like a thorn. She had seen him various times since, standing beneath the lamp on her street, watching the house, watching *her*. To show up at her father's funeral was one thing, but to attend the memorial service was audacious to say the least, but she didn't imagine he had many scruples. Not him. Not Aurelius Dupree.

She knew he wanted to get her attention, but she was determined not to let him. If she ignored him perhaps he would go away.

Beatrice was too unwell to attend the reading of the will. The meeting was held in a plush office in St. James's, and those present included Celia and her sisters Leona and Vivien, their husbands Bruce and Tarquin, and Harry, whom Celia had invited to stand in for Archie. The mood was somber and formal.

Mr. Riswold, Digby's solicitor, was not the usual plump, paternal solicitor, but as cadaverous and dour as an undertaker. He sat at the end of the table and opened his briefcase. After the usual pleasantries he lifted out a neat pile of papers held together by a staple and laid it carefully in front of him. "Let us begin," he said and the family waited expectantly to hear how their father had divided his great wealth.

Digby had in fact bequeathed everything to Beatrice, leaving it at her discretion to share money and property with their daughters. As Mr. Riswold explained, Sir Digby's money had been *gambled*—for that is the word he used, and he looked somewhat disapproving—on the Stock Exchange, which everyone present knew had crashed the year before. If Sir Digby had lived, Mr. Riswold was sure that he would have recuperated his losses in time; as it was—and at this point small beads of sweat began to sprout on his forehead—he had lost a great deal. He cleared his throat, avoided looking at any of them directly, and told them the grim truth. Digby's financial troubles had been far greater than any of them had imagined. The gambler's luck had finally run out.

"How are we going to tell Mama?" Leona asked, her long face ashen with shock. They had entered the room believing themselves very rich, only to discover that they had been left nothing.

"We're not going to tell Mama," said Celia decisively.

"I don't think we can keep this sort of information from her, Celia," said Vivien. "We will have to sell Papa's assets. That includes Deverill House in London and Deverill Rising in Wiltshire. Papa's greatest joys." Her eyes glittered with tears. Tarquin put his hand on hers and squeezed it encouragingly.

"Mama's in no state to hear that her homes are threatened," said Celia.

"Let's not be dramatic," Leona cut in. "The only person who will be doing any selling will be you, Celia. Mama is going to struggle to pay off Papa's debts with the little he has left, but there's certainly nothing in the pot to pay off yours."

Celia stiffened. "I am perfectly capable of paying off Archie's debts myself, thank you very much," she retorted crossly, aware that in truth she was incapable of paying off even half of them.

"Let's not fight," Harry interrupted.

"I agree," said Bruce. "We have to discuss this calmly, as one unit." His tidy brown mustache twitched as his mind, conditioned by a long career in the army, set about putting together a strategy.

"Celia is right," said Tarquin, who had enjoyed as many years in the armed forces as his brother-in-law and was as much excited by schemes, plans and tactics as *he* was. "There's no point upsetting Beatrice. She's much too fragile at the moment and it might tip her over the edge. I suggest we work out exactly how much is owed and then we can calculate how much is left to run both houses."

"I break out in a sweat just thinking about how much those houses cost," said Celia. "I know how much I spend on Castle Deverill—"

"This isn't about Castle Deverill," said Leona, her voice rising a tone. Vivien shot her a warning look, but Leona continued regardless. "If it wasn't for Papa throwing money at your stupid castle we might not be in the situation we are in."

"Leona, that's not fair," Vivien cut in. "Castle Deverill was Papa's dream."

"Well, it's turned into a nightmare, hasn't it."

"Please, let's not fight," said Harry again. If anyone should be upset about Castle Deverill it was him—and he wasn't.

"I never liked the place. It was cold and damp and much too big," said Leona. "You've made it into a palace. It was never meant to be a palace. I'm sure Adeline and Hubert are turning in their graves."

"Leona, enough," said her husband in the same tone he would use for an insubordinate officer cadet. "Let's be positive. There's no point dwelling on the past. Digby was perfectly within his rights to spend his money as he pleased. He'd earned it."

"And gambled it away," said Leona bitterly.

"We have to work out how to proceed." Bruce turned to the grim solicitor who had remained quiet and watchful as the temperature in the room had begun to rise. "Mr. Riswold, you know Sir Digby's affairs better than any of us, perhaps you can advise us."

Mr. Riswold pulled back his shoulders, licked his forefinger again and flicked through the pages of his document to the very end. "I anticipated your concern," he said in a monotone. "So I took the liberty of working out a plan for you . . ." Celia knew then why her father had chosen this meager, pedantic man to run his affairs; it was on account of his composure under pressure. "Prepare yourselves," he warned ominously. "For the worst." They all felt the vertiginous sensation of falling, falling inescapably toward poverty.

When Celia returned to Deverill House the butler handed her a letter on a tray. She recognized the handwriting at once and turned white. "A gentleman delivered it this afternoon," the butler explained when Celia asked, for there was no stamp on the envelope. The thought of Aurelius Dupree ringing her doorbell sent a chill coursing over her skin, like the march of a thousand ice-cold ants. She pulled herself together, calmly thanked the butler, then strode into her father's study, threw the letter in the grate with a trembling hand, and did what she had done with the others: burned it. She hoped that by destroying them the whole situation would go away.

There was only one thing to do, return to Castle Deverill. Perhaps Mr. Dupree wouldn't find her there. The following morning she explained to the butler that she was leaving for Ireland and, if that man was to turn up again, with or without a letter, he was to say that she had left indefinitely so there was no point in corresponding further. She hoped he wouldn't turn up at Deverill Rising and try to speak to her mother. If Beatrice knew what those letters had contained they'd most likely have another funeral to arrange.

ADELINE WATCHED CELIA'S return home with concern. She sensed Celia's fear as well as her determination to delve into her inner resources and find a strength she wasn't sure she had. Celia was alone. She might have Bertie in the Hunting Lodge and Kitty in the White House but she had never been as lonely as she was now. Adeline's heart went out to her; but there was nothing she could do to console her. Archie and Digby were gone from her sight; the fact that they were still with her in spirit meant nothing to someone who lacked the sensitivity to feel them.

"I envy the likes of Digby," said Barton, pushing himself up from the chair and joining Adeline at the window. "He's a lucky Deverill, after all."

"If you mean because he's free to come and go as he wishes, then you're right," said Adeline, who found herself losing patience with these cantankerous spirits. "But he's not very lucky to have left when he did. Much too early. He still had things to do."

"Didn't we all, Adeline," Barton rejoined. He sighed and watched Celia stride into the castle, leaving the servants to carry in her luggage and the nanny to take in the children. "This wasn't the first time the castle had to be rebuilt," he added.

"Oh?" said Adeline, her curiosity mounting.

"It has been burned down before."

"In your time?" she asked.

He nodded. "Aye. In my time. History does indeed repeat itself. The people of Ballinakelly rose up against me and set it alight. I was summoned back to Ireland to defend it. There's nothing like seeing your home blazing on the horizon. A great furnace, like God's own smithy at work, it was. Much like the great fire by the rebels that took Hubert."

"Those weren't rebels," said Adeline crossly. "That was personal."

"Love and hate are very closely intertwined," he said and his voice was heavy with regret.

Adeline looked at him. His face was contorted with pain, his mouth twisted with remorse. "What did you do, Barton?" she asked quietly.

He gazed out of the window but she knew he wasn't seeing anything but the face of a woman, for only love can do that to a man. "I did something unforgivable," he confessed. "And yet unavoidable."

"To whom?"

He shook his head and closed his eyes. For over two hundred and fifty years he had kept the secrets concealed safely in his heart. He had barely dared even face them himself. But now, with Adeline's light so dazzlingly bright, he wanted to release his burden. He wanted to free himself from the guilt, from the darkness that hung about him like a shroud, from the intolerable weight of shadow. He wanted to absorb some of her light. "I loved Maggie O'Leary," he said and his voice was so quiet Adeline wasn't sure she had heard him.

"You loved the woman who laid a curse on you and your descendants?" Adeline gasped. "The very same woman who condemned you to this limbo?"

"Aye. I loved her." The words left him like venom expelled from a wound. "I loved her to her core."

"But I don't understand. If you loved her, why did she not undo the curse?"

He turned to her, shook his head and gave a small, hopeless smile.

CELIA HAD NEVER felt so alone. In spite of the castle full of servants and the corridors full of ghosts, she felt isolated and abandoned and desperately lost. She barely dared look the servants in the eye for soon she would have to let them all go. She curled up in bed and felt ever more keenly the absence of her husband. His side of the mattress felt vast and cold and she dared not put her foot into it, for while she lay coiled like a snake she could pretend not to notice the chill beside her. Tears trickled onto the pillow until the cotton beneath her head was entirely wet. She felt like a puppet whose strings had been cut. The puppeteer had left her to her own devices, but she didn't want independence and uncertainty; she wanted security. She wanted things to be the way they were when she and Archie were in Italy, buying furniture and paintings for the castle. Before the money ran out, before Archie killed himself, before her father had died of a heart attack, before everything had gone so horribly wrong. She pressed her eyes shut and prayed to God. He was her last resort. The one person she could count on not to take offense at being the only remaining option. After all, wasn't His love unconditional?

The following day she went to see Kitty. She needed to be with someone who understood; someone who didn't criticize as Leona had done; someone who had suffered as much as *she* had. Only someone like Kitty could empathize with her predicament.

She found her in her sitting room wrapping Christmas presents at a round table by the window. It seemed like a lifetime ago that she had hosted Christmas. Her husband and father had been alive then. Everything had been wonderful, privileged, blessed. She appreciated her good fortune now as she had never done before. There was nothing like losing something to make one value its worth.

When Kitty saw her, standing diminished and forlorn in the doorway, she rose from her chair and walked over with her arms outstretched and her face full of compassion. Words were superfluous to cousins as close as they. Kitty wrapped her arms around Celia and squeezed her tightly. Celia gave in to her despair and bewilderment and sobbed loudly onto Kitty's shoulder. Kitty, who knew misery better than most, let her release her grief in gasps and hiccups and sighs, all the time murmuring words of encouragement and comfort. She knew time would dull the pain, it would no longer throb and burn, and Celia would eventually grow accustomed to the constant aching in her heart. Indeed, it would become as much part of her as the beat itself; she would barely notice it. Yet it would always be there, and in the quiet moments when she found herself left alone with her thoughts and her mind was not occupied with daily troubles, it would rise in her awareness and she would remember all over again the terrible agony of loss. Kitty shut her eyes and tried not to allow Jack's face to surface, as it so often did, when it caught her unawares. Hers was a loss she would carry to the grave.

They sat by the fire and Celia told Kitty how her father had gambled everything away on the Stock Exchange. She told her of Leona's resentment and Vivien's weak attempts to stand up for her. She divulged her thoughts about Harry and Boysie and was surprised when Kitty confessed that she had known for years, and she told her of her desolation and her pain, but she didn't tell her about Aurelius Dupree. She could never tell anyone about Aurelius Dupree, not even Kitty.

Then one day in early January Celia received another letter. Like those before, it was hand-delivered and presented on the silver tray as the afternoon sun sank into the sea. She was gripped by an icy fear. Aurelius Dupree was in Ireland. He had followed her here to Castle Deverill. He had invaded her fortress. She didn't dare open it. She couldn't bear to read any more about her father and what had happened in South Africa. She knew it was all lies. She knew her father would never hurt or deceive anyone. They were nothing more than vicious, evil lies. Once again she threw the letter into the fire, but this time she knew that however much the paper was consumed by the flames the information in it could never be destroyed, as long as Aurelius Dupree was alive.

She also knew it would only be a matter of time before Aurelius Dupree knocked on her castle door and she was obliged to let him in.

Chapter 25

To distract herself from her worries Celia spent a great deal of time with Kitty. Kitty's daughter, Florence, played with Celia's daughter Connie, just as Kitty and Celia had played together as little girls, while JP was too grown-up to be interested in small children. He was now a boisterous nine-year-old, as adept in the saddle as he was in the school room and handsome with it. He seemed to have inherited the finest Deverill qualities—the piercing gray gaze, the intelligent expression, the ready humor and easy charm—so no one seemed to give much thought to the qualities on his mother's side.

Kitty was careful to keep him away from Ballinakelly for fear of bumping into Michael Doyle, that brutal humbug known to all as "the Pope." The only time she had seen him had been through the car window on her way to church and she had deliberately turned her head so as not to catch his eye. She was determined he should never have contact with JP. The boy was a Deverill first and foremost—and secondly a Trench. Bridie had made her choice and started a new life in America. Kitty doubted she would ever come back. JP prayed for his mama who he believed to be in Heaven, but his prayers were hasty and careless; Kitty was everything a mother should be and he felt no less for the absence of a biological mother. He had two fathers, Robert, who was a constant presence around the house, and Bertie, whom he sought out in the Hunting Lodge as often as he was able. Indeed, as he grew up he and Bertie had grown close. They both loved the same things: fishing, hunting, tennis and croquet, tinkering in Bertie's shed and playing word games in front of the fire at teatime. Kitty knew there was nothing a Doyle could give him that he didn't already have.

Bertie and JP had constructed a large model railway in the attic of the Hunting Lodge. It took up a whole room, which had once been a storage room, and was spread across a quadrant of trestle tables. There were green hills with little model sheep grazing on grass, tunnels, bridges, lakes and tiny cottages and farm buildings. They had built a station complete with signals, moving tracks and a pedestrian crossing. There was even a fishing boat on the lake with a tiny man holding a rod, with a line and a gasping fish on the end of it. The more sophisticated parts that were unavailable in Dublin Bertie bought in London, but the hardware shop in Ballinakelly was well equipped with the essentials such as glue, paint, wood and card. It was on a particularly wet day in January that Bertie and JP, seizing on the idea to build a castle with a greenhouse and a stable block, decided to drive into Ballinakelly to buy what they needed for such an ambitious project.

Thick gray clouds rolled in off the ocean, propelled by a strong easterly wind that blew cold gusts over the water, whipping about the cliffs and whistling around the chimney stacks. Bertie, who drove a blue Model T Ford, sat at the wheel with his son by his side, relishing the project they were enjoying together. He was ashamed of having once rejected JP, of having all but disowned Kitty for insisting on keeping him when she had found the small baby on the doorstep of the Hunting Lodge. How ironic that the very child he had believed would bring about his demise had in fact given him a reason to live.

Father and son chatted excitedly about how they were going to design and build the castle. Bertie suggested various materials, but JP had his own ideas and was confident in voicing them. He wanted it to look exactly like Castle Deverill. "That might be beyond us, JP." Bertie chuckled.

"Nothing is beyond us, Papa," said JP cheerfully. "We can do anything, you and I." Bertie glanced admiringly at his son, for whom anything seemed possible. "We will build Castle Deverill with all its towers and windows and doors. We'll even make the trees and vegetable garden. I know exactly how to make the dome of the greenhouse using an onion, papier mâché and some green paint."

"I suppose the Hunting Lodge isn't enough of a challenge for you?" said Bertie, rather hoping JP would be inspired to build that instead.

JP looked horrified. "But that's not home, Papa. Castle Deverill is *home*." And Bertie shook his head because he knew *that* could only have come from Kitty.

Ballinakelly high street was busy. People were walking beneath umbrellas or hurrying to find shelter from the rain in the public houses and shops. Men in caps and jackets strode briskly down the sidewalk with their heads down and shoulders hunched and horses pulling carts plodded slowly up the road, too wet to care. Bertie parked the car outside the hardware shop and they dashed inside. Mr. O'Casey greeted them deferentially. An old man who remembered the days when the present Lord Deverill was a little boy, Mr. O'Casey had an innate respect for the aristocracy and counted the night the castle burned as one of the worst in living memory. He listened to JP's elaborate plan to make a model of the castle and shuffled about behind the counter, even climbing the ladder to reach the highest shelf, in order to find the right materials for the project. He piled them up on the counter. JP touched them excitedly. "We're going to make a fine castle," he said as Mr. O'Casey put on his spectacles and began to punch the prices into his cash register. Just as he was finishing the little bell rang above the door and a damp wind swept in with Michael Doyle.

Bertie put the money on the counter and turned to face the man the Royal Irish Constabulary had wanted in connection with the fire but had later set free. If Bertie felt any animosity toward Michael Doyle he was too polite to show it. "Good morning, Mr. Doyle," he said evenly.

Michael's eyes fell upon the child and his face softened. "Good morning, Lord Deverill." He took off his cap, freeing a halo of wild black curls. "And this would be young Master Jack Deverill?" he said with a smile.

JP nodded. "I'm JP," he said politely. "How do you do?"

Michael hadn't properly laid eyes on the child since he had carried him down on the train from Dublin. He had been a small baby then. Now he was a handsome boy with a twinkle in his eye. But in spite of his red hair he was a Doyle. *That* was certain. Michael could see it in the strength of his jaw and in the light sprinkling of freckles that covered his nose. He saw Bridie in his wide forehead and in the sweetness of his curved upper lip, but he recognized himself in the directness of the boy's gaze. For sure, JP was a bold, fearless child, just as *he* had been. He felt a surge of pride.

Bertie thanked Mr. O'Casey and lifted the paper bag of supplies from the counter. "Come on, JP," he said. "You and I have work to do." He nodded at Michael and Michael took off his cap again as Lord Deverill opened the door, then followed his son into the street. The little bell tinkled once more and the door shut behind them. Michael watched the boy climb into the car. He had already forgotten Michael and was chatting happily to his father. A moment later the car motored off and Michael was left with a strange sense of loss. JP was his nephew, but the boy would never know it.

Michael bought the items he had come for, then left for home in the car they had bought with Bridie's money. He wondered whether Grace would be sitting in his kitchen, praying with his mother and grandmother. He was quite used to her now. She had come enough times—and ignored him enough times—to convince him of her sincerity. At first he thought it a ruse to entice him back into her bed, but as the months passed and she received regular instruction from Father Quinn, attending Mass in the Catholic Church in Cork, he realized that her conversion to Catholicism had nothing to do with him. She genuinely wanted to find peace with herself and God. He understood that and respected her for it. Once they were together in sin; now they were together in Christ. Yet he could not quite forget her voracious passion and her burning skin.

As he drove off into the hills he thought of Kitty Deverill. Until he had her forgiveness he'd never lie with anyone again.

GRACE SAT ON the sofa in her sitting room while Father Quinn filled the armchair with his black robes, a glass of whiskey in his hand. Grace had stalked her prey like a patient snake with a cunning rat. She had always known it would take time. Father Quinn wasn't going to betray a secret so readily, but she knew him well enough to know that if it served his interests he would betray his own mother. He had to be coaxed, lured and gently persuaded—he had to believe that he was doing God's work. First and foremost he had to trust Grace. After all, they had plotted and schemed during the War of Independence so Father Quinn knew better than most that Grace could keep a secret. And he was well aware that she and Michael had been firm allies in the fight against the British in spite of the vast differences in their births. She was confident that she could use guile to wheedle out of Father Quinn the terrible crime Michael had committed in his past of which he was so ashamed.

She pushed the whiskey bottle across the table. "Please, Father Quinn, you need fortification in your job," she said, and she listened with half an ear as he railed against the young people and their lack of commitment.

"In our day we had a cause to fight. That united us and drove us," she said. "God knows, I wouldn't want another war, but the struggle for freedom was a cause I believed in with all my heart and I was willing to risk my life for it."

"You were a brave lady," Father Quinn said, refilling his glass.

"But I did terrible things," she said, lowering her voice in confidence. "I'll go to Hell for some of the things I did." She looked at him squarely.

"Repent ye therefore, and be converted, that your sins may be blotted out," Father Quinn quoted from the Bible.

"I lured Colonel Manley into the farmhouse. If it hadn't been for me, Jack O'Leary would never have plunged the knife into his heart. I am as guilty of murder as he is," she said in a soft voice and her eyes welled with tears. "Can God forgive me for that?"

"If you truly repent, my dear Lady Rowan-Hampton, the Lord will forgive you and wipe clean the slate."

"I truly repent, Father, with all my heart. I regret the things I have done. The things Michael and I did." She pulled a white cotton handkerchief out of her sleeve and dabbed her eyes. "How I admire him, Father. He was the worst kind of sinner— oh, the things he did in the name of freedom—and yet he turned his life around and is as pious as any priest." *And as celibate*, she thought bitterly, but she kept that complaint to herself. "If I can be half as devout as he is I shall be happy, Father Quinn."

"Michael did indeed turn his life around. He gave up the drink, you see. It awakened the Devil in him and drove him to sin."

"He told me, Father Quinn, he told me about . . ." She began to sob. "Oh, I can't believe he could have . . ." She hesitated, barely daring to breathe, hoping he would finish the sentence for her.

"But my dear Lady Rowan-Hampton, his sins are not your sins."

She turned her face away sharply. "I know that, Father, but can God forgive such depravity?"

"Indeed he can. If Michael truly repents, then the Lord will indeed forgive him. Even for that."

She gazed at him with wide, shiny eyes. "Even for that?" she repeated, desperate to know what *that* was.

Father Quinn leaned forward and rested his elbows on his knees. He stared into his glass and shook his head. "God will forgive him, but he wants more than that. He will not rest until he receives forgiveness from Kitty Deverill."

Grace let out a controlled breath and nodded gravely. She did not show her surprise nor did she reveal her delight at having snared the rat and induced him to squeak. She kept her expression steady and unchanging. "I pray that she will find it in her heart to forgive, Father."

He looked at her and frowned. "If there is anything you can do, I would be very grateful."

"As you know Kitty is a dear friend," she said, slipping the handkerchief back up her sleeve. "She took me into her confidence many years ago. Leave it with me. Now I know that Michael is ready to beg forgiveness I will see what I can do to help. I only want the best for both of them. I ask God to give me tact. It will not be an easy task."

"Indeed not," Father Quinn agreed. "But if anyone can do it, you can, Lady Rowan-Hampton. I have great faith in your abilities." *So do I*, she thought smugly.

When Father Quinn left, weaving his way to his car, which was parked on the gravel outside the house, Grace withdrew to her bedroom. She closed the door and went and stood by the window. There, in the privacy of her room, she let out a low moan and gave in to a sudden shudder that rippled across her entire body. So Kitty Deverill was the reason Michael had re-buffed her. All these years she had imagined countless different reasons, but she had never for a second imagined this. Of course she didn't believe that Michael had violated her, which Father Quinn had implied. Kitty must have seduced him, for certain, and wracked by guilt he had taken to drink. It was all Kitty's fault. Michael was a wild and passionate man, Grace reasoned, but he wasn't a rapist.

It took her a while to quell the jealousy that rose in her like a tide of putrid water, stealing her breath. She had to use all her strength to control her movements because her instinct was to pick something up and throw it against the wall. But Grace was a woman who had spent years practicing the art of self-discipline. She focused on the garden and tried to push away the picture of Michael thrusting into Kitty, which clung to her mind as if her thoughts had got stuck on one image. At length she managed to internalize her fury by hatching a plot. There was nothing like a plan to make one feel less impotent. If Grace could persuade Kitty to forgive Michael, he might return to her bed.

THAT EVENING LAUREL returned from an afternoon hacking across the hills with Ethelred Hunt. Ever since he had sug-gested that she would cut a dash on a horse, she had flirted with the idea of riding again. Indeed, she had been an accomplished horsewoman in her day, brave even, out hunting, and she wasn't planning on doing anything reckless. Hazel had thought her ridiculous; after all she was only a few years off eighty. But why should her life taper toward the end? she thought defiantly. Surely, she was as young as she felt. Ethelred Hunt certainly made her feel like a girl again, and today, riding over the cliffs with the sea crashing against the rocks below and the sea gulls circling above, she had relived a moment of her youth.

Laurel was passionately in love. There was no distinguishing it from the breathless, invigorating feelings of longing that she had experienced as a twenty-year-old. She might be an old lady now but her heart was still tender, like a rosebud opening with the first gentle caress of spring. She didn't believe herself foolish; after all, why should love be the privilege of the young? If Adeline were alive she would say that it is just the physical body that grows old, the soul is eternal and therefore cannot age. Laurel might look like a grandmother, but when Ethelred Hunt had gazed into her eyes and pressed his lips to hers he was seeing a woman.

She inhaled and closed her eyes, reliving for a wonderful moment the feeling of his mouth on hers. She could still smell the spicy scent of his skin and feel the soft hair of his beard on her face. Oh, it had been like a dream, a beautiful dream. She would never forget it for as long as she lived. "We must keep this to ourselves," he had told her, unwinding his hand from around her waist, or from where her waist had been when she was young. "Or we'll upset Hazel. I think she's sweet on me," he told her. Laurel had glowed with delight. After years fighting her sister for attention from this irresistible silver wolf he had chosen *her*.

"Oh, I can keep a secret from Hazel," she had reassured him, and indeed she would.

She walked into the house, closing the door softly behind her. She hadn't seen her sister since that morning, when they had both departed, Hazel to Bertie's for a morning at the bridge table and *she* to the hairdresser. The sound of the gramophone came wafting down the corridor from the sitting room. Laurel was surprised and wondered whether Hazel had company. It wasn't usual for her to play music just for herself. She found her sister standing by the window, gazing out onto the wintry garden where they put bird food for the hardy little robins. One hand wound around the back of her neck, the other was on her hip and she was humming distractedly and swaying slightly, Laurel thought. "Hello, Hazel," said Laurel breezily, unpinning her hat.

Hazel turned, startled. "Oh Laurel, you're back."

"Yes, I am. It was such fun to be out riding again. I feel rejuvenated." She looked at her sister and realized that *she* wasn't the only one to feel rejuvenated. Hazel's cheeks were pink and her eyes sparkled.

"At least you didn't fall off," she said in a blasé tone, as if she wasn't very interested one way or the other. Hazel didn't ask her about Ethelred and Laurel was relieved; she didn't want to betray his kiss with a schoolgirl blush.

"What have you been up to?" She perched on the arm of the sofa and placed her hat on her knee.

"This and that," Hazel replied vaguely. "Bridge was entertaining as usual. This afternoon, well . . ." She sighed dismissively. "I haven't done anything this afternoon except watch the birds. Aren't they perky?"

"Who was at bridge?"

"Just the usual crowd. Bertie and Kitty and I partnered Ethelred." She went and rang the bell for the maid. "Let's have a cup of tea and finish off that porter cake." She didn't catch

Laurel's eye as she passed her. "Tell me, what is it like to be in the saddle again? Were you afraid?"

Laurel shrugged off her sister's shifty behavior and went to sit closer to the fire. "Not afraid, no," she said, smiling at the memory. "It was the most exciting thing I've done in years." And for once neither tried to outdo the other with florid tales of Ethelred Hunt. In fact, his name was not mentioned again and the cordiality with which they had always treated each other returned in eager chatter and cheerful laughter. But every now and then both women ran their fingers over their lips and smiled secretively into their hands.

As much as Celia tried to distract herself from the cold reality of her father's death and the terrible debts Archie had left her with, she was unable to ignore the fact that she had to find money somewhere, and soon. Her father was no longer around to help her and, if he had been, she now realized that he wouldn't have had the resources. She put on smiles for her children, for the friends who came calling and for the members of her family who were always popping in to check on her, but her anxiety lay in the pit of her stomach like cement. There were moments when she stood at her bedroom window, gazing up at the stars and remembering the Deverill Castle Summer Balls of her childhood, when she, Kitty and Bridie had watched the carriages arriving, bearing County Cork's finest, and wished that she could wake up as a little girl again, with no fears or worries. The skies had always been clear on those magical nights, darkening gradually as twilight receded into night with the faint glimmer of the first star.

She dreaded having to sell the castle. This was her home

now. She had placed her heart in the heart of Ballinakelly and there it would stay.

It was a particularly windy morning when her butler walked into the drawing room to find her alone at her desk, writing letters. He knocked on the door. "There is a man here to see you, Mrs. Mayberry," he said. Celia knew who it was. She had been expecting him. The cement grew heavier in the bottom of her belly and she pressed a hand to her heart. She couldn't avoid him any longer.

"Show him in please, O'Sullivan, and ask Mrs. Connell to brew us some tea." She positioned herself in the middle of the room, straightened her skirt and cardigan and took a deep breath. A moment later the man Celia had seen at the funeral and at her father's memorial service was shown into the room.

"Mrs. Mayberry," he said, and he did not smile.

"Mr. Dupree," she replied, lifting her chin. "I've been expecting you for some time. Tea?"

Chapter 26

I don't want tea," he said in a thin, reedy voice. "Whiskey." When O'Sullivan brought it, Mr. Dupree downed it in a single gulp before replacing it on the silver salver with a quivering hand. Celia noticed his nails were cracked and ingrained with dirt. He looked at her with rheumy, bloodshot eyes. "I'll have that tea now," he said and Celia nodded at the butler, who reluctantly left the room. He was uneasy about leaving his mistress alone with this menacing vagabond.

Mr. Dupree could have been a hundred years old. His white hair was so thin that his scalp could be seen pink and scabby beneath it. His skin was sheer and mottled with age spots, scars and deep, angry lines that could have been the work of a knife. Bitterness had ravaged his lips and anger blazed behind cataracts that blurred his vision and made his eyes water. A nervous twitch had taken possession of one side of his face, snatching the muscles every few minutes and pulling his mouth into an ugly grimace, and he smelled of compacted alcohol and sweat found in men who have slept rough and lived low. The energy he emitted was as sharp and prickly as his gaze, and Celia found herself struggling to conceal her utter aversion to this man who had forced himself into her life like vermin sneaking into the castle by way of the gutter. Yet there was something evasive about the manner in which he held himself, something in the slight stoop of the shoulders and the curve of the spine, that robbed him of his menace and even aroused her pity. Beneath his anger he looked desperate.

"Please take a seat," she said and her voice was cool and as-sured; she barely recognized it as her own. She watched him perch uneasily on the edge of the armchair, then took the club fender for herself, in front of the fire. "I want you to know that I have read the letters you sent my father and I don't believe a word that's in them. The letters you sent to *me* I burned without reading them. I find it outrageous that you have the audacity to prey on a grieving family in this way."

Mr. Dupree pulled a packet of cigarettes out of the inside pocket of his jacket and tapped it against his hand. "How well did you know your father, Mrs. Mayberry?" he asked in a wretched voice, popping a cigarette between his dry lips. Celia thought his accent had traces of a brogue but couldn't place it.

"I was very close to him," she replied frostily.

Mr. Dupree shook his head. "I think you'll find you didn't know him at all," he said before bursting into a fit of coughing. "Do you believe in justice?" he asked her when the coughing had passed.

"Just tell me what you want, Mr. Dupree." Celia was infu-riated that this total stranger should assume to know anything about her relationship with her father. She watched him flick his thumb against a cheap lighter and puff on the flame with his cigarette. He put away the lighter and sat back in the armchair, crossing one scrawny leg over the other, revealing threadbare socks, dusty shoes and painfully thin ankles. "Your claims are very farfetched," she said, wishing he would get up and leave, but he didn't look as if he was planning on going anywhere for some time. Mr O'Sullivan returned with a tray of tea. He poured Mr. Dupree a cup and handed it to him. The fine bone china looked incongruous in his rough and callused hands.

"Let me start at the beginning, Mrs. Mayberry. Let me tell you about the Digby Deverill *I* knew."

Celia sighed with impatience. "All right. Go on." She had no interest in hearing his story, but as he was intent on blackmailing her, she had no choice but to listen. Mr O'Sullivan poured her a cup of tea, then left them alone, closing the door softly behind him.

Aurelius Dupree exhaled a thick cloud of smoke and narrowed his eyes. In spite of the defiance in his steady gaze the hand that held the cigarette was trembling. "When Digby Deverill arrived in Cape Town in 1885 and came out to Kimberley my elder brother, Tiberius, had already been prospecting for eight years," he began. "He knew everything there was to know about diamonds. Everything. They called him 'the Brill' because he had a nose for brilliants—he could literally smell 'em—and everyone wanted him on their team. He worked for Rhodes and Barnato—all of 'em giants and they paid him well for it. *Very* well. He called me out to join him and I came on the boat from England, traveled five hundred miles up to Kimberley and learned fast." He tapped his temple with a gnarled finger. "If you had your wits about you there was always money to be made in the mines." He grinned and Celia recoiled at the black holes where teeth had once been. "When Digby arrived, Kimberley was a great piece of cheese being eaten by ten thousand mice. Rhodes and Barnato were looking to amalgamate the mines. The place was all used up. There was nothing there for Deverill. He was just a keen boy from a good family but that counted for nothing, only money and diamonds meant a thing then and he had neither. Rhodes and Barnato were as rich as Midas. They were as rich as kings. Yet Digby arrived with his ambition and his optimism and he was a man who believed in himself. I've never met a man before or since who had the self-belief that Deverill had. He put up a tent on the edge of the mines, in the dust and the midsummer heat, with the flies—and deprivations that you can't imagine and I wouldn't want to tell you, not a refined lady like you, Mrs. Mayberry. You'd never 'ave known that he was a posh boy, thrown out of Eton at seventeen for running a gambling ring and sleeping with the matron or some other boy's mother, at least that's what he told me." He chuckled joylessly, then ejected a round of coughing from lungs full of phlegm. "They say that Lord Salisbury's son lost a hundred pounds at Deverill's table. But it wasn't with the finer class that Digby mixed in Kimberley, but with the roughest of rough diamonds you ever met. Jimmy 'Mad' McManus, who'd fought in the Crimean War and disemboweled a man with his own hands, apparently. Frank 'Stone Heart' Flint and Joshua Stein, better known as 'Spleen'—and you don't want to know how he got *that* name. He was their equal. He didn't fear them. If anything, for all his manners and his Eton tricks, these cut-throats feared *him*. He had the Devil on his side. Ruffians they were but Deverill had one thing none of 'em had: luck. He was lucky at the gambling table, so lucky that he got the name 'Lucky Deverill' soon enough, and it stuck—as did his luck."

Celia thought of her father's Derby winner—the last of his luck, before it ran out for good. "Go on, Mr. Dupree. What happened then?"

Aurelius Dupree dragged on his cigarette and Celia noticed with disgust the patches on his skin where his fingers had yellowed; he looked as if he was getting jaundice. He blew out a puff of smoke, leaned forward and flicked ash into the glass tray Celia had bought at Asprey on New Bond Street. Then he cleared his fluid-clogged chest in another round of coughing, which made Celia feel quite nauseous. "So, one day, Lucky Deverill is winning at the card table," he continued. "And Stone Heart Flint has reached the seams of his pockets. All he has left is a plot of useless farmland north of Kimberley. Deverill's luck is bound to run out at some stage, right? At some stage, certainly, but not then. Not for years! Deverill reveals his winning cards and scoops up the money. And of course, he wins the land—this supposedly useless plot of dust. Now, Tiberius and Deverill had become unlikely friends. Deverill knew nothing of diamonds, but my brother knew everything. The three of us made a pact, a gentlemen's agreement, if there were diamonds up there we were going to split it two ways. Two ways, equally, you understand, and Deverill agreed. Fifty percent for him, twenty-five each for me and my brother. It was his land but he needed us, you see. He couldn't do it without us.

"At first we found nothing. The place had been left to ruin, the mine abandoned, it didn't look like it had anything besides barren land, dust and flies and an old shack where the farmhouse had once stood. Even the well was empty and full of stones. It was a dead old pile of worthless land. But we began to dig in the places that hadn't been mined. Nothing. Deverill grew despondent and talked of quitting the place altogether, but like I said, Tiberius could smell diamonds and he smelled diamonds in the earth, right there on that supposedly barren plot of land. Deverill went and lay in the shade of the only tree for miles around, put his hat over his face and went to sleep. He wasn't interested in the land anymore. He was thinking about the next game and his next hussy. But Tiberius and me, we were hard at it. Raking the ground with our bare hands and I was following Tiberius, because he smelled those brilliants like a hound sniffing for a fox. Then he found one, just sitting by the fence, or what was left of the fence. It was sitting on the earth there, like it had just dropped out of the sky. Like I said, Tiberius knew a lot about soil and this was *alluvial* soil, loose particles of silt and clay, and he came to the conclusion that there had once been water of some sort there and the diamond had been washed downstream and deposited right at the edge of the farm. We shouted to Deverill and he came running. *Now* he was interested, all right. We climbed to the top of the koppie and dug up there, and, hallelujah, we soon found the rich yellow stuff that told us one thing: diamonds. Our blood was up and even Deverill wasn't thinking about cards and girls. We were all digging like dogs, the three of us. That ground was ripe with diamonds. Lots of 'em. We couldn't believe our luck. We set about marking our claim. Deverill went off to register in the name of Deverill Dupree." At this point Aurelius's face

THE DAUGHTERS OF IRELAND • 405

darkened with a deep and burning regret. He grimaced. "We were so busy digging we barely looked up from the ground as we put our signatures to those papers. We trusted Deverill, you see. Biggest mistake of my life, trusting Lucky Deverill." He shook his head ruefully and stubbed out his cigarette. "He had the luck of the Devil, though, there's no disputing that."

There was a long pause as he knocked back his tea and chewed on the terrible injustice he believed Celia's father had committed. Celia remained on the fender, immobile, a sick feeling growing in her stomach. Yet she couldn't stop listening, fascinated and appalled in equal measure. A new world, a new vision of her father was opening up before her like a terrible chasm. "Now Deverill wasn't just a gambler," he went on. "He was a womanizer too. No one's wife was safe when Lucky Deverill was about. Blond and blue-eyed, you'd have thought he'd been conceived by the angels. But the Devil comes in many disguises. While Tiberius and I did all the work Deverill was . . ." He hesitated and flicked his black eyes at Celia. "Well, let's just say he kept himself busy *elsewhere*. The only thing he did, while we sweated, was put up a sign that said: *A Deverill's castle is his kingdom*. He'd written on a wooden plank in black paint and I never did understand what it meant until I saw this castle right here. We laughed at him then, but we should have known," he lamented. "We really should have known. We brought our workers, hundreds of Zulus and Xhosas, and Deverill hired his old ruffians as foremen: Stone Heart, Spleen and Mad McManus. They once caught a boy stealing a diamond and beat him to death.

"Well, we needed investment to mine the diamonds, so Deverill went to Sir Sydney Shapiro. Now Shapiro was the agent of the Rothschild family—who owned the Rothschild Bank that funded Cecil Rhodes in the development of the British South Africa Company—and Deverill was sleeping with his wife. She was a looker: fair and innocent, like butter wouldn't melt in her mouth. But those ones are often the worst sluts of the lot, if you'll forgive me, Mrs. Mayberry. As for Shapiro, he had a hand in everything, like a great big fat octopus, he was, but he didn't know his quiet little wife was sneaking into Deverill's bed. With Shapiro's money Deverill formed his own company, Deverill & Co. which was owned by Deverill Dupree, but Deverill had tricked us when he registered the company, and given himself fifty-one percent of the share to our forty-nine. So Deverill came to us with an offer to buy us out. At the time five grand each seemed good enough, with the promise of shares. But he formed the World Amalgamated Mining Company, known as WAM, and sold it to De Beers for several millions. There was nothing in the agreement about our shares. Nothing. Deverill moved down to Cape Town and bought himself a mansion, setting himself up as one of the great diamond magnates, and Tiberius saw red. We decided to sue. We wanted our share and we believed we had a very strong case."

Aurelius Dupree pulled the cigarette packet out of his jacket pocket again and his hand trembled more violently. He flicked his lighter and inhaled sharply, drawing the smoke into his wheezing lungs. When he looked at Celia his eyes were no longer black but cloudy with layers of grief. "But you lost, Mr. Dupree?" Celia asked. She knew that if he had won he wouldn't be sitting here as a human wreck. She was relieved that this was all it was, a row between diamond prospectors from years ago, one man's word against that of her beloved father.

"We would have won, I'm sure of it," Mr. Dupree continued. "We would have won something. Maybe not seven million, but everyone in Kimberley knew we was owed our share."

"So what happened? Why didn't you win?"

"That's where the Devil came in, Mrs. Mayberry," he said in a voice so quiet and ominous it made Celia shiver. "Digby—"

"If you're going to talk about my father," Celia interrupted irritably, "call him *Sir* Digby."

"Oh no, Mrs. Mayberry, he'll never be Sir Digby to me. A devil in the Devil's pay, maybe, as you will see. Back then, we used to hunt. Every day almost—gazelle, antelope, zebra, elephants and even lions. Yes, even the king of the jungle. While Deverill was in Cape Town in his new palace hobnobbing with Rhodes and Barnato, we was struggling to make ends meet. But one day, we was in the Cape, outside the city. We heard of a man-eating lion from a man called Captain Kleist, a German from German South West Africa. This white hunter invited us to join the posse. It was bad manners to refuse and besides, we needed the diversion. When we arrived with our guns on the edge of the veldt, who did we find but Mad McManus, Spleen and Stone Heart with this German captain, Kleist. I doubt he was ever a real captain, but I won't digress. Anyway, there was an awkward moment, but they greeted us like old times and we didn't blame them for Deverill. So we set off into the veldt. It was dawn. Still dark and cool. But soon it grew hot. That heat like tar you can hardly move in. On and on we went. First on horse, then on foot. We saw lions, me and Tiberius, but we never saw that man-eater, *if* he ever existed. Captain Kleist was in command. He split us into pairs. He chose Tiberius and put me with McManus. The hours passed. Nothing. Mad McManus told me stories of Deverill and his immoral ways; like they say, there's no honor among thieves. Then just as we were about to give up, it was nearly midday and too hot to continue, there came shots ringing into the air nearby. We ran across the veldt. We called out. Finally we heard Kleist's voice, shouting for help. We followed it. There we came upon a terrible scene. Tiberius was lying on the earth, but he wasn't Tiberius no more. He was beyond dead, Mrs. Mayberry. Torn apart, to pieces he was. My brother looked like an impala with his insides ripped out. Looked like the man-eating lion had got 'im, Mrs. Mayberry. Nothing else could have done that and Captain Kleist and Spleen and Stone Heart were already there just looking and saying nothing. There were no words. Nothing to say. I asked Kleist what had happened. He was with him, after all. But Kleist told me they had split up and he had left my brother alone. He claimed to have fired at the lion but it was too late." Mr. Dupree's voice trailed off and he dabbed his damp forehead with his hanky.

"A most unfortunate accident," said Celia.

"And so *I* thought for a while," replied Dupree. "'A tragedy' Captain Kleist called it and all the others testified to an accident. But I took the body back to camp and washed it myself. I saw what I wasn't meant to see, Mrs. Mayberry. I saw a bullet hole in his chest, hidden among the wounds, which maybe weren't even the work of a lion's jaws but of a dagger. Perhaps my brother hadn't been killed by lions, but by man, and those men were your father's henchmen. Suddenly I knew who was behind it." He narrowed his eyes and glared across the room at Celia, who sat rigidly on the fender, her tea cold in the cup. "I told the police and they made their arrest. But it wasn't Deverill they arrested; it was *me*."

"Why on earth would they think that you had murdered your own brother?" Celia asked. "You weren't even with him on the hunt."

"No, and that's what I told the police. But Captain Kleist claimed I was with him, and McManus, Stone Heart and Spleen all agreed with him. They said it was just me and Tiberius out there so I was the only one who could have killed him. It was a setup, Mrs. Mayberry. Deverill wanted us out of the way and he got what he wanted, as he always did."

"But surely there has to be a motive for killing someone?"

"Oh, don't you worry, Mrs. Mayberry, Deverill went to great lengths to find one. He dug around and discovered that we were both in love with the same girl in our hometown of Hove. We both wanted to marry her, it's true, and it was causing a rift between us, but I'd never have killed my brother for her. Some woman testified to having heard me threatening to murder him if he married her, but if I did, it was in the heat of an argument—and that was it. I thought I was done for; I thought the judge would put on the black crêpe and hang me. But there wasn't enough proof to hang me. I was charged with conspiracy to murder and sentenced to life imprisonment. While I rotted in a South African jail, forgotten, Deverill made many a fortune. But it was built on the blood of my innocent brother." Celia put down her teacup. Aurelius Dupree stubbed out his cigarette and he did not light another. "Now I'm out, I've come for my share," he said, looking at her steadily.

"Or what? You'll sell your story to some dirty rag and sully my father's reputation? He's dead, Mr. Dupree."

"Dead men still have reputations and families live off them. I only want what is mine and I *will* have my share," he said in a quiet voice. "Your father can't give me back my life, but he can make my last years as comfortable as possible. He owes me twenty grand, Mrs. Mayberry. That'll see me out. Not greedy, me. Just want some comfort before I'm gone."

Celia stood up. "I think I have heard enough fiction for one day." She walked over to the door and opened it. "O'Sullivan, please will you show Mr. Dupree out." Mr. O'Sullivan appeared in the hall, much to Celia's relief. "Mr. Dupree is just leaving," she said in a weak voice. When she turned back into the room Mr. Dupree was right beside her. She gave a small jump as he stood so close she could smell the tobacco on his breath.

"He didn't pull the trigger, Mrs. Mayberry, but he paid the piper. He should have hanged. I will be back," he said. "I will be back to claim what is mine."

Chapter 27

Celia left the castle and set off into the hills. The winter winds were cold and brisk, raking icy fingers through the long grasses and heather. The air was damp. A light drizzle began to fall. Celia strode on as fast as she could. With her head down and her gaze lost somewhere above the ground just ahead of her, she marched into the grassy nooks and valleys she had explored as a little girl with Jack O'Leary, his pet hawk and his dog. She remembered how she, Kitty and Bridie had watched the birds and Jack had taught them all the names. Loons, shearwaters, grebes and lapwings—she could recall some of them even now. They had lain in wait for badgers, their bellies flat against the earth, their whispers full of excitement and anticipation. They had played with caterpillars, which Bridie had called hairy mollies, spiders and snails and sometimes, on balmy summer nights, they had rolled onto their backs and gazed at the stars and Celia had felt the gentle stirring of something deep within her that she could not explain. She had been drawn into the velvet blackness, into the bright twinkling of stars, into the eternal vastness of space. The sweet scent of rich soil and heather had risen on the warm air and she had felt giddy with wonder. But those days were gone and innocence had gone with them. Now all she felt was fear.

Whether or not her father was guilty of murder she didn't know. But what *was* certain was Aurelius Dupree's demand for money; money she didn't have. The scandal of his story, if told in the press, would finish her mother off for sure, and she couldn't bring herself to tell her sisters, or Harry or Boysie— she couldn't share her father's shame with *anyone*. Celia was left no choice. She *had* to find the money somehow; and she had to find it alone.

Aurelius Dupree had not only made an impossible demand, he had stripped her father of his humanity and exposed him as a brutal monster whose greed had led him to take an innocent life. A monster Celia did not recognize, or want to.

She marched on, deeper into the hills, desperate to lose herself in the mist now forming in the vales in eerie pools of expanding cloud. Eventually she walked into the trees, to hide among their sturdy trunks and branches. Tears blurred her vision, but the mossy ground was soft beneath her feet and the scent of pine and damp vegetation filled the air and began to soothe her aching spirit. Blinking away her despair and looking about her she saw that the forest was beautiful—and what is beauty if not love? The mystical energy deep within the land seemed to wrap its arms around her, giving her an unexpected feeling of strength—a feeling of not being alone. She stopped thinking about Tiberius Dupree and her father, murder and money, and gazed at the wonder of the living earth she had never really taken the trouble to notice before. There were birds in the trees, creatures in the undergrowth and perhaps hundreds of pairs of eyes watching her from the bushes. As a pale beam of sunlight shone through the thicket, falling onto the path ahead of her, Celia surrendered to the effervescence of nature and let the power of this strange presence, so much bigger than herself, carry her pain away.

When she returned to the castle she felt immeasurably stronger. She went straight to the nursery to see her children. As they fought for her attention and wrapped their small arms around her, she thought of Archie and their dream of filling the castle with a large and boisterous family. *That* would never happen now. She had two daughters who would forever connect her to their father, but brothers they would never know. *Whatever happens*, she thought as she kissed their soft faces, *I will not let the troubles affecting my life ruin yours.* She'd sell the castle if she had to and make a new home somewhere else. Surely it wasn't the bricks that made the home, but the people inside it, and it was love that held them all together—and they could take that anywhere.

With this renewed sense of determination she traveled to London to meet with Mr. Riswold, the solicitor, and Archie's bank manager and stockbroker, Mr. Charters. She explored every avenue, but when she left for Ireland she realized that selling the castle was the only option. It was time to take her head out of the sand and face up to the truth: she was on the brink of bankruptcy and only selling her beloved castle could save her.

At the beginning of spring O'Sullivan appeared at the door of the sitting room, where Celia was having tea with the Shrubs.

"I'm sorry to disturb you, Mrs. Mayberry, but there is a gentleman at the door who wishes to see you." For a moment her heart plummeted at the thought of Aurelius Dupree returning for his money and she blanched, but O'Sullivan had specifically said "gentleman," which Mr. Dupree most certainly was not.

"Did he give a name?" she asked.

"He did, madam, but I'm afraid I cannot repeat it." When Celia frowned, the butler wrung his hands. "It is a foreign name, madam."

Celia smiled. "Very well. Ask him to wait in the library."

"Oh, don't make him wait on account of us," said Hazel. "We must be leaving."

"Yes, we have lots to do, don't we, Hazel?" said Laurel.

"We most certainly do," Hazel agreed. "We are going to call in on Grace, who has a horrible cold. I've made her a tincture."

"It's an old recipe of Adeline's," Laurel told her. "It works wonders."

"Oh, it does," Hazel agreed.

"Well, if you really don't mind," said Celia, watching the two women get to their feet. In their feathered hats they looked like a pair of geese. They both smiled, for they were extremely happy these days, and as compatible as they had been before the arrival of Lord Hunt.

"Not at all. Thank you for the tea and cake. Isn't it lovely that it's spring at last," said Hazel.

"It's put a spring in my step," laughed Laurel, secretly thinking that spring wasn't the *only* thing that was putting a bounce in her step.

"In mine too," Hazel agreed, and neither sister knew that Lord Hunt had put a leap in both.

The Shrubs and the mysterious foreign gentleman passed in the hall. The Shrubs chuckled like chickens as the handsome gentleman gave a low bow and smiled, revealing bright white teeth. Ballinakelly hadn't ever seen the likes of him, they thought excitedly as they set off for Grace's. They'd be sure to give her the tincture as well as an enthusiastic description of Celia's glamorous visitor.

Celia waited for the gentleman with the unpronounceable name to be shown into the room. She straightened the skirt of her blue tea dress and stood with her hands folded, not knowing what to expect. Nothing could have prepared her, however, for the arresting charms of Count Cesare di Marcantonio. The moment he stood in the doorway he filled it with his wide, infectious smile, warm eyes and honey and lime cologne. Celia was stunned; she had not expected a man such as this. He strode up to her, took her extended hand and brought it to his lips, bowing formally. When he said his name, his pale green gaze looked deeply into hers and held it firmly. Celia didn't think she had ever met a man who exuded such self-confidence.

"Please, do sit down," she said, gesticulating at the sofa. Dressed in an immaculate gray suit with a yellow waistcoat and matching silk tie, he chose the sofa, sat back against the cushions and crossed one leg over the other, revealing stripy socks and very shiny cap-toe shoes. "Can I offer you something to drink? A cup of tea perhaps, or something stronger? My husband used to drink whiskey."

"Whiskey on the rocks, please," he said, and O'Sullivan nodded and left the room.

"So, to what do I owe the pleasure?" said Celia, but she knew why he had come; there could be no other reason.

"I am interested in buying your beautiful home," he said.

Celia's cheeks flushed with emotion. She had made the decision to sell in January but a small part of her was still in denial. That small part still hoped that Aurelius Dupree's demand for money and Archie's enormous debts would just go away. But here was a wealthy foreign count who had come to realize her fears. "I see," she said, lowering her eyes.

There was a short pause that felt like minutes, and the Count's expression softened with sympathy. "I am sorry for your loss," he said quietly.

"Which one?" Celia replied with a bitter chuckle.

"It is a terrible thing to lose a father."

"And a husband. I lost both," she said.

"And now you are going to lose your home." He shook his head and his handsome face creased with compassion. "You are a beautiful young woman. If I was not married I would buy the castle and give it to you."

Celia laughed. If it wasn't for his alluring foreign accent *that* would have sounded tasteless. "Where is your wife?" she asked, hoping to curb his flirting.

"The Countess is in New York. We live there."

"Did you, by any chance, make me an offer last summer?"

"My attorney did on my behalf. Mr Beaumont L. Williams."

"Yes, I remember. You must want it very badly."

"My wife wants it very badly, Mrs. Mayberry. When she heard it was for sale she said she wanted to have it more than anything in the world. So, I will buy it for her, whatever the cost." He cast his gaze around the room. "Now I know why she wants it so much. It is very beautiful."

"Has she seen it?"

The Count frowned. "Of course she has seen it," he replied, but he didn't look very certain. "It is a famous castle, no?"

"It's been in my family since the seventeenth century. It would break my heart to lose it. After the generations of Deverills who have treasured it, I feel I am letting them down. I'm the Deverill who will be remembered as having let it go into the hands of strangers."

"We will love it, Mrs. Mayberry. You can be sure of that."

"I have no doubt that you *would*," she said softly, still reluctant to accept the fact that the castle had to go.

O'Sullivan entered with the Count's whiskey followed by Mrs. Connell with a fresh pot of tea for Celia. The Count waited for the servants to leave, then he swilled the ice in his glass and said, "I will make you an offer you cannot refuse. I will pay you more than anyone in Europe would pay. You see, the Countess has set her heart on this place and nowhere else will do. The Countess wants it exactly as it is. She will keep the servants. No one will lose their job because of the sale. Everything will continue seamlessly. She wants it so I shall buy it for her."

Celia was perplexed. What had inspired the Countess to want it so badly? "You say your wife has seen it, but has she actually *been* here?" she asked.

He shrugged. "She has always dreamed of an Irish castle and this one is special," he told her. "It has a charming history and yet it is fully modernized. I don't think that one could say the same for the vast majority of Irish castles." He swept his eyes around the room. "Irish castles are not worth much on the whole, but this one is different from the rest. You have made it beautiful, Mrs. Mayberry. You see, I am descended from the counts Montblanca and the princes Barberini, the family of Pope Urban VIII, so I know quality when I see it."

"Are you going to come and live here?"

"Eventually, yes. The Countess is expecting our first child." He grinned bashfully. "I am going to be a father. I am very happy."

"Congratulations," said Celia. She envied the Countess her vast wealth and her good fortune. There had been a time not long ago when Celia had been blessed with both those attributes, before fate had so cruelly snatched them away. "Have you undertaken the long voyage from America just to see the castle for yourself?" Celia's curiosity was aroused by this foreign man whose wife wanted the castle so badly, in spite of never having set foot in it. There was something shifty about the whole scenario.

The Count uncrossed his legs and leaned forward, placing his elbows on his knees and looking up at her from under the glossy hair that had fallen over his forehead. "I wanted to talk to you personally, Mrs. Mayberry. I also wanted to see the castle for myself, of course. I didn't want such an important purchase to be done coldly, through my attorney. I sensed that this is a home, a family home, so I felt it was only polite to talk to you face-to-face. I understand your reluctance to sell, but I can assure you that we will take good care of it."

Celia wondered whether he had somehow read the British newspapers, which had been full of her father's financial demise and the possibility that Celia was going to have to sell the castle. But there had been no photographs of the castle itself, so how had the Countess come to set her heart so firmly upon it? "Shall I show you around, Count di Marcantonio?" she asked.

"If you have the time."

"I do," she said with a sigh, pushing herself up from the fender. "I have all the time in the world."

Celia took him on a tour of the inside first. She showed him the grand rooms, lovingly restored and rebuilt after the fire, and the furniture and paintings she had bought in Italy, which he particularly loved, being of Italian origin. She told him the history, at least the parts she knew, and he nodded earnestly and listened keenly as if wanting to learn it all by heart. He praised her style, admired the splendor of the architecture and imagined himself living there, Celia thought, as she watched him running his eager eyes over everything. She thought it odd that a foreigner with no connection to Ireland should want to move here. The landscape was beautiful, of that there was no doubt, but it was cold and damp in winter and wouldn't they miss the glamour of New York? She imagined the Countess to be a flamboyant and spoiled Italian woman with a loud voice and brash taste. She saw her striding down the hall in furs and pearls and shouting at the servants. She had no reason to imagine her so, for the Count was tastefully dressed and had impeccable manners—perhaps her envy was making her mean.

The gardens were bathed in bright spring sunshine. Birds tweeted in the trees whose branches had just begun to turn green with the fresh, phosphorescent brilliance of new leaves. Apple blossom floated on the wind like snow and sea gulls wheeled and cried above them beneath fat balls of fluffy white cloud. It could not have been a more propitious day for the

Count to see the castle. It shone in all its glory and a lump lodged itself in Celia's throat, for soon it would no longer be her home. Soon, all the love and pleasure she had poured into it would belong to someone else.

The Count marveled at the neatly trimmed borders, the recently cut lawn, the flower beds where forget-me-nots and tulips interrupted the emerging green shoots with splashes of blue and red. He admired the yew hedges and ancient cedar and the giant copper beech that rose up behind the croquet lawn in a rich display of emerging red leaves. They wandered through the vegetable garden and Celia showed him the greenhouses where she had once played as a little girl. She thought of Kitty then, and her heart gave a painful lurch. No one would suffer more than Kitty at the sale of Castle Deverill. She suppressed her guilt and tried to keep her attention on the tour and the Count.

Suddenly a shout resounded across the lawn. Celia recognized the voice at once. She turned to see Grace marching across the grass toward her in a pale floral dress. Her hand was holding her hat to stop it flying off her head into the wind. The Count also turned and Grace's face flowered into a wide and enchanting smile as she reached them. "I'm so sorry, Celia, I thought your visitor would have left by now," she said, tilting her head in that coy, flirtatious way of hers, which had won many a heart, and broken just as great a number.

"I thought you had a cold," said Celia.

"Oh, those Shrubs exaggerate everything. I'm perfectly well." She looked at the Count and smiled. "I'm sorry to interrupt," she added, giving him her hand.

The Count took it and brought it to his lips and bowed. "Count Cesare di Marcantonio," he said and his words seemed to flow over her in a delicious cascade, for she shivered with delight.

"*È un grande piacere conoscerlei,*" she replied and they smiled together as if they had suddenly come to a mutual understanding. Celia watched Grace's shameless flirting with admiration. The Count, who had been mildly flirting with Celia, now turned his full attention to Grace, and Celia realized, by the comparison, that he hadn't really been flirting with her at all. He had recognized a fellow epicurean in Grace.

"May I introduce Lady Rowan-Hampton," said Celia, and the Count gave her features a long caress with his heavy green eyes.

"How lovely to see Castle Deverill on such a day as this!" Grace continued, catching her breath.

"We were just saying the same thing," said the Count. He chuckled to himself as if surprised by his own luck. "Are all the women in Ireland as beautiful as you two *bellissime donne?*" he said. "Because, this is my first time here and I am wondering why no one told me. I would have come sooner."

"They are not," said Grace with a laugh. "I'm afraid you have seen the best West Cork has to offer."

They began to stroll toward the stable block. "Castle Deverill always had the best hunt meets," said Grace. "And Lord Deverill always had the best hunters. Do you ride, Count di Marcantonio?"

"Of course. I play polo. I have many horses in Southampton."

His reply was deeply satisfying to Grace. "What an exciting game polo is."

"I grew up in Argentina and there the ponies are the best in the world."

"And, as far as I understand, so are the riders," said Grace.

"You are not wrong. But I am much too polite to boast." He grinned broadly, showing off a perfect set of gleaming teeth.

"Oh, you don't need to be polite in front of us, does he, Celia? We're not opposed to a little boasting."

"Count di Marcantonio is looking to buy the castle, Grace," said Celia, hoping that Grace would modify her behavior accordingly, but she didn't. Her slanting cat's eyes widened and her chest puffed out with ill-concealed excitement that this dashing foreign count was going to come and live at Castle Deverill.

"I have to first convince Mrs. Mayberry that I am a suitable person to take over the responsibility of looking after such a historic castle. It is not only a castle but a much beloved home. Perhaps you are a good judge of character, Lady Rowan-Hampton, and can help me persuade her."

"I will do my best, for the both of you," said Grace, but she didn't once look at Celia. Her eyes lingered on the Count's. Celia continued to show the Count around, although she would have preferred to leave Grace to do it for her. The two of them chatted away like a pair of teenagers on a date. She wondered whether they realized that the other was married. She presumed they did and that they didn't care. The Countess was in America and Sir Ronald, well, Sir Ronald was anywhere but here in Ballinakelly.

At length Celia agreed to consider his offer. But on one condition.

"Yes?" he said, raising his eyebrows.

"There are two houses on the estate that are rented by my cousins, Lord Deverill and his daughter, Kitty Trench. I will only sell the castle if those houses continue to be let to them at the current rate. In fact, I will have it included in the documentation that the Hunting Lodge and the White House are always offered to Deverills first."

The Count shrugged. "I'm sure that will not be a problem," he said. "It is the castle that my countess wants so badly."

"While you think about it, why don't you come for dinner tomorrow night?" suggested Grace. "Celia, I hope you will come too. I will invite some nice people for you to meet. Do you play bridge?" she asked the Count.

"Of course," he replied with a shrug.

"Wonderful. Where are you staying and I will send an invitation round."

"Vickery's Coaching Inn in Bantry."

Grace's smile broadened. "If you are going to come and live here you might as well meet some of your neighbors."

Once again he kissed their hands and bowed. They stood on the steps and watched him climb into the back of his taxi and set off down the drive. "My goodness, what an attractive man! His countess is a very lucky lady," said Grace.

"Having seen the way he flirted with you, I'm not so sure she's very lucky! I wouldn't trust him as far as I could throw him."

"Oh, all Italian men are like that. If they can't flirt they might as well be denied oxygen too," said Grace dismissively. But her cheeks were flushed and her brown eyes shone with intent. Count Cesare di Marcantonio might be just the person to take her mind off Michael Doyle. In fact, in her mind, she was already at the royal suite in Vickery's Coaching Inn in Bantry. "I'm sorry you have to sell the castle, Celia," said Grace. "I truly am." She placed a soft hand on Celia's.

"He wants to buy it for his countess," said Celia. "I'm not sure why an Italian countess should want to come and live in Ballinakelly. They live in New York, and, as far as I understand, she's never even seen it."

"I agree, that *is* strange," said Grace, but she really didn't care. "You're very sweet to think of Bertie and Kitty."

"I feel guilty," said Celia.

"For what? Saving their castle and then losing it? If it wasn't for you it would never have been rebuilt. No one would be mad enough to do what you did."

"And look where it got me."

"It will make you rich," said Grace, turning serious. "This count will pay a fortune for it. He has more money than sense, I assure you. Don't accept his first offer. You can push him higher, *much* higher. If his countess wants it *that* badly, he'll pay you three times its value. He's a terrible old fraud." Grace laughed.

"What do you mean? I thought you were taken by him."

"Taken by him, yes, but not taken *in* by him. I have a sensitive nose. I can tell when someone is a phony. But still, he's very easy on the eye." She linked her arm through Celia's. "Let's go in and have a cup of tea and you can tell me how this count found out about the castle in the first place."

Celia sighed as they walked into the hall. "I'm afraid I don't know the answer to that question."

Grace narrowed her eyes. "Then we need to find out."

Chapter 28

Adeline stood by Stoke Deverill's bed and watched the old man's labored breath slowly enter and exit his body in a low rattle. His skin was gradually losing the color of life and turning the dull green of death. His mustache, once as majestic as the outstretched wings of a swan, now drooped and purple shadows stagnated in the holes where once his cheeks had been. Adeline knew his time was very near, for his son Digby, his grandson George, and other members of Stoke's family who had long departed, had come to take him home. Adeline smiled; if people knew they wouldn't die alone death would not frighten them so.

Augusta sat in a chair pulled up to the bedside and dabbed her eyes with a handkerchief. Maud perched on the end of the bed while Leona and Vivien stood by the window, wondering how long it was going to take because they had things to do. Beatrice was still languishing at Deverill Rising, unaware of the enormity of her late husband's debts. While she hid beneath the blankets her sons-in-law were fighting to keep her homes. There was little chance of success.

"It should be me," said Augusta with a sniff. "I have defied death at every turn. I'm bound to be waylaid by it sometime."

"You'll outlive us all," said Maud.

"He'd be a cruel God to inflict me with longevity! What's the fun of being down here if all one's friends are up there?" She raised her eyes to Heaven. "I think he's going now. He's stopped breathing." Leona and Vivien hurried to the bedside, relieved that the vigil was about to end. Then Stoke gave a splutter and inhaled sharply. "Oh no, he's back again!" Augusta cried. "I don't think he wants to go."

He would if he knew where he was going, Adeline thought. But Stoke was clinging on to life as if he were a climber digging his nails into the edge of a precipice, afraid of letting go. Adeline ran a hand across his brow. *Come now*, she whispered. *We'll catch you.*

Stoke opened his eyes. He stared in wonder at the faces surrounding him. Faces he hadn't seen for so long. "Digby, George," he gasped, reaching out his hand. Augusta caught her breath and stopped crying. Maud's mouth opened in amazement. Leona looked at Vivien and bit her bottom lip. Vivien's eyes sparkled with tears. Suddenly neither of Stoke's granddaughters wanted to be anywhere else but here.

Lost for words Augusta hiccuped loudly and pressed the handkerchief to her mouth. Stoke's face expanded into a wide smile, releasing the shadows and reviving his mustache. Adeline watched as Digby and George took his hands and lifted him from the bed. Surrounded by his loved ones he departed into the light. Adeline watched them go. Just before Digby disappeared he turned to Adeline and winked.

"He's gone," said Maud, peering into Stoke's lifeless face.

"Do you really think he saw Digby and George?" Augusta asked, the handkerchief trembling in her hand.

"I truly think he did, Grandmama," said Leona, putting a hand on her grandmother's shoulder. "I'm certain of it."

"I do hope they'll come for me when it's my turn," said Augusta. She looked at Maud and smiled sadly. "I haven't been that bad, have I?"

"No, you haven't, Augusta. No worse than the rest of us."

"Then I hope Stoke saves a place for me up there, because it won't be long." Leona rolled her eyes at her sister, who suppressed a grin.

"Augusta, you've been rehearsing your death for twenty years," said Maud, not unkindly.

"Then it's long overdue, wouldn't you say?" She pushed herself up from the chair and Vivien handed her her walking stick. "In the meantime, life goes on, such as it is without my beloved Stoke. Let's go and eat. I'm certainly not going to die of hunger!"

Back at Castle Deverill Adeline recounted Stoke's death to Hubert. "What a privilege it is to die like that," he said wistfully. "What a curse it is to die like *this*!" And there was nothing Adeline could say, because she wholly agreed with him. What a curse it was, indeed, for the poor unfortunate Lord Deverills to die like this.

CELIA SAT ON the window seat and stared out into the black night. Clouds obscured the stars and blinded the eye of the moon to her misery. She felt alone and fearful. There was no one she could confide in. No one she could turn to. No one to advise her how to proceed. She'd sell the castle, buy somewhere modest to live as close to Ballinakelly as possible and settle Archie's debts. As for Aurelius Dupree, when she thought of buying his silence something inside her recoiled into a tight, stubborn ball. She couldn't leave him to publish his outlandish claim, but allowing herself to be blackmailed went against every instinct. Her father would never have tolerated such an attack.

She pulled her knees to her chest and folded her arms on top, resting her forehead in the crook of her elbow and closing her eyes. She just wished the whole sorry business would go away. As she drifted off to sleep she found solace in her memories. She remembered so clearly the excitement of rebuilding the castle; the ebullient Mr. Leclaire with his plans and his ideas; the grand tour of Europe she and Archie had enjoyed together, choosing the pieces of furniture and the works of art to adorn their new home. She recalled Archie's pride, her father's pleasure, her mother's excitement and her sisters' jealousy, and the tears squeezed through her knitted lashes. It was then that she thought of Kitty, Harry and Bertie. If *she* was suffering at the prospect of selling the castle, how had *they* felt when she had bought it? It had never occurred to her that it might have caused them pain. She had expected them to share her joy, but how could they? Only now did she understand how hard it must have been for them and how valiantly they had dissembled, and she felt ashamed. She had been so selfish, so self-absorbed and arrogant. Maud, Victoria and Elspeth seemed to have no emotional connection to the place, but Kitty—and her heart swelled with compassion and sorrow at the thought of her—Kitty loved it more than anyone, even *her*. How had she endured it?

With these thoughts Celia fell asleep on the window seat. The clouds thinned and eventually the moon shone brightly through the openings, pouring its silver light through her bedroom window. She dreamed of her father. He was wrapping his arms around her, reassuring her that she was never alone, because he was with her, always. But when she looked at him he had the face of an ogre and she woke up with a jolt. She lifted her head off her knee and stared into the dark room in bewilderment. The impenetrable clouds blackened the sky and she felt cold and stiff in her limbs. She wiped the tears from her face with the back of her hand. She walked over to her bed, pulled back the blankets and climbed inside. She was too tired to think about Aurelius Dupree. Too tired even to think about her father. She'd think about them tomorrow. Other women would have given up, or paid up, or wept, but now the Deverill spirit began to emerge in Celia for the first time. She knew there was only one way to find out the truth—and to clear her father's name—and that was to go to South Africa. Her head fell onto the pillow and she was enveloped once again in sleep's embrace.

TEN DAYS LATER Celia was on the boat to Cape Town. "Has she gone mad?" said Boysie to Harry, as they sat at their usual table in White's, enjoying lunch.

"I believe so," Harry replied. "She's been very cagey. Wouldn't tell me what it was all about. Said there was something important that she had to do."

"Must be very important if she has to cross half the world to do it!" Boysie sipped his Sauvignon. "What the hell is going on? It's not like her to keep secrets from us."

"Kitty says some frightfully rich foreigner is buying the castle and everything in it," said Harry. "I can't say it's come as a surprise, but I'm sorry for her. That place is a curse."

Boysie shook his head. "The place isn't cursed, old boy, you and your family are."

"Nonsense, that's just a silly story Adeline made up. She believed in all sorts of ridiculous things. You know, she even believed in fairies." The two men laughed. "I promise you. She claimed to see garden spirits all the time."

"There's a damned eccentric streak running in your family."

"*Grandma's* family," Harry emphasized. "Look at the Shrubs."

"Yes, I do see. I suppose they see the dead, too, do they?"

"I think that would terrify them. They can barely cope with the living. That Lord Hunt is leading them a merry dance. Kitty says they're both going to have their hearts broken."

"I didn't think it was possible at their grand age. Aren't they a bit old for that sort of foolery?"

"One would have thought." Harry wiped his mouth with a napkin. "Apparently Celia has managed to get the foreigner to pay well over the sum that it's worth. She declined his offer and forced him to raise it. I dare say he wants it very much—or his wife does. He's buying it for her, you see."

"Since when is Celia a businesswoman?" asked Boysie with a chuckle.

"Maybe she has more of her father in her than we realized."

"Good. She deserves to get a lot for that place. She's selling her heart with it."

Harry frowned. "That's very sad."

"She's selling *all* your hearts with it," Boysie added, putting down his glass.

"Not mine," said Harry quietly. *"You* have my heart, Boysie, and you always will." They stared at each other across the table, suddenly serious.

"You have mine too, Harry," said Boysie. Then he looked away. There was no point in mentioning that little hotel in Soho. Harry wasn't going to change his mind. They just had to accept things as they were.

CELIA STOOD ON the deck of *Carnarvon Castle*, the seven-hundred-foot motor ship bound for Cape Town, and leaned on the railing and gazed out across the ocean. She had pawned jewelry to pay for the voyage to South Africa, which would take seventeen days. It was a long way indeed, but not very long in comparison to the personal journey Celia had made. She looked back at the girl she had been a year ago—that girl would never have imagined herself here on this boat, traveling across the world in search of the truth about her father's past. That girl would never have imagined even half of the events that had taken place in the last twelve months. She had lost her grandfather, her father, her husband and her home—and was being blackmailed by a man claiming her father had murdered his brother. *That* was more than most could handle, but Celia wasn't most, she was a Deverill and she was beginning to learn what that meant.

She looked down at the water, fizzing and foaming as the boat's gray hull cut through it at the speed of twenty knots, and felt a swell of exhilaration. The wind blew through her hair, and swept across her face, waking her from despondency. She felt a strength growing inside her, like the inflating of a balloon, filling her with confidence and a fresh sense of optimism. Out of her desolation there sprouted hope. She was a Deverill and Deverills didn't let their difficulties crush them. Tragedy could take everything dear to her, but it couldn't take her spirit. It couldn't take that. Hadn't Kitty said that those we love and lose never really leave us? She lifted her face to the wind and for the first time in months she didn't feel alone.

The elegant liner carried two hundred and sixteen first-class passengers and double the amount of second-class passengers. Among the former was the famous Irish tenor, Rafael O'Rourke, setting off on a world tour. In his mid-forties he had dark, romantic looks with pale eyes the color of an Irish morning and the heavy, soulful gaze of a matinee idol. Celia was excited to discover that he was only too happy to sing for the passengers in first class. In the evenings after dinner, he sang to the accompaniment of the pianist of the ship's show band while the gentlemen and ladies sipped champagne and cocktails at the small round tables in the bar. Candles glowed soft and warm and the lights were low and Celia drank just enough alcohol to make her forget her woes. Rafael sang of love and loss and his voice resonated with her deepest longings. She sat in the corner, alone at her table, and allowed his music to smooth down the raw edges of her grief.

The first-class deck of the boat was large and comfortable, with luxurious suites and tastefully decorated public rooms. Celia spent the day in the lounge, reading quietly by herself or playing cards with the other passengers she was slowly getting to know. She was soon adopted by an elderly couple well acquainted with the name Deverill. "Anyone who knows anything about South Africa will have heard of the name Deverill," Sir Leonard Akroyd had explained when they first met. "Edwina and I have been living in Cape Town for forty years now and Lucky Deverill is one of the great characters I remember from my past." When Celia told him that Digby Deverill was her father he had invited her to join his table every night of the voyage for dinner. "Your father once did me a great favor so I'm happy to have the opportunity to repay him by keeping an eye on his daughter." He had smiled kindly while his wife looked dutifully on. "Now let me tell you about it . . ." And he had launched into a long and rather dull anecdote that involved a stain and the lending of a fresh shirt.

Celia noticed Rafael O'Rourke whenever he came into the room, for he lit it up with his quiet charisma and easy smile. He was always surrounded by people Celia assumed to be part of his entourage. Passengers pushed themselves forward, eager to talk to him, and she imagined the only place he could be private was in his own suite. He sat smoking, reading the papers or talking to men in suits and every now and then he'd catch her looking at him from the other end of the room and she'd feel her face flush and hastily lower her eyes. She had no desire to throw herself at him like the other women did, but he did arouse her curiosity.

Soon she began to notice when he *wasn't* in the room. At those times it would feel less vibrant and strangely empty, in spite of the fact that it was full of people. Her mood would dip with disappointment until the moment he would saunter in again and inject her with a certain "aliveness" that she found confusing and slightly alarming. Was it right that a man could affect her in this way so soon after her husband's death? She felt guilty for her feelings and retreated farther into the back of the room, distracting herself with more of Sir Leonard's tedious anecdotes or the blessed relief of cards.

With only five days to go before docking in Cape Town, Celia must have been the only female in first class who hadn't introduced herself to Rafael O'Rourke. It was no surprise, therefore, when he found her on the deck one evening after dinner, and introduced himself to *her*. There is nothing as attractive for a celebrated, sought-after man like Rafael O'Rourke as a woman who holds herself back. He leaned on the railings beside her and offered her a cigarette. She looked at him in surprise but smiled and took one. "Thank you," she said, placing it between her lips.

"It's nice and quiet out here," he said and his Irish brogue caught in her chest and made her suddenly long for home. Turning out of the wind he flicked his lighter. Celia had to lean in close and cup her hands around the flame. It went out a couple of times so that on the third attempt Rafael opened his jacket wide to shield it from the gale. There was something very intimate about the way she had to bend toward his body and she was relieved it was dark so that he couldn't see her blush as she puffed on the flame. At last it lit and she stepped back and rested her elbow on the railing.

"You sing beautifully, Mr. O'Rourke, but everyone must tell you that," she said, hoping her voice sounded confident. "But what they don't tell you is that your voice has become the tonic that heals me."

"I couldn't help but notice that you're on your own," he said.

"I am," she replied.

His gaze fell softly on her face. "Might I ask why a beautiful woman like you is travelling alone?"

She laughed and wondered how many times he'd said that to strange women he met on his tours. "Because my husband is dead, Mr. O'Rourke."

He looked appalled. "I apologize. I shouldn't have asked." He turned toward the sea and looked out into the darkness.

"Please, don't apologize. It's perfectly fine. I'm getting used to being on my own."

He glanced at her and grinned. "You won't be alone for long."

"If Sir Leonard Akroyd had his way I wouldn't have a moment to myself this entire voyage. He and his wife have rather taken me under their wing."

"But you escaped out here."

"I did. They're a sweet, well-intentioned couple, but sometimes one needs a little time to oneself. I'm sure you know what I mean. From what I've noticed, you rarely have a moment's peace either."

He smiled. "So you noticed me, did you?" Before she could answer he added, "Because I noticed *you*, you see, the first day, and I've noticed you ever since. I notice when you enter a room and when you leave it." Celia blew smoke into the wind and watched the night snatch it away. "Can I show you something?" he asked.

"That depends . . ."

He laughed a deep throaty laugh. "I'm a gentleman, Mrs.—"

"My name is Celia Deverill," she said and there was something reassuring about slipping into her former identity. She almost felt as if she was regaining a little of her old self. "I'm no longer Mrs. Mayberry, you see. So you can call me Celia, if you like."

"And you can call me Rafi."

"Very well, Rafi. What is it you wish to show me?"

He walked with her along the promenade deck until they reached the end where deck chairs were lined up in rows. He stubbed out his cigarette beneath his shoe, then settled himself into one and lay back against the wood to stare up at the stars. "Aren't they grand?" he said.

Celia took the deck chair beside him and looked up at the sky. "They *are* grand," she agreed with a sigh. "They're beautiful." She remembered those stargazing evenings at Castle Deverill and the tension in her heart grew tighter.

"You see, I'm a perfect gentleman." He laughed.

"So you are," said Celia.

"Where are you from, Celia?"

"Ballinakelly in County Cork."

"I'm from Galway," he told her. "We're a long way from home."

"We are," she said quietly.

"And we have five days before we arrive in Cape Town."

"Are you married, Rafi?" she asked.

"I've been married since I was twenty-one. I have five children, all grown-up now. What would you say if I told you I'm a grandfather already?"

"That you don't look old enough. Is that what you want me to say?"

"Of course."

Celia caught her breath as he took her hand and caressed her skin with his thumb. She kept her eyes on the stars as the blood rushed to her temples. She hadn't felt a man's touch in what seemed like eons. Her heart began to pound and a warm feeling crept softly over her, reawakening the dormant buds of her sexuality. When she turned to look at him he was staring at her, his eyes shining in the moonlight. "Five days," she said, gazing back at him.

He smiled and put his hand to her face. He leaned over and pressed his lips to hers. His kiss was so tender, so sensual that it was easy to yield. *Five days*, she thought, *long enough to enjoy a delicious fantasy, short enough to walk away at the end with my heart intact. As for my virtue, isn't it time I had some fun? I'm a Deverill, after all.*

Chapter 29

The final five days on board *Carnarvon Castle* felt like another life for Celia, who threw herself into this heady adventure with the enthusiasm of someone who so badly wants to forget the world beyond the bow of the ship. On her secluded island of cabins and decks she delighted in her brief affair. Rafael O'Rourke was a sensitive and tender lover, and Celia found solace as well as a new vitality in the arms of this man who had no connection whatsoever with her family and the tragedies that had befallen it. She was able to detach from the person she really was and be someone else entirely. Someone happier, more carefree; someone closer to the untroubled girl she had once been.

In public they put on a charade of being nothing more than acquaintances. They greeted one another formally as they passed in the corridor or when they found themselves seated at next-door tables in the lounge. Rafael performed in the bar in the evenings and Celia sat at her usual table in the corner, sipping champagne and listening to the sad melodies that he sang in his rich and touching voice, only for her. In public they were strangers, but their eyes met across the room and their gazes burned, and when they found themselves alone at last in Celia's cabin they fell on each other.

At night they escaped to the deck chairs and lay in the dark, watching the stars of the Southern Cross shining brightly above them and sharing the story of their lives. As the boat gently rocked and the wind swept over the decks they lay entwined, warm from their bodies pressed together and the excitement of these stolen moments running through their veins. But five days was all they had and soon the sight of Table Mountain emerged out of the dawn mist to herald the end of their voyage and the final moments of this short chapter of their story.

Celia, so sure that she would walk away with her heart intact, found herself clinging to Rafael with a rising sense of loss. She didn't know whether her fear came from the uncertainty of where she was going and what she was going to find when she got there, from the abrupt return to real life or from the shock of their parting and the fact that they might never see each other again. He kissed her one last time, caressed her face with heavy, sorrowful eyes as if committing her features to memory and told her he would try with all his might to forget her, lest the rest of his days be dogged by longing. Then he was gone.

Celia was left with the emptiness in her heart bigger and louder than before, because, for a blissful five days, Rafael had filled it. He had made her forget who she really was and what she carried inside her. But now that she was alone again she had no alternative but to accept her position, step off the boat and face with fortitude whatever Fate threw at her. She had survived so much already, she could survive this.

IT WAS EARLY autumn in Cape Town, but for Celia it could have been midsummer because the sun was hotter than it ever was in England. The sky gleamed a bright sapphire blue and not a single cloud marred its breathtaking perfection. The light possessed a fluid quality that Celia found instantly uplifting and she turned her attention away from the shadows that preyed on her fears and squinted in the sunshine.

The city itself was tidy and clean, a sprawling mass of pale-colored Dutch-style houses simmering at the foot of the flat-topped mountain that resembled a giant's table. Having made a game of hiding from Sir Leonard and Lady Akroyd on the boat Celia was now pathetically grateful for their company as they escorted her down the gangplank and through the throng of heaving people to their chauffeur-driven car. They would deliver Celia to the Hotel Mount Nelson, where she would stay for one night, and then make sure she arrived safely at the train station and wave her on her way to Johannesburg the following morning.

Celia, who was not unacquainted with American jazz singers at her mother's Salons in London, had never seen quite so many black people all in one place before. The noise was deafening as they touted for hotels and offered to carry luggage, shouting in their eagerness to be hired in a language Celia didn't recognize. Long-legged Zulus with ebony skin in flamboyant, brightly colored costumes with vast feather-and-bone headdresses offered rides in their rickshaws and small boys scampered among the weary travelers, selling newspapers, sweets and fruit. The place smelled of humidity and dust and the salty flavor of the sea.

Celia was relieved to reach the calm seclusion of the Akroyds' plush Mercedes and sat by the window gazing out onto this famous city, which, Sir Leonard told her importantly, was "the gateway to British South Africa." She imagined her father arriving here as a boy of only seventeen and wondered at his courage and readiness for adventure. She remembered Sir Leonard's anecdote about the shirt and was confident that she would find evidence very soon to disprove Aurelius Dupree's outrageous story. She didn't doubt that the man was a liar; she simply had to prove it.

Cape Town was bustling with activity as the city awoke, stretched and set off to work. Cars weaved in and out of the double-decker trams while men in jackets and hats rode bicycles or hurried along the sidewalks on foot. Flower-sellers set up their stalls on street corners and shopkeepers opened for business. Horses and carts carried goods to sell, plodding slowly over the asphalt, and in the background Table Mountain shimmered in the morning sunshine like a large step to Heaven. As the Mercedes motored slowly up Adderley Street Sir Leonard gave Celia a brief history of the city in which he was clearly very proud to live, and Celia opened her window wide and looked out onto the main thoroughfare of grand buildings, shops and restaurants and tried to imagine what sort of place it had been when her father had first seen it.

They dropped Celia off at the very British Mount Nelson Hotel, which was positioned directly beneath Table Mountain, where she stayed for one night. The following morning Sir Leonard and Lady Akroyd saw her onto the train and insisted that she come and stay for a few days at the end of her trip. "There's so much more for you to see," said Edwina. "You can't come all this way and not see a single animal. I'm sure Leonard could persuade you to come out into the bush." Celia thought of the lion that had torn Tiberius Dupree apart and decided that she'd rather stay in the city than venture out into the bush.

The whistle blew and the Akroyds were enveloped in a cloud of steam. The train pulled out of the station and Celia set off for Johannesburg.

CELIA GAZED OUT of the window in wonder at the vast landscape. Never before had she felt so small beneath such a colossal sky. The train puffed its way through the flat and verdant plains of rich farmland, where occasional dwellings stood, bathed in sunshine. A little boy tending a herd of oxen waved as she passed, his naked torso gleaming like ebony in the early autumn light. Far away in the distance, bordering the veldt, an arresting range of mountains seemed to rise out of the earth like gigantic waves of gray rock, quivering on the horizon in the heat. Soon the veldt rose into craggy hills of low scrub and the train meandered along the valley, which eventually gave way to a wide-open landscape of dry grassland. The mountains retreated and only the sky falling softly onto the horizon shimmered in their place.

That night Celia slept fitfully in her compartment. She missed Rafael O'Rourke and wondered whether he missed her too, or whether, as she suspected, affairs were an unavoidable part of being a famous musician—a way of avoiding loneliness, which was undoubtedly also part and parcel of being on tour.

Celia feared being alone. She feared the strange rhythmic noise of the train and the unsettling sound of other passengers walking in the corridor outside her room and talking in muffled voices the other side of her wall. Yet, in spite of her fears, the movement finally rocked her into a reluctant sleep.

At last she arrived at Park Station in Johannesburg, a little stiff due to the hard mattress and raw from having slept a shallow, fretful sleep. This station was very different from the stately and immaculate station in Cape Town. It was very large and noisy and teeming with people jostling past each other impolitely. Her father's old Afrikaner foreman, Mr. Botha, was on the platform to meet her as she had arranged and because he was so tall she saw him a head above the masses, wading his way through the crowd, waving his hand in greeting. He was a large, wooly-haired man in a pair of voluminous khaki shorts with long white socks pulled up over bulging calves and scuffed brown lace-up boots on his feet. He wore a short-sleeved white shirt tucked in beneath a swollen, spherical belly and a white bush hat placed squarely above big fleshy ears. Celia imagined he must surely be in his sixties, but the thick layer of fat that covered him, as well as his bushy white beard, made him look a great deal younger. "You must be Mrs. Mayberry," he said cheerfully in a strong Afrikaans accent and extended a large, doughy hand. "It's a *murra* of a *leka dag,*" he said. "A lovely day," he translated.

She shook his hand and smiled back with gratitude. "I'm so pleased to meet you," she said, feeling immediately reassured by the confidence of this exuberant man.

"I can see the family resemblance," he said, looking her over. "You have your father's eyes. The same blue. He was a great man, your father," he added, giving a meaningful nod. "I'm sorry for your loss."

"Thank you. It was all terribly sudden."

"From what I know of Digby Deverill, he wouldn't have wanted a long, drawn-out death. Too early, certainly, but it would have been the way he'd have chosen to go."

"I think you're right, Mr. Botha."

"Come, let me help you with that." He lifted her suitcase with ease, as if it were a child's toy. "Now, I'm sure you'd like to freshen up in your hotel before we get down to business. I've taken the liberty of booking you into Jo'burg's finest, the Carlton Hotel. I think you'll find it very comfortable. Then a nice lunch." He set off down the platform and Celia had to walk fast to keep up with his long strides. "This is your first time in South Africa, I believe."

"It is," she replied.

"You've come a long way, Mrs. Mayberry."

"I hope it is worth the journey."

"It is sure to be," he replied encouragingly. "You said you need to look into your father's past. Well, there is no one better than me to help you, Mrs. Mayberry, and I am at your service."

Opened in 1906 the Carlton Hotel was grand in scale and harmoniously classical in design, with shutters and iron balconies that reminded Celia of Paris. Her suite was big and comfortable and she was relieved to be back in luxurious surroundings familiar to her. She unpacked her clothes and bathed, humming happily to herself. After her bath she changed into a light summer dress and ivory-colored cardigan, which she hooked casually over her shoulders. She felt quite restored after the long train journey and stood a moment at the window gazing out onto this foreign city that had once been home to her father. Below, a double-decker tram made its way slowly along the track on Eloff Street while a few cars motored up and down in a stately fashion, their round headlights catching the sunlight and glinting. Celia's confidence increased, for Mr. Botha was sure to dismiss Aurelius Dupree's story as invention. She was certain that she would be able to return home with her head held high—for the truth would unquestionably vindicate her faith in her father. Aurelius Dupree would crawl back into the hole out of which he had slid and never trouble her again.

Mr. Botha arrived in his car to take Celia to lunch. The restaurant was an elegant, Dutch-style building designed around a wide courtyard of shady trees and pots of red bougainvillea. Autumn was already turning the leaves on the branches but the sun was still hot and the air heavy with the lingering scent of summer. They sat at a table in the garden, shielded by the yellowing leaves of a jacaranda, and Celia felt very much herself again after a large glass of South African wine. Mr. Botha was only too happy to tell her about the young Lucky Deverill and the early days before he made his great fortune. "You knew him right from the beginning?" Celia asked.

"I did and we remained in contact right up until he died, Mrs. Mayberry. Your father was never still. He was a gambler all through his life. He liked nothing better than to take a risk. He wasn't called Lucky for nothing, now, was he?"

When they had finished their main courses, Celia felt it was time to ask the question she had come all the way to South Africa to ask. "Mr. Botha, may I speak plainly?"

"Of course." He frowned and the skin on his forehead rippled into thick folds.

"I presume you know of the Dupree brothers?" she asked.

"Everyone has heard of the Dupree brothers, but I knew them well. Tiberius was killed by a lion and his brother, Aurelius, was sentenced to life for his murder." He shook his head. "They were a rum pair of losers."

"Did my father tell you about the letters Aurelius sent him, just before he died?"

"No, he didn't. What was in them?"

Celia, now utterly confident of her father's innocence, was ready to share the contents. "Aurelius accuses Papa of murdering his brother."

Mr. Botha looked satisfyingly appalled. "That's a lie. Your father wasn't a murderer."

Celia took a deep breath. "You don't know how happy I am to hear you say that. Even though I never doubted him."

"Your father wasn't an angel either," he said, digging his chins into his sunburned neck. "They were hard times back then and competition was heavy. A man had to have a certain cunning—a certain craftiness—to succeed. But murder was not something Lucky Deverill would have dirtied his hands with."

"Aurelius told me about the hunt for the man-eating lion. He said that three men were with the white hunter. Spleen, Stone Heart and McManus. I would like to talk to them."

Mr. Botha shook his head. "They are dead, Mrs. Mayberry," he said.

"Dead? They're *all* dead?"

"*Ja,* all dead," he confirmed.

"Aurelius accuses Papa of cheating them twice. Firstly, when he registered the company Deverill Dupree and took the greater share and secondly, when he bought them out and promised them shares—"

"Let me make one thing clear, Mrs. Mayberry," Mr. Botha interrupted stridently. "Yes, Mr. Deverill registered the company Deverill Dupree in his favor, but that was because *he* had won the land in a card game, so it was right that he should have fifty-one percent to their forty-nine. As for the shares, *ja,* I know all about that too. They wanted to sue, but really, they didn't have a case. They signed all the papers willingly and Mr. Deverill paid them more than he believed it was worth at the time. How was he to have known that De Beers would buy it for millions? People are greedy, Mrs. Mayberry, and those Dupree brothers were worse than most."

"So Papa didn't cheat them . . . ?"

"He certainly did not."

Celia sat back in her chair. "Can you give me evidence to prove this odious man wrong? I'm afraid he is trying to blackmail me."

"I will give you copies of the very documents they signed," said Mr. Botha. He flicked his fingers for the waiter and asked for another bottle of wine. The sun was hot, the restaurant elegant and he was enjoying reminiscing about a man whom he had held in the highest respect.

"What was Papa like as a young man, Mr. Botha?" Celia asked, light-headed with relief to have her father's innocence confirmed.

"He was a big character. When he came out here he had very little to his name. He had lived a life of privilege, but he was the youngest of three brothers so he had to make his own way. He didn't want to go into the Army or the Church, or indeed to follow in his father's footsteps and work in the financial world, *that* sort of life would have bored him. He wanted adventure. He wanted a challenge. Not only did he have a good brain, a *sharp* brain, he had guile. You should have seen him at the gambling table. I don't know how he did it, but he rarely lost and even when he did, he looked like he was winning. No one had a better poker-face than Digby Deverill."

Celia watched the waiter fill her glass. She was already feeling pleasantly tipsy. "And what of love, Mr. Botha? Did my father have love affairs? When I was going through his office I looked at old photographs of him and he was such a handsome man. I bet half the women out here fell in love with him."

"They certainly did," said Mr. Botha with a belly laugh. "But do you know who he loved the most?"

"Tell me," said Celia, smiling at him encouragingly.

"A colored woman he called Duchess."

"Colored? Isn't that black?" she asked, fascinated.

"*Half* black, Mrs. Mayberry. Your father fell in love with a beautiful colored woman."

"What happened to her?"

He shrugged. "I don't know. She lived in a township just outside Jo'burg. If she's still alive she probably lives there now. Your father was a lady's man, that's for certain, but he was Duchess's man in his heart. She was his great love for about three years. I imagine there was no secret he kept from her."

"I want to meet her," said Celia suddenly. "I want to meet this mystery woman my father loved. She'll know him better than anyone, won't she?"

Mr. Botha shook his head. "I don't think that would be a good idea," he said and there was something shifty about the way he lowered his eyes and swilled the wine about in his glass. "I'm not even sure she still lives there. We might never find her." He waved his hand dismissively. "I can find you more interesting people to meet who knew your father. Men of distinction—"

"No, I want to meet *her*," she said. "Come on, Mr. Botha."

"It was forty years ago."

"I know and of course she's married and had children and probably grandchildren, who knows, but wouldn't it be important for me to meet her? If my father loved her once, I'd very much like to see her. She must know so much about that time. I've come a long way and I'm not going home without turning over every stone."

"Your father had other women, too . . ." he added uneasily, but Celia was undeterred.

"I know about Shapiro's wife," she said.

Mr. Botha nodded. "Yes, he had her too."

"But Duchess . . ." She shook her head and drained her glass. "I'd like you to take me to see her, Mr. Botha."

"I think you should think twice about digging into your father's past," he warned. "You might discover things you wished you hadn't. They were rough times back then. You had to be tough to succeed."

"I won't take no for an answer," said Celia, standing up.

AND SO IT was with great reluctance that Mr. Botha drove Celia out of the elegant city and into the shabby, dusty township of simple wooden huts, corrugated-iron roofs, dry mud tracks and narrow shady alleyways. Celia had never seen such poverty even during the worst of times in Ireland and her exuberance evaporated in the late-afternoon heat. Skinny dogs loped over the red earth hunting for food while men in mining caps with dirty faces bounced about in the back of horse-drawn carts on their way home from the mines. Women in brightly colored headscarves chatted in the shade while half-naked, barefooted children played happily in the sunshine. A man, clearly drunk, staggered in front of the car and Mr. Botha had to stamp his foot on the brakes to avoid running him over.

As the car drove slowly over the dusty ground people emerged from their huts and stared with curiosity at the shiny vehicle. The whites of their eyes gleamed brightly against the rich color of their skin and Celia gazed back, transfixed. She remembered Adeline's passion for feeding the poor of Ballinakelly and now, on seeing for herself the desperate quality of these people's lives, she understood Adeline's need to make a difference.

Soon the car was being followed by a small group of excited children. They ran alongside, daring each other to touch the metal, shouting in a language that Celia didn't understand. "I wish I had something to give them," she said to Mr. Botha.

"If you did, you'd never have enough," he said flatly. "Besides, you feed one and you have every child in the entire township begging for food."

After a while, Mr. Botha, now sweating profusely, was clearly lost. Celia recognized a street they had already been down. Not wanting to make him nervous she decided to pretend that she hadn't noticed, but when they drove down it for the third time she knew she had to say something. "Do you know where we're going?" she asked.

"I haven't been here for years, Mrs. Mayberry. I seem to

have lost my bearings." He buried his hand in the breast pocket of his shirt and pulled out a handkerchief with which he proceeded to pat his damp brow.

"Why don't you ask someone?" she suggested. "I'm sure these children will help us." She grinned at them through the window and they smiled back with eagerness.

Mr. Botha was reluctant to speak to the locals but he knew he had no choice. Besides, if he didn't know where he was, how would he ever find his way out? He stopped the car and asked the children now crowding around where Mampuro Street was. They all pointed enthusiastically and then started running ahead of the car, shouting and laughing at each other.

Mr. Botha followed at a gentle pace, only to discover that he had been a couple of streets away all along. Recovering his bearings he put the handkerchief back in his pocket and motored down the track, pulling up outside a small brown hut with a simple wooden door and two glass windows. "Is this where she lives?" Celia asked, climbing out of the car. The children retreated, forming a semicircle around the car, watching the beautiful blond lady in the long flowing dress and T-bar shoes with large, curious eyes.

Mr. Botha knocked on the door. There came a rustling sound from within, then the door opened and an eye looked cautiously out through the crack, accompanied by the pleasant smell of smoke. A woman's voice said something that involved a string of words Celia didn't understand interspersed by sharp clicks of the tongue. Then she seemed to recognize Mr. Botha and the door opened wider. She shuffled out on her bare feet in a heavy, brightly colored *shweshwe* dress and matching turban and craned her neck to take a closer look. On her face she had painted an array of white dots. "I've brought someone to see you, Duchess," said Mr. Botha.

Duchess turned to Celia. When she saw her the woman straightened up and a curious expression took over her face. She stared for a long moment without blinking and her lips twitched with indecision. Then the shock turned to curiosity. She glanced warily at the children who quietly scampered off and lowered her voice. "You'd better come in," she said.

"I will come with you," said Mr. Botha, but Celia raised a hand.

"No, please wait in the car," she said. Mr. Botha was not happy but he did as she requested. Celia followed the older woman into the dim interior of the hut. It was cool inside and crammed with potted plants of varying colors. There was a straw mat on the floor, a wooden table and a few chairs. The walls were painted bright blue and there was a shelf, laden with objects and a few books, above an open fireplace. Celia looked through into the other room where there was a bed positioned beneath a small window that gave onto the back of another rough dwelling. On the wall above the bed was a wooden cross, which took Celia by surprise. She hadn't imagined this woman to be Christian.

She was about to introduce herself, but the woman gesticulated to a chair with long, elegant fingers. "I know who you are," she said in a heavy accent, sitting down opposite and picking up her long-handled pipe, which she had been smoking. She was a full-bodied woman with strong arms and voluptuous breasts, graying hair just visible beneath her turban and a gauntness about her cheeks that betrayed her age, but Celia could see that she had once been beautiful. Her eyes were the color of shiny brown horse chestnuts and slanted like a cat's. When she looked at Celia they possessed a certain haughtiness that Celia imagined had earned her the name Duchess. Indeed, her skin was smooth and unlined, her cheekbones high and her eyebrows gracefully arched, giving her an air of nobility. Her full lips curved in a pretty bow shape and her teeth were very big and white. "You are Digby Deverill's girl," she said, running her intense gaze over Celia's features. "I would recognize you out of a thousand women," she added. "It's the eyes. I'd know them anywhere."

"I am Digby's daughter," said Celia, smiling. "I've just arrived in South Africa and I wanted to meet you."

The woman clicked her tongue. "How is your father?" she asked.

"I'm afraid he died," said Celia quietly. The woman blinked in horror and her head fell back a little, as if she had just been slapped. "It was a terrible shock for all of us," Celia explained, suddenly questioning her wisdom in coming. "He was still young and full of life." She proceeded to tell Duchess how he had died because the woman's grief prevented her from speaking. While Celia chattered on, Duchess's long fingers played about her trembling lips.

Eventually her eyes, now heavy with sorrow, settled on Celia. "So, you want to see me because I knew your father?"

Celia was embarrassed and lowered her gaze. What right did she have to turn up uninvited and dig up this woman's past without knowing anything about it? "Yes, I want to know who he was. From what Mr. Botha tells me, you knew him better than anyone."

Duchess's eyes seemed to gather Celia into their thrall. Celia stared back, powerless to look away. It was as if the woman was a vault of secrets that was on the point of being opened. "Your father betrayed everyone around him," she said softly, blowing out a puff of blue tobacco smoke. "And he betrayed *me*. But God knows, I've never loved anyone like I loved Digby Deverill."

"He betrayed *you*?" Celia asked, astonished. The feeling of reckless happiness that had been brought on by the verification that her father wasn't the murderer of Aurelius Dupree's story now crumbled and she felt the sickening fear return as shadows swallowing the light. "I'm sorry . . . perhaps I shouldn't have come." She made to get up.

"No, perhaps you should not have. But as you are here you might as well stay." Celia remained on the chair, wishing very much that she could leave. But Duchess had waited more than forty years to tell her story and she was determined to have her say. "God has sent you to my door, Miss Deverill. I wondered whether I would ever see your father again. But the years passed and our story faded like dye in sunlight, but not for me. My heart loves now as it loved then and it has not learned otherwise. So you will not leave with nothing, Miss Deverill. You came to see me for a reason and I am glad you have come." She pressed her lips to the pipe and Celia noticed the glass-beaded bracelets around her wrists and necklaces hanging over her breasts in elaborate designs of many colors. "My name is Sisipho, which means 'gift' in Xhosa, but your father called me Duchess. He said I was beautiful and I *was* then, Miss Deverill. I was as beautiful as you are." She lifted her chin and her sultry eyes blazed with pride. "Your father was a gentleman. He always treated me with respect, not like other white men treat black women. He listened to me. He made me feel like I was worth something. He even took me around Johannesburg in a horse and buggy." She pressed her fist to her heart. "He made me feel valued." She nodded in the direction of the bookshelf. "Those books you see there. He taught me English and he taught me to read. Digby gave them to me and I have read them all a hundred times. He spoiled me. He made me feel special and I *was* special, to him." Celia wondered if anyone since had made her feel special. From the way she was now wiping her eyes with those impossibly elegant fingers Celia doubted it. "He shared all his secrets with me. I knew everything and I have kept those secrets for over forty years. But I don't want to die with them. They're a heavy burden to carry through the gates of Heaven, Miss Deverill. I'm going to give them to you."

Celia did not want to carry the burden of Duchess's secrets either, but she had no choice. Duchess was determined to relieve herself of them. She puffed on her pipe and the smoke filled the room with a sweet, persistent smell. "Digby won a farm in a game of cards. He was so good at reading people that he rarely lost. He'd come and tell me all about it. About the foolish men who lost everything they had at the gambling tables. Not Digby. He wasn't foolish like them. He was clever and he knew it. He knew he was going to make money. He wanted to go back to London a rich man. Men would do anything to make their fortunes here. Your father was no different." She chuckled and for the first time Celia saw how her face glowed like a beautiful black dahlia when she smiled. "And he did go back to London a rich man. A *very* rich man." Now she narrowed her eyes and her smile turned fiendish. "But he was ruthless, Miss Deverill. Your father didn't make his fortune Moses's way. No, he broke a few Commandments on the path to prosperity. After all, if he had been a virtuous man he would not have loved *me*." Celia watched in fascination as this woman enlivened in the brilliance of her memories. She laid them out before her as if they were treasures, stowed away for decades and now displayed all bright and glittering for the only person interested in looking at them. And all the while her eyes shone with zeal as the words came tumbling out.

"But Digby didn't care what other people thought and he came to see me all the same. He told me about his winnings and he spent some of it on me." Her eyes were misting now as she remembered the good times. "He'd rush in all excited, like a boy with a present for his mama, and I'd scold him for spending money on me when he should have been saving what he had for the mines he was going to build. He didn't trust his own kind. White men—they might steal his diamonds, his money, but he trusted *me*. I knew he was going to strike it rich. I could see it in his ambition. If anyone was going to make it rich it was Digby Deverill—and there were thousands of men like him, with ambition and desire, all digging in the same place, but somehow I knew Digby would make it. He had the luck of the Devil. So, having won the farm north of Kimberley, he and two others went to look for diamonds there and they found them."

"Mr. Botha told me about this," said Celia, with rising interest. "Tiberius and Aurelius Dupree."

Duchess shook her head and the beads that hung from her ears swung from side to side. "Those boys were no match for Digby," she said proudly. "Their biggest mistake was in trusting him. But he looked like an angel with those big blue eyes and that halo of golden hair. He looked as innocent as a lamb. When he no longer needed them he got rid of them the old-fashioned way."

"What do you mean?" Celia asked. The smoke suddenly seemed to turn to ice and envelop her in its chilly grip. "Tiberius was killed by a lion."

Duchess watched Celia with a steady gaze. Her voice had a stillness about it now; even the smoke seemed to stagnate. "He didn't die by a lion. He died by a bullet."

"Aurelius's bullet," said Celia firmly. Her heart was thumping so violently now against her ribs that she had to put a hand there in an attempt to quieten it.

Duchess shook her head but this time the bead earrings did not move. "Captain Kleist's bullet."

Celia stared at her, eyes wide with terror. "Captain Kleist, the white hunter?"

"He was a ruffian who fought in the Prussian army. He thought nothing of killing a man. He arranged the trip and he made sure that Tiberius's death looked like it was an accident."

"But Aurelius was accused of his brother's murder and spent four decades in prison."

"He didn't do it," said Duchess matter-of-factly. "Digby framed him."

Celia began to cough. The smoke was now choking her. She stood up and staggered to the door. Outside, the sun was setting and the air had turned grainy with dusk and dust and a cool breeze swept through the township bringing the relief of autumn. She leaned against the doorframe and gasped. Mr. Botha had fallen asleep in the car. His head was thrown back against the seat and his mouth was wide open. She could hear his snores from ten feet away.

So her father was everything Aurelius Dupree had said he was. He had cheated the brothers, had one murdered and framed the other. She wanted to vomit with the shock of it. She wanted to expel what she had heard. How she wished she had never come.

"So why did you love him?" she demanded, striding back into the room.

Duchess was still sitting on her chair. She was delving into a bright beaded bag for tobacco for her pipe. "Because he was the Devil," she said simply. "No one is more attractive than the Devil." She grinned broadly and flicked her eyes up at Celia. "And he treated me like a duchess."

Celia sat down again. She ran her knuckles across her lips in thought. "You said he betrayed you too," she said.

"One day your father stopped coming to see me. He just disappeared from my world and I never heard from him again. Because of your father I was cast out of my community and disowned by my family. But I am a Christian woman now, Miss Deverill, and I have found it in my heart to forgive. I forgive them all."

With a trembling hand Celia fumbled with the catch on her handbag. "I don't have much but what I have left I want to give to you."

Duchess put up a hand to stop her. "I don't want your money. I never asked for anything from Digby and I won't accept anything from you. I have told you my story."

"But I want to give you something. For keeping Papa's secret."

"I kept it because I love him."

"But he can't thank you himself."

Duchess narrowed her eyes and grinned. "No, but I want to thank *you* for coming, child. I want to give *you* something. It was the year 1899 and my brother was a Piccanin working for an Afrikaner gold prospector who took him down to a farm in the Orange Free State. They said there was gold there. *Lots* of gold. But it was so deep they didn't have the means to mine it. So I told Digby. You see, there was a farm for sale next door that belonged to a man named van der Merwe, and no one had thought to buy that. Digby was no fool and he knew that the land might be useless then but in years to come, he said, 'Who knows what man might have created to dig deeper into the earth.' So he bought the land for nothing and it's been sitting there, untouched, for years. Now I know that the mines around Johannesburg are going real deep now. Deeper than they ever did. Why don't you think about digging there instead of digging into your father's past, and if you find gold, *then* you can give me some."

Chapter 30

Celia left Duchess smoking on her pipe. She woke Mr. Botha with a shake. He gave one final snort and sat up. "Just dozed off for a second," he said, taking the wheel.

"Thank you for bringing me, Mr. Botha. My visit was very enlightening."

"Now back to the hotel?" he asked.

"Yes please," she said, closing the passenger door and leaning back against the leather. She needed time to digest what Duchess had told her. She needed to figure out what to do. She also wondered how much of the truth Mr. Botha knew and was concealing from her. As the car motored over the lengthening shadows the children walked out into the cloud of red dust they left behind and watched the glimmer of metal disappear around the corner. "Tell me, Mr. Botha, what do you know about van der Merwe farm?"

"I don't know what you're talking about."

Celia gave him a hard stare. "You worked for my father and yet you claim to know nothing about land my father bought?"

Mr. Botha shrugged his big shoulders. "Your father's mines have all been sold to the Anglo American Corporation, to Ernest Oppenheimer. There's nothing left but some old legal papers in the safe."

"Then I'd like to see them, please," Celia told him.

"There is nothing worth seeing, Mrs. Mayberry."

Celia gave him her most charming smile. "If you don't mind, Mr. Botha, I'd like to have a look all the same. Just in case."

"Very well," Mr. Botha replied with a weary sigh. "I will take you. But I remember nothing about van der Merwe's farm. To be frank with you, Mrs. Mayberry, Duchess is old and her memory is a little vague."

"Well, while we're being frank, do you know of a man named Captain Kleist?" she asked.

"Der Kapitän," he said. "He is an old drunk and a blaggard and I don't believe he ever fought in the Franco-Prussian War. Why? Do you want to meet him too?"

Celia did not like his tone. "Yes," she replied. "I would."

Mr. Botha shook his head disapprovingly. "He's a fraud and a phony, Mrs. Mayberry. If he remembers anything it will be through the filter of alcohol or simply invented. He's nearly ninety and losing his mind."

"Where might I find him?"

"Propping up the bar in the Rand Club," he replied with a derisory snort. "But women are not permitted."

"Then I have to see him where I *am* permitted, Mr. Botha."

He sighed. "All right, I will see what I can do, Mrs. Mayberry."

MR. BOTHA'S OFFICE was on the second floor of an elegant white building that could have been in the middle of London, yet here it was in the middle of Johannesburg. He showed her into the foyer and closed the heavy wooden door on the noisy street, where trams, motorcars, men on bicycles and women on foot went about their business with the usual urgency of city dwellers. It was quiet inside the building and the woman at the front desk in a pair of glasses and blue tailored jacket smiled at Mr. Botha. He said something to her in Afrikaans and then headed off up the stairs. He showed Celia into his office and offered her a glass of water, but Celia was anxious to find the paperwork for Mr. van der Merwe's farm. Mr. Botha filled a glass for himself and then asked her to follow him to the safe, which was in a small cupboard in a room farther down the corridor. He took a while to unlock it and Celia felt he was being slow on purpose. But it opened at last and Mr. Botha leaned in and grabbed a cardboard box with his big hand. "These are your father's papers," he told her, putting it down on the desk. "You are welcome to go through them."

The box was large and held many documents. Celia pulled out the chair and sat down. "I'll have that glass of water now," she said to Mr. Botha, lifting out a beige file and opening it. Mr. Botha left her for a few minutes as he went to find a glass and fill a jug. When he returned the desk was strewn with paper and Celia had a smug and satisfied look on her face. "You're very organized," she said and her voice showed her surprise. She hadn't thought Mr. Botha would have labeled and arranged the files so clearly. "I have found the deeds to Mr. van der Merwe's farm," she said, holding up a faded pale blue file. "Now, I would like you to arrange for me to meet Captain Kleist."

Once back at the hotel Celia sat in the lounge with a large glass of whiskey. After having feared being on her own she was relieved to have time to think without the overbearing presence of Mr. Botha. She sat on the sofa and rattled the ice about in her glass. The golden liquid burned her throat but landed warmly in her stomach, swiftly taking the edge off her disquiet. Celia could not imagine her beloved father having a heart cold enough to murder, but Duchess had left little doubt. In spite of all that, the woman still claimed to love him. In spite of everything she had learned, Celia still loved him too, although she was discovering a very different father to the one she had known. She ordered another Scotch on the rocks.

Celia slept well that night. The hotel was reassuringly comfortable. The luxury was familiar and she didn't feel afraid. However, there was a new deadness in the depths of her being, a dull feeling of non-emotion, which came from resignation. Resignation to the truth, to the *terrible* truth, that her father had built his fortune on the blood and incarceration of those Dupree brothers. No amount of money could give Aurelius back those wasted years, or Tiberius. The thought was so overwhelming that her mind simply shut down. She closed her eyes and sank into blissful oblivion.

In the morning she went down to breakfast in the dining room. There was a message for her at reception. Captain Kleist was coming to meet her at the hotel at eleven. She was surprised and a little unnerved. She thought he would be reluctant to meet her. She imagined he wouldn't want to talk about so murky a past. This gave her heart a little boost and ignited a spark of hope. Surely, if he had killed on her father's behalf, he wouldn't be so keen to come and see her.

She waited in the lounge in an elegant floral dress, narrow-brimmed hat and cloth gloves, sipping a cup of tea. As the hands of the clock slowly approached eleven o'clock Celia began to feel uneasy. Her stomach churned with nerves and she could feel herself sweating. The minute hand moved beyond the twelve and seemed to gather speed as it descended toward the six. Celia watched the door. Every time anyone appeared she expected Captain Kleist, only to be disappointed. Her nerves grew still, the churning faded away and the sweat dried. She remained on the sofa for an hour until she had to resign herself to the fact that the Captain wasn't coming.

When she telephoned Mr. Botha he didn't sound at all surprised. "He's old and infirm," he explained. "I suggest you give up, Mrs. Mayberry. He has no wish to see you."

At this point many would have given up, as Mr. Botha suggested. But Celia was discovering a steely determination inside herself that she had never had cause to find before. She had traveled thousands of miles to discover whether or not Aurelius Dupree was telling the truth. She wasn't going to return to Ireland without knowing for certain. Captain Kleist was the only one who really knew what had happened that day in the veldt and she was adamant that she was going to talk to him, one way or the other. She remained on the sofa in the lounge for a further two hours, trying to think of a way of tricking him into meeting her. And then, just when her stomach was beginning to tell her that it was lunchtime, she came up with a plan—a plan that did not include Mr. Botha.

She asked the concierge for the telephone number of the Rand Club and then asked if she could use the telephone on the desk to make a quick local call. The concierge was only too happy to oblige such a pretty young woman as Mrs. Mayberry and wandered a short distance away to give her some privacy. She dialed the number and waited. Her heart was beating so loudly she thought she'd have trouble hearing the ring tone over it. There was a brief crackle down the line, then she heard it clearly. It rang a few times before a man's voice answered.

"The Rand Club, how may I help?"

"Hello, good afternoon, my name is Mrs. Temple," she said in a calm, officious voice. "I'm telephoning from the governor general's office in Cape Town. May I speak with Captain Kleist?"

"I'm afraid he hasn't come in today," replied the man.

This was as Celia had expected. "Ah, then perhaps you can help me," she said. "His Majesty's government has a very special package to send to Captain Kleist. I think it might be a medal. Would you be able to kindly give me his address so I may send it to him? It's a matter of some urgency." The man on the other end of the telephone did not hesitate in giving her the captain's address. She thanked him and put down the receiver with a rush of triumph. Flushed with her success she thanked the concierge.

Celia took a taxi to Captain Kleist's home, which was a small, modest bungalow in a quiet suburb of Johannesburg. Armed with a bottle of gin she strode up the little path to the front door. Taking a deep breath, she rang the bell. There was a long moment of silence before she heard the rattle of a chain and then the door opened a crack. A hard-faced old man with the narrow eyes of a shrew stared at her through the gap. When he saw her, in her elegant hat and dress, his face registered his surprise. "Captain Kleist?" she said. He nodded and frowned, looking her up and down with suspicion. "I'm from the governor general's office. I have a package for you."

"What sort of package?" he asked, and his German accent was pronounced.

She looked past him to see the walls cluttered with hunting trophies mounted in rows. "I hear you're a crack shot," she said. "May I come in?" Then without waiting for his reply, she pushed past him.

Kleist swung around, his face red with indignation, and Celia saw that he was holding a gun. "You know, once I would have shot someone for doing that," he said.

"But you wouldn't shoot Digby Deverill's daughter, now would you?" He stared at her in shock, lost for words. "Shall we have a drink?"

"A drink? I'm out of drink."

"Lucky then I brought a bottle with me." She held out the gin.

He took it and looked at the label. Satisfied, he walked into the small sitting room. "How do you like yours, Fräulein?" he asked.

"With ice and water," she replied.

She followed him into the room, which was decorated with animal skins and animal heads. The air was stale with the smell of old cigarette smoke, which clung to the upholstery. She sat down and tried not to look at all the dead eyes on the wall staring at her miserably.

Kleist was unshaven and perspiring, with stains on his tie and on one lapel of his crumpled linen jacket. He did not look like he was going to remember much. He handed her a glass of gin, ran his rheumy blue eyes over her features and grinned crookedly. "You are the image of your father," he said, his German accent cutting sharply into his consonants. "You remind me of him when he was a young man. You have the same eyes."

"Everyone says that," she replied coolly, not sure whether or not it was a compliment. Did they see a sliver of ice there that had been in her father's too?

Relieved that he remembered something, Celia asked him to share his memories, which he did much like the others had, with admiration. She listened as he told banal anecdotes of Digby's daring and his cunning and his unfailing luck, digressing all the time to talk about himself. Every story about her father seemed to lead into one about him. She sat back and sipped her gin while he boasted of the Franco-Prussian War and his courage in killing "natives." Indeed, he bragged, he had been awarded a medal for valor.

Celia began to tire of his long-winded tales, which might well have been total fantasy for all she knew. She didn't believe he was going to help her either confirm or deny what Duchess had told her. Was he likely to admit murdering a white person to a woman he has only just met? "Captain Kleist," she said. "Do you remember two brothers named Dupree?"

Der Kapitän nodded thoughtfully. "Of course I do. One of them, I don't remember which, got eaten by a lion."

"Yes, he did. Is it true that you arranged the hunting trip?"

"What if I did? Possibly?" He shrugged and put his empty glass on the table in front of him.

"I think you remember that day, Captain Kleist. I think you remember it well. After all, how many times have clients of yours been eaten by lions?" She watched him with an unwavering gaze. "I imagine you made a lot of money that day. More than the usual rate."

"White hunters are paid a lot," he said, then his face seemed to narrow with cunning and one side of his mouth extended into a grin. "But, it is true, I never made as much as I made that day, and I earned every penny. Your father was a very demanding client." He nodded pensively. "And the others, Mad McManus, Stone Heart and Spleen, were all working for your father too. We all earned well that day. But Deverill was a very rich man and rich men get what they want."

"You were hunting a man-eating lion, weren't you?"

"Yes, we were."

"But you didn't get him, did you?" said Celia.

"No." He shook his head. "No, we didn't."

"But you *did* get the kill my father *wanted* you to get, didn't you?" she said with care, looking at him steadily.

Captain Kleist sobered up in a moment. He returned her stare with one of equal steadiness. The stale air in that room turned as still and silent as a tomb. The Captain's face was bereft of humanity, as flat and sharp as a stone cliff. A small smile crept across it—the smile of a man too vain to conceal his triumphs. "Let's just say, Miss Deverill, that I never missed my target."

A FEW DAYS later Celia was driven to van der Merwe's farm in Bloemfontein in the Orange Free State, a five-hour drive from Johannesburg. In the group accompanying her was a young bespectacled geologist called Mr. Gerber, a Mr. Scholtz and a Mr Daniels—two prospectors who Mr. Botha insisted were vital to the project—and Mr. Botha himself, who was now taking credit for having suggested to Celia she assess her father's farm. "It was on my mind to approach Sir Digby about it just before he died," he claimed. "It is very fortunate that you, Mrs. Mayberry, chose to come to South Africa when you did. I believe the time is right to dig." Celia didn't bother to argue with him. If they found gold she wouldn't care who had suggested it.

The farm was a small huddle of trees in the middle of a vast expanse of arid yellow veldt, with a tall water tower, a dilapidated whitewashed dwelling in the Cape Dutch style with its distinctive gable and dark green shutters, surrounded by run-down wooden fences and redundant farming equipment lying abandoned on the grass like the bones of beasts long dead. To the west of the house was a field whose red earth had been recently plowed. Beyond the house were miles and miles of flat land reaching as far as the eye could see, punctuated every now and then by clusters of trees and herds of game.

A couple of scrawny goats eyed them warily as they pulled up in their cars and climbed out. Celia was happy to stretch her legs and inhale the rich country air. As they approached the front door an elderly lady walked out to greet them, followed by a pack of mongrel dogs. She was small in stature with dove-gray hair swept up into a bun pinned roughly to the top of her head and wrinkled skin browned and weathered by the harsh African summers. However, her small eyes shone brightly like two sapphires, and they settled directly on Celia. She held out her hand and smiled. "My name is Boobie van der Merwe," she said. "I am Flippy's wife, but sadly Flippy is no longer with us. I remember your father. But it was many years ago that he bought this farm. Welcome." She invited them all to freshen up in the house and then to take refreshments on the terrace. Then, while the men went off to look at the land Celia remained with Boobie in a large wicker chair that looked directly out over the veldt.

"This is a very beautiful place to live," said Celia, feeling the pull of the distant horizon tugging at her chest.

"Oh, it is," Boobie agreed with a smile. "I've lived here for seventy years."

Celia frowned. "Seventy?"

"My dear, I'm ninety-six."

"And you still farm?"

"A farmer never retires, you know. Farming is not an occupation but a way of life. Flippy died twelve years ago and I continued to farm the land with our two sons. We often wondered if your father would ever return to mine it. They're digging deep round here now. Modern technology is a wonderful thing. Perhaps Sir Digby forgot about it." *Or perhaps he had darker reasons why he never came back,* Celia thought to herself. "He certainly forgot to raise our rent," Boobie continued, her tiny eyes twinkling. "Or he *chose* to forget. He must have been a good man."

"If they mine here, Mrs van der Merwe, you have my word that you will be very well looked after. I will see that you are relocated and compensated for the loss of your home."

"You don't have to do that, my dear. We are only tenants. There is nothing to prevent you from asking us to leave, perhaps a month or two's notice. That is all. We expected to leave forty years ago." She chuckled.

"But I know what it feels like to be emotionally attached to a place. Your heart is here, Mrs van der Merwe. It will be a terrible wrench to have to leave it."

"Nothing lasts forever, Mrs. Mayberry. Everything is reduced to dust in the end. As long as I can look out over the veldt I will be happy. My boys will look after me."

"Perhaps they might consider working for *me*."

Boobie nodded thoughtfully. "Perhaps they will," she replied.

At last the men returned. They were hot and dusty but Celia could tell from Mr. Botha's face that they had reached a positive outcome. He took off his hat and fanned his sweating face. "As Sir Digby discovered forty years ago, the gold here is very deep, but it is minable. Advances in technology make it possible. If you want to persevere we will need to drill here. Or perhaps you can just sell it to Anglo American. But there's gold here. Lots of gold. This is just as large as the other deposits found in the Free State. Your father was a shrewd man, Mrs. Mayberry. What will you do?"

"I will do this myself," she said resolutely. "I will start with the men who financed my father, and their sons. They all made their fortunes with him and they will make fortunes with me. Make a list, Mr. Botha, of all his shareholders."

He replaced his hat and smiled. "I suggest you prepare to move your life to Johannesburg, Mrs. Mayberry," he said.

THE FOLLOWING DAY Celia wrote to her mother and sisters to tell them what she had discovered. There was a strong possibility that Celia would restore her family's fortune in the industry where her father had originally made it. Mr. Botha could look after her interests while she returned to England to see to the ugly business of Aurelius Dupree. Then she would return to Johannesburg with her daughters and build a new life. The castle was gone, her husband and father were gone, it was time she moved on from her losses and concentrated on rebuilding.

But there was something she had to do before she left for London.

Duchess was surprised to see her again. As the car drew up outside the humble shack she was sitting on a chair outside her front door puffing on her pipe. She looked at Celia in amazement. "I did not think I would ever see you again, Miss Deverill," she said, pushing herself up. "Will you come inside?"

Celia followed her into the dark interior of her home. She smelled the familiar scent of tobacco mixed with the herbs and spices of Duchess's cooking. "I've come to thank you for telling me about the van der Merwe farm."

Duchess chuckled and sank onto the chair. "I knew you'd find gold," she said, shaking her head. "Did I not say that you would?"

"It's very deep but, as you rightly suggested, with the machinery they have now it will be possible to dig that far into the earth."

Duchess nodded and exhaled a waft of smoke. "I'm glad. You will now be rich like your father was. Like him you are lucky."

"But unlike him my luck is not from the Devil. I will not forget the woman who made it possible, Duchess. I will not betray you as my father did."

"You have a big heart, Miss Deverill." Celia noticed that her eyes shone with emotion. "And a *good* heart, too."

Just as Celia was about to sit down the door opened, throwing light across the floor. A tall man with light brown skin stepped into the room. He was surprised to see her. The shiny car outside with the waiting driver must have aroused his curiosity and he gazed at her warily. "Miss Deverill," said Duchess, waving her long fingers. "This is my son."

Celia looked into the man's eyes and gasped. She stared at him and words failed her. It was as if she were looking into a reflection of her own eyes, for they were the same almond shape, the same pale blue, set in exactly the same way as hers. They were her father's eyes. They were Deverill eyes. She extended her hand and he took it, gazing back at her with equal wonder. "Celia Deverill," she said at last.

"Lucky," he replied, without releasing her hand. "Lucky Deverill."

Chapter 31

Grace trailed her fingers down Count Cesare's muscular chest and smiled. Her cheeks were flushed, her eyes gleamed and her greedy appetite for the gratification of the flesh was well and truly sated, for now. Indeed, the Count had not disappointed her. She had barely thought of Michael Doyle since this exotic and clearly devilish man had undone the first button of her dress. He had carried her to her bed and confirmed what she had always suspected, that Latin men know better than anyone how to pleasure a woman.

Now Michael Doyle slipped into her consciousness again. She wanted him to know what she thought of Count Cesare and she wanted him to boil with jealousy. "Now that you have bought the castle, Cesare, when are you going to move in?" she asked, propping herself up on her elbow and shaking her head so that her hair fell in tawny waves about her shoulders.

"In the fall perhaps," he replied noncommittally. "I need to sort things out in America first. Perhaps return to Buenos Aires. Play polo." He grinned and Grace devoured the beauty of it with ravenous eyes.

"I should like to watch you play polo," she said. "But I should like to see you hunt first. You cannot disappear back to America without knowing what it is like to ride a horse at full gallop over the Irish hills. There is nothing quite like it."

"I'm in no hurry to leave." He sighed and slipped his fingers through her hair to caress the back of her neck. "Now I have found entertainment here, I should like very much to enjoy a little more of what the Irish life has to offer."

She kissed his arrogant smile. "Oh, I have much more to offer and so has Ireland. You have merely scratched the surface. Stay awhile." She slid her hand beneath the covers. "I'm sure I can think of ways to keep you here."

He writhed with pleasure and groaned. "Well, the Countess is in no hurry, after all. I have bought her a castle, it is only right that I explore a little further the place where we are going to make our home."

"It most certainly is," she agreed, stroking him with deft fingers. "I shall show you everything you need to know."

KITTY RODE WITH her father up the sandy beach at Smuggler's Cove, the place where she had often walked with Jack. She gazed out across the ocean and wondered what he was doing in America and whether he ever thought of her. *Her* feelings for him had certainly not diminished with the years, but she was content with the choice she had made. She had a family of her own now and she had Ireland—always Ireland, in the heart of her heart. Only when she allowed her mind to wander freely did thoughts of Jack cut her to the quick.

News had spread fast that a handsome Italian had bought the castle and planned to bring his countess over from America to settle here. Kitty didn't imagine they would last very long. What would an Italian couple make of the gray skies and drizzle? She didn't imagine they would understand the Irish way of life. It was only a matter of time before they would move back to the glamour and sophistication of New York. A castle was a lovely fantasy for a foreigner with more money than sense but a harsh reality for strangers to this wild and unforgiving land. She didn't imagine they'd be impressed by the society here, although, from what she had witnessed at Grace's dinner parties, the Count was more than entertained by her company, in the bedroom as well as at the table.

Kitty missed Celia. She had left for South Africa without explanation, leaving her children in the care of their nanny. Kitty had kept a close eye on them, but now that Castle Deverill was no longer theirs they would surely move back to England and settle there. For all Celia's wistful reminiscences about Ballinakelly Kitty was certain that she was a Londoner at heart and would find life there very much to her liking once she'd recovered from the shock and humiliation of selling the castle. She'd be close to Boysie and Harry and her mother, of course, although Beatrice was still refusing to leave her bed and the misery of her mourning.

Celia had explained to Kitty and Bertie that the White House and the Hunting Lodge were theirs for as long as they wanted. It was even written into an agreement that Deverills should always have first refusal of those two residences, providing they didn't fall behind on their rent. The Count had promised to grant them that small concession; after all, it suited him to have the places occupied and the money coming in. It had certainly come as a relief to Bertie and Kitty to know that they could remain in their homes.

"I shall miss Celia very much," said Kitty as she rode beside her father up the wide expanse of beach.

"We have to embrace the change," said Bertie philosophically. "There's no point gnashing our teeth and wailing because that won't return things to the way they were. We have to be grateful for our memories, Kitty. We were fortunate to have lived the way we did."

"It shall grieve me very much to watch the castle inhabited by strangers."

"The Count seems a nice sort of fellow," said Bertie. "We shall probably like him very much when we get to know him."

"If he lasts long enough. I'm not sure how they are going to entertain themselves. They really are very foreign, Papa."

"They'll entertain themselves the same way we do. They'll get into the Irish way of life and it will be exciting for them because it'll be different. The spice of life is in the variety, after all."

"But surely they'll miss the glamour of New York. The society here isn't very urbane, is it?"

"Perhaps they're weary of urbane."

Kitty shrugged. "I still don't hold out much hope for them. Unless one's heart is here the mind will bore of it. The one thing that ties us to this place is love. You and I love it more than anybody and nothing can prize us from it. But the Count and his wife have no such affection, why, she has never set foot in Ireland. How can she possibly know what it is like? She must have seen a photograph in the newspapers and fancied herself living like a princess. But Ballinakelly is not a town in a fairy tale. She'll discover that as soon as she arrives and I bet you she'll be hoofing it back to New York on the next available boat with her poor count moaning behind her." She laughed. "If you and I save up all our money we might buy it when they sell."

Bertie laughed with her. "You have a fanciful imagination, my dear."

"*You* made me, Papa."

"But your imagination and your wonder at the magic of nature came directly from your grandmother."

"Which you always dismissed as rubbish," she said, smiling at him with affection.

He looked at her askance. "I have learned that it is the mark of a foolish man to scoff at things of which one knows absolutely nothing. I sense God out there, Kitty," he said, throwing his gaze across the water. "But I can't see Him with my eyes. So why not nature spirits, ghosts, goblins and leprechauns too?" He grinned at the surprised look on his daughter's face. "The idea is to grow wiser as one gets older, my dear Kitty."

"What would Grandma say?" She laughed.

"I wish I knew. I wish she were here . . ." Then he shook his head and chuckled. "But of course she *is* here, isn't she? She's always here. Didn't she insist that those we love and lose never leave us?" *Indeed I did,* said Adeline, but her voice was a sigh on the wind that only Kitty could hear.

LAUREL HAD FOUND her return to the saddle most thrilling. Hazel, on the other hand, preferred the card table. Consequently the two sisters began to find that their very different forms of entertainment took them to disparate parts of the county. In the past such regular separation would have greatly vexed them; however, now they were only too eager to be rid of each other. While Laurel stole kisses with Ethelred Hunt behind hedgerows on the windy hills above Ballinakelly, Hazel allowed him to play with her foot beneath the card table, and sometimes place his hand upon her leg when no one was looking. Kisses had to be seized in dark corridors and empty rooms and the secrecy of those moments only compounded Hazel's delight. Both women guarded their secret romances closely— until one unfortunate evening in May when a chance discovery would swipe away the veil of concealment.

Laurel had been riding, alone. She had borrowed a horse from Bertie's stable and set off on her own, for Ethelred had been summoned to the bridge table at the Hunting Lodge and it looked like he was going to be there until evening. She enjoyed riding out on her own, although she would have much preferred to have had the company of the dashing silver wolf. Little birds frolicked in the blackthorn and elder and went about building their nests while young rabbits grazed in the long grasses and heather. It was her favorite time of year and she took pleasure from spring, which had exploded onto the wintry landscape in all its glorious color.

She had stopped on the crest of the hill and gazed over the wide ocean, breathing in the bracing smells of the sea and listening to the roar of the waves breaking on the rocks below. When she set off back down the hill toward home, she was feeling light of spirit and full of joy. Everything was right with her world. She was having a delightful romance with Ethelred Hunt and she and Hazel were friends again, after months of steadily growing apart. She no longer had to feel jealous of her sister or suffer the pain of unrequited love. Ethelred Hunt loved her, of that she had no doubt. So long as Hazel never found out, everything would be fine. Poor Hazel, she thought with genuine compassion, but Ethelred had chosen *her* and she had been too weak-willed and infatuated to resist him. This was the first time in her life that she hadn't put her sister first. She wasn't proud of it, but her passion for him gave her a heady sense of carelessness and her sister's feelings were hastily and conclusively swept aside.

She walked her horse along the top of the cliff. Down below gulls and gannets pecked at sea creatures abandoned by the tide and the odd butterfly fluttered into view. Then she heard the sound of laughter that did not belong to any seabird she had ever heard. She stopped her horse and peered down onto the beach. The laughter rose on the wind and it was instantly recognizable with its distinctive warmth and flirtatiousness. The sound of a man's voice broke in then and the laughter stopped as he pulled his companion into his arms and kissed her ardently. Laurel was stunned by the vigorous passion of the man and the way the woman's knees buckled as she fell against him. So much so that she couldn't take her eyes off them. What would Sir Ronald say if he were to discover his wife in a romantic clinch with Count Cesare? Laurel thought disapprovingly—and what of the Count's wife? Laurel shook her head and tutted. Grace Rowan-Hampton should be ashamed of such licentious behavior. This wasn't the way a lady of her stature should behave. Why, anyone might stumble upon them. Laurel found it very fortunate that the only stumbling had been done by *her*. At least *she* could be trusted to keep her mouth shut.

Or could she?

Hazel didn't count, she reasoned. To gossip to one's sister

was natural and normal and Laurel knew that Hazel would ensure that it went no further. She pulled her horse away from the edge, leaving the two lovers unaware that they had just been discovered, and trotted hastily down the path toward the Hunting Lodge.

The discovery of Grace and the Count was burning on her tongue and she couldn't wait to unburden it. She hurried to the stables and, with the help of one of the grooms, dismounted and handed over the reins. She strode across the yard, removing her gloves finger by finger, impatient to find her sister. She found only Bertie and Kitty in the library. Classical music resounded from the gramophone and they were both drinking tea. "Ah, hello, Laurel. I hope you had an enjoyable ride," said Bertie from the armchair. The cards were neatly piled on the card table. The game had finished.

"Oh, I most certainly did, Bertie, thank you. It's glorious out there." She stood in the doorway, clearly not intending to join them for tea.

"I should like to go myself," said Kitty enviously. "It seems a shame to waste a lovely afternoon inside."

"There will be more," said Bertie with a chuckle.

"Has Hazel gone home?" Laurel asked, keen to find her sister.

"Not yet," Bertie replied. "She's taking a stroll around the garden with Ethelred."

"Then I shall go and find her. I have something I need to tell her," Laurel announced before leaving the room.

"I'll make sure there's a fresh pot of tea for your return," said Kitty, but Laurel had disappeared across the hall. Bertie arched his eyebrows at his daughter and Kitty shrugged. "I wonder what that's all about," she said.

"I'm sure we'll find out soon enough," Bertie replied.

The gardens at the Hunting Lodge were an assortment of lawn, vegetable garden, secret walled garden and orchard. Each was separated from the other by yew hedge, shrubs, trees or wall. These days the place had been allowed to overgrow because Bertie couldn't afford to keep on the team of gardeners who had ensured that the hedges were trimmed, the borders weeded and the annuals planted. There was a greenhouse where they used to keep cuttings and house plants during the winter months, but now it was empty, a broken pane of glass leaving an open door for rooks to enter and exit with ease along with the rain. Nothing grew in there except weeds and a small chestnut tree, which, by some miracle, had seeded itself.

Laurel set off at a brisk walk. In spite of the lack of care the gardens were full of color. Periwinkles and forget-me-nots had spread like water across the lawns and borders, and purple clematis scaled the walls with wisteria and rose. Daisies and buttercups were scattered across the grass and dandelions served as enticing landing pads for toddling bees, drunk on nectar. Monarch butterflies flew jauntily around the buddleia and swallows darted back and forth from the eaves of the house, busy nest-building. Laurel thought it all looked beautiful in a wild, overgrown kind of way. She'd like to have been young and energetic enough to have pulled out the ground elder by the roots, for it was stifling the plants and taking over the borders with bindweed and goose grass.

She marched through the secret garden, which was enclosed by yew hedge and wall. There was a bench positioned in a sun trap but the weeds had grown so tall they had almost swallowed it up. She peered around the end of the yew hedge, where a pond lay serene and quiet in the shade of a weeping willow. Pondweed grew thick and green on the surface of the water and a pair of wild ducks who had chosen to settle there were pecking at it contentedly. Laurel strained her ears for the sound of voices but heard nothing save the noisy chatter of birds. She would have called if shouting across the garden were not undignified.

She was about to give up when she saw them through the glass of the greenhouse. They were standing on the other side, in the shade, and they were holding hands—all *four* hands, Laurel noted with a jolt. And then, to her horror, she watched the man who had made her feel as if she was the only woman in the world he desired lower his head and kiss her sister on the lips. It was more than shocking, it was sickening, and she wasn't going to let him get away with it.

She strode around the greenhouse and stood a few yards away, hands on hips, scowling furiously. It took a while for them to notice her, so engrossed they were in each other. Then Hazel's eyes opened and bulged. She pushed Ethelred away with a brisk shove. "This isn't what you think," she said clumsily.

"It's *exactly* what it looks like," Laurel snapped. Ethelred swung around and stared at Laurel in surprise. *At least he has the decency to look ashamed*, she thought.

"Now, ladies," he began uncomfortably.

But Hazel interrupted him. She shook her head apologetically. "I'm sorry I didn't tell you, Laurel. I should have. Ethelred and I have been seeing each other . . ."

Laurel walked up to Lord Hunt and slapped him across the face. Hazel made to protest but Laurel turned on her. "We've been made a fool of, Hazel," she said. "I've been seeing Ethelred too!"

Hazel gazed at Lord Hunt, aghast. "Is this true?" she demanded. "Have you been seeing Laurel as well as me? You have been playing us off, one against the other?" And she pulled her hand back and slapped him on the other cheek. "How dare you."

"He's been laughing at us for months!" Laurel exclaimed, suddenly realizing the full extent of his betrayal.

"I've never felt so humiliated in all my life!" cried Hazel. "I will never get over this. Never!"

Ethelred appealed to the two sisters. "But I couldn't make a choice between the two of you," he explained, palms to the sky, face burning. "Truthfully, I fell in love with both of you."

"I've never heard anything more outrageous!" said Laurel, slipping her hand beneath Hazel's arm.

"Me neither. Outrageous!" said Hazel, glancing at her sister with tenderness. "Come, Laurel, let's leave this scoundrel to lick his wounds. I have no interest in hearing his explanations."

"But I really do love you," Ethelred pleaded, his voice cracking on the word "love." But the two sisters set off toward the house without a backwards glance.

"We mustn't tell anyone about this," said Hazel as they approached the Hunting Lodge.

"We absolutely mustn't," Laurel agreed.

"It's just too humiliating." They walked on in silence as the impact of Ethelred Hunt's dishonesty began to sink in. Then Hazel sighed sadly. "I do believe I love him, Laurel," she said in a small voice.

Laurel nodded, relieved to be able to share her pain. "So do I," she said.

"Oh, what a hopeless pair we are," lamented Hazel. "Hopeless!"

"What would Adeline say?" said Hazel.

Laurel shook her head. "She'd have no words, Hazel," she replied. "No words at all!" In the turmoil of their anguish Laurel forgot all about Grace Rowan-Hampton and the dashing count.

Chapter 32

New York, 1931

Jack waited at the front of Trapani, an elegant Sicilian restaurant on East 116th Street in Harlem. He had been expecting this call. He had known that sometime he would be needed. There was little that daunted him and no one he feared. He dragged on his cigarette and looked around him. Trapani was a classic Italian joint, wood-paneled and smelling of fried onions and garlic. The waiters were all plump Sicilians with graying hair and brown, weathered faces. They wore black trousers and white jackets and their talk rose and fell in the musical way that Italian does. He noticed there were no diners in the main restaurant, only burly bodyguards in black suits and fedoras; Salvatore Maranzano's men. Since the killing of Joe "the Boss" Masseria, Maranzano had been *capo di tutti capi*, the Boss of Bosses. The bodyguards had been expecting Jack. They had placed him at a little round table beneath the awning in front of the restaurant, offered him a cigarette, and ordered him an Italian coffee, and Jack had sat down and waited. In his line of work he spent a lot of time waiting.

"The Boss knows you're here," said one of the bodyguards with the low brow of a Neanderthal and a squashed, broken nose. "He's eating inside. He'll be ready when he's ready."

"That's grand," said Jack. "Then I'll have another one of these." And he lifted his empty coffee cup.

Jack had never met the Boss but he knew all about him. Maranzano was famously obsessed with the Roman Empire. He devoured books on the Caesars and liked to quote Caligula and Marcus Aurelius, so that he had acquired the nickname "Little Caesar," but no one dared call him that to his face. He had recently won the war against Joe Masseria and had made an alliance with the young gangsters: Charlie "Lucky" Luciano and his Jewish allies, Meyer Lansky and Ben "Bugsy" Siegel. It was a world in which everyone had nicknames—just like Ireland—and it was a world familiar to Jack, who had fought with the rebels during Ireland's War of Independence. He knew how to handle a gun and how to use it. He'd killed Captain Manley that night on the Dunashee Road and, after you've killed once, the second time comes easier. Desperate to put his past and all its pain and disappointment behind him, he had embraced the blood-filled cauldron of New York without a backward glance. He'd resolved to look after himself, and the Devil take the rest.

The quickest way to make it in New York was to join the gangs. As an Irishman newly arrived in America it wasn't difficult; New York was full of Irish. He had contacted a friend from the Old Country, who had made the necessary introductions, and soon he was running errands for Owen Madden, who ran the Cotton Club. Errands that involved riding shotgun in a truck transporting whiskey down from Canada. It wasn't long before it got around that Jack had a streak of steel in his heart. He had "earned his bones" shooting his first man, which had brought him respect, and suddenly he was in demand and earning twice the amount of money. He reflected on his meager vet's wage back in Ballinakelly and gave a derisory sniff. He had gained a reputation in New York as a cool hand on the trigger and a nickname. They called him "Mad Dog" O'Leary, and in this small, rarefied world, everyone knew who he was. He was a man of some standing and he relished his new status. He was unable to join the Mafia itself, for only Sicilians could become a "made man," but Jack didn't care. The Irish had their own gangs and rackets, and they often worked with Italians and Jews.

The Irish looked out for each other, and two and a half years after arriving in New York and getting involved in the business of bootlegging, Jack had married the daughter of one of Owen Madden's henchmen at the Cotton Club, an Irish girl whose family originated from County Wicklow. Her name was Emer and she was freckly-skinned and pretty, gentle and submissive, nothing like Kitty Deverill, whose love was passionate, her fury fiery, her determination untiring. Momentarily assaulted by the memory of her, he envisaged her running to him in the Fairy Ring and throwing her arms around him, as she had done so many times, the wind in her wild red hair, the sun turning her skin to gold, her laughter rising above the roar of waves. He pictured her face, the eagerness in her gaze, and felt the energy in her embrace as if he were living it all over again. It took a monumental effort to dispel her image from his mind and turn his thoughts to the woman he had married.

Emer was young, sweet and straightforward and, after Kitty, it was a relief to have a love that was uncomplicated. For he *did* love Emer. It was a different kind of love, but love nonetheless, and for all his longing he was certain that Emer was good for him. She understood his business, having been brought up in the world of Irish racketeers, and she didn't question him when he returned from the Cotton Club in the early hours of the morning smelling of cheap perfume, in the same way that her mother had never questioned her father. Emer accepted what he did and the risks he ran without question, and was grateful for the money he made without asking where it came from. She knew he carried a gun and she was well aware that he had used it, to deadly effect. She had given him a daughter, Alana who was now two, and she was pregnant with their second child. Their children would never know Ireland or the part their father had played in securing its independence. Jack would see that they had a better life than the one he had known back in Ballinakelly. He would do whatever it took to earn the money to make that possible.

Just then there was a flurry of activity. Lunch was breaking up and the bodyguards were pushing out their chairs, doing up the buttons on their jackets and sidling toward the door. A young Italian in a sharp suit and fedora walked across the room with the swagger of a fighter. His face was fleshy, his coarse skin marked with a long red scar that ran the whole length of his jawline. His eyes were small, dark brown and arrogant. The bodyguards fell in behind him and the ones in front walked ahead, throwing suspicious glances up and down the street before positioning themselves beside the shiny black car. Jack knew who he was. His gait and his expression were unmistakable. He was the Boss's deputy, Lucky Luciano, the man who had arranged the killing of Masseria. Luciano looked at him circumspectly, for Jack's face was new to him. Then one of the bodyguards opened his door and he climbed inside. The car rattled up the street.

"O'Leary, the Boss will see ya now." Jack stood up and walked into the restaurant. Two men patted him down and took away his pistol and the knife he always kept in a garter around his shin. Then he was shown into the back room where Salvatore Maranzano sat at a table still stained with tomato sauce and strands of spaghetti. He was about forty-five years old, compact and sturdy, in a three-piece suit that stretched over a paunch, and a traditional string tie. His face was wide and handsome with thick black hair swept off a broad forehead. He raised his eyes when Jack entered and took a few puffs of his cigar.

"Come in, O'Leary," he said in a heavy Italian accent, gesticulating through the cloud of smoke to the chair opposite.

"Don Salvatore," said Jack, giving a small bow, for he knew the Italians, especially Little Caesar, expected this sort of flattery. Maranzano offered his hand and Jack shook it.

"Take a seat . . . Coffee? Cigarette? Cognac?"

"I'm fine," Jack replied and took the chair opposite the Boss. Maranzano nodded at his bodyguards, who left, closing the door behind them.

Jack and the Boss were now alone; the small-town Irishman

and the Boss of New York City. Jack reflected on how far he had come, but he didn't have time for wistfulness, for Maranzano was staring at him intensely, his narrowed eyes appraising him to see if he really was the Mad Dog everyone said he was.

"I heard you got balls and you can take anyone down," he said quietly.

Jack gave a nonchalant shrug. "If that's what they say."

"Well, you gotta have something to be called Mad Dog— but then again there are lots of Irish boys called mad dogs. I want a dog that's mad enough but not too mad, you get what I'm saying? I want something done right and fast."

"Then maybe I'm your man," said Jack, returning Maranzano's stare with his own fearless gaze.

"You see, it can't be an Italian and it can't be a Jew, so it's gotta be a Mick, and it's gotta to be a *new* Mick. Someone fresh in town, someone not everyone knows, and someone who can shoot straight. You know what I'm saying?"

"You called and I'm here," said Jack, sounding a great deal more confident than he felt. He had wanted a job like this, a *big* job, but a cold sensation began to creep over his skin, starting at the base of his spine and crawling slowly up, and he wondered whether it was *too* big. It was one thing bootlegging, quite another working for the Mafia. But he knew that no one walked away from Little Caesar and lived.

"You know your Roman history, boy?" Maranzano asked, puffing again on his fat cigar. *Jaysus! Here we go*, thought Jack. "Let me tell you about my favorite, Julius Caesar. He taught me how to organize my army, my centurions, my legions." Maranzano's chair scraped across the floor as he got to his feet. Then he held up his forefinger in full lecture mode. "Then there was

Marcus Aurelius. He taught me the philosophy of ruling an empire. He said, 'Don't get over-Caesarified, that's dangerous, keep sharp!' You know what I'm saying? And Augustus, *he* knew an empire needed peace after war—and that's what I gotta do right now. But he ruled with Mark Antony and in the end he knew that Mark Antony had to go. *Capisci?*"

Jack did not understand but he didn't want to guess either, because if he guessed wrong, it could cost him his neck. So he played dumb. Maranzano waved his finger again. "I'll tell you about another Caesar: Caligula. He said, 'Let them hate me as long as they fear me.' He was crazy but he was no fool either, *capisci*? So, that's why I got *you* here." He sat down again and put the cigar between his lips.

"Why *have* you got me here, Boss?" Jack asked.

"I've got a job for you. It's the biggest job of your life." He jabbed his finger at Jack. "If you fuck up, you're finished in this city, but if you do it right, you'll be my guy, my Irish centurion, *capisci*? I asked you here for a reason. You saw the guy who just came out of lunch with me?" Jack nodded. "You know who he is?" Jack nodded again. "Luciano, that's who. But that fuck is trying to kill me after I made him my deputy and gave him so much." His voice grew louder and his eyes narrowed with hatred. "He's trying to kill me with his Jewboy friends, Bugsy and Meyer. You know Bugsy with his blue eyes and his movie star looks? Well, I ain't scared of no Jewboys. I got a guy in their house, and he told me, they're already planning to get me! Well, I'm going to kill Luciano first and *you're* going to do it for me."

"That's quite a job," said Jack, but he kept his eyes steady. He didn't want the Boss to see any doubt there.

"Fifty thousand dollars. Twenty-five now. Twenty-five after. That's quite a lot of money for a Mick village boy who's new in the city. Is it enough?"

"Yeah, it's enough. I'll take the job, Don Salvatore, though I got to tell you, I don't like to be called a Mick."

Maranzano came around the table and took Jack into his arms. He smelled of garlic, chives, cigars and lemon cologne. "You're a proud man, O'Leary, and I like that. I take it back. I respect your people and I like your songs. I apologize. Are we straight?"

"Yeah, sure, no problem," said Jack.

"Good." The Boss kissed him on both cheeks and sandwiched his hand between his. "Luciano's coming to my office in a couple of days. It's nine floors up but he always takes the stairs coz he don't like being trapped in an elevator. Sensible, right? And when he comes out of the meeting, he's alone and you're going to whack him between my office and the stairs. *Capisci?*"

"Sounds like a plan," said Jack, although not a very solid one.

"Here's the first twenty-five," said Maranzano, pulling out an envelope from his pocket and thumping it down on the tablecloth in front of Jack, who had never seen so much money before. Jack folded the envelope and put it in the inside pocket of his jacket. He could do a lot with fifty grand. He could buy a house for him and Emer. He could give his children a better life than he ever had.

"No one knows about this," Maranzano continued. "None of my guys outside, you understand? No one. Just you and me. That's why I'm making you a rich man. You know I own every soldier, every block, every racket in this city, O'Leary. If you let me down, if you talk, if you miss, I will crush you, and if you run, I'll chase you back to your Irish village and I will kill everyone you love in the world, you know what I'm saying? If you succeed, I will *give* you the world. You know, Jack, I've killed many men and one thing I know for sure is that you touch the end of the gun to the guy's forehead so you can feel him, right there, and that way you know it's done. Man is the hardest animal to kill. If he gets away he will come back and kill *you*."

Chapter 33

Jack perched on the edge of a desk in a little side office near the reception of Salvatore Maranzano's office. He sipped his coffee and read the newspaper, the *New York World-Telegram*, and checked the racing scores. His thoughts drifted to the showgirl from the Cotton Club he had had the night before. He could still smell her perfume and feel the dancer's muscles beneath her skin. There were benefits to being an Irish hood in New York City. He would see her that night and have fifty thousand bucks to celebrate.

He smiled to himself and turned the page. The office buzzed around him. Pretty girls in elegant dresses passed his door without casting him so much as a glance, too busy with telegrams and letters and documents to file. Others sat at desks, heads bent, typing. The offices were elegant and sumptuous, with wood paneling, high ceilings, ornately molded cornicing and shiny marble floors adorned with crimson carpets. The walls were cluttered with paintings of Rome, and Jack read the inscriptions beneath: *the Forum, the Colosseum, Palatine Hill, the Pantheon, St Peter's Basilica,* and every couple of yards was a Roman statue of some emperor or other in his toga. Jack had heard that not everyone was so impressed with the Boss's clap-trap about Caesar but no one would dare let their lack of enthusiasm show.

This building on Forty-Fifth Street was like a palace, all shiny and new, built by the same men who had built Grand Central Station. Inside, the hall was marble, the elevators gleamed, and Jack had checked himself in the doors as they closed, and rear-ranged his tie on the way up. He looked good: dark suit, slim figure, his lucky trilby, seersucker shoes in black-and-white, not bad for a country boy from Ballinakelly. He still had the gap in his teeth from where he'd been punched in prison, but his blue eyes and raffish smile were hard for women to resist. He knew why he had got the job. He had no nerves. He was preternatu-rally calm, ice-cool, and he knew exactly what to do and when to do it. He carried a Colt Super .38 in a holster under his arm. Not many people had one yet but his was already like an exten-sion of his hand. He had the cash for the hit in his suit pocket. He gave it a pat and took pleasure from the thick wad of it.

Everything was in place. He'd wait here in this room until Lucky was in the Boss's office, then he'd take up his position at the back by the stairs. When Lucky came out he'd pop him in the forehead, like the Boss had said, with the barrel right against his head, and then walk calmly along the corridor and take the elevator down before Luciano's bodyguards, waiting at the door to the stairs, would even have registered the two pops. All he had to do now was sit here and wait.

He had arrived on time at two thirty and Luciano had been due to arrive fifteen minutes later, but he had sent word that he was running late. Jack lit a cigarette and waited some more. He kept his eye on the long corridor, where the girls in silk stockings and tight skirts stalked back and forth from Salvatore Maranzano's office, and the antechamber, where dozens of ordinary men and women, city officials, workmen, politicians, and the odd gangster, waited to be received by Little Caesar. Time was passing and Luciano was late. *Very* late. Jack looked at his watch. It was now two forty-five. He turned his attention back to the newspaper. In this line of work patience was the greatest asset.

Just then four men came out of the elevator. They strode up to the reception desk, where the secretary greeted them with a smile. However, her smile swiftly disappeared, replaced by an anxious frown, and she shook her head. Jack's interest was aroused. The men were not with Luciano because he and his guards would have used the stairs. Then Jack noticed their uniforms. He lowered the newspaper and shifted so he could feel the snug weight of the Colt in his shoulder holster: if this was a police raid, he did not want to be caught with the gun or the cash. However, it was unlikely to be a police raid because the Boss was friends with the police, so who were they and why were they here? An unexpected courtesy call? He thought not. He began to feel an uneasiness crawling over him and his hackles rose like those of a dog sensing danger, but not quite knowing where it came from. He studied the men more closely. Two were in uniform, two in dark suits. The first in uniform showed his badge to the secretary, who looked at it, then nodded and shrugged. Jack watched and waited. A calmness settled upon him as his senses sharpened. If these were tax investigators and they were here when Luciano arrived, he'd have to do the hit another day. Everything had been planned but *this*.

Jack observed the tall man in the suit. It was a well-cut suit, he thought, for a government employee. He dropped his eyes to the patent-leather shoes and his stomach gave a sudden lurch. His gaze sprang up to the face and he recognized the dazzling blue eyes of Bugsy Siegel.

Then it all happened so quickly.

Bugsy's gun was drawn and the Boss's bodyguards were already on the floor, disarmed by the two men in uniform. Bugsy and his gang moved over them like cats. The secretaries froze where they were and no one screamed. Then Jack heard Maranzano's voice: "What the hell are you guys doing here?" followed by the instantly recognizable wet sounds of plunging knives and then the pops of gunfire. Jack was on his feet and running into the mail room farther down the corridor, near the stairs. He hid under the desk just as the assassins walked briskly out, passing the very place where only moments before he had been sitting. The men stopped and Bugsy spoke. "There was a guy sitting in there, a Mick—where is he? This broad will tell me. Hey, you, where is he? He can't have gone far!"

"I don't know," replied the terrified secretary. "I don't know . . . Please don't hurt me. I think he ran."

Bugsy slapped her hard. "Ran where?" The girl was now sobbing.

"Come on, let's get outta here," said one of the men in uniform.

"No, that was the Mick waiting for Lucky," said Bugsy. "I want to clip him right here. Right now."

"We gotta get outta here."

"Fine," Bugsy snapped. "But I offer fifty grand and a house in Westchester to anyone who kills that Mick, d'you hear me? Fifty grand and a house in Westchester." Then they were gone, their footsteps receding down the stairwell.

Jack had been holding the Colt in his hands and this time they were shaking. Slowly he climbed out from beneath the desk, keeping his pistol in front of him. People were emerging warily into the corridor, blinking in bewilderment. The place was eerily silent. He hurried into the reception area and found the secretary who had saved his life. He touched her tear-stained cheek. "Thank you," he said.

"You'd better get out of here," she replied. "And make it snappy." Jack jumped over a shattered Roman bust and made for the elevator, but virtually everyone on the floor had abandoned their offices and taken the elevator. He ran into Maranzano's office to find the Caesar of New York, the *capo di tutti capi*, lying dead in the middle of the floor. His legs were spread wide, his white shirt stained with blood and pulled out of his trousers to reveal his large belly still oozing crimson from the knife wound. His fingers were twitching and blood was streaming over his face from the shot to the head—the coup de grace, which he himself had always recommended, just to be sure.

Jack's mind stilled and shifted into sharp focus. He could not stay here a moment longer. He had to get Emer and Alana as quickly as possible and leave New York without a moment to waste. Luciano was now the Boss and Bugsy was Luciano's right hand, and somehow they knew that Jack had been here to kill Luciano. There was a bounty on his head and there was not a gangster in the city, Irish, Italian or Jew, who would see "Mad Dog" O'Leary without killing him on sight. He had to get out of New York and disappear forever. He would go down south, he decided, and start a new life. He'd done it before, he could do it again. Ireland flashed into his mind and his heart lurched with longing as those green hills and stony cliffs rose out of the mist like an emerald oasis in a vast barren desert. But he couldn't go home, for Ballinakelly was the first place they would look for him, and besides, there was nothing left but the ashes of his old life. No, he'd start again, far away, where no one from New York would find him.

As he was about to leave, he saw, on the desk beside a statue of Caesar, a large pile of crisp banknotes.

Jack made his way out of the building by way of the stairs, pulled his hat low over his head, and called Emer from a public telephone. "Don't ask questions and tell no one," he told her firmly, and she knew from the tone of his voice what he was going to say. "Get Alana, pack a small case and meet me at Penn Station. I'll find you under the clock. Come as quickly as you can. We're leaving New York forever, Emer, and we won't be coming back."

Chapter 34

As much as Bridie was thrilled about her pregnancy, she couldn't help but remember the last time and the brutality that she had endured on account of it. Back then Mr. Deverill had had the insensitivity to question whether the child was indeed his, before grudgingly accepting that it was and sending her off to Dublin to get rid of it as quickly and discreetly as possible. Lady Rowan-Hampton had treated her with equal callousness. She had made it perfectly clear that Bridie couldn't possibly keep her baby and gave her no choice in the decision to send her to the other side of the world. The nuns in the Convent of Our Lady Queen of Heaven must surely have had hearts of stone, for they had made her feel deeply ashamed and utterly worthless. They had regarded her as wanton and sinful, and her extended belly an affront to Mary, the Holy Mother of Jesus. Bridie had been robbed of her children without a word of sympathy or understanding, as if she were no better than a farm animal of little value. In spite of the years that had passed and the emotional distance Bridie had placed between that dark time and now, she still carried the guilt inside her like an indelible stain on her soul. However much her new situation glossed over the disgrace of her previous one, she still felt rotten in her core.

This time she was a married woman and her pregnancy was something to be celebrated and enjoyed. No one knew of the secrets she guarded or of the pain that came with the joy of this new life growing inside her, intertwined like threads, inseparable one from the other. Everyone bought her presents and congratulated her, and Bridie thought how wrong it was that a life should be worth less simply because of the lack of a wedding ring.

While Cesare was in Ireland she had a lot of time to think. She looked forward to having a child to love with a yearning born out of loss. She remembered Little Jack with a bitter sorrow and hoped that her new baby would fill the void in her heart, for not even Cesare, with all his love and devotion, had been able to. She lay on her bed, a hand on her stomach, and remembered her tiny daughter whom the nuns had spirited away before she had even held her. There was no grave, no headstone, nothing with which to remember her, only the memory of glimpsing her tiny face before the nuns had wrapped her in a towel and taken her away—and even *that* was faded like a photograph left too long in the sun. No one had considered Bridie and the irreparable tear in her heart. No one had felt any compassion for her as a human being or as a mother. Those babies had been stolen and yet there was no law to condemn the guilty and no aid to help her get back her son. She had been cast aside like a piece of refuse, sent off to America so she couldn't cause any trouble and, only now, as she prepared to become a mother again, did she realize the extent of the injustice.

At the beginning of summer, Cesare returned from Ireland. Bridie was overjoyed to see him, for she had missed him dreadfully and needed distraction from the turmoil in her spirit. She wrapped her arms around him and was sure that she could smell the salty wind and heather of home in his hair. Her heart lurched and a sudden jealousy arose in her for *he* had touched the green hills of Ballinakelly that had once belonged to her and she resented him for having breathed the air that she had been so cruelly denied. But it dropped as quickly as it had risen as Cesare reassured her that everything was ready for her just as soon as she was prepared to leave. Ireland was within her grasp, she only had to say the word and he would take her there.

But was she ready to go back? Was she ready to face Kitty, Celia, Lord Deverill and her son? Had she simply bought the castle so that *they* couldn't have it? Had she been motivated purely by spite? The moment Beaumont Williams had told her that his contacts in London had informed him that Castle Deverill was once again available to buy, Bridie had seized her chance and this time she had been firm. She wanted it whatever the cost, because she knew its value; she knew its value to the Deverills.

Bridie listened with growing rapture as Cesare described the lavishness of the refurbishment and the comfort of the new plumbing and electricity. She clapped her hands with glee and pressed him for more details, hanging on to his every word like a pirate queen being told of the latest stolen treasure. She wanted to know what all the rooms looked like and how lovely the gardens were and as he told her she envisaged it as it had been in her childhood days when she, Celia and Kitty had all been friends, playing in the castle grounds, before it had all unraveled—before she and Kitty had become enemies; before Kitty had stolen her son.

Bridie had told Cesare of her childhood in Ballinakelly and that her mother had cooked for Lady Deverill in the castle, but she hadn't told him about her son. She couldn't. She simply wasn't able to speak about Little Jack, not even to Cesare. *Especially* not to Cesare. He was so traditional, this Italian count, and so proud, too proud even to take money without embarrassment. What if he disapproved of her having a child out of wedlock? What if he loved her less because she had given him away? There were so many reasons *not* to tell him. So she kept the secret wrapped tightly around her heart and let him revel in the imminent birth of their first child together.

Cesare told her about his meeting with Celia and how he had kept Bridie's identity secret as she had asked him to. He told her that he had met Kitty at Lady Rowan-Hampton's dinner table and he watched his wife's face harden and her expression turn serious and severe. "I don't wish to hear of those two women," she said coldly. "We were friends once but that was long ago in the past." After that Cesare downplayed the amount of time he had spent with the Deverills and swiftly changed the subject to their future. He certainly didn't hint at the long hours he had enjoyed with Grace, nor at the other young women he had bedded in Cork. He decided he was going to enjoy living in Ireland—for a while at least.

They agreed that it would be madness to travel all the way

to Ireland while she was pregnant, so they planned to move the following summer, by which time Bridie would be strong enough to endure the journey. Their baby boy was born in the early hours of February in New York. The birth had been quick and relatively easy. Bridie sobbed when she finally held her child in her arms. She sobbed for the babies she had lost and for this one whom she was permitted to keep. She gazed into his face and fell in love as she had never done before. Nothing in her life compared to this. Nothing fulfilled her so completely. It was as if God had rewarded her suffering with a double dose of maternal love and she knew then that her heart would surely mend. This tiny baby had come into the world with enough love to heal all his mother's pain.

Cesare had waited in the study downstairs, pacing the floor as was tradition, while the doctor tended to Bridie in her bedroom. He was astonished when he was promptly informed that his son had been delivered, for he had expected his wife's labor to last for days. He climbed the stairs, two steps at a time, his heart racing with excitement. He opened the door to find Bridie sitting up in bed with their small son in her arms. Her face was glowing with happiness, her eyes soft and tender, a proud smile upon her lips. Cesare came to the bedside and sat down. He peered into the baby's face. "My son," he whispered in awe, and Bridie's heart brimmed with pleasure at the deeply satisfied tone of his voice. "You are a clever and beautiful wife to give me a son," he said, kissing her tenderly. "You cannot imagine what this means to me."

"What shall we call him?" Bridie asked.

"What would *you* like to call him?"

She gazed into her son's face and frowned. "I would like to

give him a name that has no connection to the past. A name that has no connection to my family. A name that is his alone."

"Very well," said Cesare, who had spent the last nine months thinking of names. "What about Leopoldo?"

"Leopoldo," said Bridie, smiling as she gazed upon her child.

"Leopoldo di Marcantonio," he said and the words slipped off his tongue as if they were soaked in olive oil. "*Count* Leopoldo di Marcantonio."

"Indeed it has majesty and grandeur," said Bridie.

"He might only be a count," said Cesare. "But he's a prince to me. Here, let me hold him."

WHEN THE SUMMER arrived, Bridie found that she was not ready to move to Ireland. She was afraid of returning to her past when her present was so happy. Afraid of seeing Kitty with her son, of not being able to be a mother to him, of having to carry so heavy a secret. Yet the castle called to her in whispers that woke her in the middle of the night but she resisted its allure and shut her ears to its insistent call. She dreamed of it, of running down the endless corridors, of chasing after Kitty, whose long red hair ran the length of the castle and was so thick that Bridie began to drown in it. She thought of the castle often and the shadow it cast across her soul grew dark and heavy and she began to fear it. She would go when she was ready, she resolved. She *would* be ready, eventually, she told herself, but not right now. Cesare was busy playing polo and enjoying the hectic round of social events; he was in no hurry to start a new life across the water. So they bought a grand house in Connecticut and delayed their move. Ireland would wait.

KITTY WAS ON her knees in the garden, pulling out bindweed and ground elder from the borders. She dug with her trowel but the roots lay deep and seemed to form a complex network of wiry tentacles beneath the soil that thwarted her efforts, for every time she thought she had got them all she discovered more. The sun was hot on her back but a cool wind blew in off the sea and was pleasantly refreshing. Robert was in his study, writing. His books were successful and he was earning good money, which kept the wolf from the door. Florence was now five and JP ten and both children gave her enormous pleasure. They were a tight, united family and in that respect Kitty felt complete. Yet Jack O'Leary was a constant presence, like her shadow, inseparable from her however hard she tried to run from him. And like her shadow, there were times, when the sun shone brightly, that his presence was stronger and other times, on cloudy days, when he seemed barely there at all. But he never left her, nor did the Jack-shaped hole he had left in her heart; no one else could fill it.

She sat back on her knees and wiped her forehead with her gardening glove, smearing her skin with earth. Her mind drifted then as if Jack was demanding her attention from the other side of the world. She could see his face clearly: the wintry blue eyes, the long brown fringe, his unshaven face, angular jaw, crooked smile and the incomplete set of teeth he revealed when he grinned. She smiled at the recollection and put a hand to her heart as a wave of nostalgia crashed against it. She wondered, as she so often did, how he was faring in America. Whether he had finally settled down and started a family with someone else. It wasn't fair to deny him happiness and yet she didn't want him to marry or have children—she wanted to think of him as belonging exclusively to her, even though it had been *her* choice not to run off with him. The image she treasured was of a solitary man, standing in the Fairy Ring, gazing lovingly at her. And in that gaze he promised to love her always. But she accepted that he would have made a new life for himself. She imagined him now as a simple, wholesome farmer in somewhere like Kansas, with his scythe in his hands, chewing on an ear of wheat, standing in the sunshine beside his pickup truck, thinking of her.

She was wrenched out of her reverie by the sound of a car crunching up the gravel. She turned to see Grace's shiny blue Austin slowly approaching. She stood up and pulled off her gloves. "What a lovely day!" Grace exclaimed, climbing out. She was wearing a floral tea dress with a rose-pink cardigan draped over her shoulders and ivory-colored T-bar shoes. Her soft brown hair was swept off her face and falling about her shoulders in extravagant curls, but nothing was more radiant than her smile.

"Hello, Grace," said Kitty, striding across the lawn to meet her.

"Goodness, you're gardening!" Grace exclaimed.

"After the rain the weeds have gone mad," Kitty replied. "Do you have time for a cup of tea? I could certainly do with a break."

"I'd love to," said Grace, linking her arm through Kitty's and walking with her into the house. "I haven't seen you for a while. I thought it would be nice to catch up."

They took their teacups outside and sat on the terrace out of the wind. Grace asked after the children and Kitty asked after Grace's father. "Well, I told you those silly Shrubs would have their hearts broken and I was right. My father played with them callously like a fox with a pair of hens. The trouble is now that he has neither he's pining like a pathetic dog. Really, you should see him, he's pitiful. He doesn't want to go out. He won't see anyone. He sits at home, smoking, reading and grumbling. He won't even play bridge. Bertie's four has broken up now that the three of them can't be in the same room together and he's begging me to do something about it. I wish Papa would pull himself together and stop behaving like a love-sick youth!"

"And the Shrubs? I haven't seen them in church . . ."

"That's because they're avoiding Papa. It's all so childish. You'd have thought they were in their twenties, not their seventies!"

"Oh dear. What a mess. I thought one stopped suffering that sort of heartache at their age."

"Clearly one never does! Tell me, much more interesting, what the devil is Celia doing in South Africa?"

"It seems like she's been gone for ages," said Kitty. "I miss her so much."

"Not a word then?"

"Nothing. Lord knows what she's doing. I haven't even been to the castle. I can't bear to see it inhabited by that peacock of a count. I bet his wife is frightful!"

"They haven't arrived yet," said Grace, masking her smile behind the rim of her cup. She couldn't wait for the Count to set up residence and for their afternoon trysts to resume. He was the only person she had encountered in the last decade who had the ability to take her mind off Michael. "I think we all have to accept change," Grace continued. "Time moves on and we have to move with it. Celia will find her old life in London, probably remarry, and you and I will find great entertainment in the di Marcantonios. Goodness, life would be dull without having people to laugh about. I do wish they'd hurry up and move. I can't imagine why they're taking so long. One would have thought that, having spent so much money buying the place, they'd be impatient to move in."

"I couldn't bear it when Celia bought the castle, but now that she's sold it to those silly people, I long for her to return. It was churlish of me to get so upset about it."

"Quite. It's only bricks and mortar." Kitty nodded and wanted very much to agree. "Now, my dear, I have something serious I need to talk to you about." Kitty put down her teacup. "Firstly, I have a confession."

"Oh?"

"Between us, just like old times."

"All right. Go on."

Grace put down her teacup too and folded her hands in her lap. "I have converted to Catholicism."

Kitty raised her eyebrows in surprise. "Catholicism? You?"

"Me," said Grace with a smile. "I have followed my heart, Kitty, and here I am a fully fledged member of the Catholic community."

"And Ronald doesn't know, so hence the need for secrecy," said Kitty.

"No one knows but you and the Doyles."

Kitty flushed at the mention of the Doyles. Bridie and Michael's faces appeared before her and she wasn't sure which one was worse. "Why the Doyles?"

"Because I needed a devout Catholic family to instruct me. Father Quinn insisted on it, seeing as I'm unable to attend Mass here in Ballinakelly and therefore unable to become part of the local Catholic community."

"What an extraordinary thing to do, Grace. But religion is a very personal matter, so I won't question your beliefs. You must want it very badly to take the trouble, not to mention the risk, of converting."

Grace sighed. "I feel light," she said happily. "I feel as if all the terrible things I did in the War of Independence have dissolved into nothing. I have been wiped clean like a dirty window."

"And you didn't feel that the Protestant God could forgive you?"

"The absolution I required was the Catholic sort. I am now in a state of grace and can enter Heaven. A relief considering the extent of my sins." Kitty wasn't sure whether or not Grace was joking. Her expression didn't commit to either gravity or humor but remained enigmatically somewhere in between.

"All right. The important thing is that *you* feel your conscience is clean," said Kitty, half expecting Grace to throw back her head and roar with laughter at her jest. But she didn't.

"Christianity is all about forgiveness," Grace continued. "I have been forgiven, through Christ, and I have forgiven those in my past who have wronged me." Her eyes suddenly looked at Kitty with more intensity. "I sense you carry a heaviness within *you*, Kitty, and I want to help alleviate it."

"Has Father Quinn asked you to seek a conversion from *me*?"

Grace shook her head. "Of course not, but I know now the lightness one feels after making one's peace with those who have wronged one."

"Are you suggesting I make peace with those who have wronged *me*?" Kitty asked, feeling her body stiffen like a threatened cat.

Grace's brown eyes bored deeper. "I am," she said.

"I carry no such weight, Grace. But thank you for offering to help me."

"But you do," Grace persisted. Kitty frowned. Grace's gaze made her feel cornered but she couldn't think of an excuse to get up and leave. "I know about you and Michael," she said quietly.

Kitty's breath caught in her chest. Her mind darted about for the leak of information—Robert, Jack . . . no one else knew. "Michael told me, Kitty," Grace lied. "Michael told me what happened. He has confessed before God. But not before *you*."

Kitty was so stunned she didn't know what to say. She stared mutely at Grace while the older woman watched her with a cold compassion. "You don't need to feel ashamed in front of me," she continued. "We have shared so many secrets. This is simply another one. But for your sanity, and for the peace of Michael's soul, you must forgive him."

Kitty was so outraged at this suggestion her voice came back to her in an explosion. "I *must* forgive him?" she snapped and Grace was so startled by her tone and the fire that blazed in her eyes that she blanched. "For *his* sanity? If you had any idea what Michael did you would not be seeking his soul's peace but the *burning* of his soul in the fires of Hell! How dare you even speak to me about it and how dare Michael send you in like a spy to seek my forgiveness on his behalf. If he was so desperate to be forgiven, why didn't he have the courage to come himself?"

"He would never presume to seek your invitation. He knows you wouldn't agree to see him." Grace frantically sought another tack. "He sent me in not as a spy but as a mediator. I'm flying the white flag, Kitty."

"I always knew you cared for Michael Doyle," she said, her

rage subsiding as Grace seemed to lose her footing. "You have always defended him. I should have known. Why, you were the only woman Michael listened to, the only woman he respected, and you, in turn, admired him back. *That* was plain to see, but I was too stupid to notice. All the while we were conspiring, carrying notes and guns and risking our lives for the cause, *you* were bedding Michael Doyle. How long have you known about the rape, Grace? Did he tell you the morning of the fire, after he burned down the castle and took me on his kitchen table? Did he betray Jack to the Tans and seek refuge in your home? Have you two been working together all along? Plotting like thieves and undermining us at every turn?" Kitty wasn't sure what she was saying, but the truth was beginning to seep into her consciousness like light slipping through a thin crack in a dark cave. She shook her head as the full extent of Grace's betrayal became clear. "If it wasn't for you, Jack and I might have had a chance. Why, Grace? What was it about our love that made you so obstructive? I thought you were my friend."

Grace's face had gone puce. "I am your friend. I came here today to help and this is the thanks I get? You accuse me of every wrong that's ever been done to you."

"And do you deny that you slept with Michael?"

"Absolutely," said Grace firmly. "Michael is a troubled soul and I have taken it upon myself, as a good Catholic, to help him. If you do not forgive him, Kitty, you will be condemning him to a life of misery."

"And what about *me*, Grace? What about *my* misery?" Kitty thumped her chest. "Do you think I walked away that morning and left my shame and my hurt and my anger in that kitchen?

No, I took it with me and I've been carrying it around with me for over ten years!"

Grace wanted to accuse her of lying. She wanted to force her to admit that her shame arose not out of any violation but out of the disgrace of her own conduct. Kitty had encouraged him, for Michael was no rapist, and Michael had done what any man would have done in his situation, when faced with the open legs of a beautiful woman like Kitty. But she was too astute to ruin her relationship with the only person who could restore Michael to her bed. "Kitty," she said calmly. "You're angry and you have every reason to be. But don't let your anger cloud your judgment. I am your friend and I have always been your friend. You have my loyalty and my compassion. I don't condone what Michael did but I see him as Jesus sees him—as an erring child of God. He has committed a terrible crime and has suffered through his guilt and regret. I only want your peace and his. But I see that I have greatly offended you and I'm sorry. I didn't come to fight with you. I hoped to be able to release you of this burden. I see now that the only person who can release it is you, when you are ready."

"I will *never* be ready, Grace," Kitty snarled and she watched the muscles in the older woman's jaw tense as she struggled to hide her ire. Kitty wondered why it was so important to Grace that she forgive Michael. She now knew her friend for what she really was and realized that there was only ever one ulterior motive and that was herself. The only person Grace was ever loyal to was herself. So how would *Grace* benefit from Kitty's forgiveness? Kitty didn't know.

Chapter 35

London

Celia returned to London to face Aurelius Dupree. The crossing was tiresome for this time there was no Rafael O'Rourke to divert her, only the truth about her father, which induced a slow hardening of the heart the more she thought of it. She resolved to keep the information she had gleaned from the rest of the family; she didn't think her mother would survive the shock of learning that Digby had a black son called Lucky! The fact that Digby was a murderer too would finish her off, if knowing about Lucky hadn't already. She would tell them instead the good news about the gold mine and watch their jaws drop when she announced that she was going back to South Africa to run it. She had called the Rothschilds, the Oppenheimers and all the other financial dynasties who had been friends with her father. Since mining companies were already investing in deep reef mining in Witwatersrand and now in the Orange Free State, and since they had known her father, she had begun to raise the money for what she had named the Free State Deep Reef Mining Company.

The mine would take many years of work, compromise and patience; she wasn't under any illusion about *that*. But it would take a special determination to raise the money and Celia would have to learn everything for herself. She'd learn about the geology of gold in the deep mines, gold that was being found not in gleaming chunks but within iron ore. She'd learn how shafts were built and cages lowered to carry the men into the mines. She'd learn how they worked in the stopes and about the chemical process of melting the iron ore to extract the gold, which was the fruit of this vast and complicated process. She'd learn how to build a small town where her workers would reside and she'd employ the technical experts to see that it was all done properly. Who would have thought that Celia, the self-proclaimed birdbrain of the family, would do all of this?

The last thing she needed was Bruce and Tarquin thinking they could do it better and coming along with her, so she would tell them that Digby's man, Mr. Botha, was going to oversee everything, although she had already resolved to find her *own* man as soon as she returned to Johannesburg.

The problem of Aurelius Dupree was not long in resurfacing. He knew she had gone and he clearly knew when she was back, because a day later he came knocking on her door in Kensington Palace Gardens. On this occasion he was invited in. Celia noticed how much he had aged in a couple of months. He seemed a little more bent, his cough had worsened and his hands shook as he steadied himself on the arms of the chair as he sat down. The fight had not gone out of his eyes, however, and he glared at her across the room as she poured the tea and handed him a cup. "I've been to South Africa," she told him. "I went to Johannesburg and met with my father's old foreman, Mr. Botha."

Aurelius Dupree nodded and his thin lips twisted with resentment. "Your father's monkey," he said. "I don't suppose he enlightened you with the truth."

"No, he didn't," said Celia.

"A long way to go to discover nothing, Mrs. Mayberry."

"I could have stopped there. That would have been very much to my satisfaction. I would have returned believing you and your brother made up a whole heap of lies and maligned my innocent father, who was an honorable man in a dirty world of cut-throats and ruffians."

Dupree raised a white eyebrow. "But you didn't?"

Celia shook her head. "I didn't. I dug deeper, Mr. Dupree, and I discovered, much to my shame, that you are right."

Aurelius Dupree put down his teacup and stared at her in bewilderment. "Sorry, Mrs. Mayberry. *What* did you say?"

"That you are right, Mr. Dupree. My father cheated you out of money and had your brother murdered and you incarcerated for a crime you did not commit." Aurelius Dupree's vision blurred as tears bled into the dry balls of his eyes and gathered there in shiny pools. "I will never speak of this again, not to anyone, and my words will never leave the four walls of this room, but I admit his crime on his behalf, and ask your forgiveness. I cannot pay you the amount you are owed and I cannot give you back the years you have lost behind bars, but I have discovered a gold mine in South Africa that my father was unable to mine because of the sheer depth of the gold. Now new machinery has made it possible and I intend to mine it. I have returned to London and have started to raise the funds. Therefore, what I can offer you, Mr. Dupree, is shares. I will also make sure you get the best medical care London has to offer. You have a shocking cough, if I may say so, and your health is in a terrible state. I would like to make the years you have left as comfortable as possible."

Aurelius Dupree pushed himself up and staggered over to where Celia was sitting and took her hands in his. The tears had now overflowed and trickled down the lines and crevices in his skin like hesitant rivulets. "You are a good woman, Mrs. Mayberry," he said huskily. "I accept your offer. When I first laid eyes on you many months ago I didn't think you were made of anything other than pretty stuffing, but you have proved me wrong. You are a woman of substance, Mrs. Mayberry. It takes courage to do what you have done. Indeed you cannot give me back the years, but you have given me something else that is almost more important: credence. I've spent thirty years protesting my innocence and my protests have been met with derision and disbelief. *You* have swept all that away with three blessed words. *You are right.* You cannot imagine what those three words mean to me." He coughed some phlegm from his lungs. "I'm undone, Mrs. Mayberry. Undone." He coughed again and Celia settled him onto the sofa. He was trembling so violently now that Celia asked one of the maids for a blanket and the butler to light the fire. She gave him a warm drink of milk and honey and some hot soup. The man who had failed to remove his hat at the funeral, who had sneaked his way into the church at the memorial service, who had terrorized her with threats and accusations, was now nothing more than a homeless old vagabond with deteriorating health and a fading heart full of gratitude. "You must stay here until you are better," she said, her own heart overflowing with compassion. "I won't take no for an answer. It is the least we can do."

"Then let me give you some advice about your mine," he said weakly. "I know a thing or two about mines and a lot about the men you're going to have to deal with." Celia listened as he shared his wisdom and for a while his pallid cheeks flushed with renewed life and his eyes flickered with forgotten pleasure, like the sudden reviving of embers in a fire that appeared to be dying. But as the day approached evening his energy waned and his eyelids drooped and he sank into a deep slumber, his breath rattling ominously in his chest.

Celia knew he wouldn't live to see his shares, nor would he require the best medical care London had to offer. She sensed that he wouldn't even survive the night. Aurelius Dupree could finally give up the fight, for he had at last found peace.

THE SECRETS OF Digby Deverill's past that threatened to devastate the family's reputation were buried with Aurelius Dupree. Only Duchess knew the truth and Celia did not doubt that she would take it to her grave. Celia informed her family of her plans to return to Johannesburg with her children and no one was more surprised than Harry and Boysie. They lunched with her at Claridge's and noticed a solemnity about her now, a depth she hadn't had before. Gone was the girl who wanted to dance at the Café de Paris and the Embassy, for whom life was "a riot," and in her place a woman who had lost so much but discovered through her loss something that she had never known was there: the Deverill spirit—the ability to overcome despair and rise beyond the limits of her own frailty. Not only had she found strength but she had found a future. She was going to restore the family fortune, and Harry and Boysie realized, as they listened to her, that she really meant to do it. "The past is gone," she told them. "And there's no point crying about it. One has to look ahead and keep one's eye on the horizon. As long as I do that, and don't look back, I'll be okay."

"But what will we do without you?" Boysie asked.

"Life won't be the same," said Harry sadly.

"You have each other," she told them with a smile. "It's always been the three of us but you've never really needed me, have you?"

"But we like to have you around," said Boysie.

"I'll come back when I'm rich and powerful."

"You're very brave, Celia," said Harry.

"Who'd have imagined it?" said Boysie.

Celia thought of Aurelius Dupree and smiled. "I didn't," she agreed. "But I've changed. There's nothing left for me here except you two and a frivolous life I no longer want. I'm going on an adventure, boys, and I'm excited. I'll write and tell you all about it and perhaps, if you both want an adventure too, you can come and join me. In the meantime, you must look after Mama and Kitty and write to me often. I want to know everything so that one day, when I come back, I won't feel I've been away."

The three of them held hands around the table and agreed to that. "Out of sight but not out of mind," said Boysie.

Harry picked up his glass. "Let's drink to that," he said.

"Good Lord!" Hazel exclaimed. "Celia's off to live in South Africa. She's going to become a miner."

"A miner?" said Laurel in horror, glancing at the letter in her sister's hand.

"That's what it says. She's going to dig for gold in an old mine of Digby's."

"What, on her own?"

"That's what it looks like."

"Does she know anything about mining?"

"Of course she doesn't."

"Oh dear. It sounds very alarming," said Laurel, sipping her tea.

"She says there's nothing left for her now that the castle has gone."

"She's running away," said Laurel with certainty. "How very disastrous. Do you think someone should go and bring her back? When did she leave?"

"My dear Laurel, she left weeks ago. I'm sure that when she realizes what it is to mine for gold she will be back. It simply isn't the place for a woman."

There was a long pause as Hazel folded up the letter and replaced it in the envelope. The silence, which had been kept at bay for the duration of their short conversation, now returned to hang heavy and sad between them like a fog. In that fog was the unavoidable presence of Ethelred Hunt.

Hazel glanced at her sister. "Are you all right, Laurel?" she asked quietly.

Laurel inhaled through her nostrils and lifted her chin. "I'm all right," she said. "And you, Hazel, are *you* all right?"

"Yes," said Hazel, but her voice quivered like the string of a badly played violin.

"No you're not, I can tell."

"No, not really."

"Me neither," conceded Laurel.

"We agree on that then."

"We agree on everything these days," said Laurel with a joyless laugh.

"I love him," said Hazel. "I love the very bones of him."

"And I love him too," said Laurel. She reached out and took her sister's hand. "But we have each other."

"Thank God for that," said Hazel. "I don't know what I'd do without you."

There was a knock at the door. "Goodness, are we expecting anyone?" Laurel asked. Hazel shook her head and looked worried.

"Who could it be?" said Laurel, getting up from the sofa.

"Let's go and see," said Hazel, following her sister into the corridor. They reached the front door and took a while to release the chain and unlock it. Since the Troubles neither Shrub had been casual about the security of their home. They opened the door a crack to see the sorry face of Ethelred Hunt, who was standing with his hat in his hands. Just as Laurel was about to slam the door in his face he wedged his shoe in the gap.

"May you permit me to speak?" he asked. The Shrubs stared through the crack with wide eyes, like a pair of terrified birds. "I have come to the conclusion that I love you both and I simply can't live without you. I can't decide between you and it seems to me that you are a job-lot, that you come together and are impossible to separate. So I have an outrageous but frankly delicious suggestion. Would you like to hear it?"

The women looked at each other. "We would," said Hazel.

"Go on," said Laurel.

"What would you say to the three of us living together?" The two sisters blinked at him in amazement. "I know it's un-conventional and I'm sure my daughter will have a lot to say about it, but I can't see another way. It's all or nothing and I'm not a man to settle for nothing. It's either the three of us or . . ." He hesitated. "Or unhappiness. The last few months have been deeply unhappy. I don't regret one moment of the past; I only wish I'd had more of it. What do you say, girls? Are we on?"

There was a brief scuffle and then the door opened. "How about a cup of tea?" said Hazel happily.

"I'll put the kettle on," said Laurel, making off toward the kitchen.

"Oh, I think something stronger," said Ethelred, placing his hat on the hook in the hall, sandwiched between two pink sunhats with blue ribbons. "After all, we've got something to celebrate."

Chapter 36

Connecticut, 1938

I won't wear that dress, do you hear!" shouted Edith, stamping her foot.

"Edith dear, Grandma bought it for you and brought it all the way back from Paris so you *will* wear it," said Mrs. Goodwin patiently. "It's Christmas Day. Let's not fight on Jesus' birthday."

"I don't care who gave it to me and I don't care that it's Jesus' birthday. I hate it. I won't wear it. You can't make me!" Edith glared at her sister, who had appeared in the doorway in an elegant blue dress with grown-up shoes and stockings, her hair pinned and curled in the sophisticated fashion of the day. "What are *you* looking at, Martha?" she raged. "Why can't I have a dress like hers, Goodwin?"

"Because you're ten and Martha is almost seventeen," the

nanny replied. "When you're seventeen you will have dresses like Martha's."

Edith sat on the edge of her bed and folded her arms. "I will not wear this stupid dress." She clenched her jaw and no amount of coercing could induce her to put on the dress.

At last Mrs. Goodwin gave up. "I'll go and tell your mother."

Edith smiled. "You do that, Goodwin. Mama won't make me wear it. She'll let me wear whatever I want."

But today was not just *any* day. It was Christmas Day and lunch at Ted and Diana Wallace's house was a large family affair. Pam was mindful of her mother-in-law's warning, that if she didn't discipline Edith, the child would grow into a monstrous adult, and she was desperate for her approval—especially as Joan and Dorothy's children were considered "delightful" and "good." It was ironic that the adopted child whom she had worried might never fit into the Wallace family clan was Diana Wallace's favorite grandchild and a paragon of good manners and gentle character, while her natural child who carried the blood of the Wallaces in her veins was Diana Wallace's *least* favorite grandchild and the family nuisance. Today was the one day of the year when Edith had to do as she was told. Pam was adamant. Edith had to wear Grandma's dress, no matter what.

When Edith heard what her mother had said she could not believe it. She jumped off the bed and marched down the corridor to her mother's room, where Pam was sitting at her dressing table clipping diamond earrings onto her ears. In the mirror Pam saw the furious figure of her youngest child standing in the doorway in her underwear and turned around. "Darling, don't look at me like that. Your grandmother gifted you the dress for today so you have no choice but to wear it."

Edith started to cry. She ran to her mother and flung her arms around her. "But I hate it," she wailed.

Pam kissed the top of her head. "How about we go shopping and find you a dress you do like."

"Now?" asked Edith, cheering up.

"Of course not, darling. The shops are closed at Christmas. When they open again it's the first thing we'll do."

Edith pushed herself away and stuck out her bottom lip. "But I want a new dress now!"

"Edith, you're behaving like a spoiled child. Pull yourself together." Pam was pleased she was asserting control.

Edith stared at her mother in horror. "You don't love me anymore," she sobbed. The other two tacks hadn't worked, so perhaps self-pity would.

But Pam was having none of it. Today her girls had to be on their best behavior, come what may. Grandma Wallace had given Edith the dress, which was very pretty, and Pam was not about to offend her by bringing Edith to lunch in a different one. "Edith, go to your room and put on the dress or, I promise you, there will be no presents for you this Christmas."

"You hate me!" Edith shouted, bolting for the door. "And *I* hate *you!*"

Pam turned back to the mirror. Her face was very pale and her eyes shone. She wanted more than anything to burn the stupid dress and let Edith wear one of her own, but she couldn't. How she resented Diana Wallace. She wiped away a tear with a tremulous finger, then patted the skin around her eyes with a fluffy powder puff.

Edith wore the dress but she didn't smile and she barely spoke as she sat in the back of the car gazing out of the window at the snowy gardens and frosted houses. She wanted to punish them all for her misery, especially her mother. *You're gonna wish you hadn't made me wear it,* she thought spitefully. The fact that Martha looked so pretty and behaved so beautifully made her all the more furious.

Pam and Larry were the last to arrive. Larry's brothers, Stephen and Charles, were already there with their wives, Dorothy and Joan. Their children, all grown up now, were among them, dressed impeccably in suits and ties and tidy frocks. Pam was acutely aware of Edith, who hadn't said a word since they'd left the house. Her face was gray with fury, her lips squeezed tightly shut; she was making no secret of the fact that she was furious. Pam overcompensated, greeting everyone enthusiastically, while Larry carried in the bag of gifts to place beneath the tree. "Oh Edith, you're wearing the dress I bought you," said Diana, running her eyes up and down with approval. Edith didn't even attempt a smile.

"It's so pretty, Ma," Pam jumped in. "You're so clever to find it. Green is a lovely color for Edith."

Diana smiled at her youngest grandchild. She had registered her silent protest and chosen to ignore it. She turned her attention to Martha. "My darling child, you look beautiful. You're growing up so fast. Come and sit next to me so I can look at you properly. Is that a new dress? It's mighty grown-up, but I suppose you are about to turn seventeen. How time flies." Martha knelt on the floor beside her grandmother's armchair while Edith, encouraged by a gentle push from her mother, shuffled off to help her father put the presents under the tree. The conversation resumed and Edith's rudeness seemed all but forgotten. Joan, however, watched Edith carelessly throwing the brightly wrapped gifts onto the floor and narrowed her eyes. She had always thought that Martha would be the one to give Pam trouble but it had turned out to be Edith. She grinned into her champagne flute. Diana Wallace was a woman for whom good manners were paramount. She despised ill-disciplined people and uncivilized children. Joan looked proudly on her own children and decided that Edith's bad character had little to do with nature and everything to do with nurture. Pam had raised Martha to be a Wallace with obvious success, but she had neglected Edith because she had expected her breeding to do it for her; it hadn't.

After lunch everyone opened their gifts. The room filled with smoke as the men lit cigars and the women cigarettes. Edith seemed unhappy with all of her gifts. She was determined to ruin everyone's day, even if it meant making hers considerably worse. When Joan gave her an exquisite sewing basket with miniature cotton reels tucked into their own little slots she threw it on the floor and folded her arms. "I hate sewing," she snapped. "That's the sort of thing Martha would like."

Pam noticed her mother-in-law's appalled face and hurried to reprimand her child. "If you cannot behave you might as well leave the room," she said, although it pained her to raise her voice at Edith.

Edith, humiliated in front of the entire family, ran out of the room in tears.

"I'm sorry," said Pam with a heavy sigh. "I don't know what's got into her today."

"Come here, Pam," said Larry, patting the sofa beside him. "She'll grow out of it. She's just going through a difficult stage."

"This difficult stage has been going on for some time," said Diana drily. "I suggest you employ a strict English governess. Goodwin is much too gentle. It's time she retired, don't you think?"

"Mother has a point," said Larry, puffing on his cigar.

"Martha will be terribly upset to lose Goodwin," said Pam.

"Then why not send the two of them to London together. Martha should see a bit of the world. She should go on a tour."

"I'm not sure that's such a good idea, Mother. Europe looks like it's sliding back into another war."

"Don't be ridiculous, Larry. There's not going to be another war. No one wants a repeat of the Great War. They'll do anything they can to avoid it. Life must go on. Really, I was in Paris in the fall and I felt quite safe."

Ted, who was standing in front of the fireplace with Stephen and Charles, joined in the conversation. "The threat to peace is from dictatorships," he said emphatically, puffing on his cigar. "We Americans might be neutral but we need to be more involved in Europe in order to avoid another war . . ."

Joan wandered into the hall. She heard sniveling coming from the top of the stairs. There, sitting on the landing, was Edith. Joan carried her ashtray up the stairs and sat beside her niece. She put the cigarette between her scarlet lips and inhaled. Edith stopped crying and looked at Joan suspiciously. "I'm sorry I gave you a sewing basket. I thought it was darling." She looked down at the child's tear-stained face. "But it isn't really about the sewing basket, is it? What's it about then?"

"Mother made me wear this horrible dress."

"Don't you like it?"

"It's ugly."

"Ma gave it to you so you had to wear it whether you liked it or not. You know, when I was a child, I never had any say over what I wore. Right up until I was sixteen. My mother chose everything and I obeyed. Children were more obedient in those days."

"Mother hates me," said Edith. She started crying again.

Joan flicked ash into the little tray. Her nails were very long and painted a glossy scarlet like her lips. "Your mother doesn't hate you, Edith. That's absurd."

"She does. She prefers Martha. Martha does everything right and never gets into trouble. Martha is perfect."

"Well, she certainly behaves well."

"Mother prefers her to me."

"You know that's not true."

"It is. If she loved me she wouldn't have made me wear this horrid dress."

"Love has nothing to do with dresses, Edith. She had to make you wear it otherwise she would have upset Ma, who bought it for you."

"Mother doesn't want me. She only wants Martha," said Edith, realizing that with Aunt Joan self-pity would guarantee her lots of attention.

"Your mother wanted you so badly," said Joan. "She longed for you from the moment she married your father, but you took a long time in coming."

"She had Martha," said Edith bitterly.

"But she wanted *you*."

Edith frowned. "She didn't know me, Aunt Joan."

Joan examined her nails and considered the secret she was about to spill. She knew she shouldn't and she was well aware that if she was caught she would be in a great deal of trouble, but the child was gazing up at her with big shiny eyes and there was something inside Joan that wanted to help her—at the expense of Martha, who was so perfect and beloved and *irritating*. "Shall I tell you a secret?" she said. Edith sniffed the gravity of this secret like a hound sniffing blood and stopped crying. She gazed at her aunt, barely daring to breathe. She nodded. "But you have to promise not to tell anyone, ever. This is between you and me, Edith."

"I promise," said Edith, who at that point would have promised the world.

"Let's shake on it, then." Joan held out her hand. Edith shook it. Joan stubbed out her cigarette. The rumble of voices from the drawing room downstairs receded as Joan leaned in closer to her niece. "Martha is adopted," she said. There, it was done. Those words had been released and they could never be recovered. Edith stared up at her in amazement. "It's true. Your parents couldn't have children so they went to Ireland and bought one. You see, they wanted a baby very badly. So badly that they were willing to buy someone else's. Then, years later, by some miracle, God granted them one of their own and you were born. You see, my darling, you might think they don't love you as much as Martha, but the truth is they love you *more* than her because you belong to them in a way that she never will."

At that moment their conversation was cut short by Pam, who appeared at the bottom of the stairs. "There you are," she said, throwing her gaze onto the landing where Edith and Joan sat huddled together like a pair of conspirators. Edith, so overwhelmed by the secret, ran down the steps and into her mother's arms. "I'm sorry, Mother. I promise to be good from now on," she said and Pam frowned up at Joan. Joan shrugged and pulled a face, feigning ignorance. Relieved that Edith had cheered up, Pam mouthed a "Thank you" at Joan and took Edith back into the drawing room.

The transformation in Edith was instant. She was polite, charming and obedient. Pam was astounded and asked Joan what she had said to her at the top of the stairs, but Joan pretended that she had simply told her that life was easier if one did as one was told. For the first time since joining the Wallace family Pam felt warmly toward her sister-in-law. "You have a magic touch," she said.

"Really, it was nothing. She's a good girl at heart," Joan replied, which made Pam even more grateful. But Edith was bursting to tell the secret. She returned home at the end of the day with a smug smile on her face and a feeling of the deepest satisfaction in her heart. Every time she looked at her sister she could barely contain the information that was making her feel so superior and had to bite her tongue to stop it from slipping off. But slip off it did, because Edith was not only bad at keeping secrets, as are most ten-year-olds, but she wanted to wound. The darkness in her nature, born out of a sense of inadequacy, compelled her to continually search for the higher ground, and when it came to Martha, the only way to achieve any advantage was by pulling her sister down. Edith had no idea how far down the secret would drag her.

It didn't take long for Martha to strike the match that started the fire. Edith goaded her on purpose until Martha rolled her eyes and snapped at her, at which point Edith raised herself to her full height and out it came. Gleeful, Edith told Martha that she didn't really belong to their mother because she was adopted. At first Martha didn't believe her. "Don't be ridiculous, Edith," she said. "Why don't you go and find something to do instead of picking fights with me."

"Oh it's true," Edith insisted. "Aunt Joan told me."

That got Martha's attention. "Aunt Joan told you?" she asked, suddenly feeling less secure.

"Yes, she did, and she made me promise not to tell anyone."

"So why have you told me?"

"Because you should know. Mother and Father aren't really yours. They're mine though. Aunt Joan told me that they wanted me so badly and were so sad that they couldn't have me that they bought you. Then they had me. It was a miracle," she said with delight. "*I* was a miracle."

Martha's eyes filled with tears. "You're making all this up."

"No, I'm not. You came from a shop."

Martha shook her head and left the room, fighting tears. She ran into the snowy garden and sat on the bench beneath a cherry tree where she could cry alone. If it was true and she *was* adopted why hadn't her parents ever told her? Why did Aunt Joan decide to tell Edith? Why would anybody confide in a ten-year-old? If it *wasn't* true, why would Aunt Joan say such a spiteful thing? Martha sat on the bench and explored all the alternatives. She tried to take herself back into her childhood and remember anything that might corroborate Edith's tale but there was nothing that gave her adoption away. She knew she looked like her mother, everyone said so, and neither parent had ever made her feel less important than Edith. There was only one person she could ask.

Martha found Mrs. Goodwin in the nursery sitting room ironing a basket of clothes. When Mrs. Goodwin saw Martha's tear-stained face she put down the iron. Martha closed the door behind her. "Where's Edith?" Mrs. Goodwin asked.

"In her room I presume, where I left her."

"Are you all right, my dear? Is she being difficult again?"

Martha stood in front of the door looking uncertain. "Mrs. Goodwin, I need to ask you something and you must tell me the truth."

Mrs. Goodwin felt a sinking sensation and sat down on the arm of the chair. "All right," she replied nervously. "I will tell you the truth."

"Am I adopted?"

The old nanny's mouth opened in a silent gasp. Her skin flushed and she shook her head vigorously, not to deny the statement but to get rid of it. But the secret was out and no amount of shaking her head would expunge it. "Martha dear, come and sit down," she said, aware that her eyes were stinging with tears.

Martha began to cry. She put her hand to her mouth and choked. "I thought Edith was lying . . ."

Mrs. Goodwin did not wait for Martha to sit with her. She hurried and pulled her into her arms, holding her fiercely. "My darling child, it doesn't mean that your parents don't love you. In fact it means quite the opposite. It means they wanted you so badly they were prepared to travel the world to find you."

"But where's my real mother?"

"It doesn't matter where she is. She's irrelevant. Pam is the woman who has loved you and taken care of you since you were a tiny baby. She was so happy when she found you in that convent in Ireland, they both were. It was as if they fell in love."

"She didn't want me then? My *real* mother."

"Your biological mother is the woman who gave birth to you but she's not the woman who has loved you and—"

"But she obviously didn't want me, Goodwin. She gave me away."

"You don't know the facts. I think it's much more likely that she was a young unmarried woman who got into trouble."

Martha pulled away and searched her old friend's eyes. "Why has no one ever told me?"

"Because it's irrelevant. You're a Wallace and a Tobin, Martha." Mrs. Goodwin's face hardened. "Did Edith tell you?" Martha nodded. "How does she know? Surely your mother wouldn't have told her."

"Aunt Joan told her."

Mrs. Goodwin was horrified. "Now why would she go and do that?"

"I don't know." Martha went and sat down on the sofa and hugged herself. "I feel sick, Goodwin. I think I'm going to throw up."

Mrs. Goodwin hurried for the wash bowl. She returned a moment later and put it on Martha's lap. "Breathe, darling. Take deep breaths and you'll feel better. It's the shock." Indeed, Martha had gone very white. "Your parents didn't want you to know because they didn't want you to suffer as you are suffering now. I can't believe Joan would be so thoughtless. How can she expect a ten-year-old child to keep a secret such as this? What was she thinking? Your mother will be furious when she finds out."

"She's not going to find out," said Martha quickly. "I'm clearly not meant to know and I don't want to upset her or

Father. Edith couldn't have known what she was doing," she added and Mrs. Goodwin's heart expanded at the goodness in Martha, for even when faced with enough evidence to condemn her sister, she chose to excuse her of any blame.

"Edith knew exactly what she was doing," said Mrs. Goodwin in an uncharacteristic outburst of vitriol. "*That's* why she told you."

Chapter 37

Learning the truth about her birth had shifted something in Martha. Mrs. Goodwin noticed the change even if no one else did. She was quiet, pensive and heavy-hearted. While Edith was more buoyant than ever, grabbing her parents' attention with both hands, Martha's solemnity was barely noticeable, but Mrs. Goodwin, who knew and loved her so well, was disturbed by it. Yet unhappiness drove her deeper into herself and in that dark and silent place she found something she had lost long ago: a sense of where she came from and who she really was. She heard whispers on the wind and saw glimpses of strange lights that hovered around the snowy garden. At night when she lay crying on her pillow she had the distinct feeling that she wasn't alone. She didn't know who it was and, having been brought up in the Christian faith, she wondered whether it was God or an angel sent to reassure her. She thought of Ireland often and imagined her mother as a frightened young woman with nowhere to turn. She didn't despise her for giving her away—such negativity was not part of Martha's nature—she *pined* for her. Somewhere, in that distant land, there was a woman who was part of her. A woman who had lost her, and the frightened young woman of her imagination made her ache with pity.

Martha refused to go anywhere and stayed in her room, staring out of the window, while Mrs. Goodwin made excuses so as not to arouse Mr. and Mrs. Wallace's suspicion that something was dreadfully wrong. Martha preferred to be alone with her thoughts. She took comfort from her inner world because the outer world had so disappointed her.

Then one night in early January she had a strange thought. It seemed to come out of nowhere. She saw the image of a shoebox at the back of her mother's bathroom cupboard and heard the words *birth certificate* very clearly, as if they had been whispered into her ear. She sat up with a jolt and looked around the room. It was dark, as usual, but she sensed she was not alone. Her heartbeat accelerated and her hands grew damp with nervousness. There was somebody in her bedroom, she was sure of it. She knew, however, that if she turned on the light the being would disappear and she didn't want it to go. She wanted very badly to see it.

After a while she lay down again and closed her eyes. But her heart was racing and she felt more awake than ever. Then a memory floated into her mind. She remembered a brownstone building and the fear of going up in a lift that looked like a cage. She remembered holding her mother's hand, but she remembered also the briskness of her mother's walk—the determination in her stride to go deeper into the building. She saw a tall man with big blue eyes bending down to inspect her as if she were an insect and her stomach clamped with panic. Then she saw a strange lamp that looked like a demonic eye and she gasped with fright. Horrified, she leaned over and switched on the light. She glanced around the room. There was no one there. No sound save the thumping in her chest. She took a deep breath and tried to recall more of the memory. The man faded, taking with him the terror, but something refused to go. She couldn't discern what it was, only that it was there, just out of reach. She worked the muscle in her brain until it began to fatigue. The more she tried to recall it, the further away it drifted. Eventually she gave up. She turned off the light and lay back down on the pillow. The vision of the shoebox must surely have been a dream, she thought, but she'd take a look the following day when her mother was out, just in case. If she could find her birth certificate she'd know who to look for—because she *was* going to look. *That* she had already decided.

The following day, as soon as her mother had left the house with Edith, Martha hurried into her bathroom. She crouched down to open the cupboard beneath the sink. Inside were neat bottles lined up in rows, bags of cotton wool and packets of medication. She was astonished to see the shoebox of her vision sitting in darkness at the back, just as she had envisaged it. With a trembling hand she carefully lifted it out. Barely daring to breathe she raised the lid. Inside were papers and a piece of old blanket. Burrowing beneath the piece of blanket she pulled out the documents. There, sitting in her hand, was her birth certificate. It took a moment for her to focus because her eyes had once again blurred with tears. But she blinked and her focus returned. *Born on January 5th, 1922, at 12:20 p.m. in Dublin at the Convent of Our Lady Queen of Heaven. Name: Mary-Joseph. Sex: female. Name and surname of father: unknown. Name and surname of mother: Grace, Lady Rowan-Hampton.* She caught her breath. Her mother was an aristocrat. She presumed she had got pregnant out of wedlock and been forced to give her child away, and her heart flooded with sympathy. She wondered whether Lady Rowan-Hampton ever thought of her and wondered how she was. Wondered whether she was happy, whether she even knew that she existed. She wondered whether she regretted giving her away or whether she had simply signed the papers and moved on with her life. Was it possible to ever forget a child you gave away? She put the box back and returned to her room, where she stared at her face in the mirror and tried to imagine what Lady Rowan-Hampton looked like. Did she resemble her mother or her father? she wondered. Her father's name was unknown, but Lady Rowan-Hampton must know who he is, she thought. If she found her mother she might be able to track down her father too. Then a horrid thought occurred to her: what if Lady Rowan-Hampton *didn't want* to be found? The idea that Martha's appearance might be unwelcome was almost enough to thwart her plan, but she dismissed that as negative. There was a fifty percent chance that her mother would be grateful and she had to bank on that.

When Mrs. Goodwin told Martha that she had been dismissed in favor of a governess who was coming to look after Edith in February, and that she would shortly be leaving for England, Martha's reaction took the old nanny by surprise. She didn't sob and beg her to stay as she had expected; she gazed into the nanny's sad face and declared that she was going with her. "But, my dear, your place is here with your family," she protested.

"I will not rest until I have found my mother," Martha replied, and the determination in her voice told Mrs. Goodwin that she had made up her mind and nothing would change it.

"But what will your parents say?" Mrs. Goodwin asked anxiously.

"I will leave them a letter explaining what I plan to do. If I tell them they will try to stop me. I have thought of nothing else since our conversation in the nursery."

"But where are you going to look?"

"I found my birth certificate, Goodwin, in Mother's bathroom cupboard, and discovered that my mother's name is Grace, Lady Rowan-Hampton."

Mrs. Goodwin's eyes widened. "Fancy that," she said, impressed. "You're a lady."

"I intend to travel to Dublin, to the convent where I was born. Surely they will have records."

"I'm sure they will." Mrs. Goodwin looked perplexed. "I don't have much money, Martha," she warned. "But I will help as much as I can."

"I came into some money on my sixteenth birthday," Martha explained. "And I have saved a little over the years. It will certainly pay for my passage to Ireland and, if I live modestly, it will enable me to manage once I'm there." She took Mrs. Goodwin's hands. "Will you come with me?"

"To Ireland?"

"To Dublin. Oh please, say you will. It will be an adventure. I'm afraid to go on my own. I've never been anywhere. But you, you've traveled. You're wise and experienced. I know I can do it if you come with me."

"Well, I do know a little more of the world than you do." The nanny smiled tenderly. "If you want me to, of course I will. But you have to promise me one thing."

"What?" Martha asked nervously.

"That you make it right with your parents when you get back."

"I will," she replied.

"They love you dearly, Martha. This is going to make them very unhappy."

"I cannot help that. Now I know the truth I cannot unknow it and I cannot let it go. My mother is out there somewhere. Perhaps she longs for me. Maybe she doesn't, but I have to know. I'm not the girl I thought I was, Goodwin. I have to find out who I really am."

"Very well," said Mrs. Goodwin briskly. "Leave everything to me."

AND FROM HER place in Spirit, Adeline smiled with satisfaction at a job well done.

BACK IN NEW York Bridie read the letter from Michael: Old Mrs. Nagle was dying and her mother was asking for her. As her eyes filled with tears she realized that she couldn't avoid her destiny any longer. She had bought the castle out of revenge but perhaps her deepest desire lay in the land on which it was built. In spite of her fears about confronting the people she loathed, she harbored a longing for those she loved that called her back to her roots. She put the letter on the table and gazed out of the window. The sky was a pale blue, the winter sun shining weakly onto the frozen earth. A robin hopped about on the snowy lawn, its red breast bright against the white flakes. Finding nothing for it there it spread its wings and flew away, and Bridie wished that she had wings too so she could fly away. Fly away home. This time for good.

JACK HAD SPENT the last seven and a half years in Buenos Aires. He had used some of the money Maranzano had given him to open an Irish pub in a neighborhood northeast of the city called Retiro, and bought a small apartment in a Parisian-style building close by. Both he and Emer had tried very hard to love their new home. After all, Buenos Aires was a beautiful city of tree-lined avenues, sun-dappled squares and leafy parks, but the prosperity it had enjoyed in the twenties had collapsed with the Great Depression and the atmosphere was now tense and uncertain. It was not the time to be running a new business. But Jack had had no option but to hide. He didn't think Luciano and Siegel would look for him there. However, every knock on the door gave his heart a jolt and every lingering glance in the street raised his suspicion. He slept with his gun beneath his pillow and he feared for his children every time they left the house. Emer was patient and calm but even she was beginning to tire of his constant wariness.

Alana was now ten, Liam was nearly seven and Emer had given birth to Aileen the year before. He worried for their safety and he worried about their future. He didn't see himself living out the rest of his days in this country where he struggled to speak the language and strove without success to find a sense of belonging. His pub had few customers; the Irish community in Buenos Aires was small and Argentines didn't appreciate Irish music or Irish stout. He had made a few bad investments and was losing money fast. He looked out of his bedroom window one morning and made a decision. It was time to go home.

Nearly eight years had passed since he had run from the Mafia; he didn't imagine they were looking for him now. He believed he'd feel safe in Ballinakelly. He trusted his children would have a better quality of life there and a better future. He wanted to put away his gun, dust off his veterinary bag and live a quiet life without looking over his shoulder and mistrusting every stranger. He tried not to think of Kitty. He tried to focus on what he had, not on what he had lost. He loved Emer. She was his present; he had no reason to fear the past.

Barton Deverill

Ballinakelly, County Cork, 1667

The day dawned gray and overcast. The air was cold and there was a hardness to the wind as if its edges had been sharpened like knives. Rooks and crows hopped about the castle walls where the fire had charred the stones to an ugly black, but Lord Deverill's flag flew high and defiant on the western tower so that all who saw it were reminded of his triumph over his enemies and discouraged to rise again.

Lord Deverill awoke with a sickening feeling in the pit of his stomach. He climbed out of bed with a groan and called his servant to bring him wine and bread. Maggie O'Leary had dominated his thoughts since the first time he had laid eyes on her, but today the whole sorry episode would be over once and for all. Today she would die. Burned at the stake the way many witches had gone before. He hoped that with her death so too would die her image, for it plagued him day and night and, however much he tried to distract himself, she was always present, always tormenting him with the power of her allure. He could see them now, those eerie green eyes staring at him with a mixture of insolence and wonder. Today they would close forever and he would be rid of her and rid of his guilt for having given in to his desire and taken her in the woods.

He dressed and summoned his horse. The ride into Ballinakelly seemed to take longer than normal. Accompanied by a small handful of men he made his way slowly, through dense woodland and on down the valley where a little stream meandered its way idly over glistening stones and craggy rocks. The hamlet, when he reached it, was unusually quiet. There was no one to be seen at the gates and the road was empty but for a young boy running as fast as his legs could carry him for fear of arriving late and missing the spectacle. For that's what it was, a spectacle, and the people of Ballinakelly were gathered in the square ready to be entertained.

Lord Deverill rode his horse up the road, past the modest stone cottages, the blacksmith's forge and the inn and farther into the heart of the hamlet. The closer he got the more his stomach cramped with fear. He did not want to see her. He did not want *her* to see *him*. He did not want to be reminded of his foolishness. At last he saw the crowd of people and, beyond, the pile of wood gathered to make a small hill and the stake that stuck aggressively out of it. He swallowed hard and gripped the reins to stop his hands from trembling. One or two people turned and saw him and then a ripple of whispering hissed through the crowd and a hush descended until it was so quiet that even the babes in arms were silenced by the shock of it.

Lord Deverill caught the eye of the little boy who had only a moment ago been running up the road and summoned him with a finger. The boy hurried to his horse and looked up at him with eager eyes. Lord Deverill bent down and whispered something that only the boy could hear. The child nodded and took the small bag Lord Deverill gave him and the reward of a shining coin with grubby hands. Then he disappeared into the crowd like an agile little ferret. A moment later there was a rattling noise as a cart appeared, carrying a woman dressed in a simple white robe. Her hair was long and tangled, hanging about her like a black veil, and she was kneeling on straw with her hands tied behind her back. She said nothing but she cast her eyes about the crowd and seemed to bewitch them all, for no one dared utter a sound. Even when she was on her way to her death they feared her.

She walked calmly to the stake and her hands were bound behind it. She did not try to resist. She did not fight, cry out or wail. She looked frail up there, like a child, but the nobility with which she stood was otherworldly. A priest read out her crime in a voice that echoed around the square, but Maggie seemed unmoved by it. All the while she ran her gaze over the people with her chin held high and an imperious expression on her beautiful face as if she pitied them all for their ignorance. She apparently did not fear death and the crowd sensed her bravery and were awed into a dreadful silence.

Just as the men with flares advanced to light the pyre she raised her eyes and looked directly at Lord Deverill, into his soul, and Barton's breath was frozen in his chest. He was powerless to move. It was as if she was looking deep into his very core and he didn't know whether the smile that curled her lips was of gratitude or defiance. He tried to look away but she held him steadily, like a snake with her prey, and as the sticks caught fire and gray smoke began to envelop her, her blazing eyes watched him still.

The flames lapped at her feet and grew higher but she remained silent and the crowd began to shuffle uneasily. Why didn't she cry out? Why did she not feel the burning? At last she let out a low moan. Barton stared in horror as the moan escalated into a shrill, piercing cry that threatened to shatter every eardrum in the square. And then the small bag of gunpowder she held in her hands caught light and exploded with a loud bang, thus releasing her as Barton had intended.

Lord Deverill realized that he hadn't breathed and took in a giant gulp of air. The crowd staggered back as sparks flew and the fire roared like the mouth of a mighty dragon. The people shielded their eyes and their cries rose with the crackling sound of burning wood and the stench of roasting flesh. He had seen enough. He turned his horse and galloped as fast as he could out of the village.

Chapter 38

Martha and Mrs. Goodwin arrived at the gates of the Convent of Our Lady Queen of Heaven. It was a bright February day, but the gray walls looked austere and formidable and Martha immediately felt uneasy. She imagined her mother arriving here as a young woman in trouble, as Mrs. Goodwin had said was the most likely scenario, and imagined her fear, for these walls looked more like a prison than a refuge.

They had telephoned ahead and booked an appointment to meet Mother Evangelist, who had sounded very kind and helpful, and Martha had felt greatly encouraged by her readiness to see her. Surely, if she had no information at all she would have told her on the telephone and saved her the trouble and cab fare. Now, however, faced with these high walls, Martha felt her hope draining away and she began to lose courage. Mrs. Goodwin sensed her anxiety and smiled reassuringly. "God's houses always look so forbidding, don't they? Be they churches, cathedrals or convents, they don't give one a warm welcome, do they?"

"This is the first time I've ever been to a convent," said Martha, hoping it would be the last.

At length the door opened and a nun in a dark blue habit with a sweet face and soft gray eyes introduced herself as Sister Constance and invited them in. Martha noticed the smell at once. It wasn't unpleasant; a mixture of wood polish, detergent and candle wax. They were taken to a waiting room where a fire burned in the grate and a candle flickered on the occasional table beside a large, leather-bound Bible, a jug of water and two glasses. "Please make yourselves comfortable. Mother Evangelist is expecting you. She'll only be a few minutes. Would you like a cup of tea?"

"Yes please," said Mrs. Goodwin. "We'd both love one, thank you."

Sister Constance left the room. Martha sat on the edge of the sofa and looked around. The walls were painted white and a high window gave little light. The room looked forlorn in spite of the fire. She knitted her fingers in her lap. Mrs. Goodwin sat beside her and put her hand on Martha's. "It's going to be all right. They'll have records. They must have lots of children coming to look for their mothers. I'm sure you're not the first and you won't be the last."

Sister Constance returned with two mugs of tea on a tray with a bowl of sugar, a jug of milk and a plate of Kimberley biscuits. She placed it on the occasional table beside the candle. "There," she said with a warm smile. "Have you come far?"

"From America," said Martha.

Sister Constance's eyes widened with surprise. "Goodness,

that is a long way. Well, I hope you enjoy Dublin. It's a lovely city. If you have time you must have tea at the Shelbourne. It's a very grand old hotel and quite lovely."

"Oh, we've heard of the Shelbourne," said Mrs. Goodwin.

"Of course you have, everyone's heard of the Shelbourne," said Sister Constance. Her eyes were drawn to the door where Mother Evangelist was now standing. The young nun scurried out of the room and Mother Evangelist walked in with an air of authority and sat down in the armchair.

"I'm sorry to have kept you waiting. I'm glad Sister Constance made you cups of tea. It's a bright day but a cold one. Now, you've come to find your mother," she said gently, looking at Martha.

"I have," said Martha, pressing a hand to her heart to quieten it.

"I would like to help you, Miss Wallace. Many young mothers come here when they get into trouble and adoption is the only option. We do our best to help them and find their children loving homes. However, it's natural that you should want to find the woman who gave birth to you and, if it is God's will, you will be successful. You told me you have the birth certificate."

"I don't have it," Martha explained. "I found it but my adoptive mother doesn't know so I was unable to bring it with me."

"Very well. What was the name of your mother and what was the date of your birth?"

"My birthday is January 5, 1922, and my mother's name is Grace, Lady Rowan-Hampton. My adoptive parents are Larry and Pamela Wallace of Connecticut in America."

Mother Evangelist nodded and wrote the details in a little

book. She stood up. "I won't be long. I just need to retrieve the records. Perhaps I can supply you with an address or at least something to set you on the right path. People do move around, you know, and your mother might have married and changed her name. However, let's get the records and take it from there, shall we?"

When she was gone Mrs. Goodwin patted Martha's hand. "You see, it's not so frightening after all, is it? Mother Evangelist wants to help. I'm sure they have reconciled many mothers with their children. It's the right thing to do and Mother Evangelist seems to want to do the right thing."

Martha nodded and picked up her mug. The tea was tepid and weak but she didn't mind. She wondered what Lady Rowan-Hampton would think when she discovered that her daughter had come to find her. It seemed a very long while before Mother Evangelist returned. Martha began to feel nervous again, but this time she sensed something wasn't right. "Why is she taking so long?" she whispered to Mrs. Goodwin.

"There must be drawers and drawers of files," she said. "Perhaps they're kept in a cellar somewhere. I'm sure she'll be back shortly."

At last Mother Evangelist appeared, but her expression had changed. She was no longer smiling. Martha watched her sit down and the anxiety seemed to creep up her leg and down her arms as if it were a creature with prickles. Mother Evangelist sighed. "I'm so sorry," she said, shaking her head. "It appears that your records have been mislaid. I took so long because I went to ask Sister Agatha, who was the mother superior at that time. She's old now and her memory is going. She didn't know why the records had been lost and has no recollection of a Lady

Rowan-Hampton, but then many of the girls only stayed for a short while and this was seventeen years ago. I'm sorry to disappoint you. However, you have the name, which is a very good start. Many of the children who come back don't even have that. It's an unusual name and with an aristocratic title she shouldn't be too hard to find."

Martha wanted to cry. She felt her face flush and pursed her lips to stop them trembling. Mrs. Goodwin took over the talking. She thanked Mother Evangelist, who seemed genuinely sorry not to be able to help. She showed them back down the corridor to the door. As Mother Evangelist unbolted the door Martha noticed an old nun standing in the doorway of a room farther down the corridor. She was staring at her with small, intense eyes, her hard face impassive and her thin lips drawn into a mean line. Martha knew instinctively that *she* was Sister Agatha. She shuddered and the nun closed the door with a slam. It seemed a deliberate act of rebuke.

Once out in the sunshine Martha let her tears flow freely. Mrs. Goodwin put her arms around her. "There there, dear, don't cry. We've only just started our search. We *will* find her, I have no doubt. It was never going to be easy. I know, let's go and give ourselves a treat. Let's go to the Shelbourne and have a nice cup of tea. The tea at the convent was weak and cold. I'm sure the tea at the Shelbourne will be exceptionally good."

The Shelbourne Hotel did not disappoint. It was grand and classical, with high ceilings, marble floors and tall windows looking out onto St. Stephen's Green. They made their way across the foyer to the Lord Mayor's Lounge, where a waiter showed them to a round table beside one of the windows and

Mrs. Goodwin asked for afternoon tea. "You'll feel restored once you've had some scones and jam," said Mrs. Goodwin. "We're not going to give up because we fell at the first hurdle, Martha."

"I know. I suppose I thought that, because we knew the name, the address would be easily come by. After all, if she was a grand lady she'd presumably come from a grand house that might have been in the family for a long time."

"Well, you're not wrong," said Mrs. Goodwin. "I know a little about British titles. I don't think it will be that difficult to find her."

"But where do we start?"

"We must go to London. Your mother might have traveled to Dublin from her home in England to have her child in secrecy. I'm wondering now whether she ever lived here. I have family in England who will help us. I suggest we start there."

"All right, then. Let's go to London," Martha agreed. The waiter brought the tea, which was far superior to the tea they had had at the convent, and scones, which tasted better than anything Martha had tasted in America. "Goodness, these are good," she said and the color began to return to her cheeks and the optimism to her heart. "While we're here we might as well enjoy the park and have a look around the city. I've been trying not to think of Mother and Father," she said quietly.

"The letter you left explained everything very clearly," said Mrs. Goodwin. "I imagine Edith might be in a bit of hot water, though," she added.

"I specifically told them not to blame her. She's only little."

"Your aunt Joan will be in trouble and with good reason."

"She shouldn't have told Edith," said Martha firmly. "But

I'm glad that she did. I have a right to know where I come from."

"You do, dear," Mrs. Goodwin agreed.

At that moment their attention was diverted by a couple of gentlemen who stepped into the room. The older gentleman wore a three-piece suit with a gray felt hat while the younger man, who stood a good few inches taller than the other, was equally well dressed but of a slimmer, more athletic build. Both had an air of old-fashioned grandeur and importance, for it seemed that the entire hotel staff had gathered around them to ensure their comfort. They were escorted slowly through the room in a stately fashion and the older gentleman greeted people he knew with a dashing smile and a raffish twinkle in his pale gray eyes. Those with whom he spoke seemed very happy to see him and Mrs. Goodwin noticed how the ladies put down their teacups and gave him their hands, giggling flirtatiously as he brought them to his lips with a courteous bow. Martha and Mrs. Goodwin watched them in fascination. Mrs. Goodwin was taken by the charm of the older man, with his flaxen hair and arresting eyes, and wondered who he was, for surely he was a man of some standing in this city. Martha stared at the redheaded boy, who must have been of a similar age to her, for she found his insouciance compelling. There was a jauntiness to his walk and a confidence to his smile, as if he had only ever encountered good in his life. The two men settled at their table, which was a short distance from Mrs. Goodwin and Martha's, and the waiters fussed about them with napkins and menus and pleasantries—although they placed their orders without consulting the menus.

"Well, that's an elegant pair of men if ever I saw one," gushed

Mrs. Goodwin. "Must be father and son, don't you think? Besides the color of their hair they look quite similar."

Martha did not reply. She was unable to take her eyes off the boy. He was handsome, certainly, with a mischievous curl to his smile and a lively, amused gleam in his eyes, but there was something besides. Something Martha had never found in anyone else. Then, sensing he was being watched, he raised his eyes and they locked into hers as if destiny had always meant them to be together. They stared at one another without blinking, stunned and delighted at the strange new feelings they aroused in each other.

"What are you looking at, JP?" asked Bertie, following the line of his gaze. He smiled then as he saw the pretty girl by the window. "An eye for the ladies, eh?" he commented with a chuckle. But JP was too electrified by her to reply. He gazed at her as if he had never before seen anyone more lovely. Bertie smiled at his son's enthusiasm and remembered the first time he had laid eyes on Maud. She had aroused the same excitement in *him*. He looked back at the young girl who realized she had drawn the attention of *both* men and hastily dropped her gaze to her plate, blushing profusely. But Bertie did not avert his eyes, for there was a familiarity about her that he wasn't quite able to put his finger on. It was in the way she blushed perhaps, or in the sweetness of her shy smile, he couldn't be sure, but he was certain he had seen her somewhere before. She began to nibble on a scone while her companion clucked away like a hen. He could tell that she was making a great effort not to look in their direction again and finding the task almost impossible. JP's eager gaze drew her like a magnet.

"Would you like me to ask them to join us?" Bertie asked.

JP was surprised. "Would you, Papa?"

Bertie grinned. "Leave it to me." He called over a waiter and said something in his ear. A moment later the waiter was passing the message on to Mrs. Goodwin, whose face revealed her pleasant surprise at Lord Deverill's invitation. The older woman raised her eyes and looked at Bertie, who bowed his head and smiled encouragement.

"Will they come?" asked JP impatiently.

"I do believe they will," said Bertie, and a moment later the two ladies were standing before them and Bertie and JP were on their feet, introducing themselves enthusiastically.

"How very kind of you to invite us to join you," said Mrs. Goodwin once she had sat down. "Martha and I have just arrived from America."

"Is it your first time in Ireland?" Bertie asked, noticing that the two young people were now too shy to look at each other and were equally flushed.

"It's Martha's first time," said Mrs. Goodwin.

"And how are you finding it, my dear?" asked Bertie, turning to the nervous young woman sitting on his left.

"Oh, it's charming," she replied. "Just charming."

"Will you be staying long?"

The girl glanced anxiously at Mrs. Goodwin. "I don't know. We haven't really made plans. We're just enjoying the visit."

"Quite right," said Bertie. "Ah, the tea," he added as fresh pots, jugs of milk, a little plate of sliced lemon and a five-tier cake-and-sandwich stand were placed in the center of the table.

"Goodness," said Mrs. Goodwin with a sigh. "What a wonderful display of treats." She helped herself to a cucumber sandwich.

"Which would you like?" Bertie asked Martha, who was gazing at the cakes with wide, delighted eyes.

"Oh, I don't know," she replied, moving her fingers up and down the plates indecisively before settling on an egg and watercress sandwich on the lowest level.

"That's *my* favorite," said JP, reaching out to take one for himself. The two young people grinned at each other as JP popped his sandwich into his mouth and Martha took a small bite of hers.

"Good, isn't it?" said JP, when he had finished it. Martha nodded.

"How would you like your tea, Mrs. Goodwin?" Bertie asked.

"With a slice of lemon, please," she replied. "Martha likes milk. Lots of milk. In fact, there's more milk in her tea than tea."

JP laughed. "That's just how I like it too," he said, frowning at Martha, astonished that two strangers should have so much in common.

"How extraordinary," said Mrs. Goodwin, enjoying herself immensely. "I don't know anyone who likes their tea as milky as Martha does."

Bertie poured the tea. JP and Martha filled their cups to the brim with milk, taking pleasure in this shared idiosyncrasy that immediately bonded them. The conversation continued as they drank their tea and ate their sandwiches. A while later Bertie was giving them a list of all the interesting things they should see in Dublin when JP and Martha's hands reached for the same chocolate sponge cake on the top level of the cake stand. They laughed as their fingers collided over the plate and withdrew as

if scalded. "We like the same cakes too," said JP softly, gazing at Martha with tenderness.

"But there's only one left," said Mrs. Goodwin.

"Then we shall share it," said JP. He put the cake on his plate and lifted the silver knife to cut it. Martha watched him slice it in two, now dizzy with infatuation. "Half for you," he said, placing one piece on the plate in front of her. "The other half for me," he added. And they lifted the small pieces to their lips and smiled at each other as if they were conspirators, sharing in a secret plot, and popped them into their mouths.

Epilogue

Ballinakelly

The air was thick and stuffy in the backroom, arranged as it was at one end of O'Donovan's public house and partitioned by a dividing wooden wall, which didn't quite reach the ceiling. The cigarette smoke and body heat from the men next door flowed freely over the top of the partition, along with the sweet smell of stout and the sound of deep voices. Set aside for the women (for women were not permitted in the public house), this was where the six elderly members of the Legion of Mary, known as the Weeping Women of Jerusalem behind their backs, met every week, sitting in a line along the bench like a row of hens in a henhouse.

There were the Two Nellies: Nellie Clifford and Nellie Moxley, Mag Keohane, who was always accompanied by her dog, Didleen, Joan Murphy, Maureen Hurley and Kit Downey. The Legion of Mary dedicated themselves to caring for the poor. They would cook them meals, take the elderly to Mass and stay in their houses if they needed nursing. Their weekly treat was to sit in the backroom at O'Donovan's and have a glass of Bulmers Cidona or a Little Norah orange crush. Mrs. O'Donovan would put a lump of ice in each glass, as she had an icebox, and provide a plate of Mikado and Kimberley biscuits, which she couldn't sell on account of them being broken. The greatest luxury, however, was that she allowed them to use her flushing lavatory upstairs. " 'Tis America at home, girl," Mag Keohane had said to Mrs. O'Donovan the first time she used it. "You're a lucky woman not to have to brave the elements to do your business and all you have to do is pull the old chain and the lot disappears. God help us, 'tis a wonder we haven't pneumonia from going out with the old chamber pot in the middle of winter." The Weeping Women of Jerusalem used it, even when they didn't need to, just for the thrill.

"Can you believe that Bridie Doyle bought the castle?" said Nellie Clifford now, nibbling her Mikado biscuit. "I remember laying out her poor dead father, God rest his soul, when she was a little thing of nine."

"She's come a long way from the streets of Ballinakelly," agreed Nellie Moxley, sipping her orange crush. "She's a countess now, which they tell me is a fine thing to be. Indeed, she's made a healthy donation to our Legion, God rain his blessings on her."

"Her new husband is eaten alive with money. A fine-looking man even if he has a foreign look about him," said Joan Murphy.

"They say that foreign cows wear long horns," said Kit Downey with a grin.

"I'm not one to say, but I hear he has an eye for the ladies,

God save us. Nonie Begley is a receptionist at the Shelbourne and says that when he stays there he has a regular lady," said Joan Murphy.

Nellie Moxley leaped to his defense. "Maybe that's a sister or a relative."

But Nellie Clifford was quick to put her straight. "You're as innocent as the suckling child, Nellie. That was no sister, girl. It's none other than Lady Rowan-Hampton." The women gasped in unison. "They were in the dining room holding hands and making sheep's eyes at each other."

"Merciful Jaysus, the maids at her place said that Michael Doyle was a regular visitor there when the master was abroad, and that he would swagger into the hall, king of all he surveyed." The women shook their heads and clicked their tongues with disapproval.

"But what does Lord Deverill make of the new mistress of the castle?" Mag Keohane asked. "She was the daughter of the cook and now she owns the place."

"Hope for us all," cackled Kit Downey.

"I heard that Kitty Deverill swore like a sailor when she heard the news."

"God save us!" muttered Nellie Moxley.

"That Michael Doyle will be above himself now. I suppose they'll all be after moving into the castle."

"I heard that Mariah won't be leaving her home for love nor money," said Kit Downey.

"She's a good woman, is Mariah. As for Old Mrs. Nagle, it won't be long now," said Nellie Moxley. There was silence for a moment as they spared their thoughts for poor Mrs. Doyle and Old Mrs. Nagle.

Then Nellie Clifford put her glass on the long shelf that ran along the partition in front of them. "It's poor Bridie Doyle we should be praying for. She might have married a rich man but, mark my words, she'll be paying for it. By Christmas he'll have a girl in every corner of the county."

A head suddenly poked through the gap at the top of the partition. "Ye are great with the prayers, girls. An example to us all. Will I walk ye home in case some blaggard tries to way-lay one of ye?"

"Get away with you, Badger, and stop codding us," said Kit Downey. "We have miraculous medals and we are like nuns, we travel in twos for safety and we have Mag's Didleen to protect us. She'd tear him limb from limb, God save the mark." Badger's chest rattled.

"That's a graveyard cough if ever I heard it," said Mag Keohane.

"I'll tell you something, girl," retorted Badger with a grin. "There's many in the graveyard who would be glad of it."

Just then a hush came over the pub as a cold wind swept in through the open door. "It's none other than the Count," Badger hissed and his wooly head disappeared behind the partition.

"The Count," said Nellie Clifford, making her mouth into an O shape as she took in a long gasp. The six women strained their ears to hear what he was saying.

"How can I help you, sir?" Mrs. O'Donovan asked from behind the bar.

"I have just arrived on the train from Dublin. I would like a cab to take me up to the castle."

There was a shuffle as the hackney cabbies looked at one another, not wanting to rush their drinks.

"Why don't ye stay for a stout and a game of cards," ventured Badger Hanratty. "You're not in a great hurry, are ye? Then one of these good men will drive you up."

The women heard the Count laugh. "A glass of stout and a game of cards? Why not? Dinner can wait. So, what are we playing?" There ensued a scraping of chairs as he made himself comfortable at one of the tables. A moment later he added in a loud, exuberant voice, "Madam, a drink for every man in the house." And a roar of appreciation rose up as the men hurried to the bar to order more stout.

"God save us, they'll be legless and good for nothing," said Nellie Moxley, shaking her head.

"He knows how to win hearts in Ballinakelly," said Joan Murphy with a smile. "I can't wait to see what happens next."

Acknowledgments

As I continue to follow the lives of Kitty, Celia and Bridie, I continue to rely on my dear friend and consultant Tim Kelly for research and guidance. Our regular meetings, over porter cake and cups of Bewley's tea, have provided me with entertainment as well as information and his wonderful stories keep me laughing long after he has left my house. I am so grateful to my books for they have given me a great friend in Tim.

I would like to thank my mother, Patty Palmer-Tomkinson, for reading the first draft and editing out all the grammatical errors and ill-chosen words, thus saving my editor at Simon & Schuster from what is probably the least interesting part of her job! My mother is patient and enthusiastic and her advice is always wise. She's also a very intuitive person and a sound judge of character, I have learned a lot from her. I'd also like to thank my father because I wouldn't be writing these books if I hadn't had the magical childhood they gave me in the most beautiful corner of England. Everything that goes into my work flows directly from them.

Writing a scene about the Derby was always going to be a challenge, but I would not have attempted it without the help of David Watt. Thank you so much, Watty, for reading it through and correcting it—and for suggesting many ways to improve it.

Thank you Emer Melody, Frank Lyons and Peter Nyhan for your warm Irish encouragement and Julia Twigg for helping me research Johannesburg.

My agent, Sheila Crowley, deserves an enormous thank you. She's the best agent a writer can have because she's there when I need a counselor, when I need a friend, when I need a strategist and when I need a warrior. Quite simply, she's always there when I need her Full Stop. Her mantra "onward and upward" reflects her positive and determined attitude and every time she says it I'm grateful that she's taking me with her!

Working with Sheila at Curtis Brown are Katie McGowan, Rebecca Ritchie, Abbie Greaves, Alice Lutyens and Luke Speed and I thank them all for working so hard on my behalf.

I'm so fortunate to be published by Simon & Schuster. I feel that it's a family and that I belong there. I'd like to thank them all for turning my career around in 2011 with my first Sunday *Times* bestseller and for continuing to put such dedication and drive into publishing my books. A massive thank you to my editor-in-chief, Suzanne Baboneau, for editing my novels with such good judgment and tact. The manuscript is always hugely improved by her appraisal and pruning and my confidence lifted by her enthusiasm and encouragement. I thank Ian Chapman for being the wind in my sails, or should I say sales! I thank him for giving me that break five years ago and for turning my books into the successes that I'd always hoped they would be. I'd also like to thank Clare Hey, my editor, and the brilliant team she works with, for putting so much energy into my books. They all do a fantastic job and I'm so grateful to every one of them: Dawn Burnett, Toby Jones, Emma Harrow, Ally Grant, Gill Richardson, Laura Hough, Dominic Brendon and Sally Wilks.

My husband, Sebag, has been key in plotting the Deverill Chronicles with me and encouraging me to challenge myself by venturing off my familiar path. He's so busy with his own books but he took the trouble to read through the manuscript and share his ideas. I'm glad I took his advice because I believe I have written something that will really entertain my readers—I have certainly entertained myself in writing it. He's my most cherished friend, my most honest critic, my most loyal ally and my greatest supporter. Thanks to Sebag I believe I am the best I can be.

And finally thank you to my daughter Lily and my son Sasha for giving me joy, laughter and love.

ALSO BY
SANTA MONTEFIORE

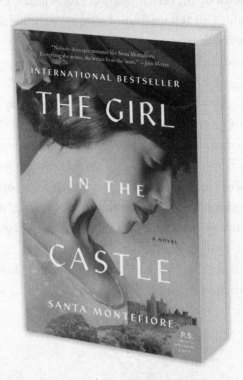

THE GIRL IN THE CASTLE
A Novel
Available in Ebook and Digital Audio

"Nobody does epic romance like Santa Montefiore.
Everything she writes, she writes from the heart."
— Jojo Moyes

Ireland. The early twentieth century.
Two girls on the cusp of womanhood. A nation on the brink of war.

A powerful story of love, loyalty, and friendship, *The Girl in the Castle* is
an exquisitely written novel set against the magical, captivating landscape of
Ireland—perfect for fans of *Downton Abbey* and Kate Morton.